TO PARTS UNKNOWN

John Anthony Miller

All the best

John A. Miller

To Parts Unknown

John Anthony Miller

ISBN: 978-1-940224-58-9

COPYRIGHT 2014

by John Anthony Miller

This book may be purchased through
Amazon.com and Amazon Kindle
Taylor and Seale Publishing.com
Barnes and Noble.com
Books a Million

This novel is a work of fiction. Names, characters, places and incidents are the product of the author's imagination and are used fictitiously. Any resemblance to actual persons, living or dead, events, or locales is entirely coincidental.

Taylor and Seale Publishing, LLC
Daytona Beach Shores, Florida 32118

Phone: 1-888-866-8248
www. taylorandseale.com

Dedication

To Cindy, Chris, Danielle, and Steffany — and the family
and friends whose constant support is so much appreciated

Special thanks to Dr. Mary Custureri and Dr. Melissa
Shaddix at Taylor and Seale Publishing, Donna Eastman
and Gloria Koehler at Parkeast Literary Agency, and the
many advanced readers, all of whom worked diligently to
make the manuscript the best that it could be.

CHAPTER 1

Singapore
February 6, 1942

The howl of air-raid sirens greeted me on my first afternoon in Singapore. I knew the city was threatened, but I wasn't prepared for a Japanese attack on the day of my arrival. I searched for enemy aircraft, wondering how the attack would be launched and how it might compare to what had happened in London.

The streets began to fill with panicked people, shoving and pushing as they rushed for safety. If I had been home in London I would have known where to go. But Singapore was confusing, with few signs posted for bomb shelters and no directions on where they were. I was only a few blocks from my hotel where a shelter existed, but I wasn't sure if I should try to get there. I watched as people swarmed through the streets, running in different directions.

The door to a nearby shop burst open, the bell affixed to it dangling loudly. A butcher, still wearing his blood-stained apron, led two women into the street, their freshly wrapped meat under their arms. They started running towards a park just past a restaurant with outdoor tables. Other shops also emptied, and patrons joined pedestrians in a frightened mass that moved chaotically in a dozen different directions.

I didn't see an immediate danger. I heard no planes. No bombs were exploding. As people continued to scatter, I decided to return to the hotel. It was only three blocks away. In London the warning sirens sounded several minutes before the attack actually started. There was ample time to reach safety. But even then, not everyone made it.

I walked briskly down Orchard Road, across the cobblestone streets, past the shops and street vendors' kiosks, where everything from fresh vegetables to books to furniture to fish was sold on a daily basis. But I had gone only a few hundred feet when I realized the farther I went the emptier the streets became. A city that had been alive with people hurrying to work, shopping for gifts and life's essentials, talking to friends, and idly passing the day, was now abandoned. Automobiles were deserted or parked haphazardly, some with their doors ajar, left by owners who valued their lives more than their vehicles. Street vendors left their wares on display, free for the taking should anyone be so inclined. Even the stray cats that wandered the sidewalks had suddenly vanished.

I wondered if I had made the wrong choice. I should have sought the nearest shelter, started towards the park, where so many others had gone. But given how far I had walked, the park was now equally distant from the hotel. I continued on, breaking into a trot.

I felt my heart pounding, its echo throbbing in my head. I had barely travelled a city block when I heard the drone of enemy aircraft. The sound of their engines increased slowly from a buzz to a roar, their distance from the city diminishing. Seconds later bombs exploded in a deafening blast. First one, then another, and finally a series of explosions scattered randomly across blocks of the city proper. Again I looked to the heavens, which were marred by only a few cottony clouds, but I saw no planes. I thought Orchard Road might be spared, just as specific targets had been chosen by the Germans when I was in London. Maybe the attack was centered on the docks, or the factories, the airport, or the naval base. Maybe it wouldn't threaten me.

After I had gone another block I slowed a bit, struggling to breathe. A plane appeared, flying so low it skimmed the tops of nearby buildings. It sped forward with no specific destination; it was either in route to a target or departing from one. I could see the pilot in the cockpit, his face hidden behind a pig-like mask. And I saw markings on the fuselage, the Japanese flag adorning its wings, machine gun barrels protruding from its belly. It had been designed for one purpose: to deliver death and destruction.

The rapid report of a machine gun sounded, and bullets burrowed into the street. A black sedan bore the brunt of the attack; holes appeared along the running board and up the passenger's side door. A string of splintered bricks then danced across the boulevard, puffs of smoke and fragments of stone spitting into the air. Bullets moved across the street, and I felt the sting of stone shards biting my legs. The firing continued, raking the wall of an adjacent bakery and shattering the shop window, sending pieces of glass onto the display of pastries.

I murmured a short prayer, then ducked into the doorway of a clothing shop. I was gasping for air. The bullets had barely missed me. My heart raced, my lungs burned, my muscles ached. I leaned against the wall, maintaining the smallest profile possible. The firing continued, spraying buildings and breaking windows. I had to think of a way to escape. If I stayed where I was, I would certainly die.

I leaned against the wall, as far back in the vestibule as possible, my chest heaving. I waited another minute and then peeked from the doorway. The plane was gone. I started running as fast as I could, my legs burning with pain.

Just as I reached Trafalgar Street, an explosion rocked the boulevard, louder than all that preceded it. I was blown from my feet, enveloped in smoke, dust and debris. I skidded across the cobblestone, scraping my elbows and tearing my shirt and trousers. I was lost in a whirling kaleidoscope as signs and cars and trees and shop windows rotated around me in a dizzying display of destruction. Visions of my parents, the London fog, a rugby game in September, a college professor, Trafalgar Square, and my first-ever kiss with Sally Westgate flashed before me. And so did the night when Maggie died.

The Malay Towers, a four-story apartment building, had burst into fragments. The front wall crumbled to the ground, falling forward in slow motion. I covered my head with my arms as it collapsed, and brick and timber and glass and bits of furniture rained from the sky. With one wall torn away, I could see the sagging floors of each succeeding level bending precariously. Fire raged from the structure, weak and distant at first, barely flickering, and then gathering strength and spreading, climbing the walls until flames licked the sky and blackened the horizon with smoke.

As debris continued to fall, fragments of wood and stone pummeled my arms, legs, and torso before something much heavier hit me in the head. My vision dimmed and darkness slowly engulfed me. I wondered if this was death: a numbing sensation that very slowly spreads through your entire body, wrapping you in a cocoon of ever decreasing sensations until the body ceases to function. The sounds of the attack - plane engines, bullets bursting, and bombs exploding - all suddenly seemed dwarfed and distant. I could see Maggie, her image shrouded in mist, her hand outstretched. I reached for her, but she eluded me. No matter how hard I tried, I couldn't touch her. And then, as seconds passed, the sounds of battle grew gradually louder, starting with a muted whisper and growing in ever increasing decibels until the world returned with a deafening roar. Her image vanished.

"Are you all right?"

I raised my head, numb to my surroundings. A woman was leaning over me, a concerned look etched on her face. She was pretty but not beautiful, with a porcelain complexion and a mane of blonde hair that danced on her shoulders. She had an upturned nose, thin lips, and blue eyes that studied me curiously.

"I think so," I said, struggling to rise. "What are you doing here?"

She smiled. And it was an amazing smile. As the corners of her lips turned upward, her eyes twinkled so brightly the skies lit in a thousand rays of color. "I was looking for someone," she said. "But I found you instead." She helped me up, and briefly checked for injuries. "You don't seem badly hurt. Can you run? We have to get out of here."

As if to punctuate her statement, a bomb exploded a few blocks away. We both cringed and ducked, not knowing where it had fallen. A Japanese plane flew past, speeding to other targets.

We started running down Orchard Road. I was bruised and dazed, but not seriously hurt. My nostrils stung from the acrid stench of gunpowder, and I choked on dust and smoke. As my senses sharpened, I realized that planes still swirled overhead, machine guns still fired, and bombs still fell.

"Where were you going?" she asked.

I pointed to the Victoria Hotel. "The bomb shelter,"

I shouted.

She nodded and kept running beside me. She had a satchel slung over her shoulder, which swayed in rhythm to her step, back and forth.

As we neared the hotel, I heard a sputtering aircraft engine. An enemy plane was flying erratically, its altitude low. A string of black smoke trailed from one wing as flames sprouted from the engine, growing denser and thicker as it plunged towards earth. The speed of its descent increased; the pilot vainly tried to straighten the dive.

I grabbed her arm and pulled her to the side of the road. We took refuge behind a delivery truck, its body neatly lettered: Fi Wong & Sons, Purveyors of Fine Foods. It was parked crookedly, its driver having disappeared, but it did offer some protection. Not much, but some.

The entrance to the hotel was marked by an expansive lawn, bordered by beds of yellow flowers and marked by brick walls anchored by fluted columns. As we approached, the pilot tried to ease his descent, but the plane skimmed across the lawn, destroyed a bed of flowers, and broke in pieces as it bounced back onto the road. Parts of one wing and a section of fuselage slid past us, skidding down the street.

The front of the plane came to rest directly in our path, battered and broken and bathed in gray smoke. As we moved around it I saw the pilot, still strapped in the cockpit, the glass shattered. The mask was torn from his smudged face, dangling from one ear, and his neck was twisted at an odd angle. Blood stained the front of his tunic and his forehead as it dripped down his face. His eyes stared vacantly forward, as if he could see his final destination, but it wasn't where he'd landed. He was young, a man who would never know manhood. I thought of Maggie. She had died too young.

I looked at the woman. She turned away, preferring not to see. She had an expression of complete revulsion on her face and looked as though she might be sick. I suspected it was the first dead body she had ever seen.

I led her around the plane's parts, pieces of wing, broken glass, and bits of fuselage that lay scattered on the lawn, and we reached the hotel entrance. The explosions continued, some distant and some near, interrupted by rapid bursts of machine-gun fire. I could hear the occasional burst of anti-aircraft guns; at least we were fighting back. And I had escaped.

"Thank you," I said to the woman. My lungs felt scorched; it was difficult for me to breathe. "I might have died if you hadn't helped me." I reached in my pocket and fished out a business card. I handed it to her. "My name is George Adams. I'm a reporter with the *London Times*. Let me know if I can ever return the favor."

"I'm glad to have helped. Are you sure you're all right?" She pointed to my forehead. "You're bleeding."

I was embarrassed that she'd had to rescue me. I should have been smarter and found a bomb shelter. I knew better. I had lived through the Blitz. "No, I'm fine. Thanks for your concern. Who are you?"

She smiled, and I was again taken by the breathtaking beauty her smile brought to an otherwise ordinary face. "A guardian angel," she said. Then she scampered down the steps and into the bomb shelter.

I entered the basement and moved to the back where I collapsed on the floor in a seated position, my back against a sturdy column. She sat nearby, taking the satchel from her shoulder and plopping it on the floor beside her.

A hundred hotel guests and employees were scattered about. Most were engaged in animated conversations, but I saw that some quietly prayed.

I closed my eyes, thankful to be alive, and fought to catch my breath. I felt blood trickling down my cheek, and I noticed my trousers were torn and tattered. A knot on my head throbbed with pain. My left elbow was scraped but not bleeding. I was fortunate. It could have been much worse.

I reached in my pocket for a handkerchief, withdrawing a pencil, a notebook, and Maggie's photograph, but my hands were trembling so badly I dropped them all on the floor. I retrieved the notebook and pencil, but the snapshot had fluttered a few feet away.

"Let me help you," the man beside me said. "You're hurt."

He picked up the photograph, looked at it briefly, and handed it back to me. Then he took the handkerchief and started dabbing at the blood on my face.

"There are some small cuts on your cheek and forehead," he said. "And a nasty bruise." He pressed the handkerchief against the lacerations, stemming the dripping blood.

"Thanks," I said. "It's a bit tender."

I glanced at his face. He was engrossed in my minor injuries, dabbing at the cuts with the handkerchief, studying the wounds. I was grateful. No one else had paid any attention. The woman had avoided me after the rescue, but I didn't know why.

"The bleeding has stopped," he said. "How about your legs?"

I thought about my reception to Singapore. The London press reports were inaccurate. I would hardly describe the city as Fortress Singapore as it commonly was. The city was under attack, but the Allies were ill-prepared to defend it. The city was surprised and overwhelmed, confused and frightened. Victory would be difficult.

I rolled up my torn pant legs to the knee. Shards of brick were imbedded in several places on my calves and one larger fragment just below the knee.

He examined them closely. "This may hurt a bit. Here, take a swig of one of these. The thermos is tea, the bottle is gin. Either one will help to calm you."

I opted for the tea. I took a sip, choking on the hot liquid before returning the thermos. I felt no pain, just an overwhelming sense of relief. I had survived. Nothing else seemed to matter.

He removed the fragments of cobblestone, laying the shards on the floor. Then he poured some gin on the handkerchief and dabbed each of the entry wounds. "I think I got everything," he said. "You'll know if I didn't. Are you all right?"

"Yes, I think so. And I do appreciate your help."

"Take another swig," he offered the thermos.

I put my lips to the container, taking a longer sip this time. It did help. I could feel the calmness coursing through my body. Still, although the pain was dissipating, the fear was not.

I studied him closely. He was about forty years old, a good dozen years my senior, and the lines of life had just begun to etch the weathered skin of his face. His eyes, which were a sparkling blue, were his most striking feature. A two or three day growth of beard shadowed his face, and a yachting cap topped an uncombed mop of brown hair.

"I'm Thomas Montclair," he said. He thrust his hand forward, shaking mine firmly.

9

"George Adams," I replied.

"That was worse than the last few attacks. They're becoming more frequent. And more severe. Didn't you hear the warning?"

"Yes, but I was several blocks away. I just arrived from London a few hours ago. I wasn't sure where to go." It sounded ridiculous. There were probably bomb shelters everywhere. I could have just followed everyone else.

He pointed to my notebook. "Are you a writer?"

"Yes, I am. I work for the *London Times.*"

"Why did you ever come to Singapore?" he asked.

I didn't want to explain my reason. Especially to a man I had known a matter of minutes. "I wanted to report from the front lines."

He raised his eyebrows. "Isn't London the front lines?"

"Yes," I admitted. "I suppose it is. But it's more than that. My predecessor was killed in an earlier air raid."

"The only people coming to Singapore now are running away from something worse," he said.

I didn't have a good answer. I wasn't about to tell him that I had to leave London, that I saw Maggie's face in every window, on every corner. I didn't want him to know that I couldn't even function, that a task as simple as choosing my shoes was utterly overwhelming.

"It was a good opportunity," I said simply.

He studied me for a moment, curiously. It was almost as if he knew something far more intriguing than a better career opportunity had brought me to Singapore. Maybe he was too polite to ask.

"Actually, I wanted to be a soldier," I said, interrupting the impasse.

"You weren't accepted?"

"No," I said. "I had a very sickly childhood. I have trouble breathing, and I don't have much stamina. I'll make more of a contribution as a reporter."

"Probably so," he said.

He was quiet, either uninterested or reflecting on what I'd said; I didn't know which. He took another sip from the bottle.

The ground shook from a bomb above. I shuddered and quickly looked upward as dust filtered from the ceiling, rattled loose by the blast. I hoped the hotel wouldn't collapse like the Malay Towers had. I shifted uncomfortably, keeping a wary eye on the beams above.

"I don't recognize your accent," I said.

He smiled. "I'm a citizen of the seven seas."

I looked at him curiously. He was being as evasive as I was.

"But of French ancestry," he added.

"From France?" I asked. "Or a colony?"

"From everywhere," he said. "My family moved frequently."

"Have you been in Singapore long?"

He shrugged. "I lose track of time."

"What does that mean?"

He nodded towards the woman who had helped me. "An interesting lady," he said.

I looked over at her. She sat upright, her back against the wall. She held a book in front of her, and the pages had her complete attention. As bombs burst above us and the sounds of machine-guns, diving planes, and whining engines drowned conversations, she calmly read. She refused to be intimidated, not by me staring at her, not by the other guests, and not by the Japanese army. I looked at the book. It was entitled, *Murder on the Suez Canal.*

That was an interesting choice. Another volume sat on the floor beside her. I squinted, reading the title on the spine. It was a far different subject: *Social Stratification of the Indian Subcontinent*.

"She helped me get to the bomb shelter," I said. "She's a brave woman."

"I may ask to borrow her book."

"The murder mystery?"

He looked at me strangely. "No, the book on India."

I hadn't expected the reply. There might be more to the man than I thought. He might have an interesting story to tell. Maybe he could form the foundation of my first article. I was planning a series for the *Times*. I wanted to call it *People of Singapore*.

"I think she arrived yesterday," he continued.

"Who is she?" I asked. "She wouldn't tell me her name."

He laughed. "I have no idea. But, as I said before, people are fleeing Singapore by the boatload. Those arriving can only be leaving something worse."

"Why are you here?" I asked.

He pointed towards the street. "The bombing has ceased."

The sirens signaling the end of the attack sounded, but I wondered for how long. When was the next attack coming and would it be worse than this one? I had to establish some contacts with the military and determine how serious the situation was. My first impression was that Singapore was in dire danger.

As we made our way to the exit, I glanced at the woman who had helped me. She was disappearing into the crowd. I didn't know why I found her so interesting. I suppose it was because she had saved me. Or maybe it was her smile. Or the assortment of books she was reading. And then I suddenly felt guilty. How could I even think about another woman, regardless of the reason? It wasn't fair to Maggie.

"I want to thank you for helping me," I said. I thought about the potential story. "Maybe I can buy you dinner?"

"How about a drink," he said. "We can meet in the hotel bar this evening."

We climbed the steps. He opened the door, and rays of sunlight streamed into the dimly lit basement.

"Yes, of course," I said. "I would like that, but something soft." I wondered if many of the hotel guests frequented the bar. I suspected they did. It might be interesting.

Singapore would be more difficult than I realized. I had to immerse myself in its culture, learn about its people, understand its motives, and predict its future. I would understand and assess its military capabilities: the strength of its defenses, the morale of its defenders, the will of its attackers and the chances for its survival. I planned to interview people, from the men who cleaned the streets to the social elite to the highest ranked military commanders I could gain access to. I must become a part of Singapore, and it would become a part of me. And I must learn why Thomas Montclair had come, and why he stayed, and why he had helped me when a dozen others had simply stared. I made a note to find out who the woman was, courageous and defiant in the face of danger, but reluctant to reveal her identity. I would learn the secrets of Singapore, but I would tell their secrets too.

CHAPTER 2

I returned to my room, continually playing the scenes of the air raid in my mind. It had been traumatic, especially for the residents, but it was far from the intense aerial assaults that London experienced. This attack didn't compare to a thousand planes harassing the city day and night, the incessant wail of sirens and ambulances, the sickening cost in injuries and deaths, or block after block of devastation and destruction. Even though I had almost lost my life, it was due to my own stupidity, my own complacency and overconfidence. I would not make that mistake again.

The magnitude of the attack showed me much about the Japanese. There were less than a hundred planes, all fighter aircraft with minimal destructive impact. And, although it came late, the British did counterattack, both with anti-aircraft guns and a handful of planes dispatched after the attack had started.

But the assault had come quickly; it had been launched from a nearby airfield, probably just across the straits on the Malay Peninsula. The air attack that killed my predecessor Miles Jackson had come from long range bombers that flew from Japanese bases in French Indo-China. Given what I had witnessed, the city's defense would be difficult. The British and their allies seemed undermanned and overwhelmed, even though reinforcements arrived daily.

While reflecting on the attack, and wondering when the next would come, I cleaned up my injuries. Thomas had removed the cobblestone splinters in my legs and glass particles in my cheek. I cleansed all the wounds, ensuring nothing else remained, and then rubbed an antiseptic on them that I had gotten in the hotel shop. My head ached where the beam had struck me, so I put a wet cloth on it and took some aspirin. Other than that there was little else I could do.

I obsessed about the woman who had rescued me. I wondered why she wouldn't tell me who she was or who she was looking for during an air raid. Assuming she was really looking for someone. The mystery was intriguing. But she wasn't why I had come to Singapore, my writing was. So I immersed myself in my work, occasionally distracted by thoughts of her smile.

I sat with my notepad and created the first in a series of articles titled, *Live from Fortress Singapore.* I gave a detailed description of the air raid, making the images vibrant and real, the emotions vivid and deep. First I focused on my experience: the machine gun attack, the collapse of the Malay Towers, my mystery rescuer, and the plane that crashed on the lawn of the Victoria Hotel. Readers always seemed to like it when I related personal experiences.

I closed the article by summarizing my thoughts on military preparedness, capturing the panic in the streets, and describing the mood in the hotel bomb shelter. I envisioned the series as a companion to my articles on the people of Singapore, and I thought it would give British subjects around the world a vivid depiction of the war in Southeast Asia.

I brought the article to the office of the *London Times*, which was across the street from the Victoria Hotel, tucked away in a string of storefronts and offices that ran the length of the entire block.

As I left the lobby, I saw that the crashed Japanese plane had marred the expanse of green lawn that wrapped around the hotel, the rich soil exposed from the aircraft skidding over it on its way to the street. Wreckage lay scattered about: pieces of a wing, a section of tail that still had the plane's identifying numbers on it, the grass singed brown by leaking gasoline, and scattered debris, mostly fragments of wood too small to tell what part of the plane they had come from.

A flower bed, one of dozens, had been destroyed, but a gardener was already working magic with what was left, rearranging the flowers, removing what was damaged, and adding more. A work crew, consisting of three uniformed workers, organized the debris, bundling it into smaller packages and loading it on the back of a small truck. Although the cockpit still sat in the midst of the street, just beyond the lawn, I saw no sign of the pilot, his remains having long since been taken away.

I entered the *Times* office to find a single room, spacious but crammed with a dozen desks situated in the center, facing each other in two rows. Each desk contained a small lamp, a typewriter, stacks of paper, file compartments, pens, and pencils. The desks were mostly occupied, and some of the reporters' fingers were flying across the keys as they fought to meet the day's deadline. Others were on the phone, frantically gathering information, confirming sources, and making arrangements. Arms waved, tongues wagged, eyes proofread. It was truly a news room, and probably the most important in Southeast Asia.

"Can I help you?" asked a young woman of Asian descent, petite and pretty with black half-glasses.

"Yes," I said. "How are you? I'm looking for Alistair Duncan."

She motioned her head towards an office at the back

of the room. I nodded and walked towards it.

Alistair Duncan was tall and very thin, with an anemic look and pale blue eyes that made him appear one day away from a hospital bed. His suit fit poorly, probably due to his irregular shape, and his tie was loosened, the top button of his shirt undone. He looked just as I would expect an editor to look after enduring a long day with too much news to cram into too little time. He spoke on a telephone as I knocked on his door, the earpiece cradled on his shoulder while he typed, slowly and methodically with two or three fingers on each hand. A moment later he hung up the phone and motioned me in.

"I'm George Adams," I said. "I arrived earlier today to replace Miles Jackson."

"Adams, nice to meet you. Alistair Duncan. Do you have anything for me?"

"Yes," I said, handing him my article. "A report on the air raid."

"That's three days in a row they've attacked," he said. "But we'll beat them back. This is *Fortress Singapore*."

As he skimmed the pages, I outlined my plans for two articles a day, focused on both the people of Singapore and the war. He occasionally looked up; he seemed to like the idea but offered no reaction. He was preoccupied with finishing his own report, his eyes glancing towards the manila sheet rolled into the typewriter. When he finished reading, he called the man whose desk was nearest his office, gave him the article and instructed him to post it.

"We need you, Adams," he said. He pointed to the office, which was chaotic, with nine or ten people alternating between phone calls and typewriters. "It's pandemonium here. Especially since the air raids started.

17

The whole world wants to know what's happening in Singapore."

"I'm glad I can help," I said. My thoughts drifted back to London. I missed it already: my office, my desk, my typewriter. "Do you have a military contact I can use?"

He scribbled some information on a notepad. "Here are three," he said. "The first, Colonel Rogers, is on General Percival's personal staff. Difficult to find, somewhat guarded, but the most knowledgeable. The other two have second-hand information, but they're still good sources. Tell them you work for me."

I looked at the contacts. I didn't recognize any of them, but I wasn't that familiar with military leaders in the Asian theater. When I looked up I saw Duncan glancing at his watch.

"Thank you," I said as I stood to rise. "I'm sure we'll be seeing a lot of each other."

The Raffles Café sat next to the *Times* office, a cozy eatery with a generous view of the expansive lawn in front of the Victoria Hotel and Orchard Road as it rolled past on its way to the harbor. Beside the wide windows were a half dozen wrought iron tables and chairs situated on the edge of the sidewalk, none showing any signs of damage from the air raid, and now occupied with an assortment of citizens idly passing the early evening. It reminded me of the Treasure Island Café, one of my favorite haunts in London and a location where I had spent many an afternoon, often with other reporters from the *Times* office.

I went in and ate dinner, selecting a local dish called Mee Siam, which was rice with seafood and vegetables. I then enjoyed a cup of tea, which was as popular in Singapore as it was in London. I quietly watched the pedestrians passing: young women with strollers, octogenarians with canes, policeman, students, housewives and businessmen, wondering how they continued with their daily lives with the Japanese at their doorstep. They strolled by, most not even looking at the downed plane across the road, intent on their destination: work or school or shopping or visiting friends and relatives. Somehow they coped, just as we had in London.

An elderly man was seated beside me, well dressed in slacks and a sports coat, his shirt unbuttoned at the collar, his white hair meticulously combed. He reeked of British upper class, an integral component of any colony. He sipped his tea, watching me curiously.

"Nasty business, the air raid," he said.

"Yes, it was," I agreed. "When do you think the next attack will be?"

"Tomorrow," he said. "They're coming daily now. In another week, they'll be sitting beside me having tea."

I liked him. He was polite and sophisticated, and he possessed the wit and wisdom that only the years seem to offer. His name was Henry Hyde, and he was a retired banker. Originally from London, he had lived in Singapore for the last forty years. He described life in the city before the war, and I did the same for him in London. The more we talked, the more I found him interesting, honest, and sincere, a man of both conviction and integrity.

"I never missed London," he told me. "At least not until now. Singapore is paradise. But apparently the Japanese have figured that out. Now they want it. The trick is not to let them have it."

"How do we do that?"

He shrugged. "We're in a precarious situation. Reinforcements arrive daily, troops and planes and canons, but the island is almost surrounded. I was out in my boat yesterday and saw Japanese on Ubin Island."

I pictured the map of Singapore and the Malay Peninsula in my mind, but I couldn't capture details that minute, even though I had memorized maps as a child.

He noticed my bewilderment. "Here, I'll show you," he offered. He drew the Malay Peninsula on a napkin. At the base he drew a rough circle, shaped like a diamond. "This is the island of Singapore. The city of Singapore is located on the southern side, just beside the lower point of the diamond. The entire island is about thirty miles east to west and fifteen miles north to south. The Japanese are on the Malay Peninsula, which wraps the northern half of the island. Now they are also on Ubin Island, to the northeast."

"So that's where the attack will come from?" I asked.

He shrugged. "You should have the answer in a few days."

Henry Hyde became the first person profiled in my *People of Singapore* series.

I strolled into the hotel lounge at 9 PM that evening, wondering how long the city would be spared another air raid. I had now acquired the habit of always knowing where the nearest bomb shelter was; I didn't want to be unprepared. I realized that Singapore was a different situation than London. The Japanese had every intention of invading the island. There were no distractions for them, no alternative targets, no reason to bypass. The invasion would come, probably in a matter of days.

As I had expected, given the impeccable reputation of the hotel, the lounge was a spacious room with an elegant décor. Ornate, cream-colored moldings framed the ceiling and divided the walls at their center. The upper portion of the room was wrapped in beige-striped wallpaper, while the lower half was whitewashed wainscoting. The outside wall contained a series of twelve-pane windows, some of which were cracked or broken from the recent bombing and haphazardly patched to keep out insects. Those windows still intact offered a generous view of Orchard Road and the landscaped lawn.

An empty stage with closed curtains that depicted the Singapore waterfront ran the length of the room. I guessed that the war had borrowed many of the city's best performers, but I envisioned happier times when crowds of people enjoyed fine food and the area's finest productions. Now only a scratchy phonograph played the year's most popular songs. I recognized the voice of Billie Holiday.

Perpendicular to the stage and jutting into the room was a horseshoe-shaped mahogany bar. Twenty people of various nationalities were scattered around its circumference, while a busy bartender manned the center. A bare dance floor occupied the area in front of the stage, while the remainder of the room was filled with small tables. Some faced the windows, where you could watch the pedestrians on the boulevard beyond, but the rest were scattered about. The majority were occupied, some by well-dressed men and women of society's elite, others by the more mundane.

I turned and walked towards the bar, my attention drawn to a woman sitting alone by the dance floor. A mane of yellow hair cascaded to her shoulders, while her face was buried in a newspaper. A glass of white wine sat on the table, beside a book. It was the woman who had rescued me during the air raid.

I considered stopping to talk to her, but then I

remembered how reluctant she was to reveal her identity. I assumed she wanted privacy. I decided to discretely nod and wave when I caught her attention, but I was no rival for the newspaper. She never looked up.

I did want to know more about her. I wondered who she was, and if she had found whomever she had been looking for, why she had come to Singapore, and where she obtained her voracious appetite for reading. If nothing else, that was a habit we shared.

I saw Thomas seated at the bar but with a different appearance. Gone were the rumpled clothes and yachting cap he had worn that day, replaced by black slacks and a white silk shirt. He had shaved, and his hair was combed.

"Mr. Adams, he called. I'm glad you could come. How are you feeling?"

"Much better, thank you." I ordered a juice for me and a cocktail for you."

"Did you write any articles about the air raid?" he asked.

"Yes, I did." I told him about the stories I had written, both on the air raid and about Henry Hyde. I described the two series I planned to create and briefly talked about my column in London. His interest seemed genuine.

"So tell me," he said, his face reflective. "What does London think of the situation here?"

"It's known as *Fortress Singapore*. Its defenses are impregnable. A universe away from what we saw today. But the English government is confident it will survive."

"Now that you are in Singapore, you should report the truth to those back home."

"And what is the truth?" I asked. "A few air attacks

and nothing more? A weakness in our defenses that has been momentarily exploited? Or an imminent defeat?"

He searched my face, wondering whether to trust me. It was a look I had seen a hundred times when conducting interviews. He glanced at those nearby, insuring he could not be heard. Then he leaned forward and whispered, "I'm afraid that *Fortress Singapore* is actually a myth, developed as a propaganda ploy to boost morale. In truth, the British are on the verge of the worst defeat in their history."

I thought about the air raid. It had been small when compared to what I had seen in London. Damage was limited to an apartment building, some broken windows and bullet-ridden cars. I suspected that was mirrored in different sections of the city. But there wasn't a significant loss of life. It seemed a gross exaggeration to admit defeat; the battle had yet to begin.

"I think you might be mistaken," I said. "And so does all of Britain. Our forces greatly outnumber the Japanese. We can deter an invasion."

"Are you sure?" he asked. "Look at what you witnessed today. Who was the aggressor?"

The Japanese did attack. And for the most part they were unopposed. Although I did see an enemy plane shot down. "We don't know what damage our forces did."

"The Japanese forces are massed on the Malay Peninsula, ready to attack. But, I've heard rumors they have also occupied Ubin Island in the northeast."

The whole world knew that the Japanese occupied the Malay Peninsula. But no one knew that they were on Ubin Island. So Thomas confirmed what Henry Hyde had told me. I thought it interesting that two such varied sources had the same information.

"Will they attack from Ubin Island?"

"I doubt it," he said. "It's probably a diversion. But it does pin some of our forces there in case they do attack. That's what the Japanese want."

"How do you know all of this?"

He shrugged. "I talk to people. I listen. There are many soldiers in the city. It only takes a liter of beer to loosen their tongues."

"Why do you trust me with this information?"

"It's nothing secret," he said. "I'm sure someone will confirm it."

"Do the residents of the island share your view of its defenses?"

"A few do," he said. "But most hope for a miracle. But the truth is, unless the British send assistance, Singapore is doomed. Maybe you can write an article that rallies that support."

"I need to confirm your assessment," I said. "Facts are more persuasive than opinions."

"I encourage you to do so," he said. "If you want, I will take you around the island tomorrow. You can see the defenses for yourself."

He was then distracted, and looked towards the dance floor and chuckled. I turned to see what captured his attention.

An American song by the Andrews sisters, an upbeat tune called *Boogie Woogie Bugle Boy* blared on the phonograph. The mystery woman sat at her table, her eyes still on the book, but consumed by the music. Her foot tapped on the floor, she was snapping her fingers, and her upper body swayed back and forth. As the song moved to the chorus, she raised her eyes from the page and mouthed the lyrics, oblivious to the rest of the room. I wondered how she could read and sing at the same time.

I looked at some of the other patrons. The Victoria Hotel was one of the most exclusive establishments in the world. Almost all its guests, except for me, were upper class socialites. Most were British. And upper class Englishman were staid and stiff. But they watched her also, amused by her behavior.

"You like her, don't you?" Thomas asked.

I was uncomfortable with the question. My mind was focused on Maggie, as it should be, not some woman I didn't even know. "I do find her interesting," I admitted.

"So do I," he said. "What do you find so appealing?"

I had asked myself the same question. "She's brave, intelligent, unconventional, daring and unafraid. She has a beautiful smile and is very attractive, particularly her blue eyes and blond hair."

"That's what you see?"

I looked at him strangely. "Yes, that's what I see. Why? What do you see?"

"I see someone hiding from the world. Someone vulnerable, afraid she'll be hurt, who acts strong and defiant so no one notices."

He surprised me. He was far more perceptive than I thought. I considered his statement, and watched the woman as she sipped her wine, oblivious to the excitement she had caused in the taproom.

"Isn't it funny," he said. "We see completely different things."

"Maybe we each see what we want to see. Not what really is."

CHAPTER 3

It was almost midnight when I prepared to depart, more than a little tired. I was not a drinker, so alcohol wasn't the cause. My father was a Protestant minister, and I experienced a strict upbringing. There had been no alcohol in my house, as we believed it was dissipation. I did have a happy childhood, at least as happy as possible when confined to bed for most of it, but I had little opportunity to develop any other vices.

Thomas was determined to remain at the bar until it closed, which I would later learn was his custom. I said my goodbyes and made my way across the empty dance floor, past the tables that surrounded it, most of which were still occupied. I glanced at the patrons as I passed and smiled. I pictured them watching the mystery woman enjoying the music. Just as I left the lounge, I felt someone lightly tap my shoulder.

"Mr. Adams?"

It was her. She held up the business card I had given her.

"I think I'll take that favor you offered."

"Of course," I said anxiously. "Just name it. But who are you? You wouldn't tell me this morning."

"I'd rather not," she said. "It's not important anyway."

"But it is to me," I said. "And I can always get it from the hotel registry."

She smiled, that beautiful smile that had so overwhelmed me earlier. "All you'll get is the name under which I registered. Which may or may not be mine."

I studied her for a moment. She was determined but polite. I tried a different tactic. "You can trust me," I said softly.

She arched her eyebrows. "I can trust a reporter? I bet I'm already in the morning papers. I'm sure you wrote about the air raid."

She was right. I did write about the air raid. And I did mention her. "I'm sorry."

"I thought so."

"But I can keep a secret."

She studied me closely, and a tense moment passed. "All right, I'll trust you," she said. Her eyes twinkled with a bit of mischief. "But if you betray me, I will make it very unpleasant for you."

"Really?" I asked, detecting a sense of humor. "How so?"

"Let me see," she said, rubbing her chin thoughtfully. "Suppose I pull out each fingernail, one by one, slowly and deliberately."

"Ouch," I said. She had probably gotten that idea from one of the murder mysteries she read. "I think that will make me keep my promise. Have I convinced you?"

She was pensive for a moment before surrendering. "I suppose."

"And you are?"

"Lady Jane Carrington Smythe," she said.

My eyes widened. I was surprised I hadn't recognized her. But why would I? Who expected to find a titled Englishwoman, especially one as well-known as she, wandering around Singapore during an air raid?

The Smythe family had been entrenched in Ulster for centuries. Her father, the Earl of Carncastle, spent the past twenty-five years as a political advisor in India, helping the crown govern the colony. Some claimed he was banished from England after the Great War because he was a relative of the German Kaiser. It had created quite a stir, there were even accusations of aiding the enemy; it was a sordid scandal at the time. So Lady Smythe had spent most of her life in New Delhi while her family maintained a dominant voice in England's oversight of the subcontinent.

"Lady Smythe," I said with a bow, "I am honored to meet you."

She rolled her eyes. "Yes, I'm sure. But you can save all that rubbish. Call me Jane."

"Lady Jane," I said, unable to entirely forego the formalities. "What can I do to assist?"

She surveyed the area and, when satisfied we were alone, she continued. "I can use your help. But no one must know who I am. Not under any circumstances. Do you understand?"

My interest was piqued. I wondered why such secrecy. And what did she need my help for. She could have, and do, whatever she wanted. All she had to do was ask.

"I understand," I said. "I will not reveal your identity."

She eyed me for a moment and, when satisfied she could trust me, she led me into the lobby. We moved past the walls of Italian marble and around a group of broad-leafed potted plants. A secluded leather sofa was hidden by the shrubbery, and it was here that she chose to sit.

The room was deserted except for the clerk manning the registration desk. He yawned while he read a newspaper through half-lens glasses. He occasionally peeked over the frame to gaze about the room, but seemed to have little interest in us, assuming he noticed us at all.

Her continued need for secrecy only heightened my

curiosity. I leaned forward, giving her both my undivided attention and the respect her social position demanded.

"I've been told that journalists have a network of global contacts," she said.

She was partially right. I was a journalist. But I had no global contacts. In fact, I had barely left London. Not even for other regions of the United Kingdom. I had no idea what she wanted, but I was intrigued. Both by her and her dilemma.

"Please, continue," I said.

"I was supposed to meet someone here, at the hotel, but he has not arrived. I would like you to help me find him."

I remembered when she had rescued me. So she really was searching for someone. But why during an aerial assault? Maybe she thought he was in the immediate vicinity and might be injured or caught unaware.

"I think anyone could help you with that," I said. "It doesn't have to be me."

"It's a personal matter," she said. "And I told you, I don't want anyone to know that I'm here. That's very important."

I studied her for a moment. She was attractive on so many different levels. I knew it was wrong, given Maggie's memory, but I hadn't been able to stop thinking about her. I wasn't sure if I could help Lady Jane. But I decided to try.

"Tell me about this person you were supposed to meet," I said.

"He's a soldier who is stationed here."

"He never arrived?"

"Not at the hotel, but I assume he's still in Singapore. And I must find him. We intend to go to

Australia."

I considered the many reasons she might be meeting the man. A love interest. He was a friend or relative. She might be helping him desert the army, or finding him for a friend, or maybe she was escaping from something worse, as Thomas had said. It was troubling that he hadn't contacted her. I considered the turmoil of the last few months. There could be a dozen legitimate reasons why he didn't. But he could also be dead.

"Do you know his regiment?"

"Yes," she said. "He's with the Twelfth Infantry Brigade. His name is Captain Balraj Patel."

I was a bit surprised. It was an Indian name. Although I knew she was also from India, it ruled out any relation.

"When was the last time you talked to him?"

"I received his last letter about three weeks ago."

If she had received his letter three weeks ago, plus the time it took to get there, he could now be anywhere. Three weeks in war equaled a lifetime in peace.

"You do realize that I've only arrived in Singapore this morning?" I said hesitantly.

"So," she said. "I only arrived yesterday. But I never expected the Japanese to be so close."

"Nor did I," I admitted. "The situation is far worse than those in London know."

I thought of racing down Orchard Road that afternoon with bullets firing and bombs bursting. I thought of the abandoned cars, panicked people, and diving planes. Singapore was a city at war.

She was staring intently, almost as if she were trying to gauge my sincerity. Eventually she seemed satisfied. She stood abruptly and turned towards the bar.

"Why don't we have a drink?"

"A marvelous idea, but I don't drink alcohol.

We returned to the taproom, and I found the same faces I had left ten minutes before. We sat at the bar, and I ordered a sparkling water with lime while she had a spark ling water with lime while she had a glass of white wine. Thomas sat directly across from us talking to an Asian man whose head was shaved. I assumed this impeccably dressed gentleman was a city businessman.

"I'm hoping you have contacts with the military who can tell me where he is," she said. "I'm afraid something happened to him. I'm frightfully worried."

"Considering the chaos of the last few days, he could be anywhere on the island," I said. I tried to think of the best way to approach this. The location of specific divisions was likely classified. Each had their own area of expertise, vital information to the enemy.

"I suppose," she said. "But I do think he is still here." She sipped her wine, her lipstick leaving a faint outline on the glass. "Do you know anyone who can find him?"

I had to think of something. I didn't want her to change her mind. Not only was she a fascinating person, but she would also be a valuable contact for my career, opening doors to a level of society that were currently closed, especially if she felt indebted to me.

I was about to admit that the issue may be more difficult than it seemed when my eyes met Thomas. I thought of the military discussion we had just shared, the specific information he had access to. He smiled broadly, nodded a greeting, and motioned discreetly to Lady Jane.

"I have met someone with detailed knowledge of military matters," I said. "I can approach him. He may be willing to help."

 "And who is that?" she asked.

 "That gentleman directly across the bar."

CHAPTER 4

"Who is he?" she asked.

"His name is Thomas Montclair."

"English?"

"No, French, but from parts unknown."

"Why do we need someone else?" she asked. "If there are more people involved, someone may find out who I am. Can't you just make a few inquiries? You should have access to the authorities. I don't."

"Yes, I do," I said. "But they may not be willing to tell me anything. Thomas is familiar with the geography of the island, and he knows a lot of local people. He may be able to get information more easily than us."

She studied him from across the bar, a hint of skepticism crossing her face. "How well do you know him?"

"I've only spent a few hours with him. But I do think we can trust him. He's an interesting person. Intelligent, well-traveled, he speaks five languages, and more importantly he knows Singapore."

Her interest was piqued. "He speaks five languages?"

I watched her closely. She seemed to respect and admire intelligence; it was a quality she possessed, judging from the books she read.

"Yes, he does," I said. "And when we were in the bomb shelter, he was looking at the book you had. He wanted to borrow it."

"What book is that?" She looked uncomfortable, as if she had caught us spying on her.

I smiled, thinking of the title. *"Social Stratification of the Indian Subcontinent."*

She seemed a bit surprised, both that we had noticed what she was reading and that he found it appealing. She glanced at him again, studying him with different eyes. "Interesting," she said slowly. "But what if he doesn't want to help?"

"Let's first see if he does."

"All right," she said. "And I agree with you. He can likely open doors that we cannot. Also, make it clear to him that money is no object. I'm saying that for your benefit also."

"Lady Jane, I would be honored and privileged to assist you," I said. "But I will not do so for monetary gain. I suspect Thomas will feel the same."

"Why do you say that? You don't even know him."

"He is staying in one of the most exclusive hotels in the world. I didn't get the impression he's in need of money."

"So you think he is a sincere, compassionate man who will gladly assist."

"Yes, I do."

"From your extremely limited exposure to him."

"I suppose," I said. I couldn't tell if she was debating with me or toying with me. Her expression gave no hint.

An awkward pause ensued as the seconds of tension ebbed away. Then she started laughing. "You shouldn't be so serious, George. You need to learn how to have fun."

I grinned. "You had me a bit nervous." I mentally added humorous to her list of attributes.

She sipped her wine and then rose from her seat. "You speak to Thomas," she said. "I'll meet both of you here tomorrow evening at 8 PM. I want to get some sleep. I plan to make inquiries of my own tomorrow."

I grabbed my drink and went to the opposite end of the bar and sat beside Thomas. He was still talking to the man with the shaved head. Any hope I had of joining the conversation ended when I realized they were speaking Mandarin Chinese.

They chatted for several minutes more, their words interrupted by sighs and laughs. Thomas turned to me occasionally, seeking my opinion, as if I could actually understand them. His Asian companion rose from his stool and laughed loudly. He nodded to me politely, and walked to the exit. Thomas laughed also and, as his friend took his leave, turned back to the bar and lit his pipe.

"What was all that about?" I asked.

"Li Ching is an old friend," he said. "He made a fortune in the shipping industry. And he tells the best jokes in Singapore." He turned to me and smiled. "So, my friend, you were not so fortunate with the lady?"

"No, it wasn't like that," I explained.

He chuckled. "No, of course not. It never is."

"Thomas, that woman is Lady Jane Carrington Smythe, an aristocrat from New Delhi."

"I didn't care for New Delhi," he said. "India is interesting enough, especially from a spiritualistic perspective, but the weather was…"

"She asked for my assistance with a difficult situation," I said. "I agreed to help her, but I'm not sure I can."

He seemed concerned. "Is she in trouble?"

"No," I said. "She is trying to find someone. A soldier. He was supposed to meet her yesterday here at the hotel."

"And he never showed up?"

"No, he didn't."

"It might be a mistake to get involved," he said. "Her friend could be dead. Especially given the recent fighting. Imagine how horrible it would be to have to tell her."

"I already considered that." I thought about Maggie. Alive one minute and gone the next.

"What do you plan to do?"

"I'm not sure," I said. "I don't know the area or the people. And the military will not release information. At least not officially. I told her that I only knew one man who might be able to help."

"And who is that?" he asked.

I paused. I had no right to impose. He was a stranger only hours before. "You," I said finally.

He showed no emotion, and merely reflected on what I'd said while puffing his pipe. "Why did you choose me?"

"I don't know, instinct, I suppose. This afternoon you helped me. And you know Singapore."

He studied the remaining patrons in the bar, smiling at the ladies. I let a moment pass without disturbing him.

"She's willing to pay whatever you ask," I said.

He puffed his pipe, still gazing around the room. "Money isn't an issue. I have enough to suit me."

His reply made me curious. I had seen no evidence of employment. And he didn't seem born to wealth, even though he was staying at a posh hotel. But I wasn't rude enough to ask, even though I wanted to.

"I'll consider it," he said abruptly. He changed the conversation to the Japanese assault.

We talked until 1 a.m. I had stayed longer than planned and was very tired. It was time to go. I got off the stool, stood a moment to steady my weak legs, and said my farewells.

The stillness of the night was shattered by air-raid sirens. Seconds later the drone of enemy aircraft, faint at first but gradually growing louder, challenged the whine of the warning whistles. The room rumbled from distant explosions; pictures on the walls shook but did not fall. I noticed my glass vibrating on the bar

"We had best get to the bomb shelter," I said. I had no desire to risk my life twice in one day.

Thomas stood, fumbled with his pipe, and filled his glass. The other patrons rushed past on their way to the basement, shouting and shoving. I started to follow.

When I was halfway across the room I paused and waited. Thomas was still at the bar, choosing the bottle of gin rather than his glass.

"Thomas! Come on!" I started for the lobby, where a stairway led to the basement.

"Let's use the outside entrance," he called. He walked to the opposite end of the room where double doors opened into the street.

A massive explosion ripped through the night, dwarfing the magnitude of the blasts before it. I watched in horror as the wall beside him shattered, exploding in an eerie, timeless motion. It burst into fragments, raining dust and debris, and he disappeared from sight.

CHAPTER 5

The blast knocked me off my feet, and I stumbled backwards onto the tiled floor. I sat for a moment, stunned and bewildered. When I regained my senses, I saw that the outside wall had collapsed. A section about twelve feet square was destroyed, crumbling into a heap of timber, stone, stucco and plaster. A few vertical posts remained, looking terribly undersized to support the floors above them, and a large opening was left, offering a gateway to the expansive lawn beyond. I peered out of the gap and saw a crater in the ground where the shell had landed, broad and shallow and adjacent to the building. Then I realized that Thomas was buried in the wreckage.

I scurried to the debris, pulling brick and stone and wooden beams and bits of a broken window off him. I choked on the dust and quickly grew weary, fighting the burning ache in my lungs and feeling the strength drain from my muscles.

"Thomas!" I called.

I heard nothing. There was no scraping, no digging. I wondered if he was unconscious. Or worse. I dug frantically, yanking and scratching and clawing, my fingertips torn and bleeding.

The bombing continued; the sound of explosions were both distant and near, close to the hotel and on other sections of the island. I heard planes whizzing, bombs dropping, machine guns firing, but unlike the air raid of that afternoon, I heard aircraft fighting in the skies, the distinct sounds of planes swooping as they evaded each other, machine guns firing continuously. The Allies were meeting the enemy over the skies of Singapore, refusing to succumb.

I knew I had to move quickly. Thomas could be suffocating. But I didn't have the stamina. "Dear God, give me the strength to help my friend." I gasped for air, coughing and choking, and struggled to continue, my muscles growing weary as each second elapsed.

I pawed at the debris with my hands, scooping it away. I grabbed wooden posts, pulled them aside, and eyed the structure they had supported. The hotel still seemed sturdy.

I removed one more beam and saw Thomas's face caked in dirt and dust. He gasped and started coughing and then, once an arm was freed, he wiped the dirt and debris from his face and nose, crying out with relief.

The rest of the rubble was harder to clear, timber and brick and plaster; it was several minutes before he was completely freed. I dragged him from the wreckage, heaving and gasping for air, and helped him to his feet. Then I wiped the dust from his eyes.

I stood before him, beads of sweat dripping from my forehead, my muscles trembling. I wiped more dirt from his face. "Are you all right?"

He coughed, spitting dust from his lungs. "Yes, I think so. Still a bit disoriented."

I led him away from the collapsed wall, over towards the bar, and guided him to a chair. "Here, sit down."

He took a moment to regain his senses. Blood dripped from his forehead and oozed from his arm. I regained my breathing, and felt the strength slowly return to my sore muscles. It took me a minute to realize what had happened. My little prayer had been answered. I was too weak to be accepted by the military, yet I had just saved another man's life.

The bombing ceased, and sirens signaling the end of the attack sounded. There were no more planes, no more machine guns. Sounds of battle were replaced by ambulance sirens and rescue vehicles. A few minutes later, emergency responders were out on the street, assessing the damage, searching for injured, clearing the roadways, and determining what was needed to insure life in Singapore continued.

"You have a nasty gash on your forehead and a jagged cut on your arm," I said. I applied pressure to the head wound. "When the others return, we'll send for a doctor."

He didn't argue. He sat in the chair, gulping fresh air. The dust was just beginning to settle, and through the opening in the outer wall, I could see a building a few blocks away. It burned furiously, the yellow flames flickering in the night.

I went to the bar and returned with a moist towel and wiped the remainder of the dirt and dust from his face, gently dabbing his injuries. I inspected the cut on his forehead. Blood dripped down his face and onto his shirt. I held the towel firmly against the wound.

"Hold this a moment," I said, moving his hand to the towel.

Patrons started to return from the bomb shelter, and Thomas addressed the first to arrive. "Mr. Chang, can you find a doctor?"

"Of course," the man replied. "One of the guests is a physician. I'll go and get him."

"What happened?" the bartender asked.

"A bomb dropped just outside. The impact collapsed part of the wall," I said. "Unfortunately, it fell on Thomas."

"Oh, dear," said Mrs. Hawkins, the elderly secretary for the Singapore Croquet Club. "How did you ever survive?"

"George dug me out," Thomas said.

"You're lucky he was here," the bartender said while surveying the damage.

"Yes, I am," he replied.

An Asian man carrying a doctor's bag hurried in, glancing at his watch. We appreciated his help because we knew he was needed for injuries far worse. He rapidly placed ten stitches in the cut on Thomas's forehead and five more in the gash on his arm. A quick examination for more serious injuries found nothing but bruises, some abrasions, and aching muscles.

"You're fortunate," the doctor said. He observed the gaping hole in the wall.

"You could have been killed.

"I would have if George hadn't saved me."

I was proud that I had helped him. I knew that if the situation were ever reversed, he would do the same.

"Get some rest," the doctor advised. "You have a few bruises, but you'll feel better in no time."

Once the crowd dissipated, Thomas and I made a toast to celebrate his survival. I handed him his glass, and he raised it.

"To my friend George," he said. "The man who saved my life."

I clinked his glass with mine. "I don't know if I saved your life, but I am your friend."

"Fair enough," he said, banging his glass on the bar top. "And our adventures continue. Tomorrow I'll show you Singapore's defenses. It won't be what you're expecting."

CHAPTER 6

The countryside sped by in the darkness, trees and hills and picket fences framing manicured lawns that bordered English country cottages with thatched roofs. The winding road led up one hill and down another, curving in and out, perched aside a cliff that led to a rock-strewn coast where waves lapped against the shore.

"I'm sorry we left so late," I said, noticing Maggie's eyelids fluttering.

She yawned and then kissed me on the cheek. "That's why we're taking a holiday. Because you work too hard."

"There's so much to write about, with air raids in London and the Nazi offensive on Moscow."

"But you work every day and you need time off. We haven't been away since the wedding. And next month is Christmas. So this is the only chance we'll get."

She brushed her hand through my hair. "And you are going to relax and we are going to have fun."

She looked out the window, studying a dog that ran by the road, and a few moments later I saw her eyes close. I continued driving as 2 a.m. came and went, my mind drifting to a story I wanted to file on Monday morning.

The road was deserted with only an occasional passing car or truck. Distant noises of the moonlit night were accented by the drone of tires rolling down the road. The sounds were so soothing and serene they caused my eyelids to droop, and my breathing slowed to a regular, relaxed rate so typical of approaching slumber.

The horn blared suddenly, and my head snapped forward disjointed and confused. The truck loomed large, its headlights growing bigger and brighter. I swerved sharply, trying to avoid it. I felt my car tip, two wheels leaving the ground, skidding forward and banging against the fragile rail. The vehicle began to roll on its side, sliding against the barrier, the cliff wall dropping to the raging sea below.

The crunching sounds of the rail breaking, the truck twisting the metal of the car and pushing it ever so slowly and unavoidably towards the cliff. The steel screeched as it bent and broke and with one last cry of protest the car hurtled over the edge, spinning in an eerie, timeless motion towards the sea.

I screamed, bolting upright in bed.

My face was covered in sweat, my body trembling. It took several minutes before my racing heart slowed. I eased onto the pillow, lying on my back, staring wide-eyed at the ceiling. I closed my eyes and cried, whispering Maggie's name trying to forget the horrid nightmare that I had lived once already.

I awoke near 8 a.m., my muscles stiff and sore, my discomfort magnified by the horrible dream. I hadn't eaten anything during last night's fray, and my stomach roared like a waterfall. My head was a knot of throbbing pain. I couldn't remember a time when I felt worse.

I tried calling each of the military contacts that Alistair Duncan provided. None were available, and, even though I waited in the room for an hour, they didn't return my call. I suspected that, with the island's defense paramount, most of the military was too consumed with the upcoming assault to have time to talk to a reporter.

When I entered the hotel dining room, I saw Thomas sitting at a table overlooking the street. The wooden shutters were open and pedestrians were wandering down Orchard Road, gawking at the most recent bomb damage. I went over and joined him.

"Thomas, how are you feeling?"

"A bit bruised, I'm afraid."

"That's to be expected," I replied. "But it could have been worse."

He motioned to a waitress. "Mr. Adams will join me."

She came to our table and prepared to take my order. I looked at the fruit, cheese, ham and croissants that Thomas was devouring and my empty stomach felt like it would leave my body and pounce on it.

"I'll have everything he's having," I said.

He stopped chewing and arched his eyebrows. "You're that hungry?"

"Yes, I am."

He returned to his meal. I wondered how he could eat so heavily after all he had drunk the night before.

The waitress returned with my coffee and I sipped it slowly, savoring the rich aroma that instantly eased my headache. I started the slow process of recovery.

A few minutes later Thomas finished eating. He laid his fork on the empty plate and sat back in his chair. He lit his pipe and blew clouds of cherry smoke in all directions. He looked at me thoughtfully for a moment, as if suddenly recalling a long-forgotten secret.

"I've borrowed a friend's car," he told me. "I'll take you to the northern part of the island and show you some of the defenses."

"I would like that," I said.

"We can also look for the lady's friend. Do you know the regiment?"

"I do," I replied. "He's with the Twelfth Infantry Brigade. His name is Captain Balraj Patel."

"We can leave as soon as you've finished breakfast."

When Thomas went to get the vehicle, I waited in front of the hotel. Two trucks were parked near a side door; one was delivering fish and the second was a beer distributor. I decided to ask some questions.

The beer truck driver was a stout, friendly man dressed in shorts and a sleeveless shirt. As he loaded cases of beer onto a hand truck, I wandered over to him.

"How are you?" I asked. "Have you been bothered by the air raids?"

"About as much as everyone else," he said. "I just hope we beat them back."

"Do you deliver all over the island?"

"Oh, yes. From the cricket club to the navy base."

"How do our defenses look?"

He shrugged. "I'm not really an expert, but we have troops everywhere. I don't know if it's enough."

"Have you seen any Indian troops? I'm looking for an old friend."

"Sure," he said. "I just got back from a delivery at the navy base. There's an Indian division there."

"Thanks," I said. "I'll take a look."

I walked away, appreciative of the information, and walked over to the fish merchant.

"How are you?" I said. "Are the fish caught locally?"

He was a thin, swarthy man who smiled as I approached. "Yes, sir," he said. "And they're fresh too. These were caught this morning off the east coast."

"Really?" I asked. "Did you see anything unusual?"

"Just Japanese," he said. "They're on Ubin Island."

"Not for long," I said enthusiastically. "We'll get them out of there."

I went to the entrance and waited for Thomas, digesting what I had just heard. Indian troops near the navy base and another confirmation of Japanese activity on Ubin Island. Maybe it was easier to obtain information just by talking to people.

The automobile, a sporty roadster with a convertible top, was parked by the entrance to the lobby.

"I'll show you some of Singapore before we investigate the countryside," Thomas said. "It's a fabulous city."

His tour started at the Victoria Hotel with a trip down Orchard Road. It was a beautiful boulevard, lined with broad sidewalks and shops that sold everything from cakes to corsets. I saw street vendors, rows of tenements, landscaped parks, waterways with small boats, buildings that touched the clouds, and people that swarmed the streets. The architecture was distinct, British and Colonial, Oriental and Indian, all intertwined and mixed in a hodgepodge of colors and shapes, bricks and limestone and turrets and tiles, merging into a twirling kaleidoscope that depicted a cultural melting pot where people of many races and places lived comfortably.

It was exciting. And it suddenly occurred to me, that Singapore held the secret for peaceful coexistence; its residents had come from around the globe: Great Britain, India, China, Australia, the Dutch West Indies, and they blended and melded and lived in peace and harmony and happiness. The city was a microcosm for what the world should be but probably never would be.

Thomas interrupted my admiration of the idealistic society. "We'll go north on Woodlands Road."

"My sources tell me there's an Indian division in the north, protecting the navy base," I said.

We saw troops when we exited the city proper, as soon as the buildings yielded to trees and farms. On one hill, which sloped gently from the road to a peak of a hundred feet, we saw a wide assortment of tents and tanks, men and mortars, sandbags and shells. A patrol was nestled along a nook in the road, a dozen men tucked within a grove of trees, warily watching the landscape. Thomas braked to a stop.

"Can you tell me where the Indian Twelfth Infantry Brigade is stationed?" he called.

"Who wants to know, mate?" a soldier asked suspiciously. I saw an Australian insignia on his uniform.

"I'm looking for a friend," he said. "An Indian captain named Balraj Patel."

He studied Thomas for a moment, and then relented, assuming he was harmless. "There's Indian troops scattered around the island," he said. "Your friend could be anywhere. The defenses are just getting organized after the retreat from the north. He may be easier to find in a few days."

"Thanks," Thomas called. "I appreciate the help."

We continued on, passing ordnance and troop carriers as well as soldiers walking in groups. Some numbered a few, others over a hundred. Thomas stopped three or four times and asked for information; no one could, or would, provide any.

We soon reached an area a few miles from the northern coast. A scenic pond sat beside the road, branches from the trees that surrounded it providing a protective canopy. Two Australian soldiers sat along the edge of the water, studying the ripples as they spread from a nearby waterfall.

Thomas guided the car beside them and stopped. They glanced at us curiously, then returned to watching the water. We got out and walked up to them.

"How are you?" Thomas asked.

They nodded, offered no reply, and pointed to the water.

"What?" Thomas asked.

"A crocodile," the soldier said.

We moved up to the pond and looked. The crocodile was along the bank, its scaly tail lounging in the mud, its long snout just below the waterline, watching us with interest. We made sure to keep a safe distance, the soldiers included.

"His jaws look pretty powerful," one soldier said. "I'd hate to make him angry."

"Best stay away then," his friend said. He turned to us and laughed. "We almost went for a swim."

"Lucky we saw him first," the other said.

"I wonder if you can help us," Thomas said. "We're looking for a friend in the Indian Twelfth Infantry Brigade. We came from the city, but we've only seen Australian troops."

"We know that an Indian division is near the naval center, but we haven't been able to determine who or exactly where," I added.

"The Indian Third Corps is protecting the base," one soldier said. "But the Twelfth isn't part of that."

"Try the west coast," the other said. "He could be there."

We thanked the soldiers and decided to head back to the city.

"This may be harder than I thought," I said.

"What's the best way to continue?" he asked.

"I don't know," I said. "I got more information from the deliverymen than we did any of the soldiers. I'll try my military contacts again. They might help. But wouldn't you think Captain Patel could get a message to Lady Jane fairly easily?"

"Yes," Thomas said. "If he's not dead or wounded."

I thought for a moment, my mind returning to the purpose of our journey. "I saw troops everywhere. So I'm not convinced we're unprepared to fight."

"You saw uniforms everywhere," he stressed. "What you didn't see was faces. And the look of defeat that consumed them."

I was silent the remainder of the ride, digesting Thomas' logic and observations. Most of the troops in Singapore had come from the Malay Peninsula. Since the initial Japanese invasion, they had retreated over three hundred miles. And Thomas was right. They had yet to taste victory.

Just as we reached the suburbs of the city of Singapore, a motorcycle sped past us, racing down Woodlands Road. The long blond hair of the driver was blowing in the breeze. It was Lady Jane Carrington Smythe.

CHAPTER 7

When we returned, I went to the Raffles Café with my notepad and sat at an outdoor table. I sipped a cup of tea, watched pedestrians passing by, and started scribbling my next article, my thoughts forming as the pencil raced across the page. I eyed the clock in the tower on the Singapore Bank building, conscious of the afternoon slipping away. I wanted to complete my article in time for the morning papers in London. I wrote quickly, ideas flowing freely. When completed, I took the handwritten article to the office and watched as the typeset appeared.

Byline: *Live From Fortress Singapore*
Japanese forces are tightening the noose around the neck of Singapore, slowly strangling the island with battle-hardened troops. Numerous sources, from fishermen to bankers to boaters, have confirmed that the enemy has occupied Ubin Island, to the northeast, complimenting Japanese strongholds to the north on the Malay Peninsula. His Majesty's troops are strategically placed for maximum defense with Australians to the west, Indians to the north, and British to the east. The strength of the enemy army is not known, but given their observed positions, reinforcements of all kinds, naval, air, and ground forces are desperately needed for the city's defenses. Further civilian reports indicate…

I thought it important to present an accurate depiction of the situation to encourage reinforcements and to sway public opinion. The defenses of Singapore had to be bolstered. The Japanese had launched two air raids since my arrival. They were clearly on the offensive. Yet I knew from other articles that not many reporters were bold enough to paint such a desolate landscape or brave enough to see it.

I posted my second article in the *People of Singapore* series. It featured the truck driver who, in his owns words, delivered beer from the cricket club to the navy base. Life in Singapore continued.

I entered the taproom at 8 p.m. that evening, assuming it would be closed from the bomb damage. Instead I found that repairs had started, a makeshift wall already in place to provide support pending permanent restoration. The rubble had been cleared away, broken windows had been replaced, the room was cleaned and mopped, and little evidence of the destruction remained.

Patrons of the prior evening, give or take a few, were busily wasting the hours away. They sat alone or in small groups, dining, drinking, and laughing. As I observed their relaxed behavior, I wondered if the recent air raid had even occurred, especially since I knew, as they did, that it was only a matter of time before the planes returned, bringing death and devastation.

Thomas was seated at the bar, a half-empty bottle of gin before him. He puffed on his pipe with obvious contentment, gazing at the other guests, smiling at the ladies and nodding at the gentlemen. He was handsomely dressed in a gray, hand-tailored suit and a blue shirt with a gray tie. I'm sure he wanted to make a good impression on Lady Jane.

As I approached I saw him eyeing a raven-haired woman on the other side of the room. Their eyes met and she smiled, no doubt flattered by his attention. Their discreet communication occurred to the obvious ignorance of her inattentive mate who was enjoying the glass of brandy that sat before him.

"How are you feeling?" I asked as I sat beside him.

"Better," he said. "But still a bit sore." He motioned for the bartender. "A sparkling water with lime for Mr. Adams, please."

I scanned the taproom. "Has Lady Jane arrived?"

"I haven't seen her. But I'm sure she'll be here shortly."

She arrived ten minutes later, pausing in the arched doorway to search the faces of the room. The dim lighting afforded her a mysterious quality and, when combined with the pale-red evening gown she wore, produced a beauty that I hadn't before appreciated. The gown hugged her frame, shyly revealing her cleavage, and her hair glowed like the moon's image in a peaceful pond.

"She looks a bit pale," Thomas said. "I wonder if the situation in Singapore is wearing her down."

I gave him a bewildered look, wondering if we were looking at the same person. "I think she looks fabulous," I said softly. As soon as I said it I thought of Maggie and felt a stab of guilt.

She started towards us, her body swaying with self-confidence, her presence filling the room and overwhelming those of us who dared to share it with her. I had underestimated her poise and sophistication, her charm and charisma. I couldn't take my eyes from her, and I doubted that anyone else could either.

"Lady Jane Carrington Smythe," I offered. "May I present Mr. Thomas Montclair?"

She nodded. "It's nice to meet you, Mr. Montclair. I've heard a lot about you."

He bowed and took her hand, kissing it lightly. "I am pleased to make your acquaintance."

He stepped aside to let her pass. Then he winked at me.

"Maybe we'd be more comfortable at a table," I suggested, ignoring his antics.

I thought of what an unusual group we were. I was from London, strictly middle class, but closer to the lower end than the upper. Thomas was French and seemed comfortable with any class, and Lady Jane was from the highest echelon of society, yet she didn't want to be and didn't act as if she was.

I ordered her a glass of white wine, and we moved to a booth in a dimly lit corner, far from most eavesdroppers. Two middle aged men occupied a nearby table. They were probably waiting for their wives to come down for dinner. They were discussing horse racing and surely had no interest in us.

When we sat down Thomas pointed to the small bandage on his forehead. "I have a souvenir from the attack last night," he said. "We were a little late getting to the bomb shelter."

"I was wondering what happened," she said. "Your arm too?

"Yes, bad luck, I suppose. George saved me."

She turned to me and smiled. "Really," she said with mild surprise. "You seem to have a penchant for danger, George."

I thought of the night in England, the car hurtling over the cliff. Maggie's lifeless body. "Nothing could be farther from the truth," I said softly.

"George tells me you need some assistance," Thomas said.

She sipped her wine. "Yes, I do. It's a rather delicate situation, and absolute discretion is required."

"Yes, of course," he said. "We understand."

"Rest assured, Lady Jane," I added.

"Can you tell us what you need?" Thomas asked.

I listened attentively while she described her dilemma to Thomas. She carefully avoided explaining why she was meeting the Indian captain. Thomas never asked.

Once she had finished providing the information, he asked a question I had never thought of.

"How do you and the captain plan to get to Australia?"

She looked sheepishly at me. "That was my next request of George."

I was stunned. "Lady Jane, that might be difficult. I know you want to protect your identity, but after we find Captain Patel, why don't you go to the authorities and ask for assistance?"

She studied us closely, assessing our sincerity, before continuing. "There are several reasons," she said. "Captain Patel will be deserting, for one."

I almost reconsidered my offer to help. Not only was desertion a serious crime, but to a man like me, who had been rejected by every branch of the military, it spit in the face of honor and integrity, courage and commitment. It denied the fight for freedom, ignored the lives lost, and rejected the sacrifices made. It was a disgrace.

Thomas sensed my revulsion. I saw him watching me, curiously, and he answered Lady Jane with an eye keenly trained on me.

"I'm certain that Captain Patel has strong and valid reasons for deserting, just as you, I'm sure, have a very solid basis for assisting him," he said. "Since your integrity is beyond question…" he glanced at me, "we have no need to know those very personal details."

His speech helped; it was very diplomatic. But I still found the whole episode distasteful. I elected to ignore it, at least for the present.

"Thank you," she said, eyeing me warily. "It is intensely personal."

"And I may be able to help," Thomas continued. "I have a friend who operates an air freight business. He can probably get you out of Singapore. But it gets more difficult with each day that passes."

"Do you think the Allies will be defeated?" she asked. There was a flicker of fear in her eyes.

"Yes, I do," he said. "I think the situation is desperate and that we should all leave the island, including George."

I looked at him. His statement was sudden and unexpected, his opinion exaggerated and dramatic. I wondered why. Did he know more than he was willing to share? Or had he already been preparing to leave the island?

"That's a pessimistic assessment," I said. "I'm not ready to admit defeat. And I made a commitment to report from Singapore. So that's what I intend to do."

"George, a Japanese victory is days away," he said. "And after they conquer the island, there will be no *London Times* office. You'll have no purpose in Singapore, other than to risk your life."

I thought about the air raids, panicked people, bombed buildings, the tired, defeated faces of the soldiers, the *Times* office, where a dozen frightened reporters talked on phones and hammered typewriters. I envisioned the geography, Ubin Island and the Malay Peninsula, and the area the Japanese already occupied. I considered Singapore, and compared it to London. And I evaluated the

Japanese and contrasted them to the Germans, realizing they had no intention of abandoning the city in search of other prey. So in the end, the only conclusion that I could possibly reach, was that Thomas was right. Regardless of the commitment I had made to Toby Fields, it did me nor the *London Times* any good at all if I vanished beneath the boot of the enemy. As long as there was a war there would be a front line. I must find it and give the British subjects of the world a window to the war.

"What do you suggest we do?" Lady Jane asked.

"My friend is flying to Batavia," Thomas said. "Probably in the next two or three days. I plan to go with him. You and Captain Patel, when we find him, are welcome to come with us. You can easily leave for Australia from there. George, I suggest that you come also."

"Can we trust your friend?" Lady Jane asked.

"I am going to see him tomorrow," Thomas said. "Why don't you both come with me? I'm sure you'll feel comfortable after you meet him."

"Where is he?" I asked. I didn't want to be gone the whole day. There were interviews I wanted to conduct.

"He's located just outside the city, on the southeast sector of the island. That's the only portion not threatened by the enemy. In the meantime, I'll have fake identities prepared for all of us. I think it's the best thing to do."

"I suppose we should be prepared," I said reluctantly. I still found it repulsive to run away. But I was also realistic enough to know the consequences if he was right.

"I agree," Lady Jane echoed.

"And we did search for your friend today," Thomas added. "But we weren't able to locate his regiment. At least not in the northern sector of the island."

"I know," she said. "I went there too. He's not in the western sector either, and I'm told that the British cover most of the eastern portion."

"Maybe we'll find him tomorrow," Thomas said.

She looked relieved. "I hope so. I am frantic with worry, wondering what might have happened to him."

"We saw you on the motorcycle earlier today," I said. "Where did you ever learn to ride?"

She smiled, and the room grew brighter. "In India. Not that my father approved. But I refused to sit in the stifling heat, being fanned by servants. I was restless, and I wanted to see the world, even if it was a small corner of countryside wrapped around New Delhi."

"So there's a bit of gypsy in your blood," Thomas said. "I can certainly relate to that. I've lived in more countries than most can count."

"How interesting," she said, her eyes studying him, perhaps seeing him for the first time. "I started as a child, venturing a little bit farther on my bicycle every day. Then I graduated to horses, cars, and motorcycles. Eventually it was airplanes. Each week I planned a different journey until I was travelling farther and farther from home."

"How far did you go?" I asked.

She looked first at me, and then at Thomas, with the utmost seriousness. "All the way to Singapore." Then she started laughing, amused to have fooled us.

"I spent some time in India," Thomas said. "Mainly in New Delhi. I loved the architecture."

She nodded in agreement. "The British plans for New Delhi have been superb, mixing Indian influences with English. The buildings rival any in the world."

They continued to share their experiences on the

subcontinent from Calcutta to New Delhi, from mountains to sea. The conversation wandered from religions to regions, castes to coasts, and history to hierarchies.

I watched as they chatted, having little to contribute even though they made efforts to include me. Curiously, I felt a tinge of jealousy; I was annoyed that they seemed to have so much in common and that they chatted so effortlessly, moving from one topic to the next. But soon my journalistic tendencies overrode my desire to participate in the conversation, and I found myself analyzing them, dissecting the personalities of these two unusual people that I had been so fortunate to meet.

Every inch of Lady Jane Carrington Smythe, every breath she took, symbolized the British aristocracy of the Indian subcontinent. But only when she wanted it to. She was far more adept at seeming ordinary, blending in, and using a dry sense of humor to keep anyone from getting too close to her. Nevertheless, her intelligence, her eloquence, and her sharp wit personified years of education and training and managed to seep into any conversation she had.

I easily visualized her in an English riding uniform, demonstrating her equestrian skills, or seated before a piano, her fingers traveling the keyboard with an ease that would amaze the less talented. But just as easily, I imagined her downing shots of tequila in a back street bar, personally offending the king, or racing a horse amidst a dozen mounted men.

Familiar with the poets of the nineteenth century, I'm sure she could quote both verse and interpretation, speaking comfortably with academics who had made those topics their lives and then a minute later read a murder mystery or a romance novel that's forgotten as soon as it's finished.

But even with all of her culture and education, I saw her rebellious side, her desire to be unconventional and innovative, and there was little doubt that Lady Jane Carrington Smythe would say or do whatever she pleased, insuring she had fun as she did so.

She was everything that Maggie wasn't.

Thomas was a mystery that left no clues, no pieces offered to complete the puzzle. A world traveler who spoke five languages, a man of French ancestry who didn't seem French, he offered just enough insight into his personal life to be interesting but not enough to understand him. A man with no obvious means of support, he lived comfortably in one of the world's most luxurious hotels, enjoying each minute life offered.

Clearly not born to wealth, Thomas still had enough intelligence and poise to mingle with those who were. Friend to princes and paupers alike, he conversed with each on a level they understood, and he relished in learning the ways of their world. Willing to help when he had no vested interest in the outcome, he seemed to skip through life, telling stories and quoting people from every layer of society, usually to provide an escape from reality for those who needed it most.

I wondered, as I watched him chat so freely with Lady Jane, what it was that motivated him. What created his obvious zest for life and his apparent love for the human race? I needed to know.

After I had dissected my companions, I thought it only fair that I examine myself. I took a swig of soda and pretended to look in the mirror.

I was a man who grew from a sickly boy, overcoming rejection, disappointment, failure, and heartache. I never gave up or considered surrender and always tried harder than everyone else just to be ordinary. I loved rugby and cricket, but would never be gifted enough to play either. I admired great literature, Shakespeare and Tennyson and Dickens, yet I would never be more than a mediocre journalist. The entire world was at war, but I was too inadequate to be a soldier. I was a lover of London, yet I felt compelled to leave. I was quiet, but inquisitive, friendly but reserved, respectful yet curious. I was loyal to friends and dedicated to family.

And I was responsible for Maggie's death.

CHAPTER 8

My thoughts, and the dialogue enjoyed by Thomas and Lady Jane, were suddenly interrupted by the hotel registration clerk. He burst into the ballroom, his face flush with excitement, his half-glasses still perched on the edge of his nose. He yelled to quiet the murmurs, waving his arms until he had everyone's attention.

"The Japanese have invaded the island!" he shouted.

The room erupted in gasps, garbled conversation, and hollered questions. I think we all had hoped the attack would never come, that it would be thwarted by the Allies before it was ever launched. Some patrons rose from their chairs, trying to get the clerk's attention, while others talked among themselves, anxious and fearful. All hoped the invasion had been halted on the beaches and that the long road to victory had begun.

"Let the man speak!" a husky voice in the back of the room bellowed. "Quiet!"

Gradually the noise subsided and the clerk continued. "The Japanese have crossed the Strait of Johore and landed on the northwest coast. The Australians are resisting fiercely, but the enemy has established a beach head. They could threaten the airport, but..."

"The airport!" gasped Charlie Li, a local real estate developer. "How will anyone escape?"

"Wait! Listen!" the spokesman said. "The commander of the British forces said the city will be held at all costs."

I realized then that the city would not be held. If the Japanese had gained a foothold on the island and were already threatening the airport, the invasion was going badly for the Allies. I thought of Thomas's warning, now an hour old. Somehow, he always seemed to know what was coming next.

Lady Jane was startled. "Will we still be able to get off the island?"

"I hope so," Thomas said, although his face showed no confidence. "Lady Jane, it may be easier for you to escape to India. There are transport vessels in the harbor now. I have some friends at the port. I can get you passage."

She looked at him for a moment, and sadness crossed her face. "I'm afraid I don't have that option," she said softly. "I think I'll go with you and George. Someday, I may return to India. But it can't be now."

I wondered what had happened. What had she done that made her unwelcome? There was the connection with Balraj Patel, a commoner from a different culture, a different race, and probably a different religion. Was he more than a friend? That much was likely. She wouldn't have come to Singapore just to meet him. They had to be in love. It was the only thing that would make her aristocratic family disown her. I could imagine her father's reaction.

"Then I must get our fake identities quickly," he said. "I think we're going to need them."

He didn't react to her reluctance to return to India. He probably shared the same thoughts I did. But he didn't show it. It wasn't like him.

The next morning at 10 a.m. we met outside the lobby. Guests were scattered about, carrying luggage and waiting for taxis or rickshaws to take them to the harbor. Although the flight for safety had started, it was still controlled and disciplined and not yet widespread. Most were cautiously observing the military situation. Waiting. Still hopeful.

We heard distant sounds of battle, the earth rumbling gently as cannons relentlessly tossed shells. The Singapore defenses responded; large guns designed to fire over the ocean now aimed at the Malay Peninsula. The Allies faced a dilemma. Even though the attack had come from the northwest, the enemy was also entrenched on Ubin Island to the northeast; it was not known if a two-pronged attack was imminent. In any event, the enemy presence pinned British troops on the eastern coast.

Thomas managed to borrow the same roadster, although now the convertible top was up. Lady Jane sat beside him while I climbed in the back. He guided the automobile through the streets of Singapore in an easterly direction, avoiding throngs of pedestrians merging onto the boulevards and competing with cars, bicycles, and trucks for the same real estate. I was perplexed by all the activity. Residents continued with their daily lives, yet the Japanese army was twenty miles away.

We traveled farther from the city's center, past the school and the park, the golf course and knitting mill, and the buildings grew sparser. Scenery transitioned to small farms, nestled in a landscape bathed in various shades of green. Thomas guided the car down a little-used lane, hidden by weeds and strewn with small rocks, which probably once formed a road. We traveled a hundred yards more and halted beside an old barn, its slate roof scarred with patches and its weathered siding missing some of its clapboards.

"We're here," Thomas said. "Come on, I'll introduce you to my friend."

As we exited the car he went to the trunk and

removed a small wooden crate; it was about a foot square and only a few inches wide. Although its contents were unknown, it appeared to be heavy. Thomas strained to carry it.

"What is that?" I asked.

"Some cargo for a delivery later today," he said.

"It looks heavy," I said. "It must be lead. Or gold."

He ignored me, and led us to a door at the side of the barn and rapped on it loudly. A distant voice called from within. He glanced furtively in all directions. When satisfied no one observed him, he entered.

We crossed the threshold, and took a moment for our eyes to adjust to the dim lighting. The barn contained a small airplane, its tail closest to us. It was a bi-wing bathed in a rich varnish and used to transport cargo. Although it was several years old and a bit weathered, it appeared well maintained.

There was a tiny office at the rear of the barn tucked beside a room that contained shelves filled with parts and tools. Thomas walked to it, knocked on the door, and then entered, carrying the crate. He emerged a minute later without it, followed by a young Chinese man.

"This is Chin, a good friend of mine," he said. "Lady Jane Carrington Smythe and George Adams."

Chin was slender and of average height, his black hair long and draping his forehead. A broad smile consumed his face, but his black eyes didn't twinkle to match it; they were dull and sad. He looked to be about twenty years old but was probably older. He wore a small gold cross around his neck.

"I'm pleased to meet you," Chin said with a slight bow of respect. "Thomas tells me that you want to leave the island."

I thought his statement curious. I wondered when they had communicated. We had just discussed leaving the prior evening. Thomas might have telephoned, informing his friend that we were coming, but then why was the visit needed? Maybe he was here only to deliver the package.

"Yes, we do," Lady Jane said. "And we expect to have another gentleman with us."

"That's fine," Chin said. "I was planning to leave for Batavia in two days, just after dusk. I don't think we should wait much longer. The Japanese could advance rapidly. This may be our only chance."

"What if the military situation deteriorates?" I asked.

"Then we'll leave tomorrow night," Chin replied. "I was waiting for some cargo. But I'll leave without it if I have to."

"Have you made this journey often?" Lady Jane asked.

"Oh, yes," he said. "Many times. I don't foresee any problems. It's about six hundred miles. But we'll stop about halfway on the island of Sumatra. I have some crates to deliver, and we can refuel there. Why? Is something wrong?"

She was hesitant, but finally expressed her concern. "You look so young."

He laughed. "I'm not as young as you think. Nowhere near."

"Chin is one of the most experienced aviators on Singapore," Thomas said. "I wouldn't trust our lives with anyone else."

"Thanks for the compliment," Chin said. "Who is the other person joining us?"

When Lady Jane seemed hesitant to speak, I replied

for her. "He's a close friend. He's with the Twelfth Infantry Brigade. We've been unable to locate him. Even though we've searched much of the island."

Chin looked at me strangely. "The Twelfth Infantry Brigade?"

"Yes," I replied. "Why?"

"You drove right past them to get here," he said. "They're stationed on the outskirts of the city."

CHAPTER 9

"That doesn't make sense," Lady Jane said. "Unless..." She paused and her complexion paled. "Is there a hospital nearby?"

"The British Military Hospital is about four miles west of the city," Chin said. "But those not seriously wounded are treated at field hospitals near their units."

"We can search on the return trip," Thomas offered. "We'll find him. Don't worry."

"I'm afraid something happened to him," Lady Jane said.

"Then let's go look," Thomas said. "Chin, we'll see you at dusk the day after tomorrow."

We got back in the car and Thomas turned the ignition. "I've known Chin for years," he said as he guided the vehicle down the lane. "He was an orphan. His parents died in some sort of accident, I forget what it was. But he ended up in the streets. I think he was about fourteen years old at the time."

"Why didn't someone take him in?" Lady Jane asked. "He must have had friends or relatives."

He shrugged. "I'm not sure."

"How did he survive?" I asked.

"He did some odd jobs, but mostly he stole. Picked pockets and the like. And he lived in an abandoned house on the outskirts of the city. Eventually he met a young woman of the Christian faith, the daughter of missionaries, and, even though they were both teenagers, they fell in love. He adopted her faith, and they married. They were expecting a child when her parents left them for a temporary assignment on the mainland. They were never seen again."

"How did the youngsters ever raise a child?" Lady Jane asked.

"They didn't," Thomas said. "Chin went to the hospital after the birth, and his wife had vanished and left the baby behind. He thinks his wife's relatives were somehow involved. The nurse told him his son would be sent to an orphanage unless Chin took him, so he did. He searched for his wife for months but she had disappeared, just like her parents had. Her relatives weren't talking, nor could he trace his wife's whereabouts through them. It's a mystery to this day."

"What did he do?" I asked.

"He raised the child."

"In an abandoned building?" Lady Jane asked. "That doesn't make much sense at all. The authorities didn't prevent him from taking the baby?"

"They didn't," Thomas said. "And initially he went to the abandoned house. But a stranger heard the story, and through the friend of a friend, he got Chin a job at the airport cleaning out hangers. The stranger also found a retired lady to help with the baby. Chin worked hard, earned enough for an apartment. Then one of the pilots took a liking to him and taught him how to fly. Eventually he saved enough money to buy a plane, and he started his own cargo route."

"That's a remarkable story," I said, already making a mental note to develop it into an article. Readers liked success stories, especially when people overcame so many obstacles.

"Chin is an amazing person," Thomas said. "He would do anything for you. He has for me. He's the closest to family that I have."

"Where is his son?" Lady Jane asked.

"They were inseparable," Thomas said. "And then a year or two ago, the boy got sick. The doctors said it was some sort of cancer. But he died shortly after that. A young boy still. Maybe nine or ten. Chin has never been the same."

Lady Jane's eyes grew moist, and a tear slowly dripped down her cheek. "I had a cousin who died as a child," she said softly. "It was horrible. He was only five years old."

I didn't know how to console her. She looked so sad, as if her whole world had come to an end. Another tear dripped down.

"Disease can be horrible," I said.

"It wasn't disease," she said, a vacant, faraway look in her eye. "He drowned. We were swimming in the pond by his house. I was seven at the time. He went under the water and didn't come up. I screamed, yelling for help and crying uncontrollably."

Neither Thomas nor I spoke.

After a short pause, she went on, her voice barely above a whisper. "I tried to pull him out. I never in all my life ever tried that hard. But I just wasn't strong enough."

"Which is why you're so strong now," I said quietly. "I'm sure that your cousin is in the arms of Jesus, and that he is at peace."

She was silent; she nodded and then answered. "I have to be strong. I can never let anything like that happen again. Not ever."

I knew what it was like to feel responsible for someone's death. I knew the pain that lives inside you, never escaping, always a reminder of those few fragile minutes when life is unalterably changed. I wanted to make her feel better, to know that she wasn't the only one who shouldered such a tragedy. But I couldn't tell her about Maggie.

I also knew what it was like to not have the strength to overcome obstacles or adversity, to not be able to continue when every cell in your body wants to and needs to.

"I'll never be strong," I said quietly.

I then told her the story of my sickly childhood and the impact it had had on me as an adult. "It started when I was seven years old. All I ever wanted was to be able to walk and breathe and run and play. My father was a minister. He'd told me if I prayed hard enough I would be able to walk. So I started praying every hour. Just for a few minutes. I realized that it was working. So I tried to stand. Every day I prayed and tried again. And finally, I was able to stand, wobbling like a new-born colt.

"And then after that, I tried to walk. I fell on the floor, gasping for air, unable to move, weary and overwhelmed. But I dragged myself up and tried again. Then finally, I was able to walk in a very cumbersome way with braces.

"I was a teenager by then. Everyone else was playing rugby and cricket. I watched them from a window. So my next battle was getting those braces off. That took years too. But I didn't give up. I prayed each night and woke each and every day and tried. When I failed, I tried again. Eventually, over the course of years, I learned to walk. Then I learned to run. But I still have trouble breathing, and I'm still not strong."

When I finished, Lady Jane wiped the last remnants of tears from her cheeks. "George, I think you may be the strongest man I know. If I can see that, why can't you?"

We were quiet then, absorbed in our own thoughts

as we headed back to the city. We drove a mile through farms, the plantings bordered by rows of trees, and then entered the outskirts of the city, past the Singapore Cricket Club and onto a more heavily traveled road. Although soldiers were visible at the clearings on the side of the road, they were British units, primarily assigned to the eastern half of the island to thwart any Japanese assaults from that direction.

"Why is this so hard?" Lady Jane asked. "It's a small island."

"They have to be assigned just east of the city," Thomas said. "Chin saw them yesterday. They couldn't have been relocated that quickly."

I pointed to an Indian soldier who was standing at an outdoor fruit vendor. "Let's ask him."

Thomas guided the car to the side of the road. "Excuse me," he called. "Do you know where the Twelfth Infantry Brigade is?"

The soldier turned, looking at us curiously. "I'm with the Twelfth."

"Where are you stationed?"

He pointed north. "About two miles up Nelson Road."

"Do you know Captain Patel?" Lady Jane asked. "He's of average height, black hair and eyes, with a black beard."

"Yes, I do," the soldier replied. "He's at the field hospital."

"Where is that?" Thomas asked.

"Down that dirt road about a mile."

"Thanks," Thomas called.

He guided the car where the soldier pointed. The road led through a wooded area, the trees and vegetation interrupted briefly by fields of flaxen grass. A short distance later we found a clearing where a handful of tents were pitched beside a stream. He stopped the car beside the road. Soldiers were scattered about the entrances to the tents, some with bandages on their faces or upper bodies, others with arms in slings. They were the walking wounded, probably removed from the Malay Peninsula. I suspected those in the tent were in worse condition.

"We're looking for Captain Patel," Thomas said to a group of soldiers standing by the road.

"Yes, he's here," said a soldier on crutches, his right leg bandaged and bent at the knee. "In that tent near the stream."

"Is he all right?" Lady Jane asked anxiously.

I realized how difficult this must be for her. She cared deeply for this man, so much that she had traveled across the Indian Ocean to find him, enough that she had forsaken family and friends. Just to be with him. But he had vanished. With no explanation. He might be injured. Or he might be dead.

"I don't know," the soldier said. "But I think the nurse is in there now."

We entered the tent. It was cramped, housing a dozen soldiers who lay on cots, neatly arranged in two rows. They were in various states of injury, some sitting up in their cots with bandages on arms or legs, while a few lay motionless, gauze covering their heads. Some of the bandages were stained with blood. The smell of disinfectant, mixed with sickness, drifted in the air.

Thomas and I stood by the entrance while Lady Jane studied their faces. She had reached the end of the first row when a petite Asian nurse, dressed in a crisp white uniform, intercepted her.

"Can I help you?"

"Yes, I'm looking for Captain Patel. Balraj Patel."

"I'm sorry," the nurse said. "I can't help you."

"But we were told that Captain Patel was here," I said, intervening on her behalf.

"That's true," the nurse said. The expression on her face showed compassion, as if she could feel our disappointment. "He is. Captain Deepak Patel is on the last cot in the next row."

Lady Jane sighed; her face mirrored despair. "Can you tell me where Captain Balraj Patel is?"

"I'm afraid not," she said. "The regiment is somewhat scattered right now. Some are stationed in the eastern edge of the city, but others are farther west."

"Where is the commander?" I asked.

"I can't tell you that," she said. "I'm sure you understand."

We returned to the car, somewhat dejected.

"At least we know the general area," I said. "We'll have to keep searching."

"I just hope he's all right," Lady Jane said. "I hate to think of the horrible things that might have happened."

"Then don't," I said as I lightly touched her arm. "Think of the wonderful things that are yet to come."

CHAPTER 10

I went to the *Times* office after breakfast the next morning. The main room was empty, with typewriters abandoned, telephones in their cradles, and pens and paper lying unused on the desks. The silence was disturbing; the room should have been loud and boisterous and chaotic, filled with questions and conversation. In the back office, Alistair Duncan sat behind his desk, his anemic frame somehow seeming even thinner than it had the day before. He was hurriedly tossing papers from his desk into a brief case. His hair was frazzled; his face was flushed. An unfolded map lay sprawled on his desk, wrinkled and stained with coffee.

"Adams, it's every man for himself. Do what you can to get out of here. The Japanese are almost at the airport. And they're poised to attack from Ubin Island in the east."

"What do you intend to do?"

"I'm leaving tonight. I'm going with a friend, an RAF commander. His division is going to India. That should tell you something. The air force is leaving so they don't get captured. What are we still doing here?"

"How about the others in the office?"

"They left this morning. What are you going to do? Do you want to come with me?"

"I have a chance to leave tomorrow."

"For where?"

"Batavia."

"Good, take it," he said. "There's a *Times* office there. It's right across from Hotel Duncan. You can work from there. Batavia will be the front line in a few weeks anyway. The Japs are unstoppable. Tell the editor I sent you. He's an old friend. I can't remember his name right now. Give me a minute, I'll think of it. How are you escaping?"

"Cargo plane," I said. "It's in a barn a few miles east of the city."

He briefly looked at the map. "Maybe you better leave today. Before you lose your chance."

I studied his face and the anxious fear that had crept upon it. If he was that rattled, maybe I should be too. He was right. I had to escape. And soon.

I returned to the hotel lobby, walking across the lawn scarred by the plane that had crashed on the day of my arrival. I stopped for a moment and thought about the dead pilot, twisted in the cockpit, barely old enough to shave. And then I thought about Maggie.

Thomas pulled up in his friend's car just as I reached the hotel entrance. The distant sound of explosions erupted, although it was difficult to determine who was firing. Echoes produced by the massive guns seemed like they came from the north, but no shells landed nearby. For the moment, the noise was only a nuisance.

Lady Jane emerged from the hotel a moment later. "Thank you for borrowing the car," she said as she climbed in.

"Let's hope we find him," Thomas said. "Then we need to focus on our escape."

"Everyone in the *Times* office left today," I told them. "With the exception of the editor. He leaves tonight. He strongly urged me to leave as soon as possible. What can we do to get out of here?"

"We can leave at any time," Thomas said. "But I think we'll be safer with the fake passports. I just checked; they'll be ready tomorrow morning. We should wait for

75

them. They might prove useful."

We motored towards the eastern edge of the city to the area where we thought the Twelfth Infantry Brigade was located. After driving up and down a few blocks, we came to a side street filled with vendors selling their wares and mobbed with potential customers.

"Let's park here," Thomas said. "We'll ask some of the soldiers mingled in the crowd."

"I don't know how people are shopping when the Japanese are so close," Lady Jane said. "Even soldiers. You would think they'd be attacking the enemy, or at least getting ready to. No wonder we're losing the war."

The narrow cobblestone alley led to a network of similar paths, all wrapped by tenements constructed of whitewashed limestone. Laundry was hung out to dry from open windows, and small children played on the buildings' back steps. An elderly man stood on a third floor balcony, wearing a sleeveless undershirt and smoking a cigarette, watching people wander by.

Rows of tables displayed fruit, crafts, old pots and pans, used books and clothes. A handful of soldiers walked among the crowds, none of whom seemed concerned with the distant rumble of guns that continued unabated.   We paused to watch one woman haggling with a vendor over the price of some fruit.

Thomas stopped an Indian soldier that was walking by. "Are you with the Twelfth Infantry Brigade?"

The man nodded his head. "Yes, I am. Why do you ask?"

"We're looking for a Captain Balraj Patel," I said. "Do you know where we can find him?"

"Captain Patel?"

"Yes," I said.

"There is a Captain Patel with the regiment, but I don't know his first name. He was camped on the outskirts of town yesterday, just off Vanguard Road."

"How do we get to Vanguard Road," Lady Jane asked.

The soldier pointed north. "Take that road a half mile. Pass the rugby field. There are a few shops on your left. One sells jewelry, I think. They are camped next to a restaurant."

"Thank you," Thomas called as we headed for the car.

We quickly found Vanguard Road and then followed the directions provided by the soldier. Soon we saw the rugby field and found the shops next to the restaurant. Tents were staged in fields on both sides of the road, covering any ground not claimed by trees, vegetation, and buildings. Thomas guided the car to a stop, and we walked up to a soldier standing in the parking lot.

"Excuse me," Thomas said. "Can you tell me where Captain Balraj Patel is?"

"Captain Patel?" he asked, caught off guard by the question.

"Yes, do you know him?"

"Of course," he replied. He pointed to some tents next to the restaurant tucked under the shade of a large tree. "He's right over there."

I had a sinking feeling in my stomach. If Balraj Patel was alive and well and only a few miles from the Victoria Hotel, there was no valid reason why he hadn't contacted Lady Jane.

"Can you wait for me in the car, please?" she asked. She sounded tense and annoyed.

She walked across the dirt parking lot, anxious but

determined, and approached a man who stood beside the tree, his back to her, smoking a cigarette. Just as she reached him, she called his name.

He turned at the sound of her voice, his face showing shock and surprise. He recovered quickly and walked towards her, holding his arms out as if happy to see her. She remained where she stood, her hands on her hips.

Her back was towards us, so we couldn't see her face. But her arms moved as she talked, energetic and animated. She seemed to be pleading, questioning, and trying to understand. Balraj Patel's expression was a mask of feigned happiness.

"She must be asking what happened," I said.

"Wouldn't you?" Thomas asked. "She gave up her life for this man, travelled across the Indian Ocean, and made her family disown her. She at least deserves an explanation."

We watched their body language, unable to hear the conversation. Lady Jane now stood with her arms folded. Balraj Patel looked like he was pleading, probably begging for forgiveness.

"Do you think they're engaged?" I asked.

He arched his eyebrows and looked at me like I was insane. "Of course," he said. "Why else would she do what she did? And why would he plan to desert? Neither are easy decisions to make."

"But what makes a titled Englishwoman fall in love with a man from another race and culture who's so far beneath her social status?"

"The same reasons anyone else falls in love, I suppose," he said.

"I'm not so sure," I replied, studying the scene unfolding before us. "She is so unconventional, so daring and defiant. I wonder if she fell in love with him to spite her family."

He shrugged. "We'll probably never know. But one thing is certain. I don't think that's a pleasant conversation."

"He may have a good explanation. She seems to be listening to him."

"For now," he said. "But before the conversation is over, I think she'll be devastated. She is a vulnerable woman. But she hides it well."

I disagreed. "I think she is strong. Like she said yesterday. I wouldn't want to be Balraj Patel right now."

The discussion continued for several minutes. They kept their distance, never getting any closer to each other. We could see Balraj's expression, changing from a smile to indignation and back to a smile, and Lady Jane's gestures, sometimes soft and caring but more often demanding and defiant. Then Balraj approached her, reaching out his arms as if to hug and kiss her.

She swung her right fist in a mighty arc, punching him in the face. He never expected the blow, and he staggered backward, his hand on his nose. Blood started to ooze between his fingers.

"You win," Thomas said. "She is strong."

"Don't say anything," I hissed. "She'll be embarrassed."

She walked back to the car, strutting angrily across the dirt. When she arrived, her face was pale, as if shocked, but her lips were taut, locked in a defiant glare. There wasn't the slightest trace of a tear. She really was strong. I admired her and found her spirit attractive, I couldn't help it. She climbed in the car, closed the door, and stared forward with no expression.

"Can we leave, please?" she said.

I knew she was hurt, but she looked even more confused and shocked, as if she'd chased a dream but found a nightmare.

"I feel like a fool," she added. "I followed this man to Singapore. I thought he loved me. And I've made a horrible mistake."

"Life would be pretty dull if we never made mistakes," Thomas said. "At least you were brave enough to try. Most would have never done that."

She raised her right hand, shook it, and then clenched it as if to stimulate the blood flow. "I think I broke the cad's nose."

Back in the city, I returned to my room and again tried to reach the military contacts that Alistair Duncan had provided. None answered. Not that it mattered. The Singapore office of the *Times* no longer existed. I had no way to post articles, no method of distributing information.

I replayed the scene of the afternoon in my mind. Lady Jane must feel horrible, humiliated and foolish. I was determined to make her feel better, to help her forget and move on, to start life anew. But first and foremost, we had to get out of Singapore. The dangers increased with each minute that passed, each foot that the Japanese advanced. We had to escape.

We met at the hotel lounge that evening. I was still anxious about our departure, as were many of the patrons, and the invasion and how to escape dominated the room's discussions. I looked around at the worried faces and wondered how many would be sitting in the same chair the next night.

Lady Jane wandered in after Thomas and I had finished a snack or two. She strolled across the floor, the aura of perfection shattered, the light that seemed to surround her dimmer. The confidence that was so apparent previously reduced to a shadow. I ordered her a glass of wine and she sat beside me.

"Are you all right?" I asked.

"Yes," she said. "Hurt and confused but fine."

"In time you'll reflect on this as one of the shining moments in your life," Thomas said.

"And why is that?" she asked with a hint of irritation.

He looked at her with the utmost seriousness. "Because it led you to George and me."

She smiled and then slowly shook her head. "I feel like such an idiot. If you had any idea what I gave up in India, you would think that I am certifiably insane. I lost family, friends..." She hesitated, and a look of anguish crossed her face. "...and loved ones."

"You lost them temporarily," I said. "You know where to find them."

"It's not like that," she said. "What I did was inexcusable. It was scandalous. And I will never be forgiven by anyone. And for what?"

"Lady Jane," I said. "The hurt will fade. And in a few weeks' time, this will be nothing more than a bad memory."

I was sickened by the statement as soon as I'd made it. Heartache does not always make you stronger; bad decisions don't always make you learn. I should know that more than anyone. I lost Maggie, and, after four months, hardly an hour passed when I didn't think about her, when I didn't miss her smile, her touch, her laugh, and her love. Who was I to preach to Lady Jane about what it took to be a better and stronger person? I certainly didn't know.

"I was able to get our passports," Thomas said.

"Then we need to leave as soon as possible," I said. "Remember what they said at the *Times* office: If the air force is evacuating, we should too."

"We'll leave in the morning," Thomas said. "Chin's cargo can't be that important. There's no reason to stay here."

"Are you sure you don't want to go to India?" I asked Lady Jane one last time. "It might be safer."

"I'm positive," she said quickly. "I'm not welcome there."

I felt sorry for her. Her whole life had collapsed, all within a few short weeks. And now the Japanese were stealing the island an inch at a time, destroying everything in their path and squeezing the Allied armies into an ever dwindling footprint. Our escape was jeopardized; our lives were at risk. The next twenty-four hours would be critical. We all knew it. Even if none of us said it.

The chandelier shook, specks of plaster drifting from the ceiling. The great guns of Singapore were firing at the enemy. A moment later, the air raid siren wailed, dwarfing the cannons, and the drone of aircraft buzzed overhead. The taproom emptied as patrons hastily made their way to the bomb shelter.

I guided Lady Jane down the steps. Thomas followed, a bottle of gin in his hand. We went to the far wall and made ourselves as comfortable as we could, listening to the distant rumbling of war. We talked for a while, discussing our escape, but after an hour had elapsed Thomas became reflective and thoughtful, finding his gin more interesting than those around him.

Lady Jane, no longer in the mood for conversation, reached into her handbag and withdrew two books. She began reading the first, *Murder on Mount Kilimanjaro.* I wondered if the murder mysteries were part of a series by the same author. She seemed to have an unlimited supply, digesting one every few days. She laid the second book on the floor. I looked at the title: *Florence During the Renaissance.*

I think we were numb to the danger. It was ever present, never more than a minute away. But life had to go on, and it did. The city still functioned: clerks sold, chefs cooked, reverends preached, and children played. But they did so with an ever-growing shadow looming over them, like night about to swallow the day.

The bombing lasted for hours. Not like the short, intense attack on the day I arrived, but a steady pounding by shot and shell, cannon and craft. The attack was distant, but steady, and the rhythm was only occasionally interrupted by the sound of an aircraft whizzing overhead. It was sometime after midnight when the bombing ceased. After several minutes of silence, the siren sounded to signal the end of the attack and those in the shelter made their way up the steps. They were quiet and subdued, anxiously awaiting information. It arrived shortly, passing through the crowd like a bullet. The Japanese had launched another attack, invading the island from the west.

CHAPTER 11

I lay in bed, staring at the ceiling as the night slowly passed. I couldn't stop thinking about the escape, the dangers wrapped around it, and its diminishing chances for success. The Japanese had attacked from both the northwest and the west. They occupied Ubin Island to the northeast, and if those troops attacked as well, the island would be sandwiched into submission. Then any chance of leaving would vanish. I thought about my colleagues in the *Times* office who had already gone, and Alistair Duncan, now on his way to India. We hadn't planned our exit in time; we shouldn't have waited for the forged passports. They couldn't be that important. If the Japanese surrounded Singapore, Chin wouldn't be able to avoid them. What would we do then?

My thoughts wandered to Lady Jane. I felt sorry for her, but there was nothing I could do to help her. There was no way to ease her pain. I could be her friend and provide a sympathetic ear. But I couldn't undo what had already been done.

I wondered what had motivated her. Was it strictly her love for Balraj Patel? Or had she come to Singapore to escape something worse, to borrow a phrase from Thomas. Maybe her rebellious streak sparked her flight. But I knew, for an action that drastic, there had to have been a catalyst, and I didn't think Balraj Patel was it.

Thomas was attracted to her. And I think the feeling was mutual. Maybe romance was blooming now that Balraj Patel had walked out of her life. I felt a tinge of jealousy thinking about them together. I was attracted to her too. Then I felt pangs of guilt. I should have been thinking about Maggie. So I did.

I remembered the time Maggie found a puppy, a sleep-eyed bulldog tucked in an alley off Whitehall Street. He was lost or abandoned, and she insisted that we take him home. We stopped along the way to buy food and toys and a little cushioned bed, and then put a notice in the newspaper stating that a lost dog had been found. When no rightful owner came forth, we eagerly adopted him. Maggie had decided that the bulldog closely resembled the English monarch Henry the Eighth, so that became his name. Before I left London the dog and I were inseparable, just like Maggie and I once were. He was with my sister now, but I thought of him often, especially when reminded of Maggie's sense of humor. Who else could imagine that a dog and a king resembled each other?

I got out of bed when dawn colored the sky a burning amber hue. I had little packing to do. I was so terrified of the Japanese that I had never unpacked. I carefully separated my money between my wallet, a pocket, and each suitcase. Then in the event of theft or a lost suitcase, I wouldn't lose everything. I also had a stack of bearer bonds the *Times* office had provided for my living expenses. Before leaving my room, I knelt down and rested my elbows on the bed.

"Dear Lord, please guide our delivery to a safe harbor, and please give me the strength to endure the journey and to be brave when I must be. Amen."

I entered the lobby around 8 a.m. and found it full, packed with panicked people checking out of the hotel, waiting to leave, or wanting to leave. There were only so many ways to get off the island. The airport was threatened by the Japanese, eliminating flight except by small cargo planes like Chin's. But the enemy had yet to conquer the seas, which left a limited number of ships with an overabundance of people.   The chaos in the lobby symbolized the panic that consumed the entire island.

The room was filled with conversation, casual and controlled, frantic and anxious, by people coming and going at a rapid rate.   Others waited, scanning the newspaper, which was probably the last local edition available, or reading magazines. Still more hoped for a miracle, a British victory.

I waited in line at the registration desk, checked out, and then started pacing the floor, waiting for the others. I studied the people. Everyone seemed rushed, all in a hurry to go nowhere.   Luggage was stacked near the door and propped against the wall, filling all unused space in the room.   I glanced out the doors and saw cars, taxis, and rickshaws cramming the circular drive that led to the lobby entrance, picking up departing passengers.   I wondered where they were all going.

Thomas arrived a few minutes later.   He wore rugged outdoor clothing, dark blue in color with a matching peasant's cap. He hadn't shaved probably for a day or so, and he had the beginnings of a beard. A half-smoked cigar, harsher than his aromatic pipe, dangled from his lips, and a white duffel bag was slung over his shoulder. He eyed the people rushing to check out, hurrying to escape, and trying to find passage to anywhere, but he didn't seem concerned. It was almost as if he'd expected it.

"Where's Lady Jane?" he asked.   He dropped his bag on the floor beside my luggage.

"She hasn't come down yet."

He went and stood in line to check out.   Five minutes later, he returned and sat beside me.   After a final glance at the chaos in the room, he reached into his duffel bag and removed a book. Within seconds he was engrossed in the pages.

I looked at the title on the spine: *Social Stratification of the Indian Subcontinent.* I was startled. The book belonged to Lady Jane. I wondered when he had borrowed it. I certainly wasn't present when he did. How much time were they spending together?

I didn't want to dwell on what Thomas and Lady Jane may or may not be doing, so I decided to interview some of the guests. I wanted to know if they were as scared as I was and if they thought their escape would be successful. I was curious to see if they were residents of Singapore or visitors. And why did they come here to begin with.

I went over to a young woman, probably in her early twenties, a cute Caucasian with red hair and freckles. A little girl, an exact replica of her mother, clung to her knee. She waited anxiously by the door, studying each taxi that pulled in front of the hotel, looking for the one that would whisk her away on the next leg of her journey. She was a bit frantic, wide-eyed and pale, and her eyes were moist. She was probably trying to be brave so she didn't frighten her daughter.

"Are you a resident?" I asked.

"Oh, no," she said. "I'm Australian. My daughter and I came to see her father. He's in the army, stationed on the west coast. We finally got a chance to see him the day before yesterday. Then the invasion came, and now I don't know what has happened to him. I hope he's all right." She dabbed her eyes with a handkerchief and whispered to me so her daughter couldn't hear. "I know it was stupid to come, but we didn't know when we'll see him again."

"How are you traveling?"

"We booked passage on a freighter," she said. "I

was lucky. It only takes a few dozen people. I just hope we make it home. And I hope my husband does too. I hate to even think of what might happen to him."

"Have faith," I said, stealing a phrase from my father the minister. "I'm sure he'll be fine. Have a safe journey."

I walked away, my heart heavy. The toll on the families and friends of front-line soldiers was unimaginable, almost unthinkable. I looked back at the young wife who might never see her husband again, the young daughter who may never know her father, and I felt a hollow feeling in the pit of my stomach. I had seen the fear in their faces, their futures uncertain, dreams delayed. I wondered how many more were just like them, how many others in the lobby were leaving loved ones behind.

I made my way to an elderly gentleman dressed in a handsome suit with a broad-brimmed hat. "Excuse me, sir. Are you a resident?"

"Sort of," he said. "I live here several months a year. I stay at the hotel. I never thought the Japanese would invade. I didn't think His Majesty's troops would let them. They wouldn't in my day, I can tell you that."

"How are you getting out?"

"By ship, along with most of the others. I'm told five vessels are leaving today, but only two or three more after that. You need to get out too."

"Where are you going?"

"Home."

"And where is that, sir?"

"London. And I can't wait to get there."

I felt my heart sink, depression washing over me like a tidal wave. I wished I was going home. "Good luck to you, sir. And have a safe journey."

I thought about London, and realized how empty I was without it. Just to stroll along the Thames, or walk through Hyde Park, or gaze upon the unbelievable architecture of Victoria Station, would be such an enviable treasure.

And then there was my family. My mother, who was sweet and considerate, kind and compassionate. And my father, the stern and staid Protestant minister, at least on the exterior. But on the inside, he got teary eyed watching a movie, emotional reading a good book. He might deceive his congregation, but he had never fooled me. My sister Angie was an interesting mix of mom and dad, and her husband Tom, was an executive with the electric company. And then there was my dog Henry the Eighth, temporarily residing with my sister. I missed them. I missed London. And I missed Maggie.

Lady Jane came down the stairs a few minutes later, looking tired and drawn. There were black circles under her eyes, and an anguish seemed to consume her. She dressed casually, wearing dark pants and a beige blouse, and her blond hair was pulled back in a neat ponytail. She carried two leather suitcases. I was worried about her. I didn't want her hurt; I didn't like to see her sad.

"I'm sorry I'm late," she said. "I overslept. I had a difficult time sleeping last night."

"It doesn't matter," Thomas said. "Chin won't leave without us."

"Did you borrow your friend's car?" I asked.

"No," Thomas said. "The best I could manage was an old wagon."

"How did you find that?" I asked.

"The driver was delivering fruit to the hotel yesterday. I asked if he would take us to Chin's. He agreed."

"I hope he shows up," Lady Jane said. "I can't wait to leave."

"He's already here," Thomas said. "He's parked just past the third taxi, next to the rickshaw that the woman and her daughter are climbing into."

It was the lady I had just interviewed. She had made her exit from the Victoria Hotel. Now she was escaping Singapore. And hopefully, someday, her husband would join her.

"Let's get our bags and get going," Thomas continued. "Can I carry something for you, Lady Jane?"

She forced a smile. "No, thank you. I can manage."

On the street beyond sat an old wagon pulled by two slouched mares. Anchored in the driver's seat was an elderly Asian whose hair, mustache, and goatee were as white as the clouds. His eyes were a pale blue, and they twinkled mischievously as he watched us approach. I suspected he was at least ninety years old, and I seriously doubted he had the strength to manage the wagon. Actually, once I saw the wrinkles etched upon his weathered face, I was surprised he was even alive.

Thomas tossed his duffel bag into the back. "I know it's not the best, but not much is available. Throw on your luggage and we'll get going."

We each took one of Lady Jane's bags and placed them behind the driver's seat. I put mine next to hers.

"Would you like to sit next to the driver?" Thomas asked her.

"No, you go ahead," she said. "I'll sit in the back with George." She smiled at me. It was a weak smile, masked by sadness, but I liked it anyway.

Thomas climbed up front while I helped Lady Jane get into the back. We were just about to depart when the whistle of the air-raid siren interrupted our plans. I helped Lady Jane back down and guided her to the shelter. I glanced at Thomas, who was slowly climbing down from the wagon, assisting the elderly owner.

"Thomas! Hurry!" I said.

I was anxious as I entered the bomb shelter; I didn't know how much longer we could avoid disaster. So far we had endured the attacks with no harm, except for Thomas's mishap in the taproom, but that was unlikely to continue. The assault might last for hours, as it had the prior evening. We would never get out in time to meet Chin. If the Japanese invaded the eastern half of the island, we would never get away.

Thomas ambled in a few moments later, among the last to enter, engaged in an animated conversation with our driver. They sat beside us, the discussion continuing. Unfortunately they spoke Mandarin, and neither Lady Jane nor I had the slightest clue what they said. Thomas acted as if he had known the man his entire life, the discussion was so congenial. That was another quality of his that I admired: the ability to talk to anyone about anything, regardless of social status, creed or color. I decided then that I would strive to behave the same way.

The air raid was brief, lasting less than fifteen minutes. The bombing must have occurred in a distant part of the city, since we'd barely heard rumbles from the explosions. Once the attack ended and the all clear sounded, Thomas and his companion were the first to leave. They were waiting at the wagon by the time Lady Jane and I emerged.

We started down Orchard Road, moving in an

easterly direction past a mile of family-owned shops, maneuvering among cars, bicycles, rickshaws and pedestrians . I looked back at the Victoria Hotel, premier lodging of Southeast Asia, and the Raffles Café, my sanctuary from the war that provided memories of London, and fondly remembered my discussions with Mr. Hyde. The mares trudged onward, and even the peak of the capital building, some six blocks from the hotel, grew distant in the background. After negotiating a series of turns and moving through blocks of well-maintained Chinese tenements, I had completely lost my sense of direction.

As our journey progressed, the skill of our driver, so suspect at the outset, became apparent. I soon realized that he was very spry. Maneuvering the wagon required little of his attention, which allowed him to continue his conversation with Thomas.

We had traveled about thirty minutes when we saw a tiny wagon pulled by an ox that had stopped on the opposite side of a broad boulevard. It was perched beside a roadside fruit stand while its driver, a woman of about thirty, sat facing the wagon. In the back, a young girl, no more than five or six years old, sang and danced. Her arms and legs moved in tandem, displaying both her talent and coordination, and her voice mimicked that of a practiced vocalist with years of experience. She sang an upbeat, cheerful tune, a coordinated tap dance providing the rhythm that accompanied it, much to the amusement of a small crowd who had gathered to watch. We also stopped and, even though we were some distance away, we were able to enjoy the show.

The brief interlude was moving; the girl seemed to symbolize so much naivety and innocence that for a few joyful moments the war and all its horrors slowly faded, dissipating like the fog on a rainy day. We were all smiling and laughing, clapping our hands and singing along, joining a dozen others in celebrating life.

The whine of the bomb was unexpected. The whistle it made offered no warning. We would never know which cannon it had come from. But somehow, with sudden and absolute finality, the shell exploded, shrouding the street in a mist of disaster.

CHAPTER 12

We leapt from the wagon, our mares whinnying and stomping their hooves in the street while we took shelter in the stairwell entrance to a basement laundry. It offered some protection but not from a direct hit. We all stood there, trembling, our breath coming in anxious gasps.

A minute passed. Two. There were no more whistles or whines, no hints of arriving bombs or exploding shells. Tentatively, we peeked from our hiding place and surveyed the landscape.

The fruit stand lay in fragments, splinters of wood and pulp scattered about the road. The wagon was damaged, the axle broken, one wheel lying flat on the ground. The ox was dead, laying by the side of the road, maimed and disfigured, its blood staining the street. People lay scattered beside the wagon, crying and bleeding. Some were motionless.

The child lay motionless too in the center of the street where the blast had thrown her. Her mother crawled to her side, calling her name, her face a mask of agony. She scooped the girl in her arms and sat in the center of the road, cradling the small body in her arms. The child's arms and legs dangled haphazardly; her head hung limply. The woman gently rocked to and fro, sobbing uncontrollably. Sorrow lived in every wrinkle of her face; she looked as though her heart had been ripped from her body.

We hurried across the boulevard, joining a dozen others drawn by the blast. Some assisted the injured, others cleared the road for emergency vehicles. I saw at least one doctor, his medical bag beside him. He briefly checked the child, muttered a word of condolence to the mother, and moved to other injured. Tears streamed down the woman's face, trickling onto her black blouse.

I looked at the sea of injured and maimed people, wanting to assist but not knowing how. It was just like when Maggie had died. I hadn't been able to help her either. I was stunned and overwhelmed, shocked and saddened. I started crying. I kept staring at the poor child.

An agonizing look covered Lady Jane's face, and tears streamed down her cheeks. She rubbed her eyes, trying to will them away.

"It's just like my cousin," she whispered. "A life ended before it began."

Thomas knelt beside the mother. He spoke in Mandarin in a soft and soothing tone. He reached for the dead child, gently stroking her hair. He retrieved a doll that lay nearby and laid it in the lap of its lifeless owner. He rose slowly, first hugging the woman and then leaning over and kissing the child's forehead.

I could see the compassion etched in his face. His actions were genuine and sincere. He was emotional, his eyes moist, his heart heavy.

When he moved away I approached the woman and expressed my condolences. I caressed the child's head, saying a brief prayer. The wagon driver followed and lingered a minute, speaking to the mother in her own tongue.

Lady Jane moved towards the mother and hugged her tightly, wrapping her arms around her and the child. She did not let go, and for several seconds she provided a protective canopy, subconsciously shielding the woman from further hurt and harm.

I watched her curiously, perplexed by her behavior. I remembered she had vowed to be strong after her cousin's death. She would never let anything like that happen again. But this was beyond her control, so she offered the only protection she could. Maybe Thomas was right. Maybe she was vulnerable. Maybe she wasn't that strong after all. I felt for her, and I wanted to wrap my arms around her just as hers were wrapped around mother and daughter.

We made sure the injured were cared for, and then we returned to the wagon. A final glance at the tragedy showed others consoling the woman who clung desperately to her child as onlookers tried to take her away. As the wagon moved forward, I closed my eyes, no longer able to watch.

It was a terrible tragedy. The child was dancing in the wagon, laughing and singing and loving life. A second later she was dead.

"That poor woman," Lady Jane said somberly. "It makes coming across the Indian Ocean to be jilted by your fiancé seem pretty trivial. Doesn't it?"

I looked at her thoughtfully. I think that was the point that her healing began, and Balraj Patel began to fade from her life.

Our journey continued, our wagon moving slowly through the streets of Singapore, as cars and taxis, rickshaws and trucks moved past us. Street vendors returned to their displays, shoppers again gazed in windows and pedestrians wandered the streets just as I had seen so many times after the bombs had stopped falling.

We traveled the route we had taken when we met Chin, leaving the city and entering a rural area dotted with farms. We continued for an hour more, the journey much slower by mare than by car. Soon we reached the weed-strewn lane that led to the barn, and the driver traveled a hundred yards more and halted.

Thomas spoke to the driver in Mandarin, apparently thanking him, and handed him some money. He jumped to the ground and started walking towards the barn.

"I'll round up Chin," he said.

Lady Jane and I thanked the driver and removed the baggage from the wagon. We stacked everything under the shade of the tree and glanced at the landscape.

"Should we go and see what's going on?" Lady Jane asked.

I hesitated. "Probably not. If he wanted us to follow he would have told us."

"I think I'll view Chin differently," Lady Jane said. "Now that Thomas told us the story about his son."

I studied the horizon. It was early afternoon, few clouds marred the sky, and for the first time in hours no bomb blasts could be heard. It was eerily quiet. I wondered why. Had the Japanese advance been stopped? Or merely suspended.

The door to the barn opened and Thomas waved us forward. "Come on," he called. "Chin is here. And he's willing to leave now."

We grabbed our luggage and entered. Chin greeted us warmly, his face framed by a smile. He went into his office for a moment while Thomas brought us to the aircraft.

We glanced inside and saw the pilot's seat and one beside it, and then twin seats behind them. A large wooden box with a hinged lid was immediately behind the passengers' seat. The remainder of the plane was cargo space. The interior had horizontal slats situated at various heights of the fuselage. Rope was attached to this framework, designed to anchor cargo. Several wooden crates were stowed towards the rear of the plane. There was no sign of the mysterious crate that Thomas had brought previously. Chin must have already delivered it.

"It seems a bit dated," I said warily. I had little experience flying and was somewhat anxious about the journey. Especially in such a small plane.

Thomas sensed my apprehension. "It may not look like much, but I assure you it's flight-worthy. Chin flies to Batavia twice a week. And I've accompanied him many times."

"I suppose it's all right," I said with some trepidation.

"How about you, Lady Jane?" he asked. "Are you comfortable?"

"Yes, I'm fine," she said. "I flew frequently in India. And in planes much worse than this. I'm willing to continue. I'm not afraid."

She was braver than I was. I eyed the plane again, looking at the struts that supported the wings. "How many times have you made this journey?"

Thomas laughed. "Many times," he said. "There's no need to worry."

Chin joined us a moment later. "Are we ready to go?"

"Yes," Thomas said. "But I want to go outside and make sure it's safe. It's so quiet, it's unnerving. Why no sounds of battle? I'll circle the barn for a quarter mile or so, up to where the vegetation starts, and make sure everything is all right."

"I'll load the luggage," Chin said.

Thomas left while Chin grabbed our suitcases and the duffle bag. He secured them to the slats with rope, and then came back to where Lady Jane and I waited near the door to the barn.

"The plane was built in 1927," he said. "It can reach speeds of about one-hundred and seventy miles per hour and has a range of eight hundred miles. Batavia is about six hundred miles away. But I as I said before, we'll stop halfway so I can drop some cargo."

"This all sounds routine to you," Lady Jane said.

"It is, to an extent," Chin said. "But we have the Japanese to contend with. It's quiet right now. Hopefully we can get out of here before the bombing starts again."

I looked at my watch. "I hope Thomas hurries."

"He's just being cautious," Chin said. "There hasn't been any activity here even though the Japanese are on Ubin Island, which really isn't far away."

"Do you think they'll attack from there?" Lady Jane asked.

"I don't know," Chin said. "It may be a diversion. The British troops guarding the east coast could have been used on the other side of the island."

"Thomas seems to know what the Japanese will do days before it happens," I said. I was curious to see how Chin reacted to my statement.

"He's a smart man," Chin replied. Then he smiled. "He seems to know what I'm going to do before it happens too."

"How long have you known him," Lady Jane asked.

"For a long time," Chin said, his smile growing even broader. It was as if his mind's eye was searching the past, watching a time that was much more pleasant.

"He seems like a good friend," Lady Jane added. She was prodding, searching for information.

"You couldn't ask for a better one," Chin said. "I owe a lot to Thomas. I wouldn't be what I am today if it wasn't for him."

"Really?" Lady Jane asked.

Her questions were intentional; they were manipulative. Not naïve or innocent. She wanted to learn about Thomas. And she found a way to do it. I wondered why she was so interested in him. Maybe he really was taking the place of Balraj Patel.

"Very much so," Chin continued. "I was abandoned with a small baby. Thomas got me a job at the airport, cleaning the hangers. And he found a retired lady who helped me with the baby. I worked hard, learned to fly, and eventually bought this plane."

I looked at Lady Jane, dumbfounded. She was as surprised as I was. Thomas had told us the story of Chin, but had omitted his involvement.

The door opened and Thomas came in. "I think we should get moving. There's a patrol about five hundred yards north of here. I can't tell who they are. They're probably British, but I don't think we should wait to find out. Especially since the military situation is changing so quickly. The Japanese may have landed from Ubin Island."

"Get in," Chin said. "I'll do the engine checks and get started."

We quickly climbed inside. Thomas withdrew two billfolds from his pocket, handing one to Lady Jane and one to me. "These are Swiss passports with false identities."

"Is this really necessary?" Lady Jane said. She glanced at her picture and mumbled the alias that Thomas had chosen for her. "Marie La Favre."

I looked at my new identity. "Jean Bassiere."

"The Swiss are neutral," Thomas explained. "If anything unexpected occurs, we won't be treated as combatants."

His statement magnified the danger, amplifying just how serious the situation was. I had fleeting thoughts of Alistair Duncan, and those at the *Times* office, and Henry Hyde at the Raffles Café, and of guests at the Victoria Hotel who I had talked to in passing. I wondered if I would ever see any of them again, or if they all would survive. I also gained an appreciation for the extensive preparations our journey demanded.

"These are excellent forgeries," I said. "How did you get them?"

He shrugged. "I have friends."

"I have friends too," I said. "But they can't produce fake passports."

Chin completed his engine checks and closed the cowling. He moved to the barn doors and swung each open on their rusty hinges. He stepped outside and peeked around the corner.

"They're coming this way," he said when he returned. "I think they're British, but why take the chance. We better hurry."

He started the aircraft, and the engine roared to life. The old plane rolled slowly from the barn and across the fields, gaining speed as the pitch of the engine deepened. No one pursued us; no shots were fired. We would never know if they were friend or foe. Chin eased back on the throttle, and the plane jerked reluctantly into the air. I glanced out the porthole and saw that we were airborne, our distance from the ground increasing. Within minutes we were over the ocean, and soon the strangled city of Singapore began to fade from sight.

I stole one last glance at the city. I was still convinced it was a microcosm for what the world should, but probably never would, be. Singapore held the secret for mankind; maybe someday I would return.

CHAPTER 13

The sun was starting to sink on the western horizon, having reached and passed its zenith. We flew towards it at a low altitude, maybe a thousand feet, and then made a wide sweeping turn to the south.

I could tell from my knowledge of geography that we had gone in the wrong direction. Studying atlases as a bed-ridden child sometimes proved valuable. "Why did we fly to the west? Isn't Batavia southeast?"

"The Japanese occupy some of the islands south and east of Singapore," Thomas said. "We decided to go west and then south to avoid them. Just to be safe."

He always surprised me with his specific knowledge of enemy activity, including their movement, strength, and intentions. He seemed to know more than our own military, at least given my limited exposure to them.

"How do you possibly know that?" I asked.

Chin cast Thomas a guarded glance, which didn't escape my attention, and then replied. "I saw them yesterday when I returned from Sumatra, so I told Thomas."

His explanation was plausible, although their behavior was odd. More important was the relevance of the information. If the Japanese now occupied islands to the south and east of Singapore, only a sliver of territory to the southwest, that which we had just flown through, remained unoccupied or uncontrolled by the enemy. The fate of Singapore became more tenuous with each passing hour.

"The Japanese are eliminating the escape routes," I said. "Our army will be trapped unless massive reinforcements arrive."

"I'm afraid that's true," Thomas said. "Singapore is almost completely surrounded. But I think we already outnumber the Japanese by three to one. This battle was fought and lost psychologically. I told you that when we saw the soldiers. Defeat was in their faces. When you get to Batavia, the first article you write should describe your escape. There won't be many more that get out after us."

The coast of Sumatra appeared a short while later bathed in the crimson shadow of the setting sun. We flew along the northern edge of the island where vegetation grew to the water's edge and then walked in elevation to the mountains that dominated the island's interior. Since we were still flying at a low altitude, I could see the occasional hamlets tucked along the coast, clinging to the sea that provided their livelihood.

As I watched the scenery move by below, I thought of the contrasts to the urban landscape of London. Sumatra was half a world away, but it could be a universe away; it was so vastly different in geography, development, culture, and climate. I suddenly felt overwhelmingly homesick as fleeting images of the city drifted through my mind: dinner at the Sherlock Holmes Pub just off Trafalgar Square, tea at the Treasure Island Café, the Thames River, Sunday services, my family. And Maggie.

I remembered a time we walked along the Thames, returning from an American movie, *The Maltese Falcon.* All the while, Maggie imitated characters from the show, primarily Humphrey Bogart and Sydney Greenstreet, repeating the most memorable lines, mimicking their voices to perfection. It was a unique talent she possessed; I often felt like she should have been a professional comedian. I laughed all the way home. And even months later, half a world away and with Maggie in heaven, it still made me smile.

My life was so different then. I would have never left London if she were still alive. Now I was flying over Sumatra, the largest of the seven thousand islands that formed the Dutch East Indies. It was a Dutch colony with no parent, the mother country overrun by Germany. So much had changed in so short a time.

Lady Jane was busy chatting with Chin and Thomas, laughing and joking and flirting a bit. There was no evidence of any heartache, but I'm sure it was there. She was so unlike Maggie. Lady Jane was sophisticated; Maggie was practical. Lady Jane was wealthy; Maggie had grown up in the east London slums. Lady Jane spoke with a clipped, upper class accent; Maggie was pure Cockney. Lady Jane was reserved with a dry sense of humor; usually only the hint of a smile suggested amusement. Maggie was an extroverted jokester, bubbling with impulsive spontaneity, who frequently laughed hilariously, not caring who saw or heard. They were very different, yet somehow they were very much the same.

I discretely watched her while they talked. She was telling them about growing up in India, what it was like to be a child in New Delhi from the foods to the festivals, the people to the poverty. She was entertaining; she was intelligent. And she was beautiful. Each time she smiled it was like the angels lit heaven with a million suns. I looked at the skin on her cheeks, smooth like porcelain, her eyes bright and blue. And even though she appeared happy and carefree, I knew she was still mired in sorrow. I wanted to ease her pain. I wanted to protect her, to make sure she was never hurt again. But I didn't know why. Maybe it was because I couldn't save Maggie, but I might be able to save Lady Jane.

"I grew up in Paris," Thomas was saying. "My mother was a saint. My father was a hard-working, heavy drinker."

"That must have been a difficult childhood," she said.

He shrugged. "It wasn't as bad as it sounds. My father was a tough man. But he did the best he could. It would be foolish to blame my faults on him, which so many people do today."

"My family always had an after dinner drink," Lady Jane said. "And they loved parties. We had a social occasion for everything. But they were just reasons to celebrate."

"My father didn't need a reason to drink," Thomas said. "I remember when I got my first job. I was a teenager. And you got paid every day in those days. I came home from my first day of work, and my father was waiting for me on the corner of my street. He made me give him my day's wages, and then he went straight to the saloon."

"That's terrible," Lady Jane said. "What did you do?"

Thomas looked at her, his face grave and serious. "I found a different way home."

They seemed to have developed quite a rapport. They were laughing and joking, chatting as if they had known each other for years. They had much in common from the books they read to the places they had been to their favorite foods. I couldn't understand why or how or when they had become so close.

We turned inland after three hours of uneventful travel, flew along a river, and reached our destination a few minutes later. The airstrip was marked by lanterns placed along its perimeter, and Chin brought the plane to the ground directly between them. The landing was smooth and precise, and we hummed along the runway for forty yards before coming to a halt. Chin shut down the engine.

We were greeted by a man with a broad chest, muscled upper arms and a battered face like a boxer that lost more fights than he won. Completing the image of a pugilist was a gold front tooth that sparkled when reflecting light and a jagged scar above his right eye. But even though his image suggested violence, his warm eyes and broad smile did not.

"Hello, Thomas. And Chin," the man called cheerfully in accented English. "It's good to see you. I've been waiting for you."

The airstrip was surrounded by jungle, trees and shrubs tightly woven to form a canopy that climbed to the mountains in the distance. I saw a monkey watching us curiously before scrambling across the branches and disappearing from sight. On the far side of the strip where the plane had entered, we could see the river, tranquil and reflective of the setting sun, a weathered fishing boat anchored by the distant shore.

Thomas made the introductions, pointing to each of us in turn. "Lady Jane Carrington Smythe and George Adams. This is William Van der Meer, a stubborn Dutchman and a close friend. He's been kind enough to offer us his facilities."

We thanked Van der Meer for his hospitality.

"I hope you'll spend the night," he offered. "It's been a long day, and I'm sure you're tired. You can continue in the morning."

"We should really fly in darkness to avoid the Japanese," Thomas said.

Van der Meer arched an eyebrow.   "Then leave before dawn. Rest for an evening."

Thomas glanced at Lady Jane and me. "Do you mind if we stay?"

"No, not at all," she said.

"Whatever you decide is fine with me," I said.

"Then come relax at the house.   My men will service the plane and unload the cargo," Van der Meer said. He motioned to two Sumatrans, dark haired men in workman's clothes, who moved towards the plane.

Chin gave directions to the workmen and showed them the cargo to unload. I watched while they rolled large metal drums of petrol towards the aircraft. They prepared a hand pump that would be used to transfer the fuel. It was apparent they had performed the operation many times.

We walked down a slender path chiseled into the underbrush, that wound past the river. Van der Meer told us we had landed at a rubber plantation which he ran for a Dutch consortium.   The airstrip, a regular stop on Chin's cargo route, was part of the facility.

The residence was a stylish home built from native timber with a raised rectangular roof in the center to collect the heat and wide, sweeping rooflines that ran from it to disperse the rains. A broad veranda dressed the length of the residence, supported by sturdy, hand-carved columns. Although the exterior was clearly Sumatran in design, the interior showed tastes of Europe. The parlor was finished in Belgian wallpaper, green and gold accented by ornate moldings painted a bright white, while the surrounding rooms were more traditional with walls of teak or mahogany paneling. I glanced into a room off the entrance to the parlor and saw that it was a small chapel. I made a note to myself to visit it later.

Van der Meer, a widower with no children, directed us to the parlor, made sure we were comfortable, and then had a maid serve us tea and biscuits while dinner was prepared. Although exhausted, we were relieved and excited to have escaped Singapore and were anxious to talk about it.

"With Singapore surrounded they have no choice but surrender," Van der Meer said as we sipped our tea. "It's surprising. The Japanese are outnumbered by three to one."

I looked at him strangely. He recited the same troop strengths that Thomas had. I didn't understand how the proprietor of a rubber plantation would know such detailed military information. I also noticed that Thomas and Chin seemed to defer to him both in conversation and mannerisms. The relationship spanned more than cargo deliveries, but I didn't know to what.

"Yes, it's true," Thomas agreed. "The Royal Air Force evacuated with all their planes. That tells me the end is near. I think the Allies were convinced of defeat before they even got to Singapore."

Van der Meer turned to Lady Jane. "You must be relieved to have escaped."

"I am," she said. "It got worse each day. I arrived on a transport ship the same day as George. If I'd had any idea of the danger, I never would have come. It was horrible. The death and destruction. I have no desire to live through that again."

Van der Meer glanced furtively at Thomas. "Hopefully you won't have to. But Batavia may not be much safer."

"Have you and Thomas known each other long?" I asked, interrupting the discussion about Singapore.

Van der Meer sat back in his chair and took a deep breath. "Oh, yes. It seems like forever, doesn't it, Thomas?"

Thomas chuckled. "That's because it has been. We knew each other in Europe. A whole lifetime ago. And Africa."

"And Shanghai," Van der Meer added quietly, almost in a whisper.

A look of sadness and pain draped Thomas's face, unexpected and unexplained. He took a deep breath, closed his eyes tightly, and turned away.

"I don't think there's anything about Thomas that I don't know," Van der Meer said loudly, changing the direction of the conversation.

Thomas looked at him, the sadness disappearing, and smiled. "But there's nothing about me that you would ever tell."

"What an interesting friendship," I said. "How is it that you've followed each other around the world?"

The maid entered and nodded to Van der Meer. He stood and motioned to the dining room.

"Dinner is served," he said, ignoring my question.

Our meal consisted of fish steaks, bathed in tomato, red bell pepper and a curry sauce accented with ginger. It was a local recipe and, although a bit spicy, it was quite good. Accompanied by bananas and coconut slices, the meal was memorable.

The war dominated the discussion. Throughout dinner, Thomas and Chin described military activities in the region, while Lady Jane discussed defense preparations in India. I added some personal experiences from London, but I found the interaction between Thomas and Van der Meer to be more interesting. Their friendship had spanned a lifetime and three continents.

As the conversation continued, I studied our host. What drove someone to leave the Netherlands to carve a rubber plantation out of the jungle a half a world away? I suspected he was practical, hardworking, and trustworthy. He seemed to have integrity and principles; he might be the type of person you could trust with your secrets. Or your life. But maybe not. He was difficult to read.

After dinner we spent a few hours in Van der Meer's study, admiring the shelves of leather-bound books. Lady Jane was mesmerized, removing volume after volume from the shelves and thumbing through them. Thomas, Chin, and Van der Meer reviewed a large map of the region that was sprawled across a desk. They discussed the war, including regions the Japanese occupied or threatened, and they provided opinions on what was next. I watched them curiously; the conversation was a lesson in military strategy. Not a common topic for three old friends. They talked until we retired several hours later around midnight.

Our sleeping quarters were adequate; the house had several spare bedrooms. We awoke at 4 a.m. and prepared to depart to insure the initial part of the journey would be cloaked in darkness, just in case Japanese scouts were in the area. But the farther we got from Singapore, the safer we were.

"We're staying at the Hotel Duncan," Thomas said as we walked to the airstrip.

"I know the place," Van der Meer said. "And I may decide to join you. It looks like the enemy will be here in a few weeks. They need our rubber and oil to fuel their war effort. Batavia could be next."

His opinions and viewpoints were much like Thomas's. But if he was right, that meant running away again. The Japanese would jump from Singapore to Sumatra to Java where Batavia was located. And then where? To Australia? It didn't seem like anywhere was safe.

We said our goodbyes and prepared to depart. We climbed aboard the plane, and, after a series of pre-start checks, Chin gunned the engine to life. He guided the aircraft down the runway, pulled the throttle, and eased the plane skyward.

We headed for Batavia. Chin again flew at a low altitude, and we drifted lazily above the coast. It was a beautiful night, cloudless with a full moon, and dawn only an hour or so away.

"We're only a few hours from Batavia," Chin informed us.

"It is such a relief to have left Singapore," Lady Jane said.

Thomas was pensive for a moment. "I can't help worrying about what will happen to those we left behind."

CHAPTER 14

The steady drone of the engine coupled with the eerie hours before dawn soon had my chin against my chest, my eyelids drooping, and I drifted off to sleep. I stirred a few times, feeling Lady Jane's head against my shoulder, but for the most part I slept soundly.

I wasn't sure how long I was asleep when I felt someone shaking me. "George. George, wake up."

I opened my eyes, feeling disjointed and confused. I blinked several times and then sat up.

"You were dreaming," Lady Jane said. "You kept thrashing about in your chair calling out for Maggie. Are you all right?"

"Yes, I'm fine," I said. I rubbed the sleep from my eyes. "Where are we?"

"I don't know," she said. "But we should be getting close. Who is Maggie?"

Chin and Thomas were staring anxiously into the clouds, their heads bobbing from left to right. Even though Chin guided the plane, he still looked about frantically, as did Thomas, who peered from the portholes and then the windshield.

I was alarmed by their behavior. "What's wrong?"

"Japanese," Thomas said ominously. "Two planes have been shadowing us for the last few minutes."

I sat upright and looked out the porthole. I could see land on one side of the plane, white beaches with lush vegetation spreading beyond them, tiptoeing away from the water. From the other direction, just behind us, were two planes, separated from each other by only a few hundred feet. On their wings were machine-gun barrels and a white flag with the red circle in its center. They

113

were Japanese.

"Why are they bothering us?" Lady Jane asked. Her face was flushed, the tension obvious in her voice. "Aren't we hundreds of miles from Singapore?"

"We've seen a lot of Japanese activity," Thomas said. "Mostly ships and landing craft. They must be getting ready to invade Sumatra. It looked like they were going to leave us alone. Until a few minutes ago."

"I'll never be able to outrun them," Chin warned.

Thomas kept a wary eye on the planes. "Just keep doing what you're doing. We're an innocent plane, flying along the coast, posing no threat to them."

"There's no such thing as an innocent plane in the middle of a war," Lady Jane said. "They probably think we're spying on them."

I felt my heart beat faster. She was right. We were at war. No one was innocent. Everyone was either an enemy or a friend. I clutched the arms of the chair, my knuckles white.

"George, what are we going to do," she hissed in my ear.

I could feel her breath coming in gasps. She was scared. But so was I. "They'll watch us for a few minutes and then leave us alone," I said, trying to calm her by displaying a confidence I didn't feel.

"One of the planes is dropping back," Chin said. "Thomas, can you see him?"

Thomas leaned behind Chin and looked out of the starboard porthole. "I can't see. I think it went to a lower altitude."

Lady Jane leaned forward. "It's right there. Just outside my window."

An enemy plane now flanked each of our wings.

114

"What are they doing?" I asked. "Will they force us to land?"

"I don't think they've decided," Thomas said warily.

My heart thumped against my chest. I couldn't believe it. All the dangers I had faced, nine months of air raids in London, canons, and invading Japanese in Singapore, only to be killed by the enemy after I'd escaped.

Lady Jane's face was pale, her lips stiff. Her hands clutched the armrest just as mine did. I don't know why I did it, but I reached over and placed my hand on hers, grasping it tightly. She looked over and smiled bravely.

"They're slowing down," Chin said.

I looked out a porthole. The planes were dropping back, allowing the distance to grow between their planes and ours. Their noses were even with our wings, and then they slowly faded away, drifting out of sight.

"Maybe they're leaving," I said hopefully, even though I knew it wasn't likely.

"I don't think so," Chin said. "Thomas, go to the tail and see what they're doing."

He undid his seat belt and climbed from the front, squeezing past Lady Jane and me on his way to the rear of the plane. Then he peered through the portholes on each side of the plane.

"The planes are directly behind us," he said. "I think they're going to attack."

Seconds later we heard the discharge of machine guns and the fuselage was ripped by bullets, the holes making linear patterns across the side of the plane, piercing the wood and ricocheting around the cabin.

"Hold on!" Chin said. "I'm going to try to lose

them."

"What should we do?" Lady Jane shrieked.

I wrapped my arm around her. "Lean forward and tuck your head in your lap. I'll protect you."

Chin jerked the plane from left to right and rapidly changed altitude. When the aircraft ascended, Thomas tumbled about the cargo bay. He grabbed the slats on the side of the fuselage, those used to anchor cargo, and made his way to the front of the plane.

He opened the tool chest behind our seat and withdrew a machine gun. Trying to get a glimpse of the enemy, he moved to a porthole and propped it open. No good. Changing tactics, he went to another vantage point and stood poised, machine gun in hand, while he observed the skies beyond.

"I can't get a shot at them," he hollered.

"Thomas," I called. "What can I do? Is there another gun?"

"No," he said. "Just stay down. Protect Lady Jane."

The plane kept climbing as Chin pulled back on the flight stick. He then changed tactics. He dove, directing the plane downward at a steep angle, plunging towards the sea. When it seemed a crash was imminent, he reversed direction. The plane arched upward.

The Japanese planes spread apart and fired from different directions. Bullets again ripped through the fuselage, tearing the plane's belly and sides, causing air to rush in, and leaving lines of holes that traveled around the plane's fragile skin. The firing continued, moving up the wall and shattering a porthole near Lady Jane.

She screamed as the glass sprayed her. I unstrapped myself from my seat and leaned on top of her, sheltering her body with mine. "Be still," I said. "It'll be over soon."

She bolted upright, not interested in protection, and almost knocked me to the floor. "There's got to be another gun in that toolbox. I'd rather shoot than get shot at."

"Will you get down!" Thomas ordered. "George! Keep her still."

I wasn't sure she was going to listen. "We just want you safe," I explained.

Reluctantly, she sat down and leaned forward, her head on her knees. I wrapped my body around her, doing what I could to shelter her. She was warm and soft and smelled of lilacs. Her hair tickled my face.

Another burst of bullets ripped the aircraft. Some imbedded in luggage; others tore through the wall above them, shredding a hole in the side of the plane, a long tear over a foot long and several inches wide. Thomas peered through the slit in the plane's skin and stuck the machine gun barrel through the opening.

I was terrified. Bullets ricocheted around us, the sides of the plane were torn and tattered, and Chin did all he possibly could to evade the enemy. But it wasn't working. We were outnumbered and outgunned. It was easy to envision the outcome. Our chance of survival was limited.

"Keep your head down," I said to Lady Jane. "And everything will be all right. You'll see. We'll get through this. We will."

She sat up and kissed my cheek. "George, you really are the strongest man I know."

Thomas started shooting. I wasn't sure how effective the machine gun would be against another plane, but it was all we had. He stood, bracing himself against the wall with a cigar clenched between his teeth, firing away, spraying the barrel the full length of the tear in the fuselage.

Another barrage of bullets splintered the cargo bay door, hammering a pattern along one jamb and across the top. The wood buckled, and with another rush of air it was torn from its hinges. It fluttered through the clouds on its way to the ocean.

Thomas moved to the open door and leaned out, holding the frame with one hand and the gun with the other. He planted his feet and fired.

"Hold the plane steady, Chin," he shouted. "Let me get a shot at them."

He fired repeatedly at the plane closest to us, aiming at the cockpit. Bullets riddled the nose and propeller, finally shattering the plane's windshield.

I couldn't believe he was battling a modern aircraft with a machine gun. I was stunned, impressed by his bravery, his courage, and the lack of concern for his own life. He seemed more interested in killing the enemy than surviving. He continued with defiance and a lust for revenge and hatred that was both astonishing and admirable.

"I think I got him!"

He kept firing. Seconds later, the plane lost control and descended towards the sea. The pilot was slumped forward, dead or dying, the target of Thomas's bullets.

I knew the shots hit their target by pure luck. And so did he. Now the element of surprise was gone. The second pilot would take us much more seriously. Even though the danger had been halved, it provided no relief. I glanced at Thomas, brave and bold, and saw another side of the man. It was one more missing piece to an incomplete puzzle.

"The other plane is behind us," Thomas said.

"Hold on," Chin called. "I'm dropping to three hundred feet."

"Thomas! How can I help?" I frantically asked again. "There must be something I can do!"

"Just stay down and cover Lady Jane!"

He again leaned out the door, holding on to the splintered jamb tightly, his knuckles white. His machine gun rattled. Smoke drifted from the barrel as the acrid stench of gunpowder floated through the cabin.

The enemy returned fire. Bullets again sprayed our cargo bay, tearing holes and splintering wood, ricocheting and whistling past us. Bullets burrowed into the edge of my seat. They ripped off an armrest, destroying Thomas's empty seat. Bullets whizzed across the dashboard. They shattered the windshield, sending splinters of glass about the cabin.

My heart was racing, my breath coming in labored gasps as sweat prickled on my forehead. I had never been so close to death, never so frightened, never so helpless. I found myself whispering the twenty-third psalm. I held Lady Jane closer, determined to protect her, resolved to save her. I wanted to do everything for her that I couldn't do for Maggie.

"Are you all right?" I asked, yelling above the noise of the machine guns

"No, I'm terrified! Aren't you?"

I didn't answer. I was just as afraid as she was, but I didn't want her to know. I glanced over my shoulder. Thomas was still firing. I looked through the holes the bullets had ripped in the floor. The ocean was close. Very close.

"Chin!" I called. "We're losing altitude!"

He didn't reply. I turned to face him. He was slumped over the dashboard. Blood stained the back of his shirt.

"Thomas!" I yelled. "Chin's been hit!"

CHAPTER 15

The engine whined and sputtered as the plane's speed decreased. The wings dipped up and down as the plane haphazardly dropped towards the ocean, making an eerie whistling sound as it faltered through the sky. The engine then stalled completely, choking and coughing and spitting black smoke, and the nose started to dive.

Thomas ran towards the controls. "Bastards!"

Lady Jane popped her head up, craning her neck past me, and looked out of the porthole. "We're going to crash!" she screamed.

The sound of splintering wood, bending and flexing and breaking, drowned the screams that filled the cabin. The plane slammed into the waves, throwing us violently forward and then backwards, before skimming and skipping across the water, bouncing like a tiny pebble tumbling down a hill. We were awash in a jumble of sound and motion, bodies slipping and sliding in all directions. Baggage broke free, tumbling about the cabin, skimming off walls and seats and ceilings and floors.

I opened my eyes slowly, my mind foggy, and groggily blinked several times. My head hurt, my vision was cloudy, and my mouth was dry. I wasn't sure how long I had been unconscious. It could have been seconds; it might have been minutes.

The plane lay on its side, water lapping against the frame, a bi-wing sticking straight in the air. The cargo hatch served as a skylight. I gazed through it, my senses still dulled, and used the wing tip as a point of reference. I was struggling to understand what had happened, fighting to remain alert. My ears rang, and my vision was still clouded. I just wanted to close my eyes and rest, sleep for a few minutes more. But I knew I couldn't.

I freed myself from some debris, the remnants of a packing crate that was lying on top of me, and moved my arms and legs and head. Everything worked. There was no pain, and, other than stiff muscles, some bruises, and bleeding from minor abrasions, I wasn't seriously hurt.

I studied the plane, my mind still muddled, and saw that the skin, riddled with holes before the crash, was now covered with fractures that increased in size, the fuselage creaking and straining under the pressure. Water seeped in at an alarming rate, rushing through cracks of every size and spilling down onto the floor. I realized we would drown in minutes. If the sharks didn't get us first.

I jumped up. I had to find Lady Jane. I had to help her. I couldn't let her die.

She was near the tail, in the last dry area of the plane, sprawled over a suitcase. Her eyes were closed; her face was gray. A large bruise marred her cheek and temple. I was sure she was dead.

I moved frantically towards her. Thomas was sloshing through knee-deep water near the pilot's seat, blood trickling down his cheek. He paused, watching me.

"How is she?" he asked.

I couldn't speak. She looked just like Maggie had on that horrible night. I bent over her, moving my hands about her neck and face, searching for signs of life. Then I scooped some sea water in my hands and splashed it on her face.

A few anxious seconds passed before her eyelids fluttered open. "What happened?" she asked.

I sighed with relief. "She's alive," I called to Thomas.

"We have to hurry," he said. "The water is rising

quickly. I'll get Chin."

I turned my attention to Lady Jane. "It's all right," I told her. "Do you feel any pain?"

She stared vacantly, the glaze in her eyes slowly clearing. "No pain, but I feel numb all over."

"Can you move?"

She wiggled her arms and legs. "Yes, I can move. I can't believe we're still alive."

I helped her sit up and then scrambled to the front of the plane. Thomas was standing still, stunned and saddened.

Chin's eyes were open, empty and vacant, staring at a world he could not see. Flesh and muscle and blood and bone protruded grotesquely from his chest.

Thomas reached forward and closed his eyes, and then lovingly caressed the boyish face. "He was such a good man. And a good friend."

"Thomas, come on," I urged. "We have to get out of here. The plane is sinking."

I grabbed his arm, pulling him away from Chin's body, and led him back to Lady Jane.

"What happened to Chin?" she asked.

"He didn't make it," Thomas said.

Her face paled and her eyes fogged; a tear dripped from her eye. "Maybe now he can be with his son," she said softly.

I had to focus them on getting out of the plane. At the rate the water was rising, we would drown in minutes. "Let's use rope to tie pieces of wreckage and luggage together," I said.

"To make a raft?" Thomas asked.

"Yes," I replied. "Or at least something we can hold on to. Come on. We don't have much time."

Lady Jane and I salvaged some rope while Thomas climbed out of the open hatchway. As he did, I realized the water level in the plane rose and fell with the waves.

"We're only a few hundred feet from shore," Thomas said. "The plane is stuck in the sand. We must be perched on a sandbar." He was quiet for a moment, searching the landscape. "The Japanese are gone."

"Do we need a raft?" I asked.

"No," replied Thomas. "I think we can easily make it to land. George, help Lady Jane up, and we'll get out of here."

She placed her hands on my shoulders and her foot in my cupped hands, using them as a stair step. I lifted her up while Thomas pulled from above. With some minor awkwardness, we got her out of the plane.

"What about sharks?" I asked.

Thomas wiped some blood dripping down his face. "Let's hope we make it to shore before the scent of blood attracts them."

I climbed from the plane, joining them on top. We slid from the fuselage into the water and started for shore. It took little time to prove the plane indeed was perched on a sandbar. We had walked only a short distance when Lady Jane cried out in surprise and slid beneath the water.

Thomas grasped her shoulders and pulled her to the surface. "Are you all right?"

"Yes, I think so," she said, coughing and spitting water.

"Hold on to my back," he said. "I'll bring you the rest of the way."

She wrapped her arms around his neck, her legs floating in the water, and Thomas started walking towards the shore. "Oh, this is much better," she said.

I trudged along behind them, easily tiring, my muscles starting to ache and my breathing growing labored. I wished I had the strength to carry her, to bring her to safety, to provide the security she wanted and needed. But I didn't.

Once we reached the beach, we collapsed on the sand, thankful to be alive. We rested for a moment, regaining our strength and catching our breath, before checking for more serious injuries.

"I have some bruises," Lady Jane said. "And a few cuts and scrapes. But I think I'm all right."

"It's the bruise on your head that worries me," Thomas said. He eyed the lump on the side of her head and then tenderly touched the swelling. "You'll have a horrible headache once the shock wears off. How about you, George?"

"Just some sore muscles and minor bruises," I said.

"We have to get Chin's body and our luggage," Thomas said.

"What about you?" Lady Jane asked. "Your head is bleeding."

"It's from the air raid in Singapore," he said. "I think the stitches broke. It's not serious; the bleeding has already slowed. I'll be fine." He sighed, his eyes dulled by sorrow.

I looked at the plane, still perched on the sandbar. It showed signs of breaking under the strain of the rolling waves. "Thomas, we had better hurry," I said quietly. "The plane may not last much longer."

He looked to the ocean, realized my concern, and then turned to Lady Jane. "Lie under those trees and rest. We'll be back shortly. Stay out of sight. We don't know where the enemy is."

Thomas and I returned to the plane. We used rope to tie the suitcases together, and then I towed them to shore. It was easier than trying to carry them. But the second trip was harder than the first, and towing the baggage made it even harder. I was breathing heavily, my muscles burning, tiring more with each step.

"We can rest a minute if you like," Thomas said.

"I'll be fine," I said, my chest heaving, my words coming in staggered gasps.

I couldn't ask him to stop, not while he carried Chin. I struggled on, determined to make the shore, each step harder than the last. I looked at Thomas, watching him as we moved through the water, the brave, mysterious man who knew no fear. He was crying but trying desperately to hide it.

CHAPTER 16

Thomas wept as he gently laid Chin's lifeless body on the sand. He looked away, his eyes clenched closed.

I watched him trying to cope, looking as if his heart had been ripped from his body. I knew what it was like. I had held the lifeless body of someone I'd loved, begging a merciful God to give her another breath, to undo what had just been done. I understood how it felt to know you would never forgive yourself. And that's what I saw on his face.

I hugged him, patting him gently on the back. "I'm sorry."

I couldn't look at Chin, even though I tried. I wanted to pay my respects, to honor a man I barely knew, but the gruesome wound made it difficult. Now he lay in the sand like Maggie had lain on a remote cliff in England, thrown from a car I couldn't control. Chin's death brought back the pain, which had been dormant and dulled, and made it feel as sharp as a knife.

Lady Jane walked up to Thomas and wrapped her arms around him. She held him tightly for a minute, sniffling and sobbing, and then pulled away.

"Are you all right?" she asked, looking into his pained eyes.

"Yes," he said, although we knew he didn't mean it. "I'm fine."

She looked at the body but immediately turned away. "I don't want to remember him like that," she said softly.

"What do we do now?" I asked quietly, my eyes moistening.

"We need to bury him," Thomas said. He pointed to a knoll that overlooked the ocean and was rimmed by palm trees. "Under those trees would be nice."

"Then let's do that," Lady Jane said. "It's too painful to see him lying here."

We collected some flat rocks to serve as shovels, and started to dig through the soft sand. It grew more difficult the deeper we went; the sand was more compacted. But we continued on, sweating and straining, and we had almost reached a suitable depth when Lady Jane asked the question we had somehow managed to forget.

"Where do you think we are?"

We stopped digging and looked up, briefly studying our surroundings. We had been so consumed with grief and sorrow, so overwhelmed with tragedy and catastrophe, and so thankful to have been saved, that we hadn't considered what dangers we might confront.

"I don't know," Thomas said. "I was going to scout around after we're settled and try to find out."

"We need to determine if we're safe," I said. "And we have to find food and water." I eyed the landscape warily. For all we knew, we were on an island occupied by the Japanese.

When we finished digging, we lined the hole with small rocks, forming a base. Then Thomas and I gently laid Chin to rest.

Tears sporadically welled in Thomas's eyes. I wanted to console him but didn't think it was the right time. He needed to grieve. So I let him.

Lady Jane was quiet. She watched Thomas, worried and willing to help if asked, to listen if requested. She didn't look at the body.

We decided to cover Chin with the flat stones, barely larger than pebbles, that littered the beach. And then we poured sand in all the voids. When the grave was filled, and everything compacted, we laid larger rocks on top of it, and fashioned a grave marker.

I turned to Thomas. His face was drawn and pale, his eyes misty. "You knew him best," I said. "It might be nice if you said a few words."

He couldn't speak; he was too emotional. He merely shook his head.

I called upon my Protestant upbringing and quietly recited the Lord's Prayer.

Lady Jane murmured, "George, why don't we give Thomas some time alone?"

"Of course," I said. "I'm sorry, Thomas, I should have thought of that." I was supposed to be so perceptive. But she saw what I couldn't see.

We left Thomas and took our luggage to a grove of palm trees out of sight of Chin's grave. We opened the lids so the air could dry our soggy belongings and checked for damage, most of which was caused by bullet holes from the enemy's machine guns.

"My books are ruined," Lady Jane groaned.

I glanced in her suitcases. There were probably ten books scattered among her clothes; a half dozen looked like the murder mysteries she absorbed every few days.

"Maybe they'll dry out," I said, assuming she meant the sea water.

"No, look," she said, holding up a book.

There was a bullet hole right through the center, destroying the cover and the pages. I looked at the title: *Life in Australia.*

"Maybe you won't need that one," I said.

She rolled her eyes but didn't reply.

We sprawled under the shade of some palm trees, lying in the sand, bruised and spent but thankful to be alive.

Neither of us spoke.

Thomas came over about fifteen minutes later. He was composed, but his eyes were red and watery. "You two rest while I explore our surroundings," he said. "Maybe I can find some clue as to where we are."

"Shouldn't we all go?" I asked.

"No, I think not," he said. A sadness still lived in his voice. "I'd rather go alone."

"Then we'll just rest a bit," said Lady Jane. "Take all the time you need."

He smiled weakly, cast a friendly wave, and disappeared over the dunes into a fringe of foliage that abutted the sand.

After a few moments of silence, Lady Jane sat up. "George, may I ask you a question?"

I had almost fallen asleep. I opened my eyes and peered up at her. "Yes, I suppose."

"Who broke your heart?"

I tensed. I really didn't want to share my personal life. Even though Maggie had been gone for months, I had never talked about it. Not to anyone. Only family and friends and coworkers knew what had happened. "No one," I said.

"Then who is Maggie?"

I hesitated. She had a compassionate look on her face, as if she wanted to help me. But it was too painful to discuss. I didn't want to share the memories. They were private and personal. Maggie was a part of me. She always would be, and I didn't want to share that.

"It's all right," she coaxed. "I won't tell a soul. I swear. And if you tell me your secret, I'll tell you mine. Then we'll form a pact and forever protect each other."

I smiled. She sounded like a child. I saw a

different side of her. She was manipulative; she had a whole arsenal of weapons at her disposal to get what she wanted.

"It's a very long story," I finally said. "And very personal."

She had the hint of a frown on her face. I wondered why she wanted to know. Did she want to provide a sympathetic ear as a friend, or did she want me to do that for her?

"I understand," she said. "And I wasn't trying to pry. I only thought I could help. I see the pain in your eyes. And I can imagine the pain in your heart."

I studied her for a moment. Her statement was moving. She seemed sincere. I noticed the pain in her eyes. We shared heartache; we shared sadness. She wanted me to know that. It was only then that I understood her motive.

"Maggie was my wife," I said softly.

She lightly brushed the hair from my forehead, moving her face close to mine, giving me her complete and undivided attention. I knew that she cared. "Tell me about her."

I smiled, as I always did when I thought about Maggie. Then I took a deep breath. "Let me see," I said, tortured between pleasant memories and sadness. "She was very different. Unlike anyone I have ever known. She was impetuous and optimistic and bubbly and funny. She was a dozen different people rolled into one: a dreamer, a comedian, a dancer, an optimist, a teacher, a partner, a friend. She could drink most men under the table and was not afraid to try. Her laugh was contagious, and once she started you couldn't help but join her. She was smart but in a practical way. And she was a beautiful person. Inside and out. I could never understand what she saw in me. I always felt like I didn't deserve her."

"You must have loved her very much," she said softly, her eyes sincere and searching. "Whatever happened?"

I paused. I felt the pain returning. It was never really gone. But sometimes it was hidden, tucked away in the shadows of my heart.

"You don't have to tell me if you don't want to."

"She died," I whispered.

She was stunned, shaken by my reply, never expecting an answer so final. "I'm so sorry," she said. "I had no idea." She hugged me. It felt really good.

The rest of the story somehow tumbled out of my mouth, like water splashing over a dam. I described the whole horrid, tragic accident: falling asleep while driving and the car hurtling over the cliff. I explained those few painful minutes that changed life forever. "I survived…but Maggie didn't."

It was the only time I had told the whole story and the first time I ever admitted what happened. I had blurted it out, rushing to finish before I broke down. I could see the sorrow in Lady Jane's face, genuine and sincere. She felt what I felt; she saw what I saw.

"Oh, George," she said, the sympathy mirrored in her eyes. "I am so sorry. I know I shouldn't have asked. But from the moment we met I could see your pain; you wear it like a halo."

I searched her face, finding only sincerity. "Just don't tell anyone," I said softly.

"I won't. But only if you promise me something."

"What is that?"

"You have to move on," she whispered. "You can't

hold on to something you can never have. You have to let her go."

Then she hugged me again. This time she held me tighter and longer. I could smell the remnants of her perfume, what hadn't been washed away by the sea, and feel her hair brushing against my face. I savored the heat of her body and the warmth of her heart.

She was the first woman I had held since Maggie died. I wanted to gently push her away, to tell her that it wasn't right, and that I couldn't do it. But she held on, pulling me closer and holding me tighter. Then I didn't want her to let go. But eventually she did.

As soon as I had finished telling her Maggie's story, I felt an immense sense of relief wash over me, like I had been carrying the universe, as if all the problems in the world had rested on my shoulders and had suddenly been peeled away. It was like I had shed all the grief and heartache and guilt and pain I had been carrying. Even if it was only gone for a few minutes, it still felt good.

Lady Jane sat quietly, and after a few moments of reflection passed, she spoke. "Do you want to hear my story?"

I suspected it was about Balraj. I wasn't sure if I wanted to hear it, not sure if I wanted to be involved. But she had tried to help me, so I would try to help her. "If you trust me enough to tell it."

"I do," she replied. "Especially after what you told me."

"All right, then tell me."

"As you know, I've spent most of my life in India. Even though my family had been in Northern Ireland for centuries."

"Yes, I do," I said. I thought of what I knew about

133

the Smythe family.   They were wealthy aristocrats, a dominate voice on the Indian subcontinent.

"Sometimes tradition dictates that families like mine choose their daughter's future husband," she continued. "This is often done at a young age and for a variety of reasons. In my case, my husband was chosen for me when I was fourteen."

"Who was it?"

"Sir Gregory Millburne," she replied.

I recalled the name. "I've heard of him. But we've never met. Hasn't his family helped to govern India for the last fifty years?"

"Yes, that's him."

"But you never married?"

Her eyes averted mine. "I delayed it as long as I could. I wasn't ready. I felt like I was in a cage, cornered and trapped."

I knew all about cages. Polio had been my cage, keeping me prisoner for my entire childhood. I knew it wasn't exactly the same, but I was sure the trapped feeling was similar.

"I had to escape," she continued. "There had to be some way to leave and start a new life. To get everyone to leave me alone. Something or someone…"

"Balraj Patel," I said tersely.

She paused, not expecting the interruption.   "I suppose it was easy to figure out."

"What better way to end your arranged engagement and get your entire family to leave you alone? Run off with a man who is not only a commoner but who is from a different culture. And a different race and religion."

"Yes," she said. "I know it sounds horrible."

"And now, as you told me, you've alienated family

and friends and loved ones. Is the loved one Sir Gregory Millburne?"

"Yes," she said. "I realized when Balraj ended our relationship just how foolish I had been. I thought I loved him, but maybe he was just a means to escape. But I'm not a horrible person, George. Really I'm not. I just wasn't ready. And Gregory did nothing wrong. All he did was love me. I could never say anything negative about him because he is a good man. He really is. With many desirable traits. And look what I've done to him."

I was quiet for a moment. I thought about my battle with polio, my cage, and how difficult that fight had been. Then I finally spoke. "No one can understand a cage unless they've been in one. Sometimes it doesn't matter how you escape. It only matters that you do."

She studied me for a moment. Then she leaned forward, her lips tantalizingly close. I kissed her, gently. She hesitated, and then her arms wrapped around me and she pulled me closer.

I marveled at the softness of her lips, the gentleness of her fingertips caressing my face. It felt so right, so natural, so inviting, that I never wanted it to end. I wanted to hold her in my arms for eternity.

Thomas's voice boomed across the dunes, his frame visible coming just over the rise. Lady Jane pulled away abruptly, but I don't think it was fast enough. I was certain he saw us as he approached, climbing gingerly over a small dune. He looked at us curiously, hid a sly grin, and dropped two buckets on the sand. One was filled with rice, while the other bulged with fruit, bananas and melons. Three fish lay in the bucket of rice.

"Dinner," he announced. "Anything interesting happen while I was gone?"

I glanced at Lady Jane. She was a bit flustered, but she recovered quickly. "I'm starved," she said. "Where did you get that?"

"There's a road a hundred feet from here," he said. "And a farmhouse a short distance away. I went and talked to the owners. They supplied us with dinner."

"Where are we?" I asked.

"Fifteen miles from Batavia," he said.

"We're in Java?" Lady Jane asked.

"Yes, we are very fortunate," Thomas said. "I hired the farmer I met today to take us to the city in the morning. We'll meet him on the road at dawn."

"What a relief," I said. "The nightmare is almost over."

"It is," Thomas agreed. "Tomorrow will be the last leg of our journey."

"Where are we staying tonight?" Lady Jane asked.

"Under the stars," Thomas explained, his arms outstretched. "And there's a pond on the other side of the road. We can wash and clean our clothes."

"That sounds marvelous," Lady Jane said.

"You two go first," Thomas said. "I'll start cooking,"

We bathed separately in the pond, washing the salt water from our bodies and doing the best we could with our clothes and what was in our suitcases, much of which was riddled with bullet holes. When we returned, Thomas had cooked dinner, frying the fish over a makeshift fire and laying some bananas and melons on a small carpet of dried seaweed. We ate dinner, quiet and subdued, grateful for our good fortune but mourning the loss of Chin.

After dinner I surveyed the cove where we now camped. The empty expanse of beach was sheltered by trees, so peaceful and picturesque, the ocean gently rolling onto the shore. The sky was cobalt and clear, sprawling across the heavens to kiss the distant horizon. Given our fateful arrival, I hadn't taken time to appreciate its beauty. I admired the scene for a moment, the peacefulness and serenity.

We sat quietly, not in the mood for conversation. An occasional remark was made, about the stars or the relief that the sea breeze offered. But for the most part, we were each lost in our own thoughts.

Thomas rose and sat beside Lady Jane, gently touching the swelling on her head. The bruise had turned a purplish color. "How are you feeling?" he asked.

"My head is throbbing," she said. "But I don't want to complain. It could be worse."

"I wish I had something to give you for the pain," I said.

"In India, we used coffee for headaches," she said. "Made very strong and drunk black. I don't know if it works for a bruise, though."

"I find that shots of gin work well in curing headaches," Thomas said.

I laughed. "That's interesting. I was taught that shots of gin create headaches."

"Did you have a nice chat while I was gone?" Thomas asked. "Or did you rest."

Lady Jane insured Thomas wasn't looking and then cast me a wink. "A little of both," she said.

We chatted for an hour more and then retired for the evening, the beach as our blanket and the moonlit sky our ceiling. As tired as I was, I found it difficult to drift off to sleep. I couldn't stop thinking about Lady Jane.

It was a restless night, the sound of waves

pounding in our ears. It was just before dawn when we awoke. When the first rays of morning danced across the sea, we were surprised to see that our plane had disappeared. Not a trace remained. The waves had consumed even the smallest portion, leaving not the slightest hint that it had ever existed.

CHAPTER 17

The sun had barely risen when a wagon ambled down the road, the wood it was constructed of weathered and cracked. Although old and a bit tired it seemed sturdy with many years of life remaining. It had a large bed and was probably used to transport farm goods, having served generations of the same family. There was ample room for us and our luggage. Two oxen pulled it, huge, methodical beasts that moved steadily but slowly.

Lady Jane turned to Thomas. "Are we leaving Singapore or going to Batavia? I'm confused. Didn't we just take this trip?" Then she laughed and playfully slapped him on the shoulder. "You sure know how to pamper a lady, don't you?"

Thomas smiled. "Lady Jane, if you live to be one hundred years old you will never repeat the adventures you've had in the last few days. And you will never tire of talking about it."

Her eyes twinkled with amusement. She probably agreed with him. "Perhaps," she said. "Or maybe the real excitement is yet to come."

I listened to the banter between them, innocent flirting, and felt a twinge of jealousy. Maybe the conversation that Lady Jane and I had had the day before, sharing secrets and baring souls, didn't mean much to her. As I watched her trade barbs with Thomas, I realized that it certainly meant something to me.

We left the cove and proceeded onward, traveling down a rural road wide enough for only our wagon, wheel ruts marring the dirt. The sea and sand dunes, rimmed by groves of palm trees, flanked one side of the road, while acres of farm fields interrupted by trees and shrubs marked the other. We passed farmers working in the fields, most with oxen pulling crude wooden plows; some had their families working beside them. We saw one elderly farmer standing by the side of the road, stooped and gray, his plow beside him. He nodded and waved as we passed, casting a toothless grin in our direction. I suspected there weren't many strangers that passed through this part of Java.

An hour later the fields and vegetation and beaches and palm trees vanished and we entered an immense mangrove swamp. It was the most sinister scenery I had ever seen, with gnarled roots stretching grotesquely from the water, animal-like in appearance. A hazy mist boiled off the brackish water, stinking of sulfur. We saw several crocodiles, black eyes watching us hungrily as we slowly meandered past them.

Lady Jane shuddered. "This is like driving through a horror movie."

She was right. The swamp was eerie and surreal; it was like hell and the River Styx. Maybe this is where bad souls went for eternity, breathing the brackish stink of the marsh and eluding crocodiles, snakes, spiders and rats. I didn't want to see it or think about it, and I couldn't wait to escape it.

"Java has many faces," Thomas said. "Swamps, beautiful beaches, volcanoes, rice paddies gracefully terraced into the hillsides, rural roads, and modern cities. There are beautiful flowers like the pink water lotus and purple lily, and unique creatures like yellow caterpillars and butterflies of blue and gold with wings as wide as your outstretched hand. And it's one of the most densely populated places in the world."

I reflected on the maps I had studied as a child, painting the topography of the Dutch East Indies in my mind's eye. The islands that comprised the colony had been hampered throughout history with violent acts of nature, primarily earthquakes and volcanoes of unbelievably destructive force. As I recalled, some of the most powerful volcanic eruptions in history had occurred in Java or Sumatra.

"Will you be staying in Batavia?" I asked him.

"For a while, I suppose. I'm in no hurry to go anywhere."

"How about you, George?" Lady Jane asked. "What are your plans?"

I thought about the hug, her body close against me, the tender kiss, and her silken fingers caressing my face. I wondered if that intimate moment would ever be repeated.

"I'm not sure," I said. "For now, it'll serve as well as Singapore. I made a commitment to report from this part of the world, and for now that's what I intend to do. How about you?"

"I don't know what I'll do," she said. Then she looked at me and smiled. "Maybe I'll just stay in Batavia."

It was late afternoon when we approached Batavia, a sprawling city that served as the capital for Dutch colonies in the southwest Pacific. We first entered suburbs, unique in their architectural blend of Dutch and Javanese influences, and then the city proper.

Canals cut the landscape, some bordered by impressive Dutch homes while others displayed multi-storied slums teetering on the water's edge, crooked and poorly constructed and at risk of collapse.

We passed an outdoor fruit market crowded with people and products and intersected by lanes filled with pedestrians, patrons, and soldiers. We drove through neighborhoods, dwellings evenly spaced along broad avenues with steeply pitched, red-tile roofs.

We saw churches built in the European style and mosques that contrasted them both architecturally and theologically.   Buddha complimented Christ, Europe merged with Asia, peasant fused with aristocrat, but the common theme throughout Batavia was people. They crammed streets, stores, alleys, restaurants, cars, trucks, rickshaws, and bicycles.

They were everywhere.   It was one crowded, clustered mass of civilization. The city itself seemed to have a heartbeat, throbbing and beating in a rhythmic sense of humanity.   Batavia was not Singapore.   And it never would be.   It lacked the sophistication, the homogeneous blend of cultures, and the promised gateway to utopia.

We came to a halt in front of the Hotel Duncan, a modern building about ten stories high with a whitewashed façade, arched windows, and a manicured lawn.   Thomas paid our driver while I unloaded our baggage and placed it in the lobby.   Our ragged appearance coupled with our bullet-riddled suitcases earned curious stares from those who passed.

We went to our rooms and enjoyed a needed wash and change of clothes.   After a brief rest, Thomas found a doctor who removed the sutures from his arm. The cut on his forehead, reopened during the plane crash, was sealed with an adhesive bandage.   Other than the pinkish scars, his injuries would vanish, taking their place among our memories of Singapore.

Late that afternoon I wandered across the street and entered the office of the *London Times.*   A female receptionist, an elderly Javanese woman with graying hair and round glasses, occupied a desk beside the door.   The lobby was arranged similarly to the office in Singapore, but the frantic atmosphere was absent. A dozen desks sat in the center of the room, all facing each other. Half were manned with reporters, some on the telephone, others typing. Three other offices adjoined the lobby. I saw that one was occupied.

"Can I help you?" the receptionist asked.

"Hello, I'm George Adams," I said as I handed her a card. "I'm with the *Times* office in London. I've spent the last week in Singapore, and I've fled here."

The man in the occupied office looked up from his desk. "Come on in," he called.

I nodded to the receptionist. "Thank you."

The man stood to greet me. He was older, maybe sixty, with wisps of white hair covering his head. He was slight, and a bit stooped, but his pale blue eyes greeted me with a sense of energy and purpose. He seemed to love his profession.

"I'm Harry Simpkins," he said as he shook my hand. "I was with the Capetown office before I came here."

"George Adams. It's a pleasure to meet you."

"Welcome. Will you be staying in Batavia?"

"I'm not sure," I said. "I suppose for the time being. May I file my articles with you?"

"Of course," he said. "How was Singapore?"

"Chaotic and confusing," I said. "I think the battle was lost before the fight began." I was surprised to hear myself repeating what Thomas had said.

He arched his eyebrows. "How so?"

"There was an air of defeat," I explained. "On the troops' faces and throughout the island."

He rubbed his chin and eyed me curiously. "That's

interesting. I hope you don't see the same thing here. What will you write about?"

I described what I had done in Singapore, my articles on the war and the people. He seemed interested.

"I like the idea of writing about ordinary people and how the war impacts them," he said. He looked at the clock. "You missed today's deadline. Can you have something for me tomorrow?"

"Sure," I said, and turned to leave.

"Hey, Adams," he said as an afterthought. "Why did you leave London?"

I managed a weak smile. "Maybe I was running from something worse."

The following day brought tragic news. The Japanese had invaded Sumatra, the island neighbor of Java, and were battling the Dutch for control. This caused widespread panic in the streets of Batavia. Most believed Java was next.

I spent the day writing about my escape from Singapore and the invasion of Sumatra and its impact on the Dutch East Indies. I created several articles about both people I had met and the impact of war: the little girl who lost her life, Chin and his son, my discussion with the guests fleeing the Victoria Hotel, the chaos of our last few days in Singapore, Balraj and Lady Jane, although I protected their identities, and Van der Meer and the rubber plantation. I brought them to Harry Simpkins in time to meet the deadline for the morning papers in London. He glanced through them, read a few closely, complimented me on style and content, and then passed them on.

If the Sumatran invasion was devastating, the events of the next day, February 15th, were cataclysmic. The island of Singapore, once thought invincible, had surrendered to the Japanese. It was one of the worst defeats in British history. The Allies faced a bleak future; they were losing the war on every front. It seemed only a miracle could save the free world from the shackles of Toto, Mussolini, and Hitler.

Thomas visited an old friend that evening, so Lady Jane and I agreed to meet for dinner. I anxiously looked forward to it; I couldn't stop thinking about the moments we shared after the plane crash. Even if they did make me feel guilty, like I was betraying Maggie's memory. I was waiting for Lady Jane in the dining room when she rushed in, waving a newspaper. She hurried to my table and dropped it in front of me.

"Did you see this?" she asked. "We escaped just in time."

I glanced at the headline: *Singapore Surrenders.* "Yes, we did. I hope Batavia is different."

We talked awkwardly through dinner, avoiding eye contact, both uncomfortable being alone. I think we each understood that we had crossed a boundary, whether wanting to or not, and it might be difficult to retrace those steps. We made casual conversation about the weather, our impressions of Batavia, what we had liked about Singapore, an hour of discussion that really meant nothing. After dinner, I had to know what she had been thinking and where she might be going.

"Do you plan to return to India?" I asked.

"I'm not welcome in India," she replied. "It'll be a long time before I can ever go back. At least to New Delhi."

An awkward silence ensued, both of us wanting to discuss an issue we were uncomfortable with, but neither knowing how.

"But everything about you is British India," I said.

She studied me closely for a moment, her eyes meeting mine for the first time that evening. "Yes," she said. "You're right. I am India."

She was silent for a moment, forming her thoughts, and then she continued, speaking slowly and clearly. "It's a fascinating place, desperate for independence, anxious to experience the unknown, willing to falter, wanting to explore, but needing to be loved. But at the same time, it's a land that clings to tradition, comfortable with the safety and security of what it's always known. As bold as it is, it's wary of independence, anxious about the unknown, terrified to falter, too timid to explore, and more importantly, afraid to love."

Her voice was moving, anxious and pleading, desperate for understanding. She watched me as I sipped on tepid water.

"Britain, it seems, has its own issues," I said. "It's mired in the past, a comfortable time when happiness reigned. And although it knows it must face the future, and grasp each opportunity offered, it seems unable to. It can't let go of what once was, so it may never know what could be and even has trouble seeing what already is."

She reached across the table and wrapped my hand in hers. "I think with patience and determination, and recognition of their weaknesses, India and Britain could forge a long-lasting alliance."

"That's an interesting theory," I said, daring to think of a different time.

She paused and glanced at nearby patrons, her eyes then returning to mine. "Do you think you'll return to London?"

I considered it for a moment. "I'm not sure. I may want to go somewhere and start over. Maybe Singapore after the war."

"George," she said softly. "You won't let yourself start over, no matter where you go."

She was right. And I knew it. But I couldn't help it.

She clasped my hand tighter. "You have to stop running away."

The next evening I saw Thomas in the hotel bar. He had shaved his beard and was dressed impeccably, his appearance the opposite of recent days. He also smoked the pipe that was such a familiar sight in Singapore. It was only then that I realized his pipe was for civilized settings, his cigar was not. He was in a joyous mood, and even though we learned that the Japanese had captured Sumatra, the surrender did little to dull his spirits.

"Java is next," he said. "And then Australia will follow. The Japanese want the whole Pacific Ocean."

His statement did have merit. Japan needed natural resources, and they were conquering the territories that had them.

I was saved a reply by the entrance of Lady Jane. She glided into the room wearing a beige dress with an ivory shawl draped carelessly over her shoulders, looking absolutely radiant.

Thomas and I rose, and I moved to seat her.

"Thomas, where have you been hiding?" she asked.

"In the darkest corners of the city," he said.

"And why am I not surprised?"

It bothered me that they were always flirting, although I knew it shouldn't. Maybe the kiss we shared was innocent, the embrace friendly. Maybe I was making too much of it. Or maybe I wasn't.

A hotel clerk approached our table. He looked at me for a moment, and then addressed us as a group.

"Mister Montclair?" he asked in accented English.

I pointed to Thomas.

"I have a letter for you," he said.

"Thank you," he said as he tore the envelope and removed the note. After glancing at the page, he handed it to me.

MONTCLAIR,

PLANTATION CAPTURED BY JAPANESE. I'M PRISONER WITH MAN FROM SINGAPORE LOOKING FOR LADY JANE.

VAN DER MEER

I passed the letter to Lady Jane. She scanned the note and then handed it back to Thomas. Her lips were taut, her face firm, but she never said a word.

CHAPTER 18

"I have to rescue Van der Meer," Thomas said firmly. "And that's not open for discussion."

My jaw dropped, and I looked at him like he had lost his mind. The Japanese had nearly killed us once already.

"Thomas, I know Van der Meer is a close friend," I said. "But it's too dangerous. You're speaking with emotion, not logic."

"He would do the same for me," Thomas said. "And with no hesitation."

I thought about Van der Meer, the muscled arms and battered face, accented by the gold tooth. He probably would rescue Thomas. And enjoy doing it.

"Lady Jane, did you expect Balraj to come looking for you?" Thomas asked.

She glanced furtively at me, and then replied hesitantly. "I'm surprised that anyone tried to find me. But how would they ever know to go to Van der Meer's?"

He shrugged. "Chin's cargo route was well advertised. And he flew to Van der Meer's two or three times a week. But even if Balraj knew that, how could he have gotten out of Singapore?"

I wondered if it really was Balraj. He didn't seem devoted enough to Lady Jane to attempt anything that difficult. And if he successfully escaped from Singapore, I couldn't imagine him going to Van der Meer's.

"Does it really matter?" I asked. "We shouldn't even think about attempting a rescue. We can't do it."

Thomas eyed me sternly, his resolve evident. "You don't understand the bond between Van der Meer and me."

I sighed, knowing I couldn't change his mind. I

also knew I couldn't desert him. "If you're that determined to proceed, then I want to help you."

He studied me for a moment, probably wondering whether to endanger my life. "I would welcome the assistance," he said. "But I would never ask."

I had been rejected by the armed forces in England. Now I had the chance to prove myself, to make a contribution to the war effort, even if it was so minuscule as to deny the Japanese the expertise needed to operate the rubber plantation. But I also realized that I lacked the physical stamina for a jungle rescue. I could be more of a hindrance.

"I'm not much of a fighter," I said. "And I don't know how much help I can be, but I'll do everything I can."

"And so will I," Lady Jane said.

"This is a task for George and me," Thomas said sternly.

"I think I should go," she said. "I'm part of this group."

"But it's no place for a woman," Thomas said.

A defiant look captured her face, an expression I had seen before. I remembered her in Singapore, flying by on a motorcycle as she searched for Balraj Patel, sitting unperturbed in a basement bomb shelter reading a murder mystery, relaxing in a taproom in a strange city with a roomful of strangers, belting out the chorus to a popular song. She was different; she grasped every branch the tree of life offered, determined to climb to the top. Thomas might think he was going to prevent her from going, but he wouldn't be successful.

"Thomas, I think we're going to need all the help we can get," I said.

"She cannot come," he said, emphasizing every

syllable. "And that is final."

"I insist," she demanded. "You can have a million reasons for not letting me go, but being a woman can't be one of them."

We were silent for a moment. The war had brought tremendous changes to the world. Women worked in factories, replacing men who went to war, building airplanes, tanks, and jeeps. They also joined the service, performing a variety of tasks previously assigned to men, and I knew, as did Thomas, that women were working as spies behind enemy lines, perhaps the most dangerous task of the entire war effort. The difference, of course, was that in each of these examples, the women had been trained.

"I'll look after her, Thomas," I said. "I promise." I wasn't very confident. I could barely look after myself. In many respects, Lady Jane was stronger than I.

He looked at us each in turn and then relented. "All right. You can come. But only George and I will participate in the actual rescue. Is that understood?"

"Yes," she said. "And don't worry. I won't disappoint you."

"I need a little time to plan this," Thomas said. "Fortunately I have some friends in Batavia that will help."

We sat in silence for several moments, reflecting on the mission looming before us. The closer it came to fruition, the more intimidating it became.

"Excuse me," Thomas said as he rose from his chair. "I'd like to explore some paths for our departure."

He went to a well-dressed Asian gentleman seated at the bar and spoke with him for several minutes. Then he chatted with a swarthy sailor who sulked in a dark corner of the taproom, nursing a bottle of beer. I didn't know the content of the conversations, but I was impressed that he knew such a diversity of people.

I also noticed that an attractive Asian woman, about thirty-five, watched him from across the room. Her hair glistened in the dim lighting, and her black eyes peeked seductively from the shelter of provocative lashes. Her attention had not gone unnoticed by him, and he now stole glances in her direction as he talked to patrons.

Eventually he strolled to the woman's table and offered a greeting. She smiled and invited him to join her.

"Why do you think Balraj changed his mind?" I asked Lady Jane.

"I don't know if he did," she said. "Maybe he's just trying to get to Australia."

She watched Thomas chat with the Asian woman, and I saw a hint of jealousy housed in her eyes. While our conversation continued, she stole furtive glances at him. It troubled me. We had the opportunity to be alone, and I wanted the conversation to be personal, like the one on the beach, not about the rescue, Singapore, or Thomas.

"If Balraj is at Van der Meer's, then he overcame tremendous odds to find you," I said. "He must really love you."

Thomas left the lounge with his companion as Lady Jane watched warily. I was hurt that she seemed so bothered by his behavior. She stood abruptly, grabbed her purse, and prepared to go.

"It may not even be Balraj," she said. "It might be Gregory."

CHAPTER 19

I went back to my room, confused by her behavior. I wasn't sure why she was so annoyed and upset. I didn't know if it was because Thomas had left with another woman or because someone had followed her to the rubber plantation. Or both.

She had made it clear that she had no interest in Balraj Patel, and that the whole incident was a mistake. Given the abrupt ending to their relationship, I doubted he would go to such lengths to find her. He may have gone to Chin's to escape from Singapore, but once he had successfully left the island there was no reason to go to such a remote part of Sumatra. It didn't make sense. I knew that, and so did Lady Jane.

The only other candidate was Sir Gregory Millburne, Lady Jane's fiancé. I found it interesting that Thomas seemed to have no idea the man existed, evidence that Lady Jane truly had confided in me. The private conversation we had on the beach really did mean something to her, just as it did to me.

If it was Millburne, what type of man followed a woman from India to Singapore to Sumatra, risking his life on each leg of the journey? Especially after she had refused his marriage proposal and left him for another man, a man of different class, culture, and race. Nothing could be more humiliating to someone in his social position. He must really love her, and I suspect she had come to the same conclusion. She had said that he was a good man, and that she had nothing negative to say about him. Maybe that's why she'd left the taproom so abruptly. Maybe Thomas's dalliance hadn't helped.

She was a brave woman. Not only was she joining

the rescue effort, confronting the Japanese, but she might also face the man she had abandoned, ruining his life and reputation. I supposed, even though the chances were slim, that she might find Balraj Patel waiting for her. I thought about the interest she enjoyed from the opposite sex: Balraj, Sir Gregory, Thomas, and even me. It was a testament to the woman who had earned it.

My articles describing the fall of Singapore and Sumatra were among the best I had ever written. With Harry Simpkins' help, I interviewed military personnel from both the British, Dutch, and Australian armies, all high-ranking officers, and then penned a detailed military analysis of each campaign. Both articles were featured in the *Batavian Journal* and the *London Times*. Within hours of their publication, a tall man in a pinstriped suit approached me in the hotel lobby.

"Mr. Adams?" he asked.

"Yes," I said.

He held out his hand and shook mine firmly. "Joe Durgan. I'm a senior editor with the Associated Press in New York. I've enjoyed your articles."

"Thank you," I said, surprised by the recognition.

"You did a first-rate job," he added. "I saw some of your stuff from Singapore too. I was impressed. Are you staying in Batavia long?"

"I haven't quite decided."

"I don't think anyone has, including me. Well, I sure hope you'll give the Associated Press first crack at your future stories."

"I'm actually employed by the *London Times*," I told him. "But they don't have exclusive rights."

"Good," he said. "Then maybe you'll send some stuff my way. Here's my card." He scribbled a brief note of introduction on the back. "Present this at any Associated Press office in the world, and they'll buy your stories. If they're up to snuff, I mean."

"Sure," I said. "I will. Thanks for the opportunity, Mr. Durgan."

"And keep up the good work," he said. "Don't forget it's the people, Adams. That's what makes you different."

"What do you mean?"

"Your style," he said. "You write about people and what events do to them. Not the other way around like a million other reporters. You have a good angle. I like it. It puts feeling in your stories. A human aspect." He looked at his watch. "Hey, I have to go, so I guess I'll see you around."

Buoyed with enthusiasm, I went back to my room and scanned the daily paper, comparing other articles to mine. While reading the accounts of the days leading to Singapore's fall, I was sickened to learn of the turmoil before the surrender. Human behavior sometimes finds its ebb during catastrophes, whether natural or man-made; I realized that, but I was annoyed by reports of several bank robberies, all accomplished in the early morning hours. The same people probably performed them all, but investigators were left with no clues or culprits.

I continued turning pages, finally arriving at the classifieds. Although I rarely read this section, a large rectangular ad caught my attention. It stated:

Anyone knowing the whereabouts of Jane Smythe contact Philip Paddington Smythe via the law office of Jackson, Tudor, and King, F20/6A Gupta Blvd., New Delhi 91-99-6832-9562

Maybe her father or his representative was at the

plantation. To me, that now made the most sense of all, especially given a classified ad that was aimed at a global audience. Her father was probably anxious to make amends, afraid of what Lady Jane could be confronting and desperate to have her returned to the aristocratic cocoon he had built in New Delhi. I didn't blame him.

When I met Thomas and Lady Jane for dinner that evening to discuss the rescue, Lady Jane showed no sign of the irritation expressed the day before. I briefly described my meeting with Joe Durgan, emphasizing what a tremendous opportunity he offered. I mentioned the bank robberies, describing my shock that people would profit from such a precarious and tragic situation. Neither seemed interested. They studied the menu and sipped their wine.

"There will always be thieves," Lady Jane said. "In good times or bad."

I was actually making casual conversation, moving towards the topic I truly wanted to explore. I had clipped the ad from the paper and put it in my pocket.

"Lady Jane," I said delicately. "I also noticed a classified ad seeking your whereabouts."

She seemed stunned, but then she shrugged. "I'm not surprised."

I read the ad to them. "Maybe your father is the one following you or someone in his employ?"

"It's possible," she said. "I'm sure they're frantic. But they also disowned me. I find it somewhat hypocritical that they're now combing the globe to find me, placing classified ads in the *London Times*."

"Maybe they realize they made a mistake, and they love you and miss you." I said, imagining myself in their position.

Her face softened. "That may be true. And I miss them, too. But too many hateful things were said. I can't pretend that nothing happened. At least, not now. Maybe in time, I will. And I'm sure that someday I'll go back to India. But it won't be for a while."

"Don't be too harsh," I said. "You never know when something will happen that changes the way you feel or even changes the entire course of your life."

I thought about Maggie's death as I always seemed to. It had certainly changed me. No matter how far I ran, or where I went, I couldn't forget her.

We were quiet for a moment, lost in our thoughts. But it was time to discuss the most important issue. I turned to Thomas. "Are we ready for the rescue?"

"Yes," he said casually, as if we battled the Japanese on a daily basis. "We leave in the morning. And don't forget your forged passports."

Our departure, though expected, was a bit sudden and jarring. "You arranged that quickly," I said numbly. "How long will we be gone?"

"Just a few days."

"How are we going to do this?" Lady Jane asked.

Her voice wavered, and the hint of fear flickered across her face. Maybe she would reconsider and stay in Batavia. She must be terrified, as any sane person would be. I was.

"Obviously we can't attack the Japanese," Thomas said. "But fortunately, I am familiar with the rubber plantation. I know where all of the outbuildings are located, the proximity to the river, the rooms of the house, where the field hands live. All that knowledge can be used to my advantage."

"How will we get there?" I asked. I couldn't

imagine flying again. And it was several hundred miles away.

"A very close friend of Van der Meer's and mine has a fishing boat. We'll meet him at the docks. Then we'll journey to Sumatra, hugging the coast and blending with other fishing vessels before we travel upriver to the rubber plantation. There's heavy traffic because the oil fields are nearby, but that may work to our advantage."

"What about the actual rescue?" I asked.

"I will go ashore during the night and assess the situation," Thomas said. "I don't expect a significant force. There could be as little as ten or twelve, if that. The Japanese have different plans for their soldiers."

"Yes," I said grimly. "World conquest."

"What time are we leaving?" Lady Jane asked.

"We'll meet in the lobby at 7 a.m.," he replied. "And don't bring luggage. Is that understood?"

We both nodded.

"Only the clothes on your back," he emphasized. "Wear something suitable for the jungle. Lady Jane, are you still going?"

"Of course," she said. "I wouldn't let you try it without me."

"It's not too late to change your mind."

She looked at him defiantly and shook her head. "I'm going."

He sighed. "Then we'll meet in the morning. I suggest we all get a good night's sleep." Then, almost as an afterthought, he added a warning. "You have no idea how dangerous this will be."

CHAPTER 20

I tossed and turned, unable to sleep, as Thomas's warning echoed in my mind. We really did have no idea of the danger. Even trained commandoes would find such an attempt difficult. Why ever dream we could do it?

I wondered what it would be like, crawling into a fortified Japanese encampment and trying to snatch two captives from under their noses. It had to be dangerous, next to impossible, and certainly not a task for two untrained men. I didn't know about Thomas's credentials, but I had only fired a gun a handful of times. I had no experience in hand-to-hand combat, had never been in a fight in my life, and certainly posed no threat to Japanese soldiers who had already conquered most of the Pacific.

I arose early the next morning and dressed in a pair of khaki pants with a matching shirt. Rolling the sleeves up past my elbows, I gazed in a full-length mirror, and grinned when I saw the image. I could easily play the part of jungle adventurer. I looked again and laughed at my scrawny body. Well, maybe not.

I left my room just as Lady Jane exited her suite.

"Good morning, George," she said.

She wore form-fitting pants tucked into knee-high boots with a beige blouse. A brown satchel hung on her shoulder. It was a functional choice of apparel. But to me, she looked beautiful in whatever she wore.

"My, you're especially quiet this morning," she added. She smiled, lighting the hallway.

I was embarrassed, certain she caught me admiring her. "Still waking up, I suppose," I countered quickly. "Come on. Let's go downstairs."

We walked down the hallway and saw Thomas

leaving his room. He wore blue pants and a matching shirt, a yachting cap crowning his head. A half-smoked cigar, proof we were destined for uncivilized territory, hung from clenched teeth.

"Do you have your fake passports?" he asked.

"Of course," I replied.

"And we left our belongings in our rooms," Lady Jane said.

"Then let's be underway," he said.

We walked down a grand stairway, one of the unique features of the Hotel Duncan, and entered the tiled lobby. It was quiet; two men sat in a corner reading the paper, and a woman chatted with the registration clerk. I thought of the lobby at the Victoria Hotel on the day we departed, the chaos, and what a contrast this was.

We exited the hotel and stopped abruptly, unprepared for the sight before us. At the curb, waiting for our arrival, sat a silver Rolls Royce.

"Today we travel in style," Thomas announced.

"Thomas, this is so unlike you," Lady Jane said. "I was expecting another wagon." She plopped onto the black leather seats. "Very nice. I haven't driven in one of these for at least two weeks," she joked.

"Borrowed from a friend," he said. "The well-dressed gentleman I spoke to in the taproom the other night. It's a nice way to exit the city."

We spent twenty minutes cruising through crowded streets, reversing the path we took on our arrival - past houses and churches and mosques and canals and shops and markets - reveling in the luxury the Rolls Royce provided. When we reached the harbor, it was much larger than I'd expected with rows of piers and wharfs and warehouses supporting ships of various size and purpose.

All too soon, however, our hopes of continued comfort faded when the car halted at a remote section of the wharf directly in front of three rustic fishing trawlers.

We reluctantly left the vehicle, and I noticed how the morning sun reflected off the brilliant silver finish. Thomas paid the driver, an elderly man in a starched suit, and chatted with him for a moment in Dutch. The limousine drove away, leaving us standing on the pier.

Thomas shaded his eyes and shouted. "Ahoy, Bennie!"

A moment later a Javanese man emerged from the cabin of the closest ship.

"Thomas!" he called. "Come aboard."

Thomas led us onto the craft. It was a bit weathered, the lacquer finish showing signs of age, but it seemed seaworthy and well cared for. I expected to be overwhelmed with the smell of fish since it was a fishing trawler, but no offensive odor was present. Rope and nets and various types of fishing gear were neatly stacked or stored on deck, most of which appeared new or little-used.

Bennie was slender, his sinewy body evidence of a seafarer's life. He had tattoos on both forearms depicting a man biting off a snake's head and a shapely woman named Lia. The tattoos were colorful, common to the ports, and provided a hint as to the character of their owner. His face was leathery, hardened by years of battling wind and waves, or from a life harder than most, I couldn't say for sure. Half of his right eyebrow was missing and scarred. My initial impression was that he was not a man to fight with even though he seemed genuine and sincere, generous and friendly. I wondered why he so readily risked his life.

"These are my good friends," Thomas continued. "George Adams and Lady Jane Carrington Smythe. This is my dear friend Bennie."

"Do you know Mr. Van der Meer?" I asked.

"I do," he said. "Although not as well as Thomas does." He looked at Thomas and chuckled. "Or should I say I don't know Thomas as well as Van der Meer does."

"I would like to hear that story some time," I said. "Van der Meer must be a good friend if you're willing to risk your life for him."

"He is," Bennie said. "But let's hope there's no danger." Then he smiled, flashing a few rotting teeth. "Or just enough to make it interesting."

His statement made me shiver as if someone had just run their fingernails across a chalkboard. I guessed that he was no stranger to risk, not adverse to danger, not one to run from a fight. Maybe he had been in more than one barroom brawl. Or maybe he had survived worse. After I'd thought about it, I realized he was just the type of man you would want on a journey like this. I'm sure that's why Thomas chose him. Or why Bennie had agreed to do it.

He turned to Lady Jane. "It's been a long time since I've had a woman on board. I hope you'll be comfortable."

She smiled politely. "I'm sure everything will be fine. Thank you so much."

Bennie called out, and a young Asian lad, about twelve years old, emerged from the cabin. He was bare-chested, wearing only a pair of short pants.

"This is Adi," Bennie said. "He was an orphan. But now I take care of him. He's a hard worker and a good companion. We make a good team." He ruffled the boy's hair.

His statement, which was innocent enough and attested to the warmth of his heart, stirred unexpected emotions. It made me think of Chin wandering the streets after his parents had died.

"Hello, young man. How are you?" Lady Jane asked. She extended a hand and shook his.

He smiled, appreciative of the attention. "I'm well," he said in heavily accented English.

Bennie gave Adi some instructions, and the lad disappeared below deck. Minutes later the diesel engines started, and Bennie cast off the mooring lines. The small trawler chugged through the harbor past vessels of varying size from Dutch battleships to small fishing boats. Then we moved out to sea, gaining speed but hugging the coastline.

Once underway, I went to a section of deck that was free of fishing gear and leaned against the railing, gazing at the outline of land on the horizon. I opened my journal and started writing. The pen moved fluidly across the page as I captured thoughts about Java, the rescue, Sumatra, fishing trawlers, Bennie and his tattoos, and his devotion to his adopted son. My plan was to have material, not only for Harry Simpkins of the *Times*, but also Joe Durgan of the *Associated Press*.

A few moments later, Lady Jane followed me on deck. She leaned on the railing, a book in her hand, the ocean breeze blowing her hair away from her face. She watched the sea, unusually pensive.

"What are you writing, George?" she asked.

"Just a few things I've been thinking about," I said.

"You love to write, don't you?"

I nodded. "It's my passion. When I get up in the morning I can't wait to get started. And as I fall asleep at night, I think about what I'm going to write the next day."

"Why don't you write novels?" she asked. She held

163

up the book in her hand. "Like this one. I'll be your editor."

I could think of nothing better than sitting on the coast somewhere, watching the sea and writing books that Lady Jane proofread. "Marvelous," I said softly, turning to face her. "I can't think of anything nicer."

"I certainly have the background," she said, not understanding that her credentials didn't really matter. "I read three or four books a month. And I edited all my father's reports and government documents. It doesn't sound like much, but it was really a full time job."

I looked at the book in her hand. It was entitled *Murder at the North Pole.*

"You certainly love those murder mysteries," I said. "And you seem to have an unlimited supply."

She laughed. "I'm addicted to them. But it varies. As soon as I finish this series, and there are fifty in total, I'll move on to something else. I change it every year. Last year it was period romances, England and Scotland in the eighteenth century."

I marveled at how her eyes sparkled when she smiled and laughed; they were so full of life. Maggie's eyes had been like that too. "What about the other books you read like *Social Stratification of the Indian Subcontinent?*"

"I always read one fiction and one non-fiction book at the same time," she said. "I like to swap back and forth."

"So you saved the books in your suitcase?" I asked. "They weren't too wet?"

"No, I couldn't do anything with them," she said. "I had to discard them. But Thomas took me to a bookstore that had a whole section of books in English. Even these." She held up her murder mystery.

My heart sank.   I didn't know she had been spending time with Thomas. "That's nice," I said quietly.

"It was," she replied. "I couldn't thank him enough. It was far from the hotel; I don't know how he found it. He took me shopping for clothes too.   What a nice man.   He looked so silly, waiting patiently for me to choose what I wanted."

I didn't know what to say. "I would have taken you shopping," I said softly.

She kissed my cheek lightly.   "You're a sweet man, George."

I forced a smile but felt nothing but hurt.   She had kissed me the same way my sister did or the way a friend would kiss me at Christmas.   It was nothing like the kiss on the beach with hints of so much more to come.   But maybe that was an isolated moment when she was overcome with emotion.   It may never happen again.

CHAPTER 21

Lady Jane walked into the cabin, chatted with Bennie and Thomas, and then went back on deck with Adi. They moved to the other end of the trawler and talked for a few minutes, but I couldn't hear what they said. Lady Jane started to read aloud from her book. I'm not sure how much English the boy understood, but he enjoyed the attention and appeared to dote on his new friend.

I went back to my writing, scribbling away, and an hour or more passed. I noticed Bennie and Thomas standing in the cabin, downing shots of gin. They were telling tales of their adventures, some dating back fifteen years, and all ending with a raucous bout of laughter. Their stories included countries on three continents, common acquaintances from all walks of life, and always ended with them solving some insurmountable problem, typically at someone else's expense. Their laughter increased with their gin intake.

Thomas's motivation was a mystery to me. What made him move from city to city, nation to nation, with no visible means of support and no apparent interests? He seemed to know everyone that mattered and some who didn't. All who knew him greeted him with a smile and a firm handshake or a warm hug. He had also helped me more than once, when he hadn't needed to and when he'd had nothing to gain.

Bennie was another matter. Squeezing out a living as a fisherman, he somehow didn't match the occupation. His tattoos and eerie grin made him seem more like a convict than an angler. Although a portion of the deck was covered with stowed nets and other gear, it didn't appear as if it had ever been used. I couldn't imagine Bennie ever using it. Far more interesting were his missing eyebrow and the tattoos on each forearm.

Lady Jane spent the entire afternoon with Adi, and the two then prepared dinner. They made fish accented with native spices and complimented with fruit. We enjoyed the meal and the casual conversation. I think we all avoided talk of the war, keeping the upcoming rescue at bay.

Darkness found us sprawled on deck while Lady Jane slept in the cabin. The moonlit sky served as our ceiling; the sound of tumbling waves sung us to sleep. I enjoyed the serenity, savoring it like a long-absent pleasure. I knew it wouldn't last.

I was still confused by Lady Jane. She almost seemed like two different people: a friend but potential love interest, wary but curious, someone who couldn't quite make up her mind. And there were also other suitors: Balraj, the diversion who may have returned, Sir Gregory, the hand-picked husband, and Thomas, the human riddle, the flirt, the man who always seemed to be there when you needed a friend. As I drifted off to sleep, I remembered how much easier it was to understand Maggie.

Bennie prepared breakfast, and we crowded around the table and drank coconut milk while we waited. The juice was sweeter and thinner than I was accustomed to, but I did acquire a taste for it. Once the meal was finished, Adi filled our plates with what looked like oatmeal. I sampled a small forkful and found it quite tasty. I learned that it was porridge made of coconut, pineapple, some tofu, and bits of fish.

After breakfast we reemerged on deck, enjoying the perfect weather. Thomas flirted with Lady Jane, much to Bennie's amusement.

"Lady Jane, you look fabulous this morning," Thomas said. "I think the life of a fisherman agrees with you."

She laughed, tossing her head back, the breeze blowing her hair away from her face. "I'm sure it does. I may never return to India."

"Why would you want to," he said. "When you have all of this?" He made a sweeping gesture with his arm, pointing to the open seas.

Bennie smiled, the grin always making me shiver. "I have room on the boat for a full-time passenger."

"Or two," Thomas said, hinting they would both join him.

I wasn't sure how I felt about it. I couldn't deny that I had feelings for her, but I also realized she was probably about to rescue either her first former fiancé or her second former fiancé from the Japanese. My thoughts always returned to the kiss, sweet and lingering, unexpected and spontaneous. Maybe I was the diversion, keeping her mind from Balraj Patel and Sir Gregory Millburne. Perhaps she was my diversion, keeping Maggie a memory, but not an obsession.

We moved up the Sumatran coast, long stretches of white beaches accented with palm trees thrusting from the sand at angles of varying degrees. The landscape was occasionally interrupted by fishing villages marked by many boats anchored to poles thrust into the seabed a short distance from shore. The land stretched from the coast, increasing in elevation towards the interior with mountains of different heights dominating the skyline. The majestic beauty of the island was overwhelming, as were the natural dangers, as we sighted several peaks that appeared to be active volcanoes with wisps of steam drifting from the cones to the clouds.

By late afternoon we reached the Musi River, a broad waterway marked with small towns, an occasional home built on stilts by the shore, and numerous vessels of varying size. Small fishing boats and barges moved downriver from the oil fields at Palembang forty miles from the coast. Van der Meer's home and plantation were located ten miles from the river's mouth.

It was shortly after dinner when the plantation lights became visible in the approaching darkness still a mile or so away. We anchored by a bend, hidden from the plantation. A handful of fishing vessels were docked within sight, allowing us to blend inconspicuously with the local populace. An occasional barge or freighter, confined to the deepest sections of the river, glided past on its way to the ocean.

The night was quiet except for the sound of the water parting for larger ships and the ticking of their engines as they passed. The shoreline was dark, covered with lush vegetation, and occasionally two small lights, eyes of animals reflecting the moon, could be seen peering from between the bushes. The night air was heavy and humid with a slight breeze offering relief from the heat.

We leaned on the rail gazing at the river, anchored trawlers, and passing barges, studying the stars that sprawled across the evening sky. We were just about to plan our reconnaissance of the plantation when a boat motored past. It then turned and came towards us.

"What is that?" I asked guardedly.

"I don't know," Thomas said. "What do you make of it, Bennie?"

"I think you should go below deck," he said. "There may be Japanese patrols in the area. I'll stay here

169

and keep watch."

We went into the kitchen and then down a slender set of steps that led to the engine room. We heard the sound of the approaching boat's engine gradually growing louder. My heart pounded against my chest.

I looked at Thomas. A mask of concern draped his face; he leaned forward, listening intently. Lady Jane was pale. I think she knew by Thomas's expression that we might be in danger.

The engine of the approaching boat throttled to an idle, and we heard it bump up against ours. Seconds ticked by as we anxiously waited for some hint as to what was happening.

"Anata wa nani o shite iru?" a voice called. "What are you doing?"

It was a Japanese patrol boat. I froze, afraid to make a sound, not even a breath. I turned to Lady Jane. Her eyes were wide with fright. She squeezed my hand.

Thomas held a finger to his lips. He crept towards the hallway, withdrawing a knife from a sheath on his shin.

"I can't understand your jibberish," Bennie said. "Leave me alone. I'm just a fisherman."

"Anata wa nani o shite iru?" the voice repeated. "What are you doing?"

"Get out of here," Bennie said nastily. "I don't want any trouble."

We heard the sound of someone climbing onto deck, heavy footsteps made by boots. They traveled the length of the deck, slow and methodical. I could imagine the soldier that owned them, probing and searching through fishing gear and toolboxes.

The footsteps edged towards the kitchen. I heard the door open. Lady Jane squeezed my hand tighter and moved closer to me. I barely breathed and said a silent prayer.

Thomas leaned against the wall, and motioned for Lady Jane and me to move towards the engine. Careful not to make any noise, we inched backward.

The footsteps came closer, approaching the stairs.

"Nani ga daundesu?" the soldier said. "What's down there?"

"It's the engine, you idiot," Bennie said.

His remark was met with silence. I could imagine the standoff, neither man understanding the other, but both clearly knowing the other's intent. Bennie had shown no fear, no intimidation, and no respect. I was sure the soldier was studying him, wondering if he was worth the bother of searching the rest of the ship. A minute passed, the silence deafening.

Then the footsteps walked out of the kitchen and across the deck. Seconds later we heard the Japanese boat pull away and return to patrolling the river.

CHAPTER 22

Bennie hurried down the steps. "They're gone," he said. "But that was close."

"Why would they ever care about a fishing boat?" I asked. "It doesn't make sense."

"It doesn't have to," Thomas said.

"Thomas is right," Lady Jane said quietly. "Nothing makes sense any more. Think about Chin or the little girl in the wagon in Singapore. Did any of that make sense?"

"We need to get out of here before they come back," Thomas said. "Let's move upriver and rescue Van der Meer and whoever. We don't have the luxury of reconnaissance anymore. There's no time to waste."

Bennie and Adi cranked the diesel engine to life, and we were soon puttering down the river. Ten minutes later we anchored a few hundred feet from shore. A dock that served the rubber plantation was just upriver, deserted and a bit weathered, but functional. It was lit by a single lantern that hung from a post on shore. It would serve as a landmark for both the rescue and the boat's location.

"George, can you come with me?" Thomas asked.

I was stunned by the question. I wasn't sure what I could do, and I was terrified of the Japanese. But then, if I hadn't been rejected by the military, I might already be fighting. I needed to go.

"Of course," I said. "If you think I can help."

"Shouldn't Bennie go?" Lady Jane asked.

At first I was offended. She didn't think I could do it. But then I understood her reasoning given how Bennie had handled the man from the patrol boat. If I had to pick someone to bring to a fight, it would be him.

Bennie grinned. "I would love to. I'll go get my knife."

"Wait," Thomas said. "Bennie should stay with the boat. The patrol may come back."

The enemy's return hadn't occurred to her and fear flickered across her face. She looked at Bennie's arm, the tattoo of the man biting off a snake's head, and seemed reassured.

A few minutes later I stood by the railing, ready to depart. I realized I might never return. I could die on the island of Sumatra, unknown to my mother and father, my sister Angie and her husband Tom, or my friends at the *London Times* office, all of whom were enduring the damp London winter and German air raids. But I knew I'd be with Maggie if I died.

"Everything will go smoothly," Bennie said. "Thomas knows what he's doing." He smiled, his eyes twinkling. "And he's done it before."

Lady Jane cast me a furtive look. It was a dramatic statement, meant to reassure us, but it birthed a dozen questions. It just wasn't the time to ask them.

"Trust me," Thomas said. "We'll be back with Van der Meer and Mr. Unknown, or your father, or whoever is there looking for you." He was armed with a pistol and a small machete housed in holsters on his belt. An ivory-handled knife was hidden in his boot.

Bennie handed me a pistol. "Take this, George. You may need it."

The weapon was heavier than I expected. I held it in my hand, getting familiar with it.

"This is the safety," he explained. "Slip it back, and you're ready to fire. It holds six shots. Here are some more bullets. Just spin the chamber and load them when it's empty."

"Thanks," I said. "Hopefully I won't need it." I was overwhelmed by the realization of what I was about to do. I was not a firearms expert; yet my life might depend on the pistol I held.

"Let's go, George," Thomas said. "We need to do this quickly and get out of here."

I was about to face the enemy. Until now it had seemed surreal, more like a dream than reality. Now I knew it wasn't. My stomach churned so violently I thought I would vomit.

Thomas looked at me quizzically. "Are you all right?"

I didn't want to admit I was afraid, so I searched for an excuse. I saw Lady Jane watching me. "Yes, I'm fine," I said. "I just want a moment to say goodbye to Lady Jane."

She smiled. "Be careful, George. I'll be waiting for you when you come back."

"If anything happens to me, I just want you to know that I…"

"Nothing will happen to you," she said. Then she kissed me lightly on the lips.

The kiss lingered, and I savored every second.

"Hey, what about me?" Thomas asked, grinning.

She rolled her eyes. "How could I ever forget you?" Then she gave him a quick kiss.

I smiled weakly, doubting I would ever be the only man in her life. Then I wondered why that thought had crossed my mind.

We swam to shore, moving slowly and maintaining a constant vigil for the enemy. Boats and barges still passed on the river, fishing trawlers glided by, and the moon lit a cloudless sky. The Japanese patrol boat was absent.

I quickly found that Thomas was a strong swimmer. I couldn't keep up and started to lag behind. I was winded and weary, my muscles starting to burn and ache. Eventually he stopped and paddled in place, waiting until I caught up.

"Watch for crocodiles," he said softly.

"Crocodiles? Where?"

"Don't worry. I've only seen one so far."

I doubted he was serious, but I did find that I could move much faster. I sped by him and kept swimming. When I reached the shore, I hid among some shrubs near the dock and waited.

He emerged from the river and came towards me. "Don't speak unless you have to," he whispered. "The Japanese could be anywhere."

With that warning echoing in my mind, I followed him into the underbrush. It was dense, but navigable, with a mixture of shrubs interrupted by palm trees. I sidestepped a large spider web, intricately spun, and spanning two branches several feet apart. The owner, a brown spider much larger than any I had ever seen in London, sat perched in the center, waiting for its prey.

"Be careful," Thomas said. "It's difficult to maneuver in the darkness. Stay close to me."

Ten minutes later we reached Van der Meer's estate. Forty feet in front of the house a tiny campfire lit the darkness, the flame flickering into the night. Five Japanese soldiers lounged around it, drinking from canteens, smoking and talking among themselves. It was my first glimpse of the enemy. I felt my body tremble, knowing any one of them would kill me if given the opportunity.

Thomas motioned me forward. We crawled through the underbrush to the far side of the house. Once shielded from the soldier's view, we scampered across the lawn and hid in the shrubs beside the building. Then we moved to a twelve-pane window and peered inside.

It was Van der Meer's study. Rows of bookshelves lined the walls, housing bright leather volumes. A mahogany desk covered with ledgers sat in the center of the room. Judging from the haphazard manner in which papers were strewn about, the enemy had searched his belongings.

A Japanese officer sat in a leather chair, gazing through black spectacles, and smoking a cigarette. He spoke to someone beyond my view.

"Move closer," Thomas whispered.

I leaned against the window and saw Van der Meer strapped to a straight-backed chair. His head drooped to his chest, and his face was marked with bruises. A guard stood beside him.

"Where's Lady Jane's friend?"

"I don't know," Thomas said. "But we'll find him."

The officer stamped out his cigarette on the hardwood floor. He walked to Van der Meer and asked a question. When no reply was offered, he smacked his face with the back of his hand. I wondered why the Japanese were so interested in the owner of a rubber plantation; what information could he possibly possess? I doubted it was worth beating him to get it.

"Wait here," Thomas said. "If anything happens, find your way back to the boat. I'll meet you there later."

"Where are you going?"

"To get Van der Meer." A second later he was gone, blending into the shadows.

I peeked in the window while the interrogation

continued. Every few seconds I surveyed the area. I could still hear the guards talking on the front lawn.

A moment later the officer looked towards the library entrance. He motioned to the guard, who exited the room, closing the door behind him.

Several tense seconds ticked by. Suddenly the door burst open and Thomas barged in. The ivory-handled knife was in his hand, the blade stained with blood. He flung it forward with frightening speed.

The knife lodged in the officer's chest. He stood upright for a moment, cast a bewildered look at Thomas, and sank to his knees. An instant later he collapsed.

I was shocked by Thomas's skill with a knife. I knew he had acquired it through determination and practice. How many other men had he killed?

Thomas quickly untied Van der Meer. He bent over the officer and withdrew his knife. He had a difficult time; the blade was lodged between the ribs. He planted his knee on the man's chest and pulled with both hands. It was buried to the hilt.

The two men moved towards the exit, disappearing from view.

I waited, hidden in the shrubs, the silence deafening. I wondered where they were, and what was happening. Maybe they were searching the rest of the house for whomever had come for Lady Jane. Or maybe the Japanese caught them as they tried to escape.

I heard laughter from the guards in front of the house. Nothing seemed amiss. I decided to keep waiting. I stared skyward as a cloud slid past the moon. Another minute passed. I glanced at my watch. I decided to wait four more minutes. Then I would make my way back to the boat, as Thomas had directed.

Three minutes later, Thomas and Van der Meer crept around the corner of the house. They hugged the wall, approaching through the bushes.

"Let's get out of here," Thomas said.

"How are you doing?" I asked Van der Meer.

"I'm a bit weary," he replied. "And bruised and sore."

"Where's the other man?" I asked. "Or whoever."

"The Japanese took him upriver," Thomas said.

"Where?"

"Quiet!" Thomas hissed. He held up his hand and motioned us downward.

We lay in the dirt, hidden by bushes. It was quiet; only the sounds of the jungle were audible: the chirp of a cricket, the scurry of a squirrel, a monkey leaping from branch to branch.

Then I realized what was wrong. It was too quiet. The guards by the campfire were no longer talking.

I looked past the corner of the house. Two soldiers walked by followed by three others. I lay completely still, the sound of my heartbeat echoing in my ears. A few minutes later, two soldiers strolled by, arriving on the path the departing men had taken. Once they were out of sight, I started to rise.

"No," Thomas whispered. "There's more." He held up three fingers.

I understood, and lay my head on the ground. Five soldiers had left, two had returned. There were three more. They were changing shifts.

I barely moved. Minutes passed slowly. I could feel Thomas and Van der Meer lying beside me. I was about to suggest leaving when I heard a laugh, followed by a cough.

Three soldiers emerged from the jungle. They came from the far side of the house where Thomas had gained entry and strolled across the lawn. They walked beside us, passing only inches away. They turned the corner and went to the campfire.

"Let's go," Thomas said.

We crept slowly away from the house and crawled into the underbrush, not speaking. We cautiously made our way towards the dock, moving slowly through the jungle, not making a sound. About fifteen minutes later, we reached the shore. We slid into the water, careful not to splash, and swam towards the trawler.

CHAPTER 23

We moved quietly through the water, protected by darkness. I was winded and weary, struggling to continue. Then I remembered Thomas's crocodile warning. I had horrific images of the massive jaws crushing my torso, the rows of teeth tearing me apart. I was suddenly able to swim much faster.

As I caught up to Thomas, I saw he was struggling to keep Van der Meer afloat. I swam towards them.

"Let me help you," I offered.

Together we towed Van der Meer to the boat, fighting the river currents. When we finally reached the trawler, Lady Jane was waiting by the rail.

"I was so worried," she said with a sigh of relief. "You were gone for a long time."

"Yes," Thomas said. "Everyone's safe."

"Where's Balraj or whoever was looking for me?" she asked.

Van der Meer waved an arm, gasping for breath. "It's not…"

"The Japanese took him to the oil fields," Thomas interrupted. "We'll go there next."

"Why would they do that?" she asked with alarm.

"I don't know," he said. "To work, I suppose. Get Bennie. We need help getting Van der Meer aboard. He's barely conscious."

"He's below deck," she said. "I'll help you."

Thomas and I raised him out of the water while she pulled from above. We got him safely on deck, and then we followed, gasping from our exertions.

"We did it," I said. "We rescued Van der Meer."

"Stay where you are," said a chilling voice.

Three Japanese emerged from the shadows, an officer and two soldiers. Their rifles were pointed at our faces, the bayonets glistening in the moonlight.

"I'm so sorry," Lady Jane said. "I couldn't warn you. They would have killed me if I had."

"It's all right," Thomas consoled her. "There was nothing you could do."

The soldiers searched us, removing our weapons and personal belongings. Then the officer issued a command we didn't understand.

They grabbed Thomas roughly and led him into the cabin. Lady Jane was next, followed by Van der Meer. A few minutes later, they came for me. They bound my hands behind my back and then forced me to the floor, tying my hands to my feet. Once my eyes grew accustomed to the darkness, I realized that Adi was there also, bound in the same manner. Bennie was not. Had the soldiers killed him?

"Lady Jane," I whispered. "What happened?"

"The patrol boat returned. They were aboard so quickly we couldn't defend ourselves."

The officer approached us. "Are you spies?" he asked in halting English. "Like Mr. Van der Meer?"

His question was met with silence. Why was he convinced Van der Meer was a spy? But then I thought about it: the strange relationship between Thomas, Bennie, and Van der Meer, the detailed knowledge of military strategy, the uncanny ability to know where the Japanese were and at what strength, and the fishing boat with all the unused gear. He might be right.

"No, I don't think you're spies," the officer said. "You're far too incompetent. But you may be smugglers.

Mr. Van der Meer is well versed in those activities also."

It was believable that Van der Meer, Thomas, and Bennie were smugglers. I thought of Thomas with no obvious means of support and unlimited funds, and Bennie, with a fishing trawler that showed no signs of fish.

"Production has increased at the oil facility since we've taken control," the officer said. "But there's a dire need for labor. You will suit that need nicely."

"You can't do that," I said defiantly. "We're Swiss citizens."

"I'm not interested in where you came from," he said. He issued a command to a soldier before turning back to us. "These two men will take you to the oil fields. I suggest you keep quiet until you get there. I have given them orders to shoot you if you don't."

The officer turned and left the cabin and stood on the bow of the boat. One soldier stood at the helm while another watched us. A few minutes later the patrol boat returned and collected the officer. He issued harsh commands to his underlings before departing.

Once he left, the engine was started and the soldier at the helm guided the trawler to the center of the river. He stood a few feet from me, his eyes trained ahead, and steered the craft forward. His companion stood by the door, his gaze alternating between us and the traffic on the river: barges, trawlers, and houseboats.

I saw fear in Lady Jane's eyes, and Adi, the young boy, was also terrified. Van der Meer was bruised and beaten, barely awake. Only Thomas seemed unperturbed. If the soldiers wanted to kill us they would have done so already. Maybe we were doomed to spend the rest of our lives laboring for the Japanese.

I tried to sleep. After an hour of unsuccessful

attempts, I opened my eyes and glanced at the others. Van der Meer slept; Lady Jane and Adi leaned against the wall. Although their eyes were closed, they shifted uncomfortably. They couldn't sleep either. We were all too scared.

Thomas's eyes were open, and he was staring blankly ahead. When he saw me watching him, he nodded towards the engine compartment.

Bennie was coming up the steps, hiding in the shadows. He held a knife in his right hand.

CHAPTER 24

Bennie crept forward, hugging the opposite wall. If either soldier turned, they would see him. Ever so slowly, he moved towards the soldier steering the ship.

The sentry by the door fumbled for a cigarette. Bennie paused, his back against the wall. The soldier lit the cigarette, exhaled a cloud of smoke, and yawned. Bennie tiptoed towards his companion.

The slightest noise would be disastrous. I looked at Thomas. He nodded discretely. Van der Meer still slept, but Lady Jane and Adi now watched intently, their eyes wide.

Bennie crept closer. He eased towards the helm, not making a sound. He was only a few feet away. The soldier at the door stirred, shifting his weight. Bennie paused. We waited tensely.

He took two more steps, slow and quiet and deliberate. Then he stood behind the driver. He raised his knife. With a rapid, fluid movement, he slid the knife across the soldier's throat. Blood spurted from his neck and splashed on the window. He collapsed to the floor.

The second soldier spun around, and Bennie flung the knife. It hit the man in the shoulder, barely penetrating his flesh, and bounced to the floor. Blood spotted his uniform, dripping onto his chest, but the injury wasn't severe. He raised his rifle.

Bennie swung his foot forward, his boot catching the soldier's crotch. The man grimaced and doubled over, but he didn't release his gun. He pulled the trigger.

Lady Jane screamed. The bullet imbedded in the wall a few feet from her head. I rolled over onto the floor, certain a second shot would follow, and blocked her body with mine.

Bennie tackled the soldier, punching him with one hand and searching for the knife with the other. The soldier pushed him away. They rolled on the floor, grunting and panting and swinging their fists. The soldier pushed Bennie down and sat astride him.

The knife lay on the floor. Bennie swept his leg across the floor until his foot hit it. He slid it forward with his leg. The soldier wrapped his hands around Bennie's neck until his eyes bulged and he gasped for air. His leg was bent at a crooked angle. He coaxed the knife towards his hand.

His face started to pale, the veins in his neck protruding. A gurgle came from his throat as if he were choking. But his mouth broke into a wicked grin. He slid the knife forward with his foot. Ever so slowly, inch by inch, it came closer to his hand.

His long thin fingers stretched forward, inches from the blade. The soldier's grasp grew tighter. Sweat dripped down his face. All his strength was focused on strangling Bennie to death.

Bennie moved the knife with his fingertips until he could grasp the handle. Once he held it firmly, he slowly pushed it into the soldier's stomach. His grin grew wider each inch the blade was imbedded. He angled the knife upward, plunging it forward.

The soldier groaned in agony. He tumbled to the floor, the knife stuck in his torso. Bennie choked and coughed, rubbing his hand over his throat to stimulate the blood flow. When he caught his breath, he pulled the knife from his victim.

He moved to Thomas and cut his ropes. Then he

went to the others. As he freed them, I stared at the two corpses that lay before me, blood spilling from their bodies and forming puddles on the floor. Their eyes were open, staring at me in protest, their lives stolen.

CHAPTER 25

Bennie got two lengths of canvas, and he and Thomas rolled the corpses onto them. Then he got two old cannonballs, large globs of cast iron, and placed one on the torso of each corpse, wrapping the arms around it. They covered the corpses with the canvas and tied them securely, wrapping them into tight packages.

"I knew I would find a use for those old cannonballs," Bennie said.

He smiled, which made me shiver. The two enemy soldiers had died brutally; they deserved a better burial. But we couldn't give it to them. The bodies were eased over the side of the ship, dropped to their graves with only a ripple in the river's murky waters.

Adi had started to clean up the cabin, and by the time the bodies were disposed of, most of the blood had been removed. Stains remained, and even though Adi scrubbed them they refused to disappear.

"When we get back to Batavia I'll get some lime," Bennie said. "That should work."

I looked at the marks on the floor, remnants of two human lives. They were the first enemy soldiers to die in front of me. When I was in London and the city was being bombed, German planes were downed but they rarely crashed in the city; they normally made it to the suburbs or countryside. It was a different war in the Pacific. It was personal, staring into the face of the enemy, looking in their eyes as they took their last breaths.

Lady Jane and I tended to Van der Meer, cleaning the bruises and abrasions. He was still weary, his chest battered and sore, his ribs bruised but not broken. He drifted off to sleep.

187

"We're only an hour from the oil fields," Thomas said. "I had hoped Van der Meer could guide us. He's familiar with the area."

"He can't do it," Lady Jane said firmly. "He's too badly injured."

"She's right," Bennie said. "I'll go with you. I've been there before."

I looked at Van der Meer, barely conscious, and then to Bennie, who had just killed two Japanese. Somehow, I didn't think they were the first men he had killed.

"I vote for Bennie," I said.

He grinned and moved to the helm, piloting the trawler through enemy waters. We sat in the cabin, trying to rest, but none of us could sleep. We were weary and afraid, each reflecting on what we were about to face.

I should have been thinking about the rescue, the enemy we would encounter, the danger, and the mystery man we were about to rescue. But I wasn't. For some unexplainable reason, I thought only of London. I realized how badly I missed it.

Lady Jane sat on the floor with her back against the wall. I wondered what she was thinking. But even with her hair mussed, her clothes wrinkled, and a smudge of grease on her left cheek, she looked beautiful to me. I studied her for a moment and felt myself smile.

"We're as close as I dare to get," Bennie said about forty minutes later.

He and Adi went on deck and lowered the anchor, easing it into the water. We were a hundred feet from shore, hidden behind a small island, maybe fifty feet across, tucked behind the main shipping channel. An oil barge passed in each direction, one low in the water, laden with product; the other sat high, ready to be filled.

"What time is it?" I asked.

"About 3 a.m.," Thomas said. "The oil fields are just around the bend. We'll attempt the rescue, but we should try to get out of here before dawn."

Bennie motioned us out on deck. "I'm familiar with the layout," he said. "There are several buildings on the site, mostly for field hands. Lady Jane's friend is probably held in one of those."

He drew a map for Thomas on a smudged piece of paper. "Fortunately for us, everything is near the river. But the docks will be heavily guarded."

Thomas studied the map. "What do you suggest?"

"You, George, and I will go ashore. If we find him, we'll attempt a rescue. If not, we'll use the evening to develop our strategy. Maybe risk staying one more day."

"Who will guard the boat?" I asked. "The Japanese have already boarded twice."

"I don't know that anyone can," Thomas said. "If the Japanese want to take it, they will. We just have to hope they don't find us. Or don't care about us."

I looked out on the river. I could see a dozen other fishing boats sprawled across the horizon most near the distant shore. The Japanese might not even notice us, but Lady Jane was still in danger.

"Are you sure I shouldn't stay with Lady Jane?" I asked.

"Adi will," Bennie said. "We need your help on shore."

I remembered how casually Bennie had slit the throat of the Japanese soldier and how deftly Thomas had flung the knife into the chest of the officer at the rubber plantation. Now they calmly discussed sneaking into a fortified enemy installation to rescue a man they didn't even know. I wondered why. I didn't think it was due to any allegiance to Lady Jane. It was because they thrived on the adventure; it was the life they lived. It was a secret life.

"And what happens to Lady Jane, Adi, and Van der Meer if the Japanese return?" I asked.

Bennie looked at me with the same grin he showed after he had killed the intruders. "Then we'll rescue them too."

We climbed over the side of the boat and slid into the water, paddling quietly towards the shore. Bennie led us to a spot just before the bend that was only a short distance from the trawler. Once we reached the bank, we found the vegetation thick but passable.

Thomas stripped a foot-long piece of bark from a tree. "I'll leave a path so we can find our way back."

"Mark a tree every five or six yards," Bennie said. "That should be easy to follow."

Thomas repeated the process as we moved through the brush. Thick vegetation was interrupted by small clearings where the moon filtered in to light the jungle. Twenty minutes later we reached the perimeter of the installation.

A high fence constructed of wooden posts and multiple strands of barbed wire surrounded the facility. Oil derricks stretched into the horizon, their arms swaying as they pumped crude from the ground. Tanks and docks hugged the river, connected to a series of pipes and valves. The area was well lit and patrolled by armed sentries.

"We could spend days searching the workman's huts let alone the outbuildings," I whispered.

"We knew it wouldn't be easy," Thomas said.

"We've come this far," Bennie said. "Let's at least

give it a try."

We continued further inland away from the river. After traveling two hundred feet, we found an area cast in shadows from a missing light. It was near the last of the outbuildings.

Bennie told us to remain in the underbrush while he moved to the fence. The soil was sandy, and he used a flat rock to start scooping the dirt from underneath the fence. In a matter of minutes he had dug an area large enough for us to scoot through. He slid into the facility and then motioned us to follow.

"Where should we begin?" Thomas asked. He eyed the rows of thatched huts.

"We may as well start with the closest one," I suggested.

My heart pounded as if it was about to burst. Bennie and Thomas appeared calm as if going on an evening stroll.

"That's fine with me," Thomas replied. He turned to Bennie. "George and I will search in that direction." He pointed away from the fence.

"I'll go towards the river," Bennie replied. He looked at his watch. "Let's meet back here in fifteen minutes."

Thomas and I moved towards the barracks, remaining in the shadows. We had barely passed the first hut when we heard footsteps behind us. I turned, expecting the enemy. Instead I saw a young Sumatran boy. He faced us confidently, not yet a teenager, and wore a look of awareness and curiosity.

Thomas knelt beside him and spoke in a pidgin that sounded like a mixture of Dutch and Chinese. They conversed for a moment; at one point their discussion became animated.   I was afraid their hushed whispers would alert the Japanese, but their discussion was brief. They apparently reached an understanding, and the boy disappeared into the shadows.

"Come on," Thomas said.   He led me to a dark corner behind the last hut close to the hole we had dug under the fence.

"What are we doing?" I asked.

"We'll wait here," he said. "The boy will bring us the stranger."

"Can we trust him?

"I think so."

"What is he doing wandering around in the middle of the night?"

"He's working," Thomas said.   "The Japanese captured some local orphans."

"But he's a child," I said.

He shrugged and eyed me curiously. "They don't care."

"Why is he helping us?"

"I offered to rescue him too."

I heard the crunch of footsteps on the small tufts of grass that sprung from the sandy soil. I froze and grabbed Thomas's arm. He tensed. We listened intently.

There was almost total silence, only the swish of the sliding arms of the oil platforms audible in the distance. An occasional bird screeched in the jungle, complimented by insects humming in the night. But for the most part it was quiet. We slowly relaxed.

A moment later we heard it again, but the sound was more distinct and pronounced. I was certain it was footsteps, but they seemed uneven, as if their owner stepped carefully, trying not to make noise.

I started to whisper my suspicion, but Thomas stopped me, holding his finger to his lips. He pointed to the other side of the hut. He signaled for me to follow and then carefully took a step forward.

Just as he reached the edge of the building, a sentry rounded the corner. He was startled, but recovered quickly. He issued a harsh command and motioned upward with his rifle. We had no alternative but to raise our hands.

The guard yelled for help. An astonished companion appeared, and the two looked at us closely. The first soldier spoke to the second who ran from the area.

Seconds later the young Sumatran arrived, accompanied by a dark-haired man with a small goatee. He was dressed in clothes that were far too expensive for the jungle, brown slacks and a tweed jacket that didn't seem to fit the man or the locale. He stood tall and straight, his posture rigid and his air a bit pretentious, as if he were temporarily subjected to a situation far beneath his social standing. He seemed annoyed, but patient. Unfortunately, they rounded the corner of the hut and passed directly in front of the soldier. Fearful of a coordinated assault, the guard frantically ordered them to join us. He watched nervously while waiting for assistance.

"Who are you?" Thomas asked.

"I'm Sir Gregory Millburne," he replied. "Who are you?"

I was prepared for the answer, but Thomas wasn't. "It's Lady Jane's fiancé from India," I interjected.

I knew he didn't know the story, but by phrasing my sentence carefully, I thought he would decipher it.

The soldier trained his rifle on us, shouting commands we didn't understand. We stood, arms raised, and continued to study each other.

Thomas recovered quickly. "Lady Jane sent us," he said. "We're here to rescue you."

"Really?" he asked. "How did she know I was here?"

An alarm siren sounded. I could hear voices in the distance. More soldiers were approaching.

Thomas saw the desperation cross my face. He consoled me with a confident smile. "Don't worry, George," he said. "I have them right where I want them."

CHAPTER 26

Thomas's comment was so absurd I started laughing.

The enemy wasn't amused. *"Sutoppu!"* he shouted. "Stop!" He thrust the bayonet towards me.

Thomas took advantage of the distraction. He bent over, withdrew the knife from his boot, and flung it forward.

He missed. The blade whistled past the sentry and imbedded in the wall of the barracks.

"Teiryuu!" the guard yelled. "Halt!" He leveled his rifle, pointing the barrel at Thomas, giving every indication he would shoot.

A shadow appeared in the dim lighting, growing larger as a figure rounded the corner of the building. I looked at Thomas. He saw it also. The soldier did not.

It was Bennie. He assessed the situation and then slowly moved forward, walking stealthily across the sand. The soldier was twenty feet in front of him.

The sirens wailed, and voices could still be heard. The Japanese were organizing a defense, preparing for an attack that would never come. More soldiers would be sent to aid the guard who held us captive. We had to act quickly.

Bennie crept forward. He removed the knife from his belt, the blade long and thin and glistening in the moonlight. The soldier stood, his rifle trained on us. He was vigilant and wary. Bennie came closer and paused. The soldier remained still. Bennie took a step, and then another, closing the distance between them. He raised his knife.

Bennie slid the blade across his throat. It was the

same way he had killed on the trawler. The shock on the soldier's face was replaced by pain, and blood gushed from the wound.

The rifle discharged, the sound echoing through the compound, as the soldier fell to the ground. He went limp, his legs twitching uncontrollably, blood spewing from the mortal wound and staining the sand around him.

I stared at him holding his throat as if his hands could keep the blood in his body. His eyes met mine, anguished and pained, and I shivered as I watched the life drain from his body. He was gradually consumed with a look of serenity, and then he lay still, his eyes open and vacant and staring skyward.

"Let's go!" Bennie hissed. He sprinted to the fence followed closely by Lord Millburne and the boy.

I waited for Thomas to retrieve his knife from the wall. I could see soldiers in the distance, approaching from different directions.

"Thomas, hurry!" I called.

We ran to the fence, slid underneath it, and raced into the jungle. Most of the Japanese were scattered about the barracks, searching for intruders, but some found the hole we had dug and chased after us.

We crashed through the underbrush, breaking branches and trampling shrubs, leaving an easy trail for them to follow. Six or seven soldiers rapidly pursued us.

"They're right behind us!" I shouted.

The warning seemed to panic Lord Millburne. He quickened his pace but tripped and fell. Thomas and I stopped to help him. He brushed himself off and raced forward, pursuing the boy and Bennie who was leading the escape.

The interruption was costly. One soldier was now

clearly visible, approaching through the underbrush. Others were close behind.

"Run, George!" Thomas said. He crouched behind a bush.

"Thomas, don't. Come on, we can outrun them."

"No, you go ahead. I'll catch up."

I stood beside him. I refused to desert him.

"Go!" he screamed.

I realized he had something planned. I started running. A few seconds later, I turned to see if he followed. The soldier stood five feet from him, aiming his rifle. I was his target.

I stopped, terrified. My feet were rooted to the soil. I could only stare at the barrel of the rifle, waiting for the bullet to come.

Thomas leaped forward, plunging his knife in the enemy. He withdrew it before the soldier fell and scampered after me.

"Come on, George! There's more. And they're gaining on us."

I continued onward as Thomas pushed me from behind. We raced down the path we had marked earlier, twisting through the dense underbrush. When we reached the river we saw the others swimming towards the boat.

Thomas glanced behind us. "No one is coming," he said. "They must have found the body. Now they're cautious, afraid of an ambush. If we hurry, we'll elude them."

All the energy had drained from my body. The exertion and anxiety were starting to overwhelm me. I followed Thomas into the water and started to swim for the trawler, breathing heavily, my arms and legs moving slowly. After thirty or forty feet my muscles were aching, but I continued, my head hurting, throbbing with fatigue. My vision clouded, and blackness started to overcome me.

I refused to surrender. I remembered trying to walk as a child: the pain, the heartache, and failure after failure. But I never gave up, and I wouldn't give up now. I took large gulps of air, fighting the desire to close my eyes and sink slowly beneath the surface to savor the serenity that death would bring.

My pace slowed even though I continued to kick and thrash, flailing at the endless water. I could see the trawler still a hundred feet away. Bennie and Lord Millburne and the young lad were climbing aboard. Thomas was well in front of me, almost to the boat.

I struggled to stay afloat, my body feeling heavier and heavier. I kept swimming, certain I couldn't go on but determined to survive. Thomas had reached the trawler; I still had some distance to go. I pushed relentlessly, every muscle of my body crying for rest, my breath coming in gasps and gulps, my field of vision narrowed, almost entirely circled by blackness.

I realized I was hardly moving even though I was fighting and flailing and pushing. I was afloat but barely, and I still had fifty feet to go. I pushed onward, water spilling into my mouth and lungs; I coughed and spit, barely conscious and just above the water's surface. I used every ounce of strength I had, determined to reach the boat. Inch by inch, I closed the distance.

Water washed over me as I dropped below the surface. I managed to raise my head, breaking through and gulping for air, and then I fought harder. I could see the boat, more like a shadow than a vessel, and I pushed forward, ignoring the pain. Then, too weak to fight, I sunk again.

Images of London overwhelmed me. I saw pubs and parks, Mom and Dad with their hands outstretched to welcome me, my sister and her husband raising a pint of beer in toast, my dog Henry the Eighth, wagging his tail and barking. There were cricket matches and the championship rugby game when Birmingham beat Plymouth. I could feel the fog, dense and moist, and the Thames River, Victoria Station, and St. Paul's Cathedral. And then I was standing on Trafalgar Square, walking to the Sherlock Homes Pub. Maggie was there, waving me away, forcing me to leave her. Then Lady Jane was with me. Her hand was holding mine, and she was smiling.

Vaguely, I recall Bennie pulling me over the side of the boat. Thomas was still in the water, lifting me from below. I sprawled on deck, weak and weary, my senses dulled. I could see all the faces standing over me, vague and distorted and draped with concern. Thomas and Bennie, Lady Jane and Lord Millburne, Van der Meer and the two young lads stared at me anxiously.

"Are you still with us?" Thomas asked, his voice dwarfed and distant.

"Yes, I think so," I said. I gasped, coughed and spit out water, my muscles burning and aching. But I felt my strength slowly returning, the blood flowing through my veins. "I was dreaming of London."

"He's all right," I heard Thomas say to the others. "I was afraid he wasn't going to make it."

"Oh, thank God," Lady Jane said, breathing a loud sigh of relief.

I looked up at her standing beside Lord Millburne. Her face was framed by the light of the approaching dawn like an angel, sympathetic and sincere.

"You were with me the whole time," I said to her,

still faint. "You were holding my hand."

CHAPTER 27

I looked at the faces studying me and saw a mixture of emotions: shock, annoyance, and appreciation. As my head cleared, I realized I should have kept the images private. But it was too late.

After a few minutes had passed I was able to sit up, still winded but feeling much better. The others stood over me, but they looked much less concerned. Lady Jane introduced Lord Millburne to the group. He seemed a likable man who thanked us profusely for rescuing him. We called him Sir Gregory. The young boy we had rescued, an orphan named Nugi, had already found a friend in Adi.

Bennie went to the helm and steered the trawler downriver, using the last remnants of darkness to distance us from the oil fields and maximize our chance for escape. Van der Meer returned to the cabin, hunched over from his bruised ribs. Adi gave Nugi a tour of the boat, and Lady Jane and Sir Gregory moved to the other side of the deck. They sat on a bench, some distance between them. Thomas stayed beside me.

When I fully regained my senses, I realized I had almost died. "I want to thank you for saving my life," I said to him.

He waved his hand in dismissal as if the act was commonplace. "You would do the same for me."

His statement made me think. He was right. I wondered why. I barely knew him, but when mired in the nightmares created by war, it seemed we were lifelong friends. Tragedy forms bonds that are hard to break.

Thomas motioned to the other end of the deck.

Lady Jane was talking to Lord Millburne, surprised and confused. She looked at him warily with a feigned smile framed by defeat and despair. I remembered our discussion about the cage. She thought she'd escaped, but she hadn't.

I watched her protectively. Her facial expressions hinted of both disbelief and exasperation with a spattering of guilt. The discussion was animated at times, but as daylight came they seemed to arrive at some sort of truce. At one point, he brushed the hair from her forehead. She didn't resist. I turned away with pangs of jealousy.

As the sun appeared fully, Thomas collected everyone and brought us below deck. We assembled in a small room beside the engine compartment.

"It's best if we stay out of sight until the river traffic decreases," he said.

Once we were comfortable, or at least as comfortable as conditions permitted, I studied Sir Gregory. He was a handsome man, tall and straight, his brown eyes serious, but inquisitive. His hair and goatee were perfectly trimmed, although I didn't know how he had managed that while captured by the Japanese. He seemed friendly but distant, courteous but wary. He appeared to be assessing both us and his personal situation. I had to admire him and his trek across the continents to pursue his beloved. I wondered if he would win her back. That act alone made it seem likely. He must really love her. He kept Lady Jane sequestered in one corner of the room where they spoke in hushed whispers. We knew they had much to discuss, so we left them alone.

"Why were the Japanese beating you?" I asked Van der Meer.

"I don't think they needed a reason," he replied.

"It seemed so brutal," I said.

"They thought I had information on Allied troop movements," he explained. "Like I would know what goes on in the world from a remote rubber plantation."

"How about you, Thomas," I said. "Ever had trouble with the Japanese?"

He looked at Van der Meer, and a knowing glance passed between them. "Not until yesterday."

Their answers didn't ring true. There was a link between them. And Bennie, too. But it was a secret, and secrets were kept for a reason. Van der Meer seemed to command respect from both Thomas and Bennie. Maybe he was their leader. I might never know the answer, but I did know that they were more than just good friends.

"How are you feeling?" Lady Jane asked Van der Meer. "I was worried about you yesterday."

"I'm doing much better," he replied. "Thank you all for rescuing me."

"I echo Mr. Van der Meer's gratitude," said Sir Gregory, thanking us again. "You had no reason to risk your lives for me. Your actions are greatly appreciated."

"I'm glad we could help," Thomas said.

I studied Lady Jane. Had she expected Balraj, her father, her father's emissary, or Sir Gregory? She seemed to accept the situation even though it might not be what she'd wanted.

We traveled down river, sharing the channel with oil barges, container ships, and fishermen. When we approached the rubber plantation later that morning, Bennie watched the shore closely.

"There's a lot of activity by the dock," he called down to us. "But I can't tell what it is."

Thomas traded glances with Van der Meer. "Stay near the distant shore," he said.

"I am," Bennie said. "There are three Japanese patrol boats by the dock."

"What are they doing?" Thomas asked.

I looked at Lady Jane. She sat beside Sir Gregory though their bodies didn't touch. She was listening to Bennie's reports. Her eyes were wide, her face pale.

"They're looking for us," Bennie said. "There are dead bodies lying on the dock. Van der Meer, can you come up here?"

He didn't ask for Thomas. Van der Meer was injured, and Bennie had requested him anyway, which reinforced my suspicion of who the leader was.

"Thomas, should we go up and look?" I asked.

"No," he said. "The fewer people in the cabin the better. The Japanese may be using binoculars to check the boats. Just listen."

Van der Meer grimaced as he rose, but he made his way up the stairs to the helm.

"This doesn't look good," Bennie said. "I sense trouble."

"It is trouble," Van der Meer said. "We need to slip by them."

"What is going on?" Thomas asked.

"There are a dozen Japanese standing on the dock at the rubber plantation," Bennie said. "The men we killed at the house are lying on the dock."

"And there are three enemy patrol boats gathered around the wharf," Van der Meer added. "The cabins are all facing the river. I'm sure they're watching traffic, prepared to attack any suspicious boats."

"How do we slip by them?" Bennie asked.

There was silence. I could sense the two of them surveying the situation and determining a course of action.

"Slow down," Van der Meer said. "Let that oil barge catch up to us. Then move closer to shore and stay by its side while we move upriver. That should keep us out of their view."

"I don't know if I can," Bennie said. "I may run aground that far from the channel. I don't know how deep the water is."

"We have to take the chance," Van der Meer said. "If the bottom of the boat scrapes, move towards the channel."

The boat slowed for a few minutes. Then the turbulence in the river increased, the trawler rocking gently in the rippled waves. I suspected we rocked in the barge's wake.

"Speed up," Van der Meer said.

We moved forward, the turbulence consistent, our speed constant. We sat quietly, watching the hands of the clock move forward, the sound of the barge's engines drowning our own. Several minutes passed. No one spoke.

Suddenly we heard a loud grinding sound. The boat was scraping bottom.

"Move into the channel," Van der Meer said calmly. "But slowly."

The boat jerked forward, then became sluggish. The hull scraped harder on the bottom, the length of the craft now catching on the sand. Bennie eased the wheel towards the channel and gradually the boat was freed. The turbulence from the barge's wake increased as we remained hidden behind it, but now just off her port side.

We sat quietly, listening to the engines of both boats, waiting for reports from the cabin. Minutes passed, and so did the first mile. It remained silent except for the puttering of motors. The boat continued forward, foot by foot, edging past the rubber plantation. Another minute passed.

"We did it," Bennie called down to us. "We're past the plantation."

Van der Meer came down the steps as the speed of our boat increased. Now that we were out of sight, we had to get to the ocean as quickly as possible.

"That was close," he said. "But I think we're safe now."

We left the Musi River and charted a course into the Pacific. We were in the kitchen all day, but Thomas let us spend the early evening, that tranquil time when dusk shadows the horizon, out on deck.

Van der Meer, Sir Gregory, and Thomas started discussing Dutch colonial possessions around the world. It was clear that Sir Gregory was very intelligent. It was also evident that Van der Meer was far more versed in world events than the simple owner of a rubber plantation. Once they were fully engaged in the conversation, I took the opportunity to chat with Lady Jane.

"How are you doing?" I asked when I was sure the others weren't listening.

"I'm exhausted," she said. "And you must be too."

"Yes, I am. Almost drowning wears a man out." I managed a weak smile. "Is your visitor who you expected?"

"I suppose, but I really wasn't sure who it would be. I doubted it was Balraj. But I was surprised that Gregory made such an effort to find me. After the newspaper ad, I assumed it was someone my father had sent."

"Are you disappointed it wasn't Balraj?"

"Absolutely not," she said. "I told you what a mistake that was. It was just an escape, my way out of the cage."

I didn't want to ask the next question, I think because I already knew the answer. But I had to know for sure. "Are you glad that Sir Gregory found you?"

She sighed. "I wasn't at first. But I have to admit I'm flattered he did."

"He really loves you," I said flatly.

"I know," she said softly. "And I'm touched. I really am. Maybe in India I couldn't see what was right in front of me."

Early the next morning Bennie appeared in the kitchen. "A Japanese fleet is approaching," he said.

"Are they after us?" Lady Jane asked.

"No, I don't think so," Thomas said.

"We should still be careful," I said.

"I'll go topside and watch them," Bennie said. "The boys will deliver messages."

We waited tensely. As the minutes passed, the convoy moved on, taking little interest in the trawler. We were told that most of the vessels were landing craft, destined for Sumatra.

"The Japanese are going to invade Java," Thomas said. "That's what the landing craft are for."

"That's true," Sir Gregory added. "I overhead the guards at the oil fields talking about it. The attack will come from several directions, Sumatra being one of them."

"Will we reach Batavia before the Japanese do?" I asked.

"I think so," Thomas replied. "They aren't organized yet. The landing craft have yet to be staged."

"How do you know that," I asked.

"Just a theory."

"What will happen when they get there?" Lady Jane

asked.

"Probably the same outcome as Singapore," I said.

"Then we shouldn't return to Batavia," she said. "We should go to Australia instead."

"We're not prepared," Thomas said. "Let's get to Batavia first. Then if we decide to go elsewhere, we'll have time to plan our departure."

We would be running again. Singapore to Batavia, Batavia to Sumatra, Sumatra to Batavia, Batavia to who knows where. Australia? Another island? I thought about returning to London. I'd had vivid recollections when I'd almost drowned. It made me realize how important what you normally take for granted really is: family, friends, your favorite pub, an auburn sunset, the scent of a flower, listening to raindrops, a good meal, your dog, beautiful buildings, a wise old man. The list was endless; it was comprised of the things on God's great earth you never have time to notice, at least not until they are about to vanish forever. But from this point forward I vowed to savor them, and then I realized it was time to go home.

CHAPTER 28

We were all relieved when Batavia appeared on the horizon, the sprawling, crowded metropolis that so contrasted the remote areas of Sumatra we had just left. Bennie guided the trawler into the harbor, and we docked at the pier that marked the start of our journey.

We disembarked amid the warm wishes of the sailor and his two young cohorts, Adi and Nugi. Bennie proudly announced that Nugi would become part of his family, much to the boys' delight. Adi had already started teaching Nugi to read the one book that was aboard the trawler, an old Charles Dickens novel.

"Thanks for everything," I said as I shook his hand.

I studied his face and the sly grin that always consumed it and wondered what kind of man had the kindness to adopt two orphans yet the cruelty to slit the throat of an enemy. I sensed he would do anything to help you if you were a friend and anything to hurt you if you were not.

"You're welcome," he said. "It was a lot of fun. I enjoyed it. If you ever need anything, just ask."

I smiled. Neither rescue mission was my idea of fun. I suspected any sane human being would agree with me.

We left the dock and walked towards the city. Thomas went to hire a car while the rest of us waited. We sat on a bench, chatting while we watched longshoremen and fishermen and street vendors - and even a lady of the evening or two - wander about the waterfront. Batavia was always bustling, the streets clogged with people who seemed to be in such a hurry to go nowhere.

Thomas returned an hour later with the same limousine that had dropped us at the dock a few days before. We enjoyed the ride, feeling buoyant but spent, and soon reached the colonial façade of the Hotel Duncan.

We then went to our rooms, promising to meet for dinner that evening. First we would enjoy an afternoon of rest and relaxation, privileges that had been absent the last few days.

The next day I was sitting in the office of the *London Times.*

"George, I'm impressed," said Harry Simpkins. He had just read my article, *A Journey Down the Musi River*, that I had started on the trip and finished that morning.

"Thanks," I said with pride. "I'm glad you like it."

"What a sense of adventure," he continued. "And danger. Are you sure you won't reveal the identities of those involved? The rescue is exciting enough, but if we knew it was fact and not fiction, it could really lend credibility to the tale."

"It is fact," I explained. "But I need to protect those involved. Why not add a disclaimer? State that the story is true, but identities have been protected."

"That works," said Simpkins. "When can I expect your next article? Will you be in Batavia long? Or are you off to some exotic location?"

I thought about London and how badly I missed being home. But it came with the overwhelming heartache of Maggie. I remembered my inability to function at the most basic level before I left for Singapore; I was overcome with grief. Batavia offered the chance to live history, to be an eye-witness to changing nations, cultures, people, boundaries, and borders. And Lady Jane was in Batavia, just at my fingertips, but not within my grasp. She was strength contrasted by vulnerability, beauty balanced by brains. I was tugged and torn in two different directions: London or Batavia.

I entered the restaurant that evening and found Thomas sitting alone at a table, nursing a drink. I joined him.

"Where are the others?" I asked.

"They're not here yet," he said. "I saw Van der Meer a few minutes ago. I think he went to get a newspaper."

"He seems like an interesting man," I said. "Tell me about him."

He thought for a moment. "I'm not sure where to begin. I've known him for many years. He's like a guardian angel. And he's the smartest man I've ever met."

"Really?" I asked. Thomas was very intelligent. So Van der Meer must be absolutely brilliant, especially to impress Thomas.

"And the bravest."

"What about Bennie?"

He chuckled. "Van der Meer makes Bennie look like a schoolgirl."

I thought of Bennie killing the Japanese soldiers. "I find that hard to believe."

"Then you should get him to tell you some stories sometime," he said. "He was a hero during the Great War."

I thought for a moment. "He doesn't seem old enough to have been in the Great War."

"He's not. At least not legally. He joined the French army when he was sixteen. Although he's Dutch, he had moved to Paris as a child. He lied about his age to prove his patriotism and then spent four years in the trenches. By the end of the war his chest was full of medals."

I was impressed. "For what?"

"He captured thirty Germans single-handedly. One of them was a Field Marshall. Van der Meer fooled them all somehow. Cornered them in a narrow ravine and convinced them they were surrounded by a whole brigade. He kept them there until help arrived. I think he was seventeen at the time."

"That's amazing," I said with disbelief. The words of an article on old war heroes were rolling through my mind. I couldn't wait to start writing it. I could also compare acts of heroism in the Great War with the current conflict. And battles, too.

"He was also wounded. He was at Ypres for one of those mustard gas attacks. I think he was blinded for almost a month. His eyes still tear very easily. Just a windy day can make him cry like a baby."

"Do you and Van der Meer and Bennie all work together?" I asked. "And did Chin help you, too?"

He studied me for a moment and then smiled. "Here he comes now."

Van der Meer walked into the dining room, and by the time he reached us, Sir Gregory entered just behind him. As they sat down, those at a neighboring table were discussing the anticipated Japanese invasion, and we listened attentively to the latest information. It seemed we had escaped one disaster only to walk back into another.

"I've seen what the Japanese are capable of," Sir Gregory said. "I think the invasion is imminent and, when it comes, it will be swift, coordinated, and deadly."

I studied him closely. He had been captured by the enemy. That much was true. But what other exposure to them did he have? His choice of words was deliberate; he spoke from experience. I suspected there was more to Sir Gregory than Lady Jane knew. Or wanted to know.

"The island of Java, or the city of Batavia, can't be defended," Van der Meer said. "Not against an assault like the Japanese will launch."

I remembered the panic that had overwhelmed Singapore. Batavia would be absolute chaos. It was cramped and crowed, overflowing with people. I could imagine human stampedes as people tried to evacuate. I started to think more seriously about departing, regardless of commitments made to the *London Times*.

Lady Jane arrived, strolling across the room. She wore a white dress, her hair curled into a bun on the top of her head. Jade earrings dangled from her ears, complimenting her necklace. She smiled as she entered, lighting the room. All eyes turned to meet her, including my own.

"We don't think the Dutch can defend the island," Van der Meer informed her.

She sat beside Sir Gregory, although not close to him, and quickly assessed the glum faces around her. "So we're about to relive Singapore?"

"I think so," I said. "We should plan to escape. If we stay and the island is captured it will be much more difficult to get away."

"Why not Australia?" she said.

"Maybe we should hire Bennie and explore the Southern Seas," Thomas suggested. "That would be interesting."

I considered his statement. Where did he get his money? How could anyone nonchalantly sail the seas with no visible means of support? Maybe Lady Jane and Sir Gregory could. And Van der Meer perhaps. But not me.

"I suppose I can stay here and write for the *Times*," I said. "Even if the island is captured."

"You won't be able to publish," Sir Gregory said. "The Japanese will censor everything."

"And look at what happened in Singapore," Lady Jane said reminded me. "The whole *Times* office evacuated. You would be here by yourself."

"A friend of mine from Oxford lives in Australia," Sir Gregory said. "In Perth, I think. He can probably help us."

Sir Gregory didn't know Thomas or Van der Meer. He thought they were normal people, men who worked for a living that knew little of world affairs. I didn't know them that much better. But there was one thing I was sure of. They didn't need help from anyone.

The glasses emptied as the hours passed, and each guest in turn said good night and returned to his or her room. Finally, only Thomas and I remained. I swallowed the last few drops of my now warm ginger ale and started to stand, planning to retire.

"Wait a minute, George," he said. "I want to talk to you for a minute."

I sat back down. "Is something wrong?"

"I wanted to make sure you were alright."

I was confused. "Sure. Why wouldn't I be?"

"I was afraid you might be upset with Sir Gregory's arrival."

I started to feel uncomfortable. "Why would Sir Gregory upset me?"

His eyes met mine, serious and searching. "Because you're in love with Lady Jane."

I was stunned. Maybe Lady Jane wasn't a diversion; maybe she was much more. I suppose it showed, even if I hadn't admitted it to myself. I thought about Maggie. The memory would always be there, but the feelings were fading. I realized then that I didn't have to choose. I could love them both. There was room in my heart for Maggie and Lady Jane

"Is it that easy to see?" I asked.

"It is for me," he said. "But maybe no one else. I'm right. Aren't I?"

"Yes," I said softly. "I suppose you are."

I studied my drink for a moment, reflecting on his statement. Then I turned to face him.

"What about you? I think you're in love with her too."

He smiled and rolled his eyes. "Love has many faces, my friend."

CHAPTER 29

The invasion of Java came sooner than expected. The Japanese established beachheads east and west of Batavia and also threatened a large naval base in the city of Surabaya. Dutch and Indonesian forces resisted, complimented by a small contingent of Australian, British, and American troops that mainly provided anti-aircraft support. The Japanese quickly established footholds and then advanced with little resistance from the Allied troops.

I had contacts in the military; Harry Simpkins of the *Times* office had provided me with several sources, all of whom proved valuable. My favorite was a Dutch colonel named Haak who was on the staff of General Hein ter Poorten, Commander of Allied forces. But he was difficult to contact after the invasion, ignoring my requests for information. I finally reached him after several unsuccessful attempts, and he briefed me on Allied defenses, Japanese advances, and military strategies. I learned that Allied commanders were more focused on saving their armies than Java.

I posted continual dispatches throughout these events, often working sixteen hours or more each day. I placed most of the articles with the *London Times*, while the rest were purchased by the Associated Press. Joe Durgan's business card proved to be a valuable asset.

I saw little of my companions in the days following the invasion. I asked for Thomas and Van der Meer at the registration desk and was told that, although they had not checked out of the hotel, they had left the city for a few days. I thought their absence mysterious, but consistent with their secretive lifestyles. I wondered what they were doing.   Maybe they were spying on the enemy, documenting their troop strengths and movements, or smuggling assets out of Java before the Japanese arrived. Or maybe both.   I might never know, but I did enjoy speculating.

I saw Lady Jane and Sir Gregory in the hotel restaurant during one of my longer work days.   I had stopped in for a quick dinner, and they were seated at a distant table.   Lady Jane looked tired, weary from conflict and confrontations, both personal and public.   Sir Gregory was strong and dominant.   I suspected he was gradually wearing her down, reestablishing the submissive state that she had so courageously shattered when she left India. Although I wanted to help her, I didn't know how.

The following morning, as Dutch forces and government officials frantically evacuated the city of Batavia, I saw Lady Jane in the lobby, scanning a newspaper.

"Lady Jane, how are you?" I asked.

She looked up from the paper.   Wrinkles of worry were etched in her forehead; her lips were formed in a thoughtful frown.   "Oh, George, it's so good to see you. What in the world is going on?   The Dutch are retreating?"

"Yes," I said.   "They're planning to evacuate.   They want to save as much of their army as possible."

She took my arm and discreetly led me to a sofa in a corner of the lobby.   "What are we going to do?"

"I'm not sure we can do anything right now.   But we have to find a way to escape."

"I've checked the harbor and some rural airports," she said.   "Nothing is available."

"What is going on with Sir Gregory?"

She smiled, and then softly caressed my cheek with

her fingertips. "George, nothing is going on with Gregory. But it is admirable that he came halfway around the world to find me." She paused, reflective for a moment. "He seems so different now. It's as if the whole ordeal changed him. Or maybe it changed me. But he is a good man. He really is."

"Jane," a voice boomed as Sir Gregory hurried across the lobby. "I was able to contact my friend in Perth. He may be able to help us." He looked at me and nodded. "Hello, George."

"What can your friend do?" I asked.

"He knows a high-ranking government official," he said. "He'll arrange our departure."

Lady Jane handed him the morning newspaper. "He's too late. The government evacuated. The Japanese will be here tomorrow."

Once the authorities departed, the Dutch army retreated and left the city to the enemy. Pandemonium reigned: looting, vandalism, ransacked businesses, and robbed banks. The army's retreat left a vacuum of authority, and I think that some in Batavia welcomed the enemy, even if it was only to restore order. I found the chaos repulsive, and wrote several filler articles on the behavior of the few that threatened the populace as a whole.

When the enemy arrived, I watched them from the hotel entrance. I took out my notebook, scribbling a description of their victorious march down the boulevard. A few of the Javanese cheered, believing the new conqueror had rescued them from centuries of Dutch colonial rule. But most recognized that the immediate future would be much harsher and more difficult than the past.

I knew I witnessed a new world order. The Japanese ruled the Pacific; the Germans ruled Europe. As the free nations of the world were falling like leaves from a dying tree, the Allies seemed powerless to defend them. I didn't know what would happen to me. It was frightening, watching the enemy walk through the city wearing the arrogant sneer reserved for the victor.

For some reason, on the day Batavia fell, I wondered what my parents were doing in London, and if my sister and her husband were at the local pub. They knew where I was from my articles in the *Times* and from the cables and letters I had sent them. But I had been so preoccupied with striving to be the best reporter that the *Times* had ever known, worrying about what was important to me and how I could stay one step ahead of the Japanese, that I had forgotten about them. Now I missed them terribly.

I studied the faces of those around me and saw the same fear and uncertainty that I felt. I was becoming weary of the Japanese advance; it seemed I could never avoid them. I had escaped them in Singapore and confronted - and then eluded - them numerous times in Sumatra only to yield to their control in Batavia.

"Did you ever think this would happen?" I asked a Caucasian gentleman, hoping he spoke English.

"No, never," he said. His Dutch accent was thick, his vocabulary limited. His face was consumed with sorrow; his eyes were lit with an anxious fear. "My daughter is in Surabaya. I can't reach her. I don't know if she's all right." He turned and walked away.

I noticed a woman by the curb. She was middle-aged and well-dressed; her clothes hinted of wealth and sophistication. I approached her, my notebook drawn.

"It's a horrible day," I commented.

She studied me for a moment, her eyes moist. I sensed she was apprehensive, wondering if she could speak freely. She glanced at the notebook.

"I'm a reporter," I said. "I'm from London."

"Why come here?"

She had a point. "I wonder myself sometimes," I said softly.

She nodded; maybe she shared the same thoughts. "I came from Amsterdam. Two years ago. To flee the Nazis."

"Only to face the Japanese."

"I had nowhere else to go. And the Japanese may not be as bad as the Germans."

"I wouldn't be too sure of that."

"If you were a Jew, you would know what I mean."

I looked in her eyes and saw the pain, the quiet agony of someone who had suffered more than most can imagine. I had heard rumors of what the Nazis did to Jews. Everyone had, but no one seemed to know the facts.

"What was it like?"

She hesitated, afraid to reveal the truth. "They steal your belongings. They steal your family. Then they steal your dignity. And finally, they steal your soul. If you're lucky enough to survive, you're just a shadow."

She nodded politely and walked away.

I watched her depart and was overwhelmed with anxiety. What intrigued me most was that only a few weeks ago I was in London. Before I left for Singapore, I had sat in the Sherlock Homes Pub and had Yorkshire pudding and a pint of Boddingtons with my sister Angie and her husband Tom. And just before that, I had enjoyed an afternoon playing chess with my father, walked along the Thames in the winter fog, and helped clear rubble from the buildings bombed by the German Luftwaffe.

Only a few months ago I had held Maggie in my arms. Now everything was different. The war had changed the world. And it had changed me.

I went to the *London Times* office after the Japanese marched into Batavia. The populace was returning to its normal routine, wary and fearful, and the streets had once again become a throng of humanity. Only now a sprinkling of enemy soldiers were mixed among the city's residents.

Harry Simpkins sat behind his desk, the office's only occupant. His wisps of white hair were a bit frazzled; his pale blue eyes were dulled and defeated. He was obviously despondent. He had a pad of paper before him, and, as I sat in front of his desk, I saw that it contained a few scribbled notes.

"It's a sad day for Java," he said. "Somehow I had convinced myself that Batavia would not fall. Denial is a dangerous trait for a reporter."

"Then we all suffer from the same shortcoming," I said. "I came to the Pacific to see the Allies turn the tide, to fight their way back to victory."

"And you were proved wrong." He sighed. "Look at the world we've given to our children."

"If there's even a world left to give them," I said. I tried to imagine what was to come. I suppose the Japanese would take Australia; the Germans would conquer Russia, then turn their attention to America. It was a horrific vision.

"I received some disturbing news a few minutes ago," he said. "And it affects both of us. I'm told the Japanese will intern over one hundred thousand people, including government officials, civic leaders, businessmen, and journalists."

I was alarmed. Somehow I thought I could continue to write but with limitations imposed by an oppressive society. I had hoped that if I peacefully existed and didn't threaten the new regime I wouldn't be bothered. I should have known better.

"What do you plan to do?" I asked.

"I'm leaving tomorrow," he said. "My family has a small ranch in the mountains. I think we can live there without being harassed. It's remote and self-sufficient. So the real question is what are you going to do?"

"I don't know," I said. "I'm traveling with some friends. We had hoped to escape together."

Simpkins jotted directions on a scrap of paper. "This is where the ranch is. It's near Bayah, on the southeast coast. You and your friends can go there if you have to. But you need to get out of here."

Feeling defeated and depressed, I wandered into the taproom the first evening of the Japanese occupation. Thomas sat at a table near the center of the room, waving his arms and relating one of his wild tales. Van der Meer was beside him with a smug smile pasted on his face.

"Where have you two been?" I asked.

"To the east," Thomas said as he looked at Van der Meer. "We wanted to see the invasion."

I looked at him like he had lost his mind. What type of man watched an invasion for entertainment? "What was it like?"

"Ruthless."

I studied the look of disgust on his face. It took a lot to affect him. Especially that noticeably. "What happened?" I asked softly.

Van der Meer looked at Thomas and then began his

tale. "We saw a small military hospital maybe thirty miles from the edge of the city. I guess it had about two hundred beds in it. The Japanese captured it."

"There were no guards or soldiers or machine guns," Thomas said. "It was just a simple medical facility."

"We never saw anyone carrying a gun," Van der Meer said. "It was filled with wounded soldiers, doctors, and nurses. There were men on crutches and in wheelchairs, doctors with stethoscopes around their necks, nurses in starched white uniforms. But not much else."

"And the Japanese systematically bayoneted every single person to death," Thomas said coldly.

I gasped. "My Lord! Are you serious?"

"Absolutely," Van der Meer said.

"Have you ever seen anything like that before?"

Thomas looked at Van der Meer. He didn't reply.

Sir Gregory and Lady Jane then entered the restaurant. We made room for them at our table.

"Have you given any thought to leaving Batavia?" Lady Jane asked. "The sight of the Japanese marching down the boulevards should be our hint to depart."

"She's right," I said. I was still shaken by Thomas's story, but I didn't want her to know it; I didn't want to frighten her. Instead, I shared my conversation with Harry Simpkins and described Japanese plans for the internment of some citizens.

"What do you propose, George?" Thomas asked.

"Obviously we're not safe here. I just hope it's not too late to leave."

"No, we'll manage," he assured me. "What do you think of my island sightseeing plan?"

I again wondered what motivated the man. I couldn't sail around the southwest Pacific, playing a game of hide-and-seek with the Japanese. I didn't understand why he wanted to do that. But then, his real motivation might be to see exactly where the Japanese were.

"I don't think that will work," Sir Gregory said. "We should make plans to get out of Batavia and go to Australia. It's the safest course of action. But we need to leave soon. Life, at least as it's known in Batavia, is about to change drastically."

As if his prophetic statement had been heard, the ambiance of the room was shattered by a loud command in Japanese. Six soldiers stormed into the restaurant, the heels of their boots echoing off the floor. Two officers strutted in just behind them.

CHAPTER 30

The first officer strode to the center of the room and stood defiantly, his hands on his hips. The six soldiers flanked him, three to a side. Then the second officer, the higher rank given the medals and braids that adorned his uniform, moved next to him. He spoke to his aide softly. The restaurant was silent; all eyes were trained on the enemy.

"Hij is Algemene Hakkan," the second officer said in Dutch, pointing to his superior. "He is General Hakkan."

Van der Meer grasped Thomas's arm. "Don't do it," he whispered.

Thomas's face was taut; his eyes burned with anger. He was so tense the muscles in his arms bulged, the veins visible. But I couldn't explain his reaction. Everyone else in the room was terrified.

The general stared around the room, daring someone to defy him. His soldiers stood behind him, weapons poised.

"Dit hotel zal ons hoofdkwartier zijn," the second officer said. "This hotel will be our headquarters."

General Hakkan gazed at a middle-aged woman a few tables away. She was well-dressed, wearing a pearl necklace and diamond earrings. He turned to his assistant and spoke in Japanese.

The second officer strutted to the woman, sneering with contempt. He pointed to her earrings and held out his hand.

She was indignant. "No, you cannot have my earrings. You heathen."

The officer reached forward and savagely ripped the

right earring from her ear. She gasped, her lobe torn; blood dripped onto the shoulder of her white silk blouse.

The room buzzed with anger as her gentleman companion stood in protest. The officer withdrew a pistol and held it against his chest. He quickly sat down, and those in the room quieted.

An elderly lady seated beside the woman nervously helped her remove the left earring. The Japanese officer took it, eyed it carefully, and then gave it to the general. The woman cried softly, holding a napkin to her ear.

I looked around the room. Most people didn't understand what was happening. They were frightened and confused. They hadn't realized that a conqueror takes what he wants, that anything they had was no longer theirs, but I think they understood now.

Hakkan observed the room's inhabitants, searching each face. He was enjoying the effect his actions had on the crowd. He wanted those in the room to be terrified. It amused him. His eyes came to rest on Lady Jane.

She turned away, averting her gaze. He walked towards her, his leather boots pounding the floor. I took her hand and squeezed it.

The general stood beside her, so close that his body brushed against hers. He touched her hair, caressing the blonde locks between his fingers.

"Stop!" I demanded, reaching for the general's arm.

I saw the butt of the soldier's rifle coming towards me, but I couldn't move quickly enough to avoid it. It hit me on the head, and I crashed to the ground, dazed and disoriented. My vision clouded, and the lights dimmed. I felt blood trickle from my head, wetting my hair.

"Enough of this nonsense," Sir Gregory said angrily. He rose from his seat but got no further.

A soldier placed a rifle barrel in his face about an inch from his nose and motioned him back to his seat.

Lady Jane used the distraction to rise and spin, pushing the general away. She stood and faced him, firm and defiant. Her lip was quivering, her hands on her hips. A fiery glare consumed her eyes. She refused to be intimidated.

Thomas loudly emptied his pipe into an ashtray, banging the bowl repeatedly. The noise attracted everyone's attention, including Hakkan's. Once again, Van der Meer touched his arm as if to restrain him.

The general looked at him. Briefly forgetting Lady Jane, he moved around the table towards Thomas.

He then issued a harsh command, which his assistant interpreted. *"Uw documenten!"*

Thomas pretended not to understand even though I knew he spoke Dutch. He sat with a quizzical look on his face.

"Paspoort!" the assistant clarified.

Two soldiers moved to the general's side. Two more guarded the door. Their weapons were drawn. The room was silent. The people were afraid even to breathe.

Lady Jane moved to the floor beside me and tenderly touched the welt on my head. "Are you alright?" she asked softly.

My head was swimming. "I think so," I said. "Are you?"

She nodded, moving closer.

The perplexed look on Thomas's face had changed to one of vague understanding. He nodded politely and withdrew the forged passport from his pocket. He handed it to the Japanese officer.

The general studied the document. Then he laid it

on the table.

Montclair filled his pipe with tobacco. He lit it and puffed a few times, directing the cherry smoke at Hakkan's face.

The general spoke to his aide.

"*U bent Zwitsers?*" the officer asked.

Thomas didn't reply. He looked at the general's aide with a faint smile.

"*Parlez vous Francais?*" the aide then inquired.

"*Mais oui!*" Thomas replied.

Lady Jane whispered in my ear. "We have to stop this!"

I tried to rise but was stopped by a soldier, his rifle poking my temple.

Thomas stared at the general, his eyes burning with hatred. Neither blinked; neither flinched. The general withdrew his pistol from the holster. He opened the chamber, spun the cylinder, and emptied five of the six bullets into his hand. Then he closed the chamber and whispered to his aide.

"*Laten we eens kijken hoe gelukkig je bent,*" the aide sneered. "Let's see how lucky you are."

General Hakkan placed the barrel of the revolver against Thomas's forehead. He waited a few seconds, ensuring the entire room could see what he was doing.

Then he pulled the trigger.

The click of the empty chamber ricocheted around the room. The patrons, frozen in fear, gasped collectively, then sighed in relief.

Thomas never blinked.

Hakkan laughed, motioning first to Thomas and then to his men. Once prompted, they laughed, also.

Thomas still didn't move. He continued to glare at

Hakkan.

The general turned towards the door followed by his contingent. His objective, to instill fear and terror into Batavia's inhabitants, had been successful.

Van der Meer patted his friend on the back. "Thomas, that was some display of nerves!"

"And you saved Lady Jane," I added with a tinge of jealousy. If only I had reacted differently. I would have gladly given my life to save hers.

"How?" he asked innocently.

"You diverted the general's attention from her," I said.

"Jane, darling, are you all right?" Sir Gregory asked. He hugged her, kissing her lightly on the cheek.

She sighed with relief and sat down. "I'm fine," she said bravely. She reached for her wine, her hand trembling. Then she raised the glass to her lips and drained the contents.

"That's the first of many encounters," Van der Meer warned. "The Japanese can no longer be avoided."

His statement, combined with meeting the enemy, sparked our interest in leaving the island. We discussed our escape for the next hour.

Few of the other patrons departed. I suspect their conversations were similar to ours, focused on their safety in a society dominated by the Japanese. The choices were obvious: endure the enemy or escape.

After we discussed some proposals, Thomas said, "At dawn we'll go to the harbor. We'll book passage wherever we can."

"What about Bennie?" I asked. He seemed to be just the type to aid our escape.

"He's not available right now," Van der Meer said.

"We'll need a different plan."

"We can't take luggage," Thomas added. "Maybe a small bag but nothing more. We won't check out of the hotel either. We have to act like we're only leaving for a few hours. The Japanese are already watching the guests."

"Is that acceptable to everyone?" I asked.

"It is to us," Sir Gregory said, speaking for both he and Lady Jane.

I looked at her. She rolled her eyes and shrugged. I was beginning to understand the cage she had described.

Considering the late hour and our early departure, we chose to retire. When I started for my room I saw sentries posted at the hotel entrance. We were wise to leave. The longer the Japanese were in Batavia, the stronger their hold would become.

Later that night I was awakened abruptly by someone banging on my door. I turned on the light and looked at my watch. It was 2 a.m. I put on a robe and stumbled across the room, expecting disaster. Were the Japanese commandeering my room?

I opened the door to find a distraught Lady Jane standing in the hallway. She was crying.

"George!" she shrieked. "You've got to help me!"

CHAPTER 31

I ushered her into the room and closed the door. I was confused. She was in some sort of trouble, but she had come to me for help. Not to Sir Gregory. And not to Thomas.

She wiped her tears away and folded her arms protectively across her chest.

"Tell me what's wrong," I said.

She bit her lip, tried to compose herself, but only cried harder.

I held her shoulders. "Lady Jane, I want to help you. I really do. But you have to tell me what happened."

"The Japanese general," she said.

"What about him?"

She took a deep breath, trying to collect herself. "When I went in my room he was waiting for me."

"Waiting for you? Why?"

"He had a knife. And he demanded I take my clothes off."

I felt the blood surge to my face. "The bastard! I'll kill him!"

She grabbed my arm. "You don't have to."

"Why? He deserves to die."

"He's already dead."

I stopped, my hand on the doorknob. "He's dead? How?"

"He tried to force to me to lie on the bed," she said. "I stopped in front of the nightstand where I kept a pair of scissors. As he approached me, I grabbed them and... and..."

"You stabbed him?"

She nodded. She was trembling.

"Are you sure he's dead?"

"I think so."

I paced the floor, trying to plan our next move. It was difficult to think. My head was throbbing; the butt of the rifle had left a large knot beside my ear. But I had to concentrate. Something had to be done with the general, and we had to get out of Batavia.

"We better tell Thomas," I said.

I dressed quickly and opened the door, cautiously checking the hallway. It was deserted. But soldiers could be anywhere. We crept to the room adjoining mine and tapped on the door. A moment later it opened a crack, and Thomas peered out.

"Thomas, we need your help," I said.

The door opened with no hesitation. He rubbed the slumber from his eyes, pulled his robe tighter, and led us to two chairs in the parlor.

"Tell me what happened," he said.

I related the tragedy, repeating Lady Jane's description.

He was calm and composed. He didn't ask why she came to my room for help, but I'm sure he wondered why.

"He didn't hurt you?"

She shook her head.

He eyed her for a moment. "Is the general dead?"

"I think so." She closed her eyes tightly.

"Is the door to your room locked?"

"Yes."

"Let me have the key."

She removed the key from her robe and handed it to him.

"George, you come with me," he directed.

"No, don't," Lady Jane said softly. "I don't want to

be alone."

"We're going to make sure the general is dead," Thomas said. He went in the bathroom and dressed, then removed his knife from a bureau drawer. "Lock the door behind us. We'll be back in a few minutes."

"Do you have to go?"

"If the general is still alive, it may take both of us to subdue him," Thomas said. "You'll be safe here."

We quietly made our way down the hallway. Lady Jane's room was in the floor above ours. When we reached the stairs, Thomas held his hand up. I stopped.

He leaned close to my ear. "I think I hear voices."

He cracked open the door into the stairwell. Two men were talking in Japanese. We quietly retreated, carefully making our way to the stairs at the opposite end of the long hallway.

When we reached the stairway, I opened the door slowly. We heard no sounds. Tentatively we tiptoed up the steps. When we reached the next landing, we paused at the entrance. Thomas cracked the door open and peered out.

"There's a soldier at the far end of the hall," he said. "Let's wait and see if he leaves."

"What should we do if the general is still alive?" I asked.

"We have to delay discovery until we can leave the city," Thomas replied. "We can tie him up. It might be morning before he escapes or is found. Or we can kill him."

I reconsidered my earlier threat of revenge. "Will it be harder for us if he's killed?"

He paused and turned to face me. "It doesn't matter. But I would rather kill him. You don't know Hakkan. You don't know what he's done."

"And you do?"

"Come on. The soldier left. We have to hurry."

"Tell me about Hakkan," I hissed.

"Later."

When we entered Lady Jane's suite, we heard someone groaning. We moved through the parlor and into the bedroom.

A lamp and a clock had been knocked off the nightstand and were lying on the hardwood floor. The lampshade was crumpled, the clock face cracked. A few feet away was an opened book, cast aside and askew, the partially removed dust jacket beside it. It was titled, *Murder in Moldavia*.

General Hakkan lay on the floor. He was far from dead and was just beginning to rise. The scissors were lodged in his upper back, blood dripping from the wound. He staggered to his knees, muttering in Japanese. He turned to face us.

Thomas leaped upon him. He drove his right arm forward, piercing the general's midsection with the knife. Blood oozed across his torso, dripping onto the sheets.

Hakkan groaned, cursed, and pushed Thomas away. He was a strong man, built like a bull, and he grabbed the knife, twisting Thomas's arm at such a savage angle I feared it would break.

I leaped forward, punching Hakkan in the face. He didn't flinch. He was focused on the blade, inching it closer to Thomas's torso. I punched him again. He growled, as if he were shaking an annoying dog off his pant leg.

"Grab the knife," Thomas hissed.

I added my hands to his, and between us, we managed to direct the blade away from his stomach. It pointed to the side, away from either body, with all of our hands wrapped around it.

I removed my right hand and again punched Hakkan in the face. I hit him repeatedly, and each punch I flung vented the hatred I felt for what he had done to Lady Jane.

Hakkan's strength was fading as blood seeped from his body. I stopped punching him and dug the nails of my finger into his left wrist. He tensed, gasped, and his grip loosened. I pulled his hand off the knife and subdued it with both of mine.

Thomas seized the opportunity and threw three punches directly to Hakkan's face. Blood spattered, his nose broken.

The knife dropped, and Thomas pushed Hakkan to the floor. I sat on the general's left arm, neutralizing it with the weight of my body. Thomas climbed on top of him, holding both hands around his throat.

Hakkan clawed at Thomas's face, trying to rip at his eyes. I fought to control his other arm. Thomas squeezed harder.

"I want to look in your eyes while I kill you," Thomas hissed.

Hakkan's face turned crimson; his veins bulged in his neck. He coughed, his eyes protruding from the sockets.

"You don't remember me, do you?" Thomas asked.

Hakkan glared at him, and a vague recognition crossed his face.

"Shanghai," Thomas said. He squeezed harder, his hands wringing the life from the general.

"Yes," Hakkan choked. "I remember." He grinned wickedly. "I enjoyed it."

Thomas's eyes grew wide, burning with hatred. He spat in Hakkan's face and squeezed harder, but Hakkan refused to die.

Hakkan flung one punch after another, some hitting their mark, but most missing. Each grew a little weaker. Thomas did not relinquish his hold. He squeezed harder, sticking his knee in Hakkan's wounded chest, using the added leverage to his advantage.

Hakkan slowly stopped struggling and a blue tinge crept over his face like a blanket over a sheet.

Thomas stepped back off the bed, breathing heavily, sweat dripping from his forehead, and studied Hakkan. The general didn't move.

Thomas checked for vital signs. "He's dead."

I looked at the corpse lying beside me. I wanted no forgiveness for taking a life, not this one, anyway, and was glad Hakkan was dead. Hakkan had to pay for what he'd done to Lady Jane.

Thomas stared at the body, breathing heavily. Tears were streaming down his face.

I hugged him, holding him for just a second, trying to will some of my strength to him. "Tell me about Shanghai."

He hugged me tightly and then pulled away. He wiped his tears on his shirt sleeve. "We have to hurry."

He went to the bathroom and washed up, but his clothes were stained with blood. Mine were too. It would be easy for the Japanese to track the killers.

Thomas rooted through the bureau drawers, selecting some of Lady Jane's clothing to pack. He found the outfit she wore to Palembang and rolled it under his arm. Next he selected some undergarments. He rolled up a few more items and placed them in a suede satchel. We then went into the bathroom to find Lady Jane's personal effects neatly lined up on the counter beside the sink. Cosmetics and French perfume, soaps, shampoos, and oils were swept into the bag.

I picked the book off the floor and added it to the satchel. I saw two others on the bureau: *Earthquakes and Volcanoes* and *Murder in Patagonia.* I added them to the bag.

We went to the door, listened closely, then peeked into the hallway. We saw no sentries. Cautiously, we returned to Thomas's room and tapped on the door. Seconds later we heard the tumblers of the lock reposition and a nervous Lady Jane peered into the hallway.

"Here are some of your things," Thomas said softly. He was aware of her fragile mental state and realized how horrible we looked in our bloody clothes. "Go and get dressed. We have to leave."

When she took her clothes and went into the bathroom, Thomas changed quickly and packed a small bag. He paced the floor while she got dressed, planning and plotting. By the time she emerged he had formulated a course of action.

"Go change your clothes, George," he said. "And be prepared for travel. Don't bring anything you can't carry in a small bag. Get Sir Gregory and Van der Meer, and have them do the same."

He guided Lady Jane to a chair and gently brushed the hair away from her face with his hand.

"I'll be right back," I said.

"Make sure you explain what happened to Sir Gregory and Van der Meer," he added. "And stress that we have very little time. When the other soldiers find the general's body they'll come after Lady Jane. We have to get as far away as possible by dawn. It's our only hope."

"What are you going to do?" I asked.   His tenderness confused me. I watched while he caressed her hair. I didn't like it. He was so immersed in her that at first I didn't think he heard me.

"I need to speak to Lady Jane," he said, his eyes not leaving hers.   When a few seconds passed and I had not left, he turned to find me watching. "Alone, George."

I cast Lady Jane a questioning look. I didn't want her to be alone with Thomas.   Not while she was so vulnerable, and not while I was falling in love with her.

"Go ahead, George," she said. "I'll be fine."

CHAPTER 32

The murder of a Japanese general, especially given Hakkan's importance, would be dealt with severely. The enemy would spare no effort to find us, combing the entire city of Batavia and the nearby countryside. We had to hurry. We had to get as far away as possible.

I suddenly had mixed emotions about killing him, even if I didn't think he deserved to live. But I knew a tremendous emotional burden came with taking someone's life. Although I finally uttered a prayer, a plea for forgiveness, I knew I would be haunted forever by Hakkan's vacant eyes and lifeless body.

And then there was Shanghai. What did it mean? What was the link between Thomas and Hakkan? How did Van der Meer know? These and a thousand other questions raced through my mind as I entered my room.

I dressed quickly and gathered some personal belongings, putting them in a leather travel bag. I stuffed all the cash I had into my pocket, and hid the remainder of the bearer bonds that the *Times* had provided for my expenses in the lining of my bag. As I put my passport beside them, I remembered my fake passport. It was at the registration desk. Hotels always held passports; it was their process. But our fake passports included our photographs. If the Japanese got them they would know what we looked like.

I moved cautiously into the hallway, finding no sentries. My breath was rapid and shallow, as I tiptoed across the tiled floor. I knew I could be discovered any second, challenged by the enemy, taken captive, or shot. I made my way to Van der Meer's room and rapped lightly on his door. It was a few moments before he answered, foggy and bleary-eyed. I explained the situation to him, including the sordid details. I stressed the need for haste.

"I'm glad Thomas was the one to kill him," he said with morbid satisfaction. "I only wish I could have seen it."

He dressed quickly and then packed some belongings in a ragged suitcase he had purchased on his arrival. He wasn't one for frills; he made do with the bare necessities. Once he was ready, we went to Sir Gregory's suite.

Just as we rounded a corner in the hallway, Van der Meer stopped abruptly. He leaned back against the wall. Then he motioned for me to look.

I peeked around the corner. Sir Gregory's door was nearest to us, just around the bend, but a Japanese soldier stood in front of it. He was barely five feet away.

Van der Meer pointed down the hallway. A stairwell stood at the far end. Anyone exiting from it would see us. We were vulnerable and exposed.

We waited, daring not to breath. Van der Meer poked his head around the corner. The guard was still there. He glanced at his watch.

My heart was beating wildly. There was no place to hide. Van der Meer again studied the hallway. Then he looked at me and shrugged. He motioned for me to follow him.

We crept forward. Van der Meer stepped around the corner, reached in front of the soldier's face, and grabbed his chin with his right hand. He pulled his hand back forcefully.

I winced as I heard the neck snap. The soldier slumped, headed for the ground, but Van der Meer grabbed the collar of his uniform, holding him upright with his left hand. He dragged him towards Sir Gregory's door.

"I don't want anyone to find him," he whispered.

I didn't reply. I was stunned by both his display of strength and how quickly and ruthlessly he killed. I looked at his heavily muscled arms with a new respect.

He saw the look on my face. "We had no choice. Hurry and wake Sir Gregory."

I knocked on the door as we waited anxiously in the corridor. A minute or two passed. I kept knocking, glancing furtively down the hallway. He finally answered, wearing silk pajamas that cost more than most earn in a week.

He stared wide-eyed at the dead soldier. "What is going on?"

"Forgive the intrusion, Sir Gregory," I said.

We burst into his room, and Van der Meer shoved the corpse into an empty closet. We recounted the evening's events. Sir Gregory frowned repeatedly as we told the story.

"Is Jane alright?" he asked, his face fraught and anxious.

"She's still upset," I said. "It was a trying ordeal."

"Yes, I'm sure," Sir Gregory muttered, his mind wandering. "I can't help but feel responsible for her. I always have." He looked at us, sorrow etched on his face.

"She's fine," Van der Meer said, interrupting him. "Come on. We have to hurry."

"Of course," he said. "You're right. I know what the Japanese are capable of. I still have nightmares about what they did to me at the oil fields. You're sure she wasn't harmed?"

"She's all right," I said, although I now saw him in a new light. It was only then that I realized he had probably been tortured, just like Van der Meer. With pangs of guilt and jealousy, I realized how much he loved Lady Jane.

He dressed quickly, glancing at his watch several times, and took a small satchel from the closet. "How much can I bring?"

"Just pack that bag," Van der Meer directed. "We have to be able to move quickly."

He selected some clothing and then filled the remainder of the satchel with personal effects. He started for the door and then paused. He returned to his bureau, retrieved a photograph of Lady Jane, and put it in the bag.

"I'm ready," he said tersely.

We checked the hallway, searching for soldiers. There were none visible; there were no audible sounds. We hurried to Thomas's room and tapped on the door. Seconds later, he let us in.

Lady Jane sat quietly, waiting for us. Her face was still ashen, but she was composed. Sir Gregory hugged her.

"Come on," Thomas urged. "We have to leave. The soldiers will search the entire island for us."

"And they'll kill us if they find us," Sir Gregory said grimly.

"How do we escape?" I asked.

"By railroad," Van der Meer replied. "The terminal is closer than the harbor. So we'll get farther in less time. That's important right now."

"Where will we go?" I asked.

"Madura," Thomas said.

"Where's that?" Lady Jane asked.

"It's where Van der Meer and I just were," he said. "It's a day's ride by train."

"Why go there?" she asked. "There must be other

options."

Thomas looked at Van der Meer before replying. "That's where Bennie is."

"Come on," Van der Meer said. "We have to go before the others find the body. They'll seal off the exits."

Thomas glanced at his watch. "I just hope there's a train before dawn. We'll have to avoid patrols on our way to the station."

With Thomas's warning echoing in our ears, we crept down the carpeted halls. We found a rarely used fire escape at the rear of the building and disappeared into an alley behind the hotel. It was dark and narrow, bordered by tenements and the back of stores from an adjacent street. It was raining lightly, and a quarter moon was pinned in the sky.

Van der Meer led us down one lane and then another littered with trash cans and stray animals, an occasional vehicle, crates and bicycles and storage boxes. There were no street lamps to guide us, and since we advanced cautiously, both time and distance passed slowly. I feared the sun would rise before we departed.

After we had traveled about a mile, we heard the distant sound of an approaching vehicle. Van der Meer motioned for us to take cover, so we hid behind some trash barrels.

"Don't move," Thomas hissed.

Lady Jane leaned up against me, wrapping her arm around my waist. She was so close I could feel her breath, her heart throbbing, her body trembling.

"Everything will be all right," I said softly. I glanced furtively at Sir Gregory. He wasn't watching, so I wrapped my arms around her, pulling her towards me.

A small truck drove into the end of the alley, crept

forward a short distance, and stopped. It sat there, silent, a shadow blending with the darkness. There was an audible click, and a blinding searchlight scanned the pathway, passing over our hiding place.

We waited as seconds passed. Then a cat leaped from a corner, rattling the lid of a metal can before scampering away. The beam moved up and down the alley and then slowly retreated. Eventually the driver seemed satisfied. He turned the light off, guided the vehicle into the street, and drove away.

Just as the threat passed, the rain ceased, and we continued. As we got closer to the terminal, the Japanese presence increased. They wandered nearby streets even though it was not yet dawn or waited aimlessly on corners. We suspected the enemy was using the railroad for troop movements. The soldiers must be waiting for trains.

It was shortly after 5 a.m., the sun just beginning to rise, when we reached a row of tenements bordering the edge of the railroad station. Hundreds of soldiers milled about the yard, talking in small groups, smoking cigarettes, idly passing the time. We crouched behind the last building, hidden by some shrubbery, and surveyed the situation.

There were several sets of tracks in and out of the rail yard, entering from the west and departing to the southeast. A train sat on the closest set of tracks, the locomotive adjacent to the terminal, and the last car curved past the edge of the yard. From my vantage point twenty yards from the tracks, it would be challenging to reach from our location. But the last few cars were in the darkest part of the yard and not as visible from the terminal, so it was doable.

We watched and waited. The soldiers began

boarding the first seven cars of the train. They swarmed forward, quickly and silently filing into the rail cars. First the yard and terminal emptied, and then the soldiers standing in the streets came forward, following their companions onto the train. As the soldiers boarded, the last car was loaded with crates of various sizes, probably ammunition and supplies. When all of the cargo was in place, the rest of the car was filled with burlap bags. Activity in the area soon diminished and, after twenty minutes, only a few sentries remained.

The train prepared to depart. Black smoke spiraled from the stack; steam leaked from the pistons. Workers shoveled coal to fuel the engine's furnace as the engineer performed his last visual checks of the locomotive.

Van der Meer whispered to Thomas and me. "I'll take George and Sir Gregory first. I don't want everyone at risk if this doesn't work."

"Where are you taking us?" I asked.

"To the train," he replied.

"It's a Japanese troop train," I said. "There must be a thousand soldiers on it."

He smiled. "I know. It's the last place they'll look for us."

CHAPTER 33

Even though Van der Meer's theory seemed absurd, I realized he did have a point. Who would ever look for fugitives on a train filled with Japanese troops?

The rail yard was lit by overhead lamps arranged along the periphery, but none were very bright. Since the position of the lights cast eerie shadows across the landscape, we could get to the train without being seen. Small shrubs that defined the lot's boundaries also provided cover.

"Stay in the shadows," Van der Meer said. "And keep close to the ground."

We had just reached the halfway point when two sentries strolled towards us.

They stopped thirty feet away, chatting. They were so close we could see their faces. We waited patiently, lying in the dirt and cinders, knowing that to advance further was not worth the risk.

A minute later they walked away. When we were satisfied we wouldn't be seen, we continued. Van der Meer was waiting in the shadows when we reached the train, and he led us to the opposite side of the boxcar, away from the station.

"See if anyone is around," he whispered. "I don't want them to hear the door open."

Sir Gregory ducked under the rail car. He emerged a few seconds later. "It's clear."

Van der Meer slid the metal door in the rail, opening it just enough for us to get in. He motioned to Thomas and Lady Jane. Sir Gregory and I climbed aboard and cleared enough space for everyone to fit comfortably, tossing burlap bags on top of each other and pushing crates towards the back of the car. When we'd finished, we joined Van der Meer.

Thomas and Lady Jane were halfway to the car. I watched them, jealous that I wasn't with her. I wanted to be the one to take care of her, not Thomas or Sir Gregory. They should stay in the roles I mentally assigned them, former fiancé and new friend and nothing more.

They had a more difficult time than us. The approaching sunlight and the wandering guards forced them to move slowly and more cautiously. At times they came so close to sentries that discovery seemed certain; yet, they managed to elude them.

"They'll never make it," I whispered.

"Yes, they will," Van der Meer said.

"The sun is coming up," I pointed out. "They're bound to be seen."

They hid in the shadows, crawling through the shrubs, until they finally disappeared underneath the train. We climbed into the car, waiting for them. Then a soldier appeared, straying down the tracks, wandering towards us. He stopped directly in front of our car, standing so close I could see the shadow of his hat visor across his nose.

I held my breath, leaning against the wall. Sir Gregory moved behind a crate; Van der Meer was on the other side of the door. Thomas and Lady Jane were beneath the car, their chance to escape disappearing with each passing second.

The sentry had no intention of leaving. He slung his rifle over his shoulder and withdrew a pack of cigarettes from his pocket. He lit one and puffed pensively, surveying the area. He didn't seem to notice that the door was ajar.

Minutes passed. The sentry watched the sunrise and enjoyed his cigarette. He had little to do but wait for the train to depart.

The engine belched a plume of steam. I glanced at Van der Meer, hoping he could offer a solution. His frantic look told me we were in serious trouble.

We heard someone call out in Japanese. I peeked from the car. The sentry turned abruptly and started walking towards the locomotive.

A series of shrieks came from the rails. The train started to grind down the tracks. Thomas and Lady Jane appeared from underneath the boxcar. Thomas threw his duffel bag on board and helped Lady Jane into the car, but when Thomas started to climb in, a soldier raced towards him, waving a large machete.

"Thomas!" I said. "Look out!"

He turned at my warning and caught the enemy's arm before the blade ripped his head from his body. A brief struggle ensued, and the pair fell to the ground.

The train gained momentum.

"We have to help him," I said.

"But then we'll all be at risk," Sir Gregory argued.

Thomas rolled his opponent over and pummeled his face. He then jumped up and ran for the train. It was ten feet away.

"Thomas! Hurry!" I shouted.

He came closer. The soldier rose and leveled his rifle.

"Come on, Thomas!" Van der Meer said.

"Hurry!" cried Lady Jane.

Two shots were fired. The bullets ricocheted off the ground, making plumes of dirt around him as they missed their mark.

Thomas drew even with the doorway. I reached out to assist him. Van der Meer and Sir Gregory leaned forward, prepared to help.

He reached for my outstretched hand, grabbing it tightly. He was about to leap aboard when another shot was fired. He cringed. His eyes mirrored pain, and his grasp loosened. I struggled to pull him aboard. The train increased speed.

"Thomas!" I said. "Hold on!"

His grasp weakened. With a sense of helplessness, I felt him lose his grip entirely.

CHAPTER 34

.

"No!" I screamed. "Thomas!"

Lady Jane leaped past me, almost knocking me from the car, and jumped into the yard. She held a tiny pistol in her right hand.

"Jane!" Sir Gregory bellowed. "What are you doing?"

Van der Meer followed, bolting from the railcar.

I heard a shot, different from the others, and an instant later Van der Meer helped Thomas up into the car. His shirt showed a blood stain from a wound near his left shoulder.

Lady Jane jumped in. The train was gaining speed; the car was almost visible from the terminal.

"Help me," Van der Meer called.

He lifted up the body of the dead soldier as Sir Gregory and I assisted. The soldier had a small bullet hole in his forehead. Van der Meer got in after him, winded and weary.

"I had to take him," he said of the soldier. "The others may have heard the shots, but with no body they have no reason to stop the train. It'll be a while before they realize anyone is missing."

I looked at the soldier. His eyes were open, glazed and vacant. Blood dripped from his head.

My eyes moved from the bullet hole to Lady Jane. "You?" I asked in disbelief.

She shrugged and sat passively, her face pale, and stared vacantly forward. Her whole body was trembling.

I remembered how I'd felt when I helped kill Hakkan. It wasn't a feeling of satisfaction; it was a sense of overwhelming emotion. I was flooded with thoughts of his life: wife, children, parents, siblings, teachers, friends, hobbies, favorite foods. I had removed all those memories from the face of the earth. It was just like Maggie. She had vanished forever, and sometimes I felt like she'd never existed, like she'd been nothing more than a dream.

Lady Jane looked sickly. She kept staring at the soldier. Her eyes grew moist.

"Let's get the body out of the way," I said, eyeing her carefully.

"Help me throw it over the boxes," Van der Meer said.

We lifted the corpse and shoved it past the crates. Then we stacked bags in front of it. When we finished, Van der Meer turned to Thomas and inspected his wound.

"It looks like the bullet passed through just above the armpit," he said. "It's more of a graze than a puncture. I think you'll be fine."

He removed a bottle of gin from Thomas's satchel. Then he soaked a clean sock and dabbed the entrance and exit wound. Thomas cringed but said nothing.

Lady Jane seemed sad and reflective. Was the impact from Hakkan's attack the need to kill? Was that her revenge? When she'd arrived in Singapore she had been so confident, so independent, and so exuberant. Now she seemed like an eggshell, the façade covered with tiny cracks. Balraj had been the first fracture, and each tragedy we'd faced had added another. Now the eggshell seemed about to shatter.

"Where did you ever get that pistol, darling?" Sir Gregory asked.

She cringed. No one else noticed, but I did. She didn't like the term of endearment. "I bought it in Batavia. The owner showed me how to use it."

"Why didn't you use it on Hakkan," I asked quietly.

"It was in my suitcase," she said, her voice a measured monotone. "I didn't even think of it."

"You saved my life," Thomas said. "And I'll never forget that. Thank you."

She stared forward, not even acknowledging she was being spoken to.

"Jane, did you hear what Thomas said?" Sir Gregory asked.

She nodded and then turned to face Thomas in a robotic fashion, a look of shock consuming her face. "You would do the same for me," she said. Then for what seemed to be no reason at all, she leaned forward and kissed him lightly on the lips.

Sir Gregory was taken aback. He looked at her as if he really didn't know her at all.

I looked at her the same way.

A few hours later, after I was lulled to a light sleep by the chugging of the engine's pistons, I felt the train's speed decrease slightly. I looked out the door and saw a mountainous terrain, heavily vegetated and dressed in varying shades of green. The ground seemed to rise steadily skyward, with some peaks tickling the clouds that hung on an azure horizon. Terraced rice paddies climbed the hillsides bordered by banana trees and farmers' thatched huts. On the slope of one mountain I saw a large stone statue of Buddha, a remnant of a distant age that straddled time to sit comfortably in the present just as it had in the past.

Being vaguely familiar with the geography of Java, I suspected we were somewhere in the central part of the country. But I wasn't sure where. I attempted to reproduce the maps of the nation in my mind's eye but I wasn't entirely successful.

"I know we're in central Java," I said. "But I don't know exactly where."

"We are nearing the city of Djokjakarta," Thomas said. "I think it may be held by the Japanese. If the train stops there, we will likely be captured."

"Do we risk it?" Van der Meer asked. "Or do we jump off."

"I suppose it depends on where we think these troops are dispatched to." Sir Gregory said, referring to the soldiers on the train.

"But we don't know that," I said.

"The train has served its purpose," Van der Meer said, finalizing the discussion. "We need to find a different way to reach Madura."

"Come on," Thomas urged. "We had better get ready. There's little time."

We stood by the doorway and waited. I watched the scenery rush past. We were moving much faster than I'd anticipated. I realized that leaping from a speeding train was hardly a simple task; it was dangerous.

"There's a bend ahead," Van der Meer said. "The train will slow when it gets there. Thomas, Sir Gregory, and Lady Jane will jump first. George and I will follow."

"I'll throw out the bags," I said.

The train slowed slightly when it reached the bend, but not as much as I had hoped. Thomas, Sir Gregory, and Lady Jane stood poised in the doorway, waiting for the right moment.

They leaped from the boxcar. I tossed the bags out after them as Van der Meer and I watched them land, hurtling forward with their arms and legs flailing wildly. Then we followed. As I rolled on the ground, I looked back to see the train moving forward; our departure seemed to go unnoticed.

The hill on which we landed was steeper than I'd expected. Our momentum propelled us forward so rapidly that we rolled uncontrollably down the hillside, our bags tumbling around us. We stumbled forward amid shrieks and screams, bumping and bouncing off each imperfection in the landscape.

I landed roughly on a crude road some two hundred feet lower than our starting point. I settled into a sitting position, shaken but not injured.

The others had already come to rest. Van der Meer was beside me, flanked by Sir Gregory and Lady Jane. They were unhurt but disheveled, their hair mussed and their faces flushed. Thomas was a few feet away. His left arm hung limply at his side, the blood stain a bit larger. Our bags were scattered around us.

A Japanese truck appeared on the horizon. Although still some distance away, it was moving down the dirt road in our direction.

Thomas pointed at the approaching vehicle. "We've got to keep moving."

"Let's circle the city and catch another train," Van der Meer said. "By now every soldier in Java is looking for us. And it'll only get worse."

I shivered, knowing the enemy would not give up until they found us. I peered at the truck, still a speck in the distance. We had to get away before they saw us.

"Can you travel?" I asked Thomas.

"Yes," he said simply. "There's not much pain."

We quickly left the roadway and darted into a field of chest-high reeds. I couldn't tell if the high grass was natural or planted, but it did screen us from the road.

Thomas and Van der Meer led us in the general direction of Djokjakarta, the city we hoped to bypass.

After traveling about forty yards, I glanced at the road and saw that the truck had stopped. The driver leaped from the vehicle and pointed across the field.

"They've seen us," I warned the others.

"Hurry," Thomas said. "We have to elude them. They'll kill us if they catch us."

We quickened our pace. A minute later I looked back again. I saw fifteen or twenty soldiers hurrying across the field, rapidly closing the distance.

CHAPTER 35

"They're chasing us!" I said.

A flicker of fear and anxiety crossed everyone's face. The Japanese would never give up. They would chase us to the most remote corner of the earth in relentless pursuit until their thirst for revenge was quenched.

I looked at Lady Jane. It seemed the shock from killing a man had worn off. Now her face was taut, her upper lip firm. She was determined and defiant but still afraid. The others had grim expressions, prepared to confront the enemy, but tiring of the constant battle.

"We'll never escape," Sir Gregory said. "There are too many of them."

"No, we'll make it," Van der Meer assured us.

"I have an idea," Thomas said. "Crouch down so they can't see you."

We knelt in the field and watched the reeds wave in the breeze. Thomas stood a moment longer, observing the approaching soldiers and then scanning the horizon. He didn't seem concerned.

"Make sure you stay low in the grass," he again directed. He knelt down and guided us forward.

Our crouched position was uncomfortable, but we managed. We pressed onward, resisting the temptation to stand and relieve the strain on our aching backs.

"I feel like a duck," Sir Gregory mumbled.

"Just keep moving," Van der Meer hissed. "And keep quiet."

We had trekked onward for almost thirty minutes, wading through reeds, occasionally interrupted by a lonely tree, when we heard angry voices.

Thomas held a finger to his lips and pointed to the

ground.   We waited, lying flat and motionless, barely breathing.

The voices grew louder.   There were two soldiers. They were coming closer.   From the noises they made, I suspected they were poking their rifles through the grass, bayonets fixed to the barrels. I heard their boots crunching. They continued talking.   Then one voice grew fainter; a soldier was moving away from us.   But the other voice got louder.

I squinted, peering through the grass, and saw the black boots of a Japanese soldier.   He was swinging his rifle in an arc, the bayonet slicing eerily through the grass. His back was to us.

He took a step.   He was barely five feet away.   I lay on my side, smelling the moist earth, not daring to move. The boots came towards me.   They were only a few feet from my face.   He moved again but sideways, distancing himself from me.   He neared Lady Jane.

I glanced at Thomas.   He removed the knife from the sheath on his shin and held it menacingly.   He looked at Van der Meer, almost as if asking for permission.

The soldier took another step, swinging away from Lady Jane.   A few steps more and the distance grew. We waited a minute.   The soldier stepped continually away from us.   When we could no longer hear him, Thomas motioned for us to start moving again.

We continued for ten more minutes uninterrupted by the soldiers.   When it seemed we were going nowhere, we abruptly came to the edge of the grass.   Thomas held a finger to his lips, signaling us to remain quiet.   We stayed hidden while Van der Meer and he crept forward.

They left the reeds and disappeared.   We waited, terrified the soldiers would creep up behind us.   We listened closely, but heard only the rustling of the reeds in the breeze. Thomas returned a few minutes later. He had a Japanese rifle.

"How did you get that?" I asked.

"Come on," he said. "We have to hurry."

He led us forward. When we cleared the field, I was surprised to find we were on the dirt road again. Van der Meer was waiting for us. An occasional tear rolled down his cheeks. I stared at him oddly as he wiped them away. Then I remembered the story that Thomas told me about the Great War. Van der Meer had survived a gas attack, but his eyes were so sensitive a strong wind made him cry.

I looked at him for a moment, our unofficial leader. He was calm and composed, confident and cocky. He had earned a medal for bravery when he was seventeen years old, and he could do it again if he had to. Even though Thomas now led our escape through the reeds, Van der Meer provided his silent approval for every move that we made.

"We've gone in a big circle," Lady Jane said.

"Exactly," Thomas acknowledged.

"So our efforts have all been in vain," Sir Gregory said.

"Not really," Thomas replied.

We negotiated a curve and saw the truck parked in the center of the road. An enemy soldier lay on the ground beside it.

"What are we going to do?" Sir Gregory asked.

"I thought we'd be more comfortable driving," Thomas explained. He looked in the cab. "Oh, how nice. They were kind enough to leave the key in the ignition."

Thomas handed Van der Meer the rifle and he

climbed in the rear of the truck with Sir Gregory and Lady Jane. We threw our baggage in after them. Thomas got in the driver's seat. I climbed in beside him.

"Watch for the other soldiers," he said.

He started the truck and drove away. We barreled down the road as the men who had been fanned across the field raced towards us. But we were too far away. They never even ventured a shot.

"Where are we going?" I asked. "Are we still circling Djokjakarta?"

"I'm not sure where the road leads, but we should use the truck since we have it. It may be a better option. But we need to find food first. We should try to stay in the rural areas and reach the east coast. Then we can find Bennie and get out of here."

We traveled for an hour more. Our progress was slow. The roads were rough and rutted; our journey would be a long one. Although we were in a rural area, the mountainous terrain was heavily populated. Thatched huts lined the roadway and the areas adjacent to it, which were surrounded by rice paddies terraced into the hillsides. The fields swarmed with workers, but our presence earned only a glance from the local populace. It made me think that Japanese trucks were already a common sight.

We soon reached a small hamlet, nothing more than a series of houses and huts nestled near the road, and Thomas brought the truck to a halt in front of a general store. Although several villagers milled about and wandered down the road, none seemed interested in us.

"I think it best that I don't go in," he said, referring to his bloody shirt. "Can you pick me up a few things?"

"Of course," I replied. "What do you need?"

"A few shirts, some cigars, and gin, if they have it.

Get all the food you can carry and something to put it in. Try and purchase a three-day supply just to be safe."

"I'll get some medical supplies too," I said, eyeing his injured shoulder.

He handed me some money. "Get some personal items too. Soap, combs - you know, stuff like that."

I nodded and joined Sir Gregory, Lady Jane, and Van der Meer who were already in the store. We made our way through the aisles, enduring an occasional stare from local patrons. The shelves were sparsely stocked but did contain an assortment of local foods, some clothing, and personal items. We made our selections quickly; it was dangerous for us to linger. When we left the store we found Thomas hanging out of the truck window, engaged in a conversation with two men.

"I've found a place where we can rest," he told me when I returned.

Just as we all got into the cab, a small truck screeched to a halt in front of the store. One of the soldiers got out and hammered a poster on the wall beside the entrance.

"Get down!" Thomas hissed.

We crouched low in the front seat. If the soldiers searched the store and found no comrades, they might come to the truck. We were trapped.

I could imagine Van der Meer in the back, his rifle drawn. He intended to go down fighting. Lady Jane had her pistol ready, but I didn't know if she had the nerve to use it again. Sir Gregory was still a mystery. Although he had been tortured by the enemy, and he probably hated them, I couldn't predict his reaction. Would he fight or surrender?

We could hear the soldiers talking. They were

260

questioning some of the locals. I held my breath, hoping they didn't talk to anyone who had seen us. The discussion lasted a few minutes, and then it was quiet. We cringed, not knowing if they were coming towards us.

A minute passed, tense and quiet. We heard the vehicle start, the engine cranking over and rumbling to life, and then it drove away. They had ignored our truck, never questioning why it was there, never searching for the troops who had come with it.

"See what the poster is," Thomas said.

I walked over to the entrance and saw the flyer the men had attached to the wall. It was a picture of Lady Jane with some description underneath it. Two smaller portraits were below it at the bottom of the page. One was of Thomas; the other was me. I removed it from the wall and hurried back to the truck.

I handed it to Thomas. He scanned it briefly and then laid it on the seat. "I was afraid of that," he said. "They have our fake passports so they know what we look like. We have to get out of here. They probably posted flyers all over Java."

He drove away. After another mile, he turned off the road and went across a grassy field, before guiding the truck into a grove of trees. When he was sure the vehicle was well-hidden and couldn't be seen from the road, he stopped and we got out.

Thomas led us through the underbrush, comparing the area to the description he'd gotten from the men at the store. We soon reached a small pond rimmed by thick green vegetation and circled by large flat stones. The water, which was about six feet deep, was so clean that the gray sand at the bottom was visible.

We lounged on the rocks while we gorged on a meal

of rice, cheese and pineapple juice.   We ate ravenously. When our appetites were sated, we prepared to wash.

Lady Jane was the first to bathe, so we waited by the truck to ensure her privacy. When she called for our return, we found her clothes draped over a limb to dry. Her hair was flat and wet, and she was dressed in a batrik, a colorful local garment purchased at the store.

We bathed in the pond while Lady Jane wandered into the adjacent shrubbery. The water was soothing, and it was the most peaceful moment we had in some time.   I savored it as I would any other long-absent pleasure.   It made me think of London and a hot bath in my apartment after braving a damp winter day. As soon as I thought of home, the hurt returned, like a knife in my heart, and memories of Maggie washed over me, one after the other like the scenes of a motion picture.

After we finished, Van der Meer attended to Thomas's wound. He cleansed the damaged flesh, dabbed on an ointment he had obtained at the store, and then bandaged it. "I think your recovery will be rapid."

We were about to call for Lady Jane's return when she came running through the trees, pointing to the road, her face frantic and flushed.

"The Japanese are coming!"

CHAPTER 36

We ran from the pond across the flat rocks and through the trees to our vehicle. It was tucked a few hundred feet from the road in a natural cove of dense shrubs and overhanging limbs. Lady Jane stood beside it, pointing to a troop truck that had stopped on the side of the road.

"Are they here for us?" she asked.

"It looks like it," Van der Meer said.

Troops started climbing from the back of the truck. I counted a total of ten, including the driver and an officer who had been in the cab. The soldiers stood on the side of the road and were soon joined by two civilians.

"Thomas, look," I said. "It's the men we saw at the store."

"We have to get out of here," Sir Gregory warned. "If they catch us they'll kill us."

"We can use the truck," Van der Meer said. "We'll wait until they're almost here, and then we'll drive away. They'll have to run back to their vehicle before they can come after us. Sir Gregory, Thomas, quick. Go get our belongings."

The two disappeared while we watched the enemy approach. I was tired of running, and I knew the others were too, but if we stayed it meant certain capture and death. Especially for Lady Jane.

The troops moved slowly, cautiously crossing the field that lay between us, searching the occasional islands of shrubs and trees, and even taking a moment to study a rice paddy that lay on the distant edge of the road. It was if they knew we were nearby, and they knew we were dangerous.

No soldiers remained at the truck. That was good; Van der Meer's plan might work. For a moment I studied the contrast offered by the rural landscape. A man was leading two goats down the road, briefly looking at the men and then minding the animals. He was followed by a cart of bananas pulled by a slouched donkey and driven by an elderly man with a broad hat. The civilians studied the invaders, no doubt wondering what they were doing in such a remote part of the island.

Lady Jane had her pistol clenched firmly in her right hand, her knuckles white. Her face was pale, her eyes focused on the short barrel of the gun. She was trembling.

She noticed me watching her. After making sure Van der Meer was preoccupied with the enemy, she furtively handed me the pistol.

"I can't kill anyone else," she whispered.

I grabbed the pistol. Then I tenderly took her hand in mine and squeezed it.

"Get in the back of the truck," Van der Meer said. "Be quiet though. Climb over the tailgate."

We did as he said, waiting for Thomas and Sir Gregory. They returned a moment later, handing us our bags and the extra sacks containing the provisions we had purchased at the store. Sir Gregory had the rifle we had taken from the soldier. The soldiers were closer, barely a hundred feet away.

"Thomas, you drive," Van der Meer said. "Go with him, Sir Gregory."

"Look!" I hissed.

I pointed to a grove of trees on our left. Two soldiers were emerging from the thickets, barely fifty feet away. They hadn't seen us; their attention was focused on their approaching comrades. I suspected they were scouting for the others, exploring our flank. They had probably gotten out of the truck before Lady Jane saw them. They were close enough to stop us, maybe without firing a shot. Just level their rifles and demand our surrender.

Thomas and Sir Gregory moved quietly towards the cab. Van der Meer gingerly climbed in the back with Lady Jane and me, stepping over the tailgate so he made no noise.

I heard the doors open and close almost in unison, and then the engine started. The soldiers closest to us turned towards the noise and shouted for us to stop. Thomas threw the truck in gear. The wheels momentarily spun in the soft soil before finally catching; the rear end of the vehicle swerved. As we sped away, I looked out the back of the truck and saw the soldiers pointing their rifles, preparing to shoot.

"Get down!" I said.

I pushed Lady Jane to the floor. Using my body as a shelter, I wrapped myself around her, trying to protect her.

"George, I'm frightened," she whispered.

"Just stay down," I said. "I promise nothing will happen to you."

The Japanese started firing as the truck bounced over the rugged terrain. I heard the shots. Bullets punctured the canvas that wrapped the back of the truck and pinged off the sideboard and tailgate, almost hitting the tire. One bullet whistled past me. Then I heard a thud like a snowball hitting a wall.

We bounced about the back of the truck as Thomas turned continually, battling bumps and ruts, running over shrubs and bushes, until he got back to the road. He sped as fast as the truck could travel, turning onto a side road to elude the enemy.   I lifted my head and peeked over the tailgate.   Our plan had worked.   By the time they'd recovered and come after us, we had already disappeared on the twisting roads that curved along the mountainside.

Van der Meer was sitting up, his face pale, leaning against the side of the truck. He was wheezing, struggling to breathe.   He stared vacantly forward; his shirt was stained with red.

"Van der Meer's been shot!" I shouted.

I moved to his side, a sickening feeling in the pit of my stomach. He was our leader and a friend. He had saved our lives on more than one occasion.   I was determined not to let him lose his.

I tore his shirt open. The bullet had entered the left side of his left chest near the heart. Blood oozed from the wound, dripping down his torso.

"Lady Jane, get the medical supplies out of our bags."

She handed me some gauze and a cleansing agent. I cleaned the wound, rubbing the lotion on it.   There was a gurgling sound coming from deep in his throat. I wondered if he was choking on his own blood. His eyes started to roll back in his head as if he were losing consciousness, but then his head snapped forward; he refused to succumb.   I pressed the gauze against the bullet hole, trying to stem the flow of blood, and held it firmly.

"Hang on," I said. "You'll be all right."

He looked at me, his eyes barely open, but he nodded his head. He seemed to recognize my efforts and appreciate them.

"It doesn't look bad," I said, although I knew differently.

He coughed and sputtered and then arched his

eyebrows. "I think you're wrong," he said. He winced, fighting the pain.

"George, we have to do something," Lady Jane said anxiously.

She was right. We had to find a doctor or a hospital. The wound was far more serious than our minor medical skills could cope with. We had to save his life. It was worth whatever risk we had to take to do it.

I thought of his contribution in the Great War, his bravery, his courage, all demonstrated as a boy, seventeen years old. It didn't seem fair that someone that heroic should die in the back of an enemy truck in the remote mountains of Java.

I pressed the gauze against his chest and examined his back, searching for an exit wound. There was none; the bullet was lodged inside him. There were no other wounds. I eased him from a sitting position down to the floor, holding the gauze tightly against the bullet hole. Then I put one of our bags under his head to elevate it. He seemed to breathe easier.

"Is he bad?" Lady Jane asked.

I looked to see if he was watching. His eyes were closed. I nodded my head.

A tear rolled slowly down her cheek, but she quickly wiped it away. Then she got more bandages from the bag.

"Here," she said. "Wrap this around him."

Between us, we managed to pack the wound with gauze and wrap a bandage around his chest. I rolled up some clothes in a ball and made a pillow, replacing the bag. His face was ashen, his breathing labored, but for the moment, it was all we could do.

I peeked out the back of the truck. We were

traveling down a dirt road that increased in elevation, approaching the next mountain. Small shacks abutted the road; farm fields sprawled behind them. Men worked the fields, women tended children and an assortment of animals: goats, dogs, oxen, and a few scattered donkeys dotted the landscape. We were moving rapidly. There was no one behind us.

"We should tell them to stop," I said. "They need to know about Van de Meer."

I took the water bottle and wet some gauze. I placed it on Van der Meer's forehead.

Lady Jane banged on the window, holding the curtain back for Sir Gregory to see. When he turned around, she pointed to the back of the truck where Van der Meer lay supine, eyes closed.

A startled look crossed Sir Gregory's face, and he turned to Thomas. He too glanced back, and they engaged in an animated discussion. They knew, as I did, that we had to find a place to stop. We needed to take care of Van der Meer; we needed to get help.

Again I glanced behind us. As we passed a side road, I saw the Japanese truck approaching. They quickly turned the corner and were again in rapid pursuit.

CHAPTER 37

The soldier on the passenger's side leaned out of the window, pointing his rifle at our truck. He aimed carefully, staring through the site, and then fired. The bullet hit the bumper and ricocheted onto the road.

He had been trying to shoot the gas tank. I briefly thought of our truck exploding into a ball of fire, flames spiraling into the sky, but I dismissed it. I had enough to worry about. I couldn't imagine disasters that might never occur.

Sir Gregory was firing from the front seat. His first shot missed, but his second shattered the mirror on the passenger's side of the Japanese truck. Then the driver veered to the side of the road, hiding behind our vehicle. Sir Gregory continued to fire, but he made no impact; the bullets missed the vehicle completely.

I looked at Lady Jane's gun. It was small, a Derringer that held five shots. I wasn't comfortable with firearms. My father was a Protestant minister; there were no guns in the house I was raised in.

"Do you have more bullets?" I asked.

The gun was light, almost like a toy. I could manage it easily.

"Yes," she said. "They're in my satchel. I'll get them."

"Stay down," I told her. "Lay on the floor."

I hid behind the tailgate, using it as shelter. Then I eased the corner of the canvas aside. The enemy's truck was right behind us, barely thirty feet away. I pointed Lady Jane's pistol at the driver and fired.

I missed. It was hard to keep the weapon steady

with the truck bouncing on the rutted road. The bullet hit the windshield in the center, near the top. The glass cracked and the vehicle swerved, but it then returned to the road.

The soldier fired again, only now I was his target. I ducked when he seemed ready to pull the trigger, crouching against the floorboards. The bullet whistled by, ripping through the canvas above my head.

Sweat dripped down my forehead. My skin was cold and clammy. I took a deep breath, ready to fight back.

"George, can I help?" Lady Jane asked. Her voice was trembling.

I saw a small crate at the front of the truck tucked under a bench. "See what's in the tool box. But stay down, and be careful."

I peeked past the canvas. The soldier again took aim and fired. The bullet shattered a tail light.

My heart pounded against my chest. Escape seemed unlikely, London and the hope of ever seeing it again, impossible. I had to be smarter than the enemy.

Lady Jane found more bullets and then crawled to the toolbox and opened the lid. "There are some tools and a jack," she said. "At least we can throw them."

As she slid the box forward, I took aim and fired again. I was way off. The bullet hit the edge of the windshield on the driver's side. The glass punctured, forming a small hole. Then a crack walked across the front of the windshield and the glass shattered, spraying fragments on the road.

"Stay down," I reminded her.

She laid on the floor, covering her head with her hands. "Do something, George! I don't want to die."

I started throwing tools out the back of the truck: a

wrench, a tire iron, the jack, the base for the jack, and a can of oil. The can bounced off the hood of the truck and bounced into the cab, striking the driver.

As the truck swerved I changed tactics and fired the remaining three bullets directly into the truck's radiator. I don't know if they all hit, but at least one did. Water began to belch from the front of the vehicle.

"You got them!" Lady Jane shrieked. "You did it, George."

I smiled, peering cautiously at the enemy, feeling proud and strong and awash with accomplishment. I reloaded the pistol, eager to renew the attack.

The leak worsened and steam billowed from the front of the truck, blocking the driver's vision. The vehicle slowed, and the distance between us grew. Eventually they faded from sight. We continued for a few miles more and then the truck screeched to a halt.

A moment later, Thomas and Sir Gregory opened the canvas and peered into the back.

"How's Van der Meer?" Thomas asked anxiously.

He was frantic and fraught, his eyes wide and his face pale. I had never seen him so worried, so afraid, and so utterly overwhelmed. The panicked, helpless look that consumed his face was so vivid I could almost feel his pain.

"Not good," I said, trying to be compassionate. "The bullet is still inside his chest. He's weak and gasping, but I think we stopped the bleeding. He needs a doctor."

"I'll find one," Thomas said. "We have to save him. Make him as comfortable as you can. I'll do whatever it takes to get him help."

"Jane, are you all right?" Sir Gregory asked.

"Yes, I'm fine." Then she looked at me and smiled. "George protected me."

Her statement surprised me. But I liked it.

We were quickly underway, the truck again bouncing over the crude roads. I checked Van der Meer. He was resting peacefully. I didn't know what damage the bullet had done; his bandage was stained with blood, the wound still seeping. I assumed his heart and major arteries had been spared, since the blood flow had diminished. But maybe a lung was damaged. I didn't know.

"George, thanks for saving us," Lady Jane said.

My eyes moved from Van der Meer, a friend who lay on his deathbed, to Lady Jane. I looked at her eyes, blue like a tropical sea, and her upturned nose. "I'm falling in love with you," I said softly.

As soon as I'd said it I felt guilty. I should be focused on saving Van der Meer's life, not on my new obsession for Lady Jane.

She smiled and brushed the hair from my forehead. "Do you think they'll find a doctor?"

I sighed, regretting what I had said. "I don't see how. We're not near any large cities."

The full realization of what had happened overwhelmed me. A dozen Japanese had been in pursuit, intent on killing us and wounding Van der Meer. I had fought them off with a tiny pistol. And I had done it, not through the brute strength that I would never possess, but with craft and cunning. I had disabled the vehicle, not the enemy, but the result was the same. I had saved us. Not Thomas, not Sir Gregory, but me.

We drove until dusk, with periodic stops to check on Van der Meer. He did not regain consciousness, but his condition didn't seem worse. When we reached a village, a hamlet with many streets that stretched haphazardly in all directions, Thomas drove through the town slowly.

Although the population would probably support a physician based on the amount of dwellings and myriad people who seemed to wander the streets, we couldn't find one. When we reached the village's outskirts, Thomas guided the truck into a wooded area that hugged the road before climbing to a higher elevation. A mountain in the distance spewed steam from its peak, a white trail that marred the approaching darkness.

Thomas's face appeared in the back of the truck. "You two stay here," he said. "Sir Gregory and I will find a doctor."

"We didn't see any when we drove through the town," I said. "Maybe we should keep going."

"I have to try," he said. "I would never forgive myself if I didn't."

We were quiet after they had left, the two of us minding Van der Meer. When I turned to look at Lady Jane, I saw that she was staring at me. When I met her gaze, she smiled.

"He seems to be resting comfortably," she said. "I hope he's all right. I would miss him terribly."

He was a remarkable man. And a true friend. There was no doubt he would do whatever was needed to help me, or Lady Jane, or Sir Gregory, even though we had only known him a few weeks. I never regretted risking my life to rescue him, although I have to admit I didn't support the effort initially, but I'd do it a thousand times again, if it meant he would live.

We were quiet for a moment, reflecting on a man who had made such an impact on our lives.

"What about you, George?" Lady Jane asked. "What are you going to do if we ever get out of here?"

"I'm not sure," I said.

273

I had promised my London editor six weeks in Singapore. That seemed like a lifetime ago, and I had only been there a few days. Then on to Batavia, Sumatra, back to Batavia. Now we traveled through Java, the enemy around every bend.

I really didn't know what I wanted. I was confused, conflicted by mixed emotions, both personal and professional. I wanted to be part of the war effort; I wanted to prove I could do what other men could, even without their physical stamina.

Then there was my obsession with Maggie. It was fading, replaced by Lady Jane. The hurt was still there, but it was softer. And sometimes it was traded for a memory that made me smile. Sometimes it wasn't, but one thing was certain: the distance to London could no longer be measured in miles.

"Do you want to go back to London?"

"I never wanted to leave," I said softly. "But I had to."

"It wasn't your career, was it?"

I was overwhelmed with sadness; my thoughts were flooded with memories of Maggie. I loved Maggie, and so did everyone who knew her.

"It was Maggie," she said, reading my thoughts. "Wasn't it? You had to escape. It was the only way you could try to forget."

"I saw her everywhere," I whispered.

She leaned forward and kissed me, tentatively at first, our lips barely touching, and then more forcefully. I wrapped my arms around her, pulling her close, drinking her scent, feeling her hair against my cheek, her arms wrapped around me, her heart beating against my chest.

She pulled away, flustered, and cleared her throat.

Her cheeks were flushed; her eyes avoided mine.

"I don't know what I'm going to do," she said, acting like nothing had happened, as if the intimate moment were only a dream.

"Will you go back to India with Sir Gregory?" I asked.

I probably shouldn't have said it, but I had to know. I was confused. I was angry. I felt like I was being toyed with. First there was Balraj who came and went like a streaking meteor. Then Sir Gregory arrived from nowhere to merge the past with the present. Thomas was a friend and a flirt, a man who might be the future. I didn't understand what was happening.

"He's a good man," she said. "And what better way to prove your love than travel halfway around the world to find someone. Even after I'd hurt him terribly. Look at what he's been through. He was captured by the enemy, tortured, worked to death, and almost killed. He did all that for me."

I was quiet for a moment. "That wasn't what I asked you."

Suddenly, Van der Meer groaned. He raised his arm, clutching mine. "Take care of Thomas," he said softly. "He's not as strong as he seems."

CHAPTER 38

Thomas and Sir Gregory returned with a Javanese woman, her hair long and untamed, her eyes as black as the volcanic soil.   She carried a satchel woven from local fabrics in a pattern of decorative flowers.   She nodded, smiled timidly, and climbed into the back of the truck with an agility that surprised me.

"All we could find was a midwife," Sir Gregory said. "This is Mita."

She bent over Van der Meer, laying her cloth bag beside him.   She felt his forehead, touched his lips with a fingertip, placed her palm on his check, and then fingered his wrist to feel his pulse.   She reached into her bag and withdrew several glass vials and small leather pouches.   Then she took a bottle of water, wet her finger and rubbed the moisture on his lips.   She followed the same process with an unidentified liquid.

"Is he going to be all right?" Lady Jane asked.

She mumbled and shrugged, not understanding the language but somehow knowing the question.   As she delicately removed the bandage, blood oozed slowly from the wound.   Then she took a vial and poured the liquid over both the bullet hole and her hands.   A lavender powder followed, sprinkled on the wound and the surrounding area.

She said something to Thomas.   I recognized a smattering of Dutch.

"She's cleaning the wound and using local equivalents of anesthetics," he told us.

I wondered if she knew what she was doing.   Her techniques seemed so strange, especially when compared to the medical care provided in London.   I hoped she wasn't making matters worse.   But there was no alternative.   If we did nothing, he would die.

She delicately poked the wound. Her finger lightly touched the circumference of the bullet hole, and then she inserted it to the first knuckle. She withdrew it, reached for another pouch and added a pinch of green powder.

"The vials and pouches remind me of some of the medicines in India," Sir Gregory said. "Don't they, Jane?"

"Yes," she said, watching Mita closely. "At least for doctors not trained in England."

"Is what she's doing dangerous?" I asked. "You would never see a doctor in London with a bag of powder or a glass bottle filled with strange liquids."

"As long as it works, I don't care what she uses," Thomas said.

"The medicines are from local plants and herbs," Sir Gregory said.

"And the cures have been handed down through generations," Lady Jane added.

I looked at the midwife with new eyes, watching her curiously, wanting to learn about tried treatments I might never see again. I would have asked her what they were, where the powders and liquids came from, and how she obtained them, but I didn't want to distract her; she needed to focus on Van der Meer.

She continued the examination, tenderly touching the area around the wound. It seemed she hoped the bullet was near the surface, but it wasn't. She removed a slender metal tool with a flat, curved edge, washed it off, and again started probing.

Then she deftly spun and twisted the metal tool, flipping it upward. Blood squirted from the wound and she stemmed the flow with gauze.

She spoke in a blend of Dutch and Javanese,

stringing long sentences together. She then paused and eyed Thomas, ensuring he understood.

"She wants to take him to her home," he said. "It's the only way she can remove the bullet. He'll die if she doesn't. And she says he can't be moved for at least a week."

"Thomas, we can't be delayed," Sir Gregory said. "We have to keep moving. The Japanese will track us down if we don't."

"She claims she can hide him."

"Yes, she can hide him," Sir Gregory said, compassion framing every word. "But not all of us."

"I won't leave him," Thomas declared.

We then heard a voice calling in Japanese.

"Quiet!" Thomas hissed, holding up his finger.

The voices continued. They were distant but coming closer.

"Can you understand them?" I asked.

Thomas shook his head.

I was sure we were surrounded. With posters of Lady Jane all over the country and the Japanese combing the area looking for her, capture seemed inevitable. Even though we continued to elude them, they somehow returned, creating a swirling circle framed by relentless pursuit through forest and field, river and ravine.

I looked at Lady Jane. She was listening intently, her face drawn and tired. I furtively reached for her hand and squeezed it tightly, ensuring Sir Gregory could not see. It had become a secret signal between us, clutching her hand. It showed I would protect her.

Thomas whispered to the midwife, explaining the situation. She nodded. A look of concern was replaced by one of understanding, and her attention returned to Van der

Meer.

"They're coming closer," I warned.

"We have to get out of here," Thomas said. "Sir Gregory, come in the cab with me."

They eased themselves out of the truck, careful to make no noise, and made their way to the cab. The sound of the doors opening and slamming shut was sharp and distinct, echoing through the woods. The engine turned, grinding to life. Thomas slipped the transmission into gear, and the truck lurched forward.

The Japanese shouted; I could hear three distinct voices. I looked from the back of the truck but saw only darkness and the grisly shadows that the moon cast. From the sound of their voices I guessed that they were separated, maybe thirty feet apart. They were walking, but they must have a vehicle nearby.

"Are they coming after us?" Lady Jane asked.

"I don't think so," I said, still peering into the night. "They're on foot. And they seem disorientated."

"What are we going to do?"

"I don't know," I said. "I think we should leave Van der Meer with the midwife and then get out of here. At least there's a chance she can save his life. That's something we could never do."

"Thomas won't leave him."

"He'll have to. There's no other choice."

I grabbed a map that had been in the tool box. I scanned over it, roughly aware of our location, looking for the name of the midwife's village. I eventually found it and then located the railroad. We were only a few miles from the tracks.

"Have you found anything?"

"We're close to the railroad. That can be our means

of escape."

"I'm convinced," she said. "Now you have to persuade Thomas."

CHAPTER 39

We left the woods, driving over shrubs and small trees, making our own path back to the road. I kept watch behind us. No one pursued. The Japanese who were searching for us, if they were searching at all, were on foot. They must have left their vehicle in a different location.

We traveled to another crude road, just prior to the village, and turned. We passed a small lake, glistening in the moonlight, and after a few hundred yards we turned again, reaching a thatched cottage that sat by the distant edge of the water. It was typical Javanese architecture with a high rectangular shape in the center of the roof that allowed the heat to collect and a steep slope that diverted water away during the rainy season.

I lowered the tailgate and let Lady Jane and Mita out. Van der Meer still rested, but was groaning slightly. Thomas and Sir Gregory joined us, and the woman pointed to a small outbuilding that sat beside the lake.

We went to investigate. It was probably an animal hut originally, upgraded and modernized; it was clean and well maintained. A chair and cot were in the center of the room along with shelves of medical supplies that flanked the walls. Another chair, strangely shaped with an open seat was at one end of the room; I suspected it was used to birth babies. I had read that many cultures gave birth in a vertical position, letting gravity assist the delivery.

The woman gave several sentences of direction to Thomas. She took a blanket from the shelf, unfolded it, and laid it on the cot. Then she reached for some vials of medicine, laying them on a small table.

"Can you help me?" Thomas asked us. "We have to carry Van der Meer in here."

Sir Gregory and I followed him. Together we lifted Van der Meer as gently as we could. Thomas, who favored his injured arm, and I were at his head; Sir Gregory was at his feet. We carried him inside and laid him on the table, propping his head up on more blankets. I went back to get his bag.

When I returned, Thomas and the midwife were in an animated discussion.

"What's wrong?" I asked.

"She says it's too risky for all of us to stay," he said.

"It is," I said solemnly. "Van der Meer's only hope lies with her. We decrease his chances if we stay. She can never hide all of us. Especially Lady Jane."

"George is right," Lady Jane said. "And it's the best situation for Van der Meer."

Mita again started talking, more sternly, and directing her comments to Thomas.

"We can always come back for him," Sir Gregory said.

Thomas sighed, wavering. He knew we were right but he wasn't thinking logically. He was thinking emotionally.

"The railroad is a few miles away," I added. "We should drive to the tracks and jump on the next train. When the Japanese find the vehicle and figure out what happened, they'll stop looking here. Van der Meer will be safe."

A moment of silence ensued. "You're right," he said softly. "We have no choice."

"And we have to hurry," Sir Gregory said. "Before the Japanese find us here."

Thomas gave the midwife some money and then some instructions. She nodded throughout the discussion, and seemed to assure him that his friend would be all right. We each said our goodbyes, both to Van der Meer and the midwife. Thomas hugged his friend, lingering longer than he should have.

"Hang in there," he whispered. "Everything will be all right. I won't let anything happen to you."

"Thomas, we have to go," I reminded him.

He took a deep breath and grasped Van der Meer's hand, holding it tightly, as if to send some secret signal.

"Thomas," Lady Jane urged. "Come on."

I had to ease him away. Gently, taking his shoulders, and turning him to the door. When he reached the exit, he cast one last look at his friend, as if to etch his features in his memory. Then he nodded his thanks to Mita.

We returned to the truck and left, driving slowly. When we reached the main road we traveled a few miles more past the spot where we had previously stopped. We found another dirt road that brought us farther, closer to where I suspected the railroad was. Ten minutes later I directed Thomas to stop, and he guided the truck into a grove of trees and turned off the engine.

"The railroad tracks should be cut into the mountainside. But I don't know at what elevation," I said. "Just on the other side of this hill."

It didn't seem like we would ever escape. If Lady Jane's picture had made it to a general store in a small mountain village a hundred miles from Batavia, it was posted everywhere.

I knew the climb over the hill would be difficult, especially considering how tiring our journey had already been. I hoped I could make it. We had covered a lot of territory: Singapore, Sumatra, and Batavia. Now we moved relentlessly towards Surabaya, and hopefully

Surabaya led to London.

We covered the truck with tree limbs and broad leaves, hiding it as best we could. After we had distanced ourselves from the vehicle, traveling a mile or so, we paused to eat. The cheese, bananas, and pineapple juice that had satisfied us at breakfast worked just as well for dinner. After completing our meal and resting a bit, we continued.

It was a wearying trek. The hill was much steeper than observation suggested. The vegetation was thicker, the incline more pronounced, and the altitude higher than we had thought. I had difficulty breathing before we were half way to the top, and I was embarrassed as the others paused to allow me to catch my breath. We trudged onward, however, and sometime before midnight we reached the railroad tracks.

"We can only board a train if it's traveling slowly," Thomas said. "We'll have to find a curve or incline where the train decreases speed."

We walked down the tracks, which were hugged by trees and shrubs, until we found a bend a mile farther. The tracks led around a steep curve and onto an iron-truss bridge that was about six hundred feet long. Four hundred feet below the bridge lay the rocky floor of a narrow valley. Looking down the steep slope made my knees tremble. I backed away from the edge.

We spent a restless night, hidden among the trees that lined the tracks. It was a ghostly location, by far the most secluded spot we had encountered, and the only sounds we heard were the animal noises that whispered on the southern winds. I was sure snakes slithered through the grass, but I decided not to think about it, trying to rest while the opportunity existed.

We woke at dawn, ate a light breakfast, and discussed our strategy.

"George and I will go down the tracks and wait for a train," Thomas said. "Once we're sure no troops are on it, we'll jump into the last car. If there are soldiers on it, we'll let it pass. Is that understood?"

We nodded.

"Lady Jane and Sir Gregory will remain hidden until the last car comes into view," he continued. "If it's safe, we'll signal you. Sir Gregory can lift Lady Jane while we pull her in, then he'll throw the baggage up and jump in after her. If you don't see us on the last car, remain hidden."

We carried the knapsacks containing our supplies and moved a half mile around the bend. We waited for a train's arrival. A few hours passed. There were no trains, no people, no animals, just an uneasy silence.

"Thomas, look!" I said. I pointed down the hill. There were six Japanese, weaving through the grass and shrubs.

"Where did they come from?" he asked. "Stay down. Don't let them see you."

He motioned down the tracks to Lady Jane and Sir Gregory. Once he had their attention, he pointed downward. When they saw the enemy, they retreated back into the vegetation that lined the hill that the track was carved into.

"Do you think they're looking for us?" I asked.

"I don't know," he said. "But they're certainly looking for something."

We watched them for fifteen minutes. They were systematically moving through the underbrush, searching. As they completed examining one area, they climbed the hill and continued at a higher plateau. If they proceeded, they would reach us in thirty minutes, but if we weren't careful, they would see us much sooner.

"What are we going to do?" I asked.

"Maybe we should start moving down the tracks, towards Surabaya. At least we'll put some distance between them."

"Thomas, get down. They have binoculars."

We lay flat against the side of the rails. My heart was thumping into the ground below me. I ventured a peek down the hill. The binoculars were pointed right at me.

"They've seen us!" I hissed.

The ground started to rumble; a train was approaching. I looked down the hill. The soldiers were starting to climb. In minutes they would reach us.

"Stay down," Thomas said. "Let the train pass between us and them. If we try to run now, they'll shoot us."

Sir Gregory and Lady Jane remained hidden a few hundred feet down the track. But they could see the soldiers struggling up the hill just as we had. We had little time.

The rumbling of the ground was superseded by chugging of the train's engine as it gradually approached. The soldiers scrambled up the hill; the train eased down the tracks. It would be a slow motion race. If the train arrived first, we escaped. If the Japanese did, we were dead.

Thomas studied the train. "There are no troops that I can see. It looks like a freight train. Probably bringing supplies to Surabaya."

"We don't have any choice," I said. "The soldiers are only seventy yards away. We have to catch the train."

As the engine passed, we rose and drew even with

the cars. It was traveling slowly but still much faster than I had expected. I began to doubt if I was spry enough to leap on board.

"Run with it," Thomas yelled.

I did as he said but was confused when he ran in the opposite direction, towards the back of the train. I then realized he planned to be on board well before me. He needed time to assess conditions on the boxcar, and to then help me. The second car of the ten-car train had passed me when Thomas reached the last car. He leaped into the open door, holding on to the frame to avoid falling out.

He started throwing out cargo to make room for four people. The car contained burlap bags, contents unknown, which soon lay scattered along the side of the tracks, haphazardly landing wherever they were tossed. There were no Japanese in sight.

I was now even with the last car. I threw our luggage on. Thomas held out his hand. I grasped it and leaped, closing my eyes. I felt myself pulled upward just as the train neared the bend, its brakes screeching in protest.

I heard a rifle shot, and a bullet ricocheted off the railcar, followed by another. The Japanese had climbed the hill. One soldier stood beside the tracks, rooted to the soil, his rifle aimed at us. Others were getting into position as two Japanese started running down the tracks. As the train slowed even more to maneuver the bend, they might be able to catch us.

"Throw out more bags," Thomas said. "We need more room."

I was winded, breathing heavily from exertion and anxiety, but I helped him toss thirty-pound burlap bags out of the doorway. One broke open and spilled its contents. They were filled with rice, probably destined for the troops.

We continued to discard them until we had enough space.

The soldiers fired more shots, most hitting the back of the metal railcar and then bouncing to the ground. Occasionally one pierced the inside of the compartment, a ping followed by the hollow thud of a bullet burrowing into the rice bags.

"We'll make more room later," Thomas said above the noise of the braking train. He pointed ahead to where the bridge was visible. He leaned out of the doorway and waved his arm. Sir Gregory and Lady Jane emerged from the shrubbery and stood poised by the rails, ready to leap aboard.

The train had maneuvered around the bend, the Japanese hidden by the foliage next to the curve in the tracks. Just as the car reached Lady Jane and Sir Gregory, I heard more shots. The two soldiers who chased us were at the edge of the bend, barely visible. One kneeled, his rifle on his shoulder, aiming at the train. The other stood. Lady Jane and Sir Gregory made good targets.

When the boxcar reached them, Sir Gregory threw their bags aboard. The shots continued, and one bullet ricocheted off the edge of our doorframe. Thomas leaned down while I held my arms around his waist and acted as his anchor. He grasped Lady Jane and, with a show of strength that amazed me, flung her into the car like a small child.

She screamed in surprise, landing on her derriere in the narrow space. She looked startled, as if she weren't sure how she'd arrived there.

The shots continued, ricocheting off the railcar, bullets bouncing in all directions. Puffs of dirt surfaced near Sir Gregory's feet born by stray bullets, the cinders stinging his legs. The shots were coming closer; the onslaught grew stronger. Sir Gregory ran beside the slowly moving train. Thomas reached down and grabbed his outstretched hands.

"Jump on the count of three," Thomas shouted.

More shots sounded as those firing were joined by their comrades. A half dozen soldiers were now aiming at us. A barrage of bullets bounced off the train, the rail bed, the doorframe; some bullets burrowed into the bags of rice. Leaves and branches of nearby trees split and splintered, bullets tearing them apart.

The bridge was approaching rapidly. Little time remained. We had to get Sir Gregory aboard.

Thomas yelled his count. Sir Gregory leaped, jumping on board just as the ground below him disappeared and the train chugged over the bridge.

Lady Jane's timing was not as perfect. She rose from her sitting position and collided clumsily into her former fiancé.

"Gregory!" she shouted.

Screaming hysterically, she fell from the doorway and plunged towards the valley below.

CHAPTER 40

I lunged towards Lady Jane as she fell from the car, barely catching her leg as she tumbled past me, grabbing her calf and knee with both hands. Her momentum pulled me forward, almost dragging me with her. I managed to wedge one of my legs between the edge of the door and a stack of burlap bags, which kept me anchored in the car.

Thomas reached for her belt but missed. He managed to grasp her other leg near the ankle and then clutched the side of the door frame to prevent us all from falling forward. We held her tentatively, clenching her legs, forming a human chain as she dangled head first from the railcar.

"Sir Gregory! Help us!" I shouted.

I was gasping, struggling to breathe, overwhelmed with excitement and anxiety and exertion. It was difficult to maintain my balance and hold on to her; I struggled to stay in the car and not get pulled out. Every muscle I had strained to hold her. My leg, caught between the bags of rice, was gradually sliding loose, but my arms remained tightly wrapped around her leg. The pulling, burning sensation coursed through my limbs. A sudden ache knifed across my head as I yanked backwards with all the strength I possessed. It resulted in nothing more than a dangerous stalemate as I fought to save Lady Jane.

Thomas held the doorframe with his injured arm and leaned out the exit, his face contorted with pain. His right arm held Lady Jane's ankle, maintaining her link to life.

I looked out the door, staring at empty sky and open space. We were approaching a mountain face, a smaller sister fading in the distance. Lady Jane's arms flailed wildly, her head facing the valley floor. Her screams were hideous, a high-pitched wail, eerie and piercing and ripping the heart from all who could hear it. She was losing the battle. Inch by inch, she slid from our grasp.

"Help me!" she screamed.

Sir Gregory moved to Thomas's side, his arms around his waist. "Just hold on to Jane," he shouted. "I'll pull you backwards, and she'll come into the car with you."

Thomas was tiring. I could see the strain on his face. And I was too.

"I can't hold her much longer," he said.

Sir Gregory eased Thomas backwards. "Let go of the doorframe. I've got hold of you."

As Sir Gregory pulled Thomas into the car, they dragged Lady Jane towards them. Thomas now had the use of both hands, and he transferred his hold from her ankle to her knee, securing her foot under his good arm. I assumed the same position. We now held her firmly, even if the majority of her body thrashed in the wind. We had to slowly ease her into the car, gently moving our hands higher on her body: ankle to thigh, thigh to waist.

"Let's pull her up," Thomas said.

Lady Jane's screams echoed through the valley, ricocheting off the mountain walls. The appalling pitch provided an unbearable tale of death and disaster and the minutes that lead to it.

Tears welled in my eyes, born by pain and the disaster I couldn't control. I had to hold on. I just had to. No matter what. I couldn't let go. I couldn't let what happened to Maggie happen to Lady Jane.

Thomas and I stood, raising her upward. Once we had her legs in the car, we moved our hold to her thighs. We continued pulling, sliding her in.

"Thomas!" I screamed. "Look!"

The train was approaching the end of the bridge. A tunnel loomed ahead, carved into the mountain. Only inches separated the train from the rock wall.

"Pull!" Thomas bellowed. "Hurry."

We jerked backward, using all the space available and raising our grasp to Lady Jane's torso and then her arms. With the added leverage, we pulled her towards us with one last heave.

The instant we yanked her aboard, we were overcome by the muffled roar of the train entering the tunnel. Darkness overwhelmed us.

Gasps and curses and sobs and prayers filled the boxcar. We remained in blackness for several seconds while we sped through the tunnel, the clanking of the train's wheels on the rail the only sound. When the end of the tunnel approached and light filtered in, Lady Jane clung to Thomas with tears streaming down her face.

CHAPTER 41

I was stunned to see her in Thomas's arms. She cried, mentally shattered and destroyed, physically scraped and pummeled, but more or less unhurt. He stroked her hair, caressing the strands between his fingers, and consoled her. I didn't understand why she hadn't come to Sir Gregory or me.

I tried to rationalize her behavior. Maybe she'd just hugged the person closest to her. She needed support, an emotional bond, and some assurance that she was safe. But I still found it distressing and confusing. Especially after the intimate moments we had shared.

Sir Gregory was overcome with hurt and despair. The pain on his face and the sadness in his eyes made me realize how much he loved her. I had thought he'd come from India to recover his pride, not to claim his lost love, but I was wrong. He was a good man, sincere and just and honorable, the type you could always trust to do the right thing. Just like Thomas. And even though he knew he wasn't welcome, he made the best of it. He had endured capture by the Japanese and all the disasters that had followed, because he loved Lady Jane, and he wanted to win her back. I think for the first time since he'd arrived, he realized that was unlikely.

He stood by awkwardly while she clung to Thomas. Then he leaned forward and lightly touched her shoulder. "You're safe now, darling."

Five minutes elapsed before her sobbing subsided. Thomas gently wiped the tears from her cheeks and spoke to her quietly, occasionally saying something that forced a smile. Sir Gregory and I stood by clumsily, wishing we were somewhere else. Finally, Thomas pulled away.

"It's all right now," he said. "You'll be fine."

With a final sniffle and a whispered word of gratitude, she moved away from him and sat on a rice bag. She then expressed her appreciation to Sir Gregory and me.

"You saved my life," she said, facing us with a vacant gaze. "I don't know how to thank you." Then she looked away, her eyes trained on the passing countryside.

I noticed that she was behaving strangely, probably from the shock. She stared vacantly ahead, quiet and pale, her arms folded protectively across her chest. Her bout with death had left a vivid vision that would haunt her forever. Why did I expect her to act normally? Of course she had clung to the first person she saw. I was convinced it was the trauma and nothing more that had caused her actions.

As for Thomas, he had merely responded. When Lady Jane embraced him, wanting desperately to be consoled and protected, he had complied just as any true friend would.

When I was sure she was all right, I attended to Thomas's wound. "Take off your shirt," I said. "And let me take a look."

He stripped to the waist. I found that the exit wound on his shoulder had reopened, cracking the scab and oozing blood. I got some gauze from his knapsack and held it against the wound. After a minute of direct pressure, the bleeding ceased.

"Pour some gin on it," he said. "It fights infection."

I smiled, and instead got some of the ointment we had bought at the store and dabbed at the wound.

"Ouch," he said, feigning pain. "Gin would have been better."

"Is it healing?" Sir Gregory asked.

"Yes, it is," Thomas said, pushing his cap back on an uncombed mop of brown hair. "It just stings a bit right now."

We approached the outskirts of Surabaya twenty minutes later, evidenced by the transition from mountain to coast and farm to suburb. We were quiet, knowing another encounter with the enemy was likely.

"The city is held by the Japanese," Thomas warned. "We may have a difficult time escaping."

"Should we jump off now?" I asked. I wanted to avoid a confrontation. I felt like a cat with few of his nine lives remaining.

"I don't want to leap from the train," a still-shaken Lady Jane informed us. "Especially after what just happened."

"You're right," Thomas said. "We'll wait for the train to stop. That's a better plan."

I frowned. The decision was risky. We could end up in the arms of the enemy.

"I understand the dangers of leaping from a moving train," I said. "But does that outweigh the risks of capture? I'm sure the Japanese will be at the terminal."

"Let's see if the train passes through to Madura," Thomas suggested.

The train slowed, at first appearing to stop, but it was soon apparent the reduced speed was needed to travel through the city, one of the largest in Java. We peeked from our boxcar, observing the metropolis while we moved through it. It was every bit as large as Batavia, with buildings several floors in height dotting the urban landscape. Red-tiled roofs, so prominent to the area, were sprinkled among the taller structures. Throngs of people milled about the street, traveling on bicycles, in rickshaws, taxis, and cars, and on foot. Japanese soldiers and their vehicles wandered through the city, mingling with the local residents. I knew the metropolis housed a massive naval base, but it wasn't visible from the train.

"We're not stopping," Thomas said when the bridge to the island of Madura became visible. "The soldiers we escaped from must not have warned the authorities."

Seconds later we were over the strait that separated Java from Madura.

"Where are we going?" Sir Gregory asked.

"To Pamekasan," Thomas replied. "It's the largest city on the island. We'll have to avoid the Japanese and contact Bennie."

We crossed the bridge, and a mountainous island similar to Java's terrain became visible. As we approached the distant shore, I saw a row of shacks along the water with fishing boats of many different colors anchored in the cove. A large pagoda, a tiered tower with multiple eaves, overlooked the harbor, signaling the presence and protection of Buddha. Once on the island, we passed a throng of villages bound together by an overflowing population before we entered the outskirts of Pamekasan. A boulevard bordered the railroad; a row of enemy trucks patrolled beside us.

"Won't the Japanese be at the terminal?" I asked.

"Probably," Thomas said. "We'll just have to be careful."

Pamekasan, which was originally an old fishing town that grew to an urban center, hugged the coast and sprawled around an ancient harbor. It was a quaint city but hardly spectacular, marked by narrow, winding streets crammed with crowds. The natives were mainly working class, fishermen and merchants, and most of the city's dwellings reflected these occupations.

The train chugged into the terminal, belching steam as it crawled to a stop. A sizable Japanese force, numbering a hundred or more, wandered around the rail yard and the adjacent streets, intermingled with a thousand city residents. If nothing else, the Dutch East Indies had no shortage of people.

Once the train stopped, we peered out cautiously, watching the enemy make preparations to unload. Thomas inched forward and surveyed the area.

"Wait here," he whispered. Then he disappeared.

Sir Gregory had his arm wrapped protectively around Lady Jane. She was afraid; he was apprehensive. I was tired and frightened. The Japanese were everywhere, no matter where we went. Several minutes later, Thomas reappeared.

"Lady Jane," he said. "Follow me. I'll be back for you two."

"Hurry!" I hissed. I didn't like sitting in a train with a hundred of the enemy nearby, all within shooting distance.

Lady Jane climbed from the boxcar, and they vanished beneath it. Sir Gregory and I had no idea where they were going. There was nothing to do but wait.

He returned a few moments later and motioned us to follow. We slipped beneath the boxcar and were about to dash for safety when we heard Japanese voices. Soldiers were approaching.

Five men appeared, surveying the train and its contents. They paused at the boxcar in front of ours, engaged in an animated discussion. As the minutes passed their conversation continued; they didn't seem to be leaving.

We waited, open and vulnerable, hidden only by the framework of the railcar. Ten feet from us vegetation provided an adequate screen, but those few feet seemed like miles.

One soldier walked away, but the others continued their discussion. I held my breath; my heart felt like it was in my throat.

A few minutes later the men strolled towards the front of the train. Once they were gone, Thomas led us a hundred feet down the tracks, moving through the foliage that skirted the rails and into a wooded area beyond.

When we entered the underbrush, we found Lady Jane waiting. "Why did you leave me alone?" she asked, alarmed and confused. "You were gone for a long time. Someone could have found me. What happened?"

"Nothing really," Thomas said, downplaying the potential altercation. "Just a minor delay."

"Did the soldiers see you?" she asked. Her blue eyes, normally twinkling with life, were piercing and accusing.

He shook his head. "No, they have no idea we're here. So let's keep it that way. Come on. We'd better hurry."

Thomas led us through the trees and shrubs that bordered the rail yard. After traveling about a quarter mile, dragging our bags behind us, we emerged from the woods and into a jungle of whitewashed houses and stores cluttered on narrow lanes. The harbor was visible in the distance, and the sun sparkled off the blue-green water.

We wandered through the crowded streets amid the stares of curious people. Since the island was a Dutch colony there was a sprinkling of Caucasians, but Lady Jane seemed to attract the attention of those we passed. I'm not sure if it was due to her poignant beauty or the golden color of her hair, and I hoped it wasn't due to posters placed by the Japanese. I dreaded the consequences should the enemy ask the locals if they had seen any strangers. She finally withdrew a scarf from her bag and wrapped it around her head, blending more closely with the resident women, many of whom covered their hair.

I watched her as we walked through the streets, her head high, her cheeks flushed. She had been quiet during the last leg of our journey. I suspected she was not only rattled by her near death but also confused by her emotions. There was a bond between Thomas and her; their embrace had proved that. I supposed the light banter and flirting they continually exchanged was not as innocent as I'd thought.

And then there was Sir Gregory. Proud and confident, rigid and disciplined, he had spent a lifetime waiting for her. He desperately held on to that dream, watching helplessly as it slowly slipped away. But I was also part of the equation. Although Maggie kept one of my feet firmly planted in London, the other trailed Lady Jane wherever she went.

There were a few Japanese soldiers mixed with the pedestrians, but we stayed a few feet apart, shielded by the locals, and none seemed to notice. There were so many people mingling in the streets, native, foreigner, and conqueror, that faces merged in a collage of motion and soon became indistinguishable. Even for the enemy.

After a twenty-minute walk, we left the populated area and entered a more suburban setting that marked the outer reaches of the city. We climbed a small hill that sat beside the harbor where we could see fishing boats fanned across the waves. The docks were directly below us, functional and teeming with activity. The enemy didn't interfere with daily life; they knew a thriving economy meant less risk of resistance.

The houses grew sparser the farther we traveled. Thomas led us to one dwelling that faced the harbor, a charming white-washed bungalow with a red-tiled roof. It was nicely landscaped with shrubs spaced around a small yard and offered generous views of the ocean, the city of Pamekasan, and the coast of Java, near Surabaya, which was almost a hundred miles away.

"Who lives here?" Sir Gregory asked when Thomas led us to the door.

"A friend," Thomas replied. "Although it's vacant now. We'll be safe here while we arrange our escape with Bennie."

"What if we can't find Bennie?" Lady Jane asked. "How will we get out of here?"

Thomas pointed to the boats rolling on the waves. "There are a thousand ways."

CHAPTER 42

We entered the cottage to find it clean, functionally furnished, and cozy. A large telescope was placed against a corner window in the front room facing the sea. I imagined the owner had spent many pleasant hours watching ships or the rolling ocean waves. But as we toured our temporary home, I suspected it had another purpose. In the back room, which served as a kitchen, a short wave radio was propped on a table. A stack of maps sat beside it. Suddenly the cottage no longer reminded me of a bucolic, seacoast retreat. I envisioned it was much more.

"Relax," Thomas said. "Treat the home as your own." He moved to the radio, made some adjustments to the dials that decorated its face, and started speaking into the microphone.

"Java Three, Java Three, come in."

He repositioned a toggle switch and I heard a raspy, crackling sound. He turned it back off.

"Java Three, Java Three, come in."

We stood there staring at him, our mouths agape.

"What are you doing?" Lady Jane asked.

"I'm trying to find Bennie," he said.

"Java Three, Java Three, come in."

I thought his behavior peculiar, but I wasn't that surprised. I had long suspected that Van der Meer, Bennie and Thomas, and possibly Chin, were much more than what they seemed. Smugglers, spies, I couldn't say for sure, but the pieces of the puzzle were starting to fit together.

"Java Three, Java Three, come in."

I walked into the front room, keeping an ear trained on the short wave communication. I couldn't resist the telescope, and I walked over to peer through it. It was locked into position: the angle, direction, and magnification were fixed. I placed my eye up to the lens and peered through.

I was startled by the image it displayed. The telescope was trained on the naval base at Surabaya. I was staring directly at a Japanese cruiser. I could see it perfectly: its name and serial number stenciled on the hull, the number of guns pointing skyward, Japanese sailors strolling on deck, and officers manning the control tower.

I returned to the kitchen, my suspicions answered. Thomas still sat at the radio, frantically trying to reach Bennie, while Lady Jane and Sir Gregory observed with befuddled looks upon their faces.

"Java Three, Java Three, come in."

The radio crackled and hissed, and then the answer came. "This is Java Three. Identify."

"Java Three, this is Java Two, current location Pamekasan. In need of transport. Can you assist?"

"Negative. Current location Timor. Can arrive in three days."

"Negative. Too late. Will advise of meet location later. Signing off."

He switched off the radio, sighing as he did so. "That's not good," he said. Bennie is three days away. On the island of Timor. We have to find another way to Australia."

"You're spies, aren't you?" I asked.

He didn't answer; his stern expression didn't change.

"I looked through the telescope," I added.

He studied me for a moment, and then he glanced at Sir Gregory and Lady Jane. But his eyes fixed on Lady

Jane. "We all make different contributions to the war effort."

"I suspected as much," Sir Gregory said. "I wondered how you knew so much about what the Japanese were doing. And you're way too comfortable with that knife."

"Who is Java One?" Lady Jane asked.

"Van der Meer," Thomas replied. "He runs the operation."

"Why did you ever become a spy?" I asked. I had to admit I found it interesting, but it was also extremely dangerous. I guessed that spies had short life spans.

He took a deep breath and then met my gaze. "Shanghai," he said tersely.

"What happened in Shanghai?" I asked. It was the third time he had mentioned it.

"Stay here," he said. He walked to the door. "I'm going to the waterfront to find a sympathetic captain."

After he left we exchanged apprehensive glances, puzzled by his behavior, somewhat stunned by his revelation.

"Are the Japanese chasing us because of Jane, or are they trying to catch Thomas?" Sir Gregory asked.

He had a valid point. Maybe the Japanese knew Thomas was a spy, and they thought Lady Jane was with him. It was an interesting theory, extremely credible, and one that should influence our future decisions.

"That certainly changes everything," I said. "If the Japanese are on to Thomas, they probably also know he was involved in killing Hakkan. Maybe it isn't Lady Jane they're chasing."

"Does it really matter?" Lady Jane posed. "They are after us regardless. We need to focus on getting to

Australia, which Thomas is doing."

I made a mental note of how she'd defended him. "How could we not know they were spies," I said. "Think of all the clues. Were we denying it or just ignoring it?"

"Probably both," said Sir Gregory. "But it places us in a dangerous position."

"I think it's intriguing," Lady Jane remarked. "They're doing more to end the war than we are, at risk of capture or discovery on a daily basis, forsaking any personal life to serve the war effort. I think they're very brave, not to mention how cunning they must be to continually outsmart the enemy. Actually, I find the whole concept extremely exciting. I wish I was part of it."

I didn't reply. I was surprised by her reaction, but maybe it explained her interest in Thomas.

We spent the remainder of the day relaxing, watching ships waltz in the harbor below, and waiting for Thomas to return. I took out my notebook, having neglected my writing for the last few days, and filled pages with descriptions of all we had seen and experienced, and what we now faced. I also detailed Japanese activity in Java and Madura, focusing on the Surabaya naval base. In a section reserved for personal reflection I wrote about Lady Jane.

Each day I notice something different about her, unless it's just a change in the way I perceive her, or maybe it's a change in me. When I'd first met her, I was overwhelmed by her smile; it seemed like it lit the universe it was so bright and warm, and I was sure it was a reflection of her as a person. But maybe it was only what I'd wanted to see. Or more accurately, what I'd needed to see.

I appreciate characteristics that Thomas and Sir

Gregory will never detect: how cute her upturned nose is, how infectious her laugh can be, how intently she listens, eyebrows flexed, when something interests her. Or the subtle differences in how she arranges her hair and how stunning she looks when she pins it up on her head and exposes the graceful curve of her neck. And they aren't aware of how caring and compassionate she is; they can't sense her need to protect the weak from the strong. Nor can they see that she views each day as a new adventure, determined to make it better than the last. They don't see any of this. But I do.

I often wonder what her future holds. She stands at a crossroads in her life. Will she turn back, returning to India and a time and place she's already known, mired in tradition and history and conformity? Or will she forge ahead, to parts unknown, seeking new adventures and challenges. And more importantly, who will stand beside her?

Thomas returned just as we were about to have dinner. "There are a few potentials," he said. "I'm going back later tonight."

"You found some willing captains?" I asked.

He shrugged. "It depends. It's amazing how interested someone becomes when you offer them enough money."

"What happens to the cottage when we leave?" Lady Jane asked.

"It stays as is," he said. "Van der Meer owns it. Along with several others. He established the outposts for our use."

We finished our dinner, cheese and fruit and juice, while we watched the activity on the harbor. It was a serene setting, fishing vessels returning with their day's catch, a few pleasure vessels, and an occasional Japanese patrol boat. We retired early. Lady Jane used one bedroom while Sir Gregory, Thomas, and I shared the other.

The night was hot and humid, and I slept restlessly. I awoke near 1 a.m., wet with perspiration, and realized Thomas was gone. I searched the yard and cottage with the exception of Lady Jane's room, but I couldn't find him. I assumed he went for a walk along the harbor, seeking the ocean breeze to escape the heat. I went back to sleep.

The sun had just risen when I heard the cottage door open followed by the sound of light footsteps. A few seconds later I felt a hand on my shoulder.

"I'm sorry, George," Thomas whispered. "I don't mean to startle you. But it's time to leave. I arranged passage on one of the ships. We have to hurry."

I awoke Sir Gregory. We gathered our belongings while Thomas tapped on Lady Jane's door. In hushed whispers he explained our situation.

"Do you trust this captain?" Lady Jane asked.

"I don't really know him," Thomas said. "But he's leaving for New Guinea. It's not Australia, but at least it gets us out of here. He said he would only wait one hour, so we have to hurry."

"Why aren't the Japanese harassing ships?" Lady Jane asked.

"They don't want to disrupt the local economy," Thomas said. "The more people that earn a living, the less will be dependent on them. And whatever they produce can be purchased or a percentage confiscated by the Japanese."

"Then we should be able to come and go as we

please," she replied. "There's no one to stop us."

"It's not that simple," he said. "The Japanese still watch the waterfront, and I'm sure they have patrol boats randomly search vessels as they leave the harbor."

We left for the docks, maintaining a wary eye for the enemy. The full face of the sun still rested on the eastern horizon, sitting on the ocean and spreading hues of yellow, orange, magenta, and red across the sky. A truck approached as we passed the main road, but we hid behind some vegetation and then hurried down the hillside. When we reached the wharf, Thomas led us to a distant section of the pier where some of the larger boats prepared to cast off. After scanning the area, he came to an abrupt halt, startled and confused.

"They left without us," he said. "I was sure he was going to wait."

"What made you so certain?" Sir Gregory asked.

"The captain was a fellow Frenchman," Thomas said. "I trusted him."

"So what do we do now?" Sir Gregory wondered.

"Can we find another boat?" Lady Jane asked.

We were in a dangerous position. Although there were many white people on the docks intermixed with locals, it was clear they all earned a living from the sea: fisherman, tenders, laborers, and the merchants who supplied them. We had no reason to be there, no purpose or position. We looked suspicious, standing there with our baggage, and even those who worked the docks and were accustomed to minding their own business had started to stare.

I saw a Javanese man on the deck of the boat beside us. He was watching us closely, eavesdropping on our conversation.

"U schijnt om in probleem te zijn," he said in Dutch. "You seem to be in trouble."

We looked at him suspiciously, wondering if he had ulterior motives. We didn't know who to trust.

"I'll talk to him," Thomas said.

He boarded the trawler, and he and the man conversed in hushed tones.

"Look!" Lady Jane said.

A truck was at the end of the dock. It was moving slowly in our direction, the driver stopping periodically to pose questions to those on the wharf.

"Thomas," I called. I pointed at the approaching enemy.

The conversation became more animated. After several seconds of discussion, Thomas handed the captain some money. The man smiled and crossed his arms. He looked towards the Japanese truck.

"Hurry, Thomas!" Lady Jane said.

The vehicle came closer. Thomas looked at the truck and then handed the man more money. The captain shook his head.

"Thomas, do something!" shrieked Lady Jane.

"We've got to get out of here," Sir Gregory said, eyeing the captain with disgust. "Let's try another boat."

Thomas started to retreat when the captain grabbed his arm. They traded words, the discussion brief, and then he again held out his hand. Thomas gave him one more bill, but I couldn't see the denomination. They shook hands.

"He'll take us," Thomas said, the irritation on his face evident. "Come on. Let's hurry."

The truck driver saw us boarding and increased his speed. The docks were filled with people, preparing to cast off for their daily excursion, and they hampered the enemy's progress.

The captain motioned to the crew and issued a command in Javanese. A half dozen sailors reacted, the engines started, and the lines were cast off. We chugged out to sea, just as the truck halted in front of our vessel.

The soldiers scampered to the edge of the dock, pointing to the ship and yelling. Some leveled their rifles, but no shots were fired. The distance between us grew, and they eventually got back in the truck and drove away. We continued cruising through the harbor, and minutes later we sped to the sanctity of the open seas. No Japanese patrol boats were nearby, but one was visible on the distant horizon, towards Surabaya. It didn't pursue us.

Once our safety was assured, we were introduced to the captain. He seemed friendly enough, a thin man with black hair and a smile that never left his face even when it shouldn't be there. I just didn't like his negotiating tactics.

"Where are we going?" I asked.

"Australia," Thomas said. ""We should be in Darwin in three or four days."

The crew were all Javanese, none of whom spoke English. Most knew a spattering of Dutch while the captain spoke the language fluently. I suspected from some of his reactions to our conversations that he spoke English also. After proper introductions, we were led to two cabins. They were small, as you'd expect on a trawler, but clean. Lady Jane would occupy one while Thomas, Sir Gregory, and I shared the second.

"Not exactly a world-class hotel," Sir Gregory observed with a grin.

"I suppose it's better than sleeping on deck," I said.

"Not by much," he replied. "But I'm not

complaining given where we've slept recently."

We stowed our belongings and went topside, watching Madura disappear behind us and the coast of Java pass beside us. We had escaped. The Japanese were gone; we were destined for Australia and the next chapter of our lives.

Thomas went to the bridge to discuss something with the captain while Sir Gregory and Lady Jane sat on a bench by the stern. They seemed to be involved in a personal discussion, one that didn't deserve to be interrupted. I hesitated a second before I strolled away and overheard a bit of the conversation. Sir Gregory was asking Lady Jane to come back to India with him, and he seemed to present a strong case. They had spent most of their lives together, their families were intertwined, they were of the same culture, class, and custom. I couldn't hear Lady Jane, so I wasn't sure if she commented or concurred. As badly as I wanted to move closer so I could eavesdrop, I respected their privacy and walked away.

I went to the ship's bow and leaned against the railing. With the enemy behind us, and Australia in front of us, I needed to make some decisions. My original commitment to my boss at the *Times* had been hopelessly blown off course; I had barely spent a week in Singapore. Now I had the opportunity to return to London. Or I could stay in Australia, still running from Maggie's memory. Somehow, I didn't think that was the right thing to do. I couldn't escape from a shadow. I had to accept what had happened and move on. I still had a life to live. I resolved to return to London.

Even though I had arrived at a logical conclusion, I still hadn't convinced myself. As badly as I missed London and my family and my dog and the *London Times* office and the dozens of other things that make someplace home, there was something that London didn't have, and that was Lady Jane.

CHAPTER 43

The sun streamed through the porthole, announcing the arrival of another perfect day. I stretched and yawned, saw that Sir Gregory slept soundly, snoring just a bit, but Thomas had already departed. He probably wandered the ship, talking to the crew and learning the unknown. I listened to the waves beat against the hull for a few moments, mystified by the perfect rhythm they maintained, before I dressed and went topside.

We traveled due east, using the calmer seas near the many islands that stretched from the shores of Java. I made a mental note of where we were. I knew we had left the southeast coast of Java, passed just south of Bali and then skimmed beside the irregular coast of Sumbawa. I studied the scenery as masses of land, green and mountainous and majestic, glided by on the horizon. Vessels of various sizes, from tiny fishing boats with a single occupant to massive ships carrying the world's cargo, sailed the same waters. And so did a Japanese patrol boat.

It had appeared just as we reached the shores of Sumbawa, cruising through the waves, hugging the coast. It maintained a measured distance, not close enough for us to see those on board, but near enough to see the Japanese flag and the guns that sat on deck. The captain and crew watched it warily. We did too. It was hard to determine if they were following us, had the same destination, or were only traveling beside us for a brief stretch of our journey.

Later that day after we neared the western coast of the island of Sumba, we charted a southeasterly course to the open seas. Our Japanese shadow did the same. The possibility of a coincidence was rapidly diminishing. Now we wondered when and where they would attack.

Thomas and I were watching the enemy, wary of their motives, when Sir Gregory told us the captain wanted us. He collected Lady Jane, and then met Thomas and me on the bridge. The captain and his mate were there with one of the crew. They faced us with grim looks on their faces. The remaining crewman then gathered near the two entrances. They had rifles with them.

"I forgot to mention that I had actually planned on going to Sumba," the captain said in broken English. "That's where I unload my cargo."

The tension was suffocating. The crew fingered their rifles; the captain studied us arrogantly, his arms folded across his chest.

"That's not a problem," Thomas said. "We can get off in Sumba. We'll find another way to Australia."

"It's not that simple," the captain replied.

"Why not?" Thomas asked.

"Because I don't want to take you to Sumba."

"But we paid for transport to Australia," Sir Gregory reminded him.

I could tell by the crew's expression that nothing pleasant would result from this conversation. I looked at Lady Jane. She showed defiance, a bit of anger, a little fear.

"Your money was well invested," the captain said. "You escaped the Japanese."

"What are you going to do with us?" I asked.

He nodded to the crew. A sailor approached each of us with rifles drawn, the barrels poking our backs. Amid our protests they prodded us on deck, opposite the patrol boat trailing us. They led us towards the stern where a wooden rowboat was waiting. Our bags were already in it.

"I'm too kind to kill you," the captain said.

"So you cast us adrift?" Thomas asked.

The captain shrugged. "It seems like a good compromise."

"We'll never survive," Sir Gregory interjected.

"That's your problem, not mine," he said. "I want no trouble with the Japanese. And they've followed us for a day. If they decide to board this ship, you won't be on it. And that's not negotiable."

The crew lowered the rowboat over the side, and it splashed into the water. Two ropes attached to each end kept it tethered to the ship's rail. Once the boat was situated, the crew forced us over the side and down a rope ladder. They motioned for Sir Gregory to go first. Lady Jane followed.

"You're next," the captain said to me. He was smiling, as he always did, and I remembered why I didn't like it. Bennie had worn the same sly smile when he'd slit the Japanese soldiers' throats.

I climbed down into the rowboat. Thomas was last. Then they let the line loose. The boat bobbed on the waves, moving slowly away from the mother ship. The ocean stretched before us, reaching the horizon in all directions. There was no land in sight.

The captain waved. "Have a nice trip."

CHAPTER 44

The freighter and Japanese patrol boat continued on course and were soon just specks on the horizon. Either the enemy wasn't interested, or they'd never even seen us. Both ships chugged along, heading southeast with no decrease in speed.

I didn't think anything could be worse than fleeing the Japanese, but the vast expanse of water surrounding us offered a more formidable enemy: Mother Nature. The rolling waves and surging tides controlled our destiny. We would probably die of thirst or starvation before we were ever found. Every prior obstacle we had faced could be attacked and confronted, combated and conquered. But not the ocean.

It was an overwhelming realization with no conceivable outcome but death. I thought about how I would live my life differently if I survived. I would treasure family and friends, savoring every second I shared with those I loved. I would make amends with those I hadn't treated well and thank those who influenced me or shaped my future. I would strive to be a better person, to appreciate the beauty that surrounds us, and to enjoy every waking moment I was fortunate enough to experience. If I only had another chance.

"We do have oars," Sir Gregory offered. "And I was a champion oarsman at Oxford."

"We don't even know which direction to go," Thomas said. "George, do you have any idea where we are?"

I thought about it for a moment. I recalled the islands we passed, comparing them to maps I had memorized as a child and those that were on the table in the cottage, beside the radio. I definitely wasn't as sharp as I used to be. If I could only remember more detail.

"I'm not completely sure," I said. "But I think we're southwest of the island of Sumba. If we row northeast we should reach land. But I don't know how far away it is."

"Then we'll row northeast," Lady Jane said, confident in my mental abilities.

Sir Gregory and I started rowing. He quickly showed the technique he had learned in college, and we were propelled across the waves. Unfortunately, given the size of the boat compared to the strength of the sea, it didn't appear that we were making much progress.

It took very little time for me to tire. I didn't have the physical stamina to continue, especially not at the pace Sir Gregory set.

"Can you keep up with me, George?" he asked, eyeing me with concern.

"I'm trying," I said, pulling the oars forcefully, sweat dripping from my forehead.

"That's it," he coaxed. "Keep rowing. You're doing well. Establish a rhythm. Use your legs and body weight more than your arms."

I was gasping. My muscles burned. "I tire very easily. It's from a childhood illness."

"We should stop rowing," Thomas said. "We're at the mercy of the tides anyway. Let's just drift on the waves."

"While we die of thirst," Sir Gregory mumbled. He put down the oars and surveyed the horizon.

"I have some gin," Thomas said. He withdrew a bottle from his knapsack.

Sir Gregory frowned. "That will make us thirstier."

Thomas emptied his knapsack. It contained two quarts of gin, a box of cigars, some fruit and cheese, several sets of clothes and five large bundles of money.

"We won't last two days with those provisions," Sir Gregory said. "We'll have to find a way to get water. And maybe catch fish."

It could have been worse. The men on the freighter could have killed us. Or they could have kept our belongings. At least we had some hope.

Thomas repacked his knapsack, leaving out a bottle of gin. "We won't eat until morning." He took a healthy swig.

He handed the bottle to me. I passed and offered the gin to Lady Jane and Sir Gregory. Each took a sip but refused when offered more.

The skies were overcast, clouds hiding the sun, and rain seemed imminent. Thomas spent the next hour arranging some canvas in an attempt to capture raindrops. It was a good idea, although I doubted it would work. We had to try something, and, if nothing else, it occupied our time.

When night arrived, the cloudy sky produced a blackness so opaque we could barely see our hands in front of our faces. Sounds from the rolling waves lulled us to sleep, soothing and serene and interrupted only by our boat's creaking clapboards as they protested the strain the ocean placed on them.

We slept sporadically. It was difficult to be comfortable in the body of the boat, and the strangeness from complete darkness, the moon and stars not offering any light, made us uneasy. We knew we were in danger; we just didn't know from what. Thomas, Sir Gregory, and I took turns standing watch, but if land was near, it was invisible in the dark. We barely even saw the relentless waves.

When the sun peeked over the horizon, we found that a light rain had left about four ounces of water in Thomas's container. We rejoiced at our good fortune and decided to enjoy the precious liquid. Thomas carefully poured some water into the lid of the gin bottle and gave it to Lady Jane. She savored it thankfully, like a fine French wine. He refilled the cap.

"Keep the moisture in your mouth for a moment," he suggested. "You'll enjoy it even more."

She followed his advice. As the liquid bathed her gums, a look of bliss crossed her face.

I was served next. I gratefully consumed my portion and was amazed at how enjoyable two sips of water could be.

Sir Gregory took his two sips, and then Thomas drained the remainder of the life-saving fluid into his mouth. It might be the last water we ever tasted.

When the sun crept higher the heat became unbearable. After a brief discussion, we voted to skip our midday meal, hoping to conserve what little rations remained. We tried to catch fish, fashioning a spear out of one end of an oar, but it was far more difficult than we'd believed. As our efforts continued, we spent the afternoon talking about the war, Singapore, Europe, and then more personal matters.

"I've known Jane since she was a child," Sir Gregory said. "I'm twelve years older than her, so I watched her grow up. Even as a youngster she was different, a bit difficult. No one could tell her what to do. And if they tried, she did the opposite."

"Gregory, I'm sure they don't want to hear about

my childhood," Lady Jane said sweetly.

"No, we would," Thomas said, urging him on. "Tell us."

Sir Gregory continued. "My first memory of Jane was when she had just arrived in India. Our families were driving in New Delhi when we approached a traffic light. Jane had never seen one, and was fascinated by the device. She was convinced that little fairies were inside, changing the colors. I think that's when I fell in love with her. And the years since haven't changed that."

He made me feel guilty. I had no right to love her. Sir Gregory had lived his entire life for her, seeing no future without her in it.

"You're certainly quiet, George," Thomas said. "What's bothering you?"

I didn't want my jealousy to show. I decided to change the subject.

"Shanghai," I said.

Thomas tensed noticeably, and his face was consumed with a look of absolute anguish. "I don't want to talk about it," he said.

Lady Jane moved beside him, her blond hair blowing in the breeze. "Maybe it would help if you did."

Sir Gregory studied him curiously, stroking his goatee as he often did when deep in thought. "Yes, it might. Any psychiatrist would tell you that. And you can trust us."

"It's very personal," he said softly. "And very painful. I don't think it's a good idea."

I looked at the horizon; water stretched in all directions. The sun streamed from the sky, burning our skin and parching our lips. There was no land in sight. We were unable to catch any fish, and we had a limited amount of food and water.

"It's not like any of us will live to tell anyone," I said quietly.

There was silence for a moment, and I think we all confronted our own demons. They suddenly seemed dwarfed when compared to what we now faced.

"It might lessen the pain," Lady Jane said. "Or at least mute the voices that won't let you forget."

Her statement seemed to move him and he closed his eyes tightly for a moment, willing away the unwanted images. He took a deep breath, searched our faces for signs of sincerity, his blue eyes dim and lacking the love of life they normally displayed, and finally wavered.

"I worked for a French bank," he said softly. "I was involved in international investments. The bank sent me to Shanghai. Van der Meer was there too."

He paused. It was difficult for him to maintain his composure; his voice cracked, his face was gray, his lips quivered. But he continued. "I had a family. A wonderful wife named Jeanette. We were childhood sweethearts."

He smiled for a moment, forgetting the pain. "On the first day of school, when we were five or six years old, she gave me half of her raspberry pastry at lunch. And from that day forward, I had no interest in anyone else."

The smile faded and the pain returned. "She was so fascinating: intelligent, loving, kind, and compassionate. And she was funny. Everyone liked her because she made them laugh. She was such a beautiful woman with long flowing blond hair and blue eyes that seemed to hold the secrets of the universe."

I looked at Lady Jane. She hadn't noticed the physical similarity, but I did. Her image mirrored Jeannette's. Maybe the Japanese thought Lady Jane was

Jeannette and she and Thomas had killed Hakkan together. It was an interesting theory.

"She sounds like a remarkable woman," Sir Gregory said softly.

"She was," he said, pain distorting his face, his heart twisted and torn and tattered, teaching us all what it meant to truly love someone.

Lady Jane touched his arm, her fingers lightly caressing him, urging him to continue.

"We had two enchanting little daughters, Emilie and Chantel. They were four and six years old. Emilie looked like her mother, blond hair and blue eyes. She was a little comedienne who loved to play practical jokes." He paused, finding it difficult to speak. "Chantel was like me, a mop of brown hair, blue eyes as deep as a tropical sea, and the curiosity of a cat. We had a fabulous life together."

He stopped talking, his lips taut. I envisioned the images of the two children, etched forever in his mind, frozen in time.

"What happened?" I asked quietly.

"The Japanese invaded. They were ruthless barbarians, capable of unimaginable acts of brutality. Hakkan led the attack." He took a deep breath and raised his head. His eyes, misty and dull, met each of ours in turn. "He killed my wife and daughters."

My heart was in my throat, tears clouding my eyes. I remembered the attack. It was in 1938. I had written several articles about it. By all accounts, the Japanese had been brutal, but I never understood how deeply that knife had sliced until now.

I could feel his pain like a hand grasping my heart and ripping it from my body. He had lost Jeannette. His anguish only highlighted mine, bringing it back to life. I wasn't the only one to grieve and suffer. Thomas did too. And much worse than me. My hurt was magnified in him many times over.

I was also overcome by how quickly life can change. It had taken only a few minutes, one bad decision, to take Maggie away. Thomas had lost his family just as quickly. Minutes come and go as life goes on, so trivial and routine, but during the course of a lifetime, there are a handful that make and shape you, determine your future and define your past. Sometimes we don't even notice them.

"Thomas, that is so tragic," Lady Jane whispered. She took him in her arms, cradling him in a protective canopy.

"I'm sorry," I said. I regretted having asked him. It was a reporter's instinct, I suppose, but I had to know the truth. It was a personal characteristic that was both a blessing and a curse.

"My condolences also," Sir Gregory added. "You said Hakkan personally?"

"Yes, my home was commandeered by the occupation forces. Hakkan tied me to a chair, murdered Jeannette in front of me, then went after my daughters."

Tears started to drip down his face. He made no effort to wipe them away. "Jeanette was left lying on the floor in front of me, her eyes locked with mine, the life draining from her body. She told me over and over and over again how much she loved me. Then she died. In reality, I died too. Emilie and Chantel were murdered, each holding their favorite dolls, like two little angels. Their screams will haunt me for all of eternity."

He finally broke down, crying uncontrollably, his body heaving, tears flowing down his face and dripping onto his shirt. He looked at us, pain and sorrow chiseled in every wrinkle of his face, trying to understand why something so horrible had ever happened.

"Why didn't they kill me?" he sobbed. "Why didn't they just kill me?"

We cried with him.

By early evening our lips were parched and dry, and both thirst and fatigue had started to overwhelm us. When twilight shadowed the waves, we ate the remainder of the cheese and a quarter of our melons, the latter serving to quench our thirst.

Darkness arrived, but there were fewer clouds, and the hint of a moon and a sky sprinkled with stars made the evening less eerie. There was still no land visible in any direction. We were all quiet; an aura of despair had shrouded the boat. I think we were all reflecting on our lives, and, unavoidably, our deaths. I wasn't afraid to die, but I wasn't yet ready either.

"I had hoped to see Paris again," Thomas said softly. "It's such a charming city, alive and vibrant with the greatest culture and architecture in the world. Even the bridges that cross the River Seine are beautiful. I was born there. Not in the best neighborhood, but one that offered a happy childhood. To this day I can still smell the pastries at the corner bakery even though the store closed many years ago."

Lady Jane smiled. "I have limited memories of Ulster where I was born at our country estate southwest of Belfast. I remember the moss that covered the ground near a swift country stream. I would lie there and imagine shapes in the clouds drifting by."

"When did you go to India?" I asked.

"When I was very young," she said. "Five years

old, I think. After my father was accused of helping the Kaiser during the Great War. We rarely returned to Ulster after that, maybe two or three times, but we did holiday in London. I liked living in India. It was different, mystical but mundane."

"I miss London," I said softly. "My family, my favorite pub, the excitement of living in the most important city in the world." I was quiet for a moment. "But I treasure the memories."

"Memories are nice," Lady Jane said. "But dreams are better."

We again took turns standing watch, still maintaining hope that we would soon be washed upon some distant shore. The boat, though now familiar, had become cramped and crowded. Our plight, tentative and anxious, had become frustrating and desperate and intolerable. Its outcome was beyond our control.

Not having slept well the last two evenings, we were weary enough to sleep soundly. We even ignored the gnawing hunger pangs, and the rhythmic breathing of slumber was soon upon us.

When Thomas awakened me to stand my watch, I found my mouth drier than I had ever thought possible. I sat upright, sensing the fatigue, and struggled to survey the horizon. I took a swig of gathered water, and it alleviated my obsessive desire for moisture.

I slumped in my seat and scanned the sea, my view encompassing all directions. Since it was our first evening truly free of clouds, I was soon preoccupied by the stars that lit the southern skies.

"The stars are quite beautiful tonight, aren't they?"

It was Thomas. His voice startled me. I was surprised he was still awake.

"Yes," I said. "They're very bright."

"I was always interested in the stars," he continued. "Did you know that navigators since the beginning of time have determined their location by using the stars?"

"That's right," I said. "They have. And maybe we can too."

He went on to name many of the stars that sparkled in the pre-dawn skies. I was impressed with his knowledge, and I was certain he could steer us to safety, just as mariners had done for centuries.

"So where are we now?" I asked.

He gazed at the sky for several seconds and rubbed his chin. He looked at me gravely and replied with the utmost seriousness. "I have absolutely no idea." He broke into a fit of laughter.

I laughed too.

"You've been a good friend," I said after some reflection. "Probably the best I've ever had."

"The same to you," he replied. "I've always been close to Van der Meer; our lives have been intertwined for many years. But I also count you as a dear friend."

"If we ever get out of this, I would like to preserve that."

"No question," he said, as if the mere thought of anything else was unthinkable. "Our lives will be shared, just like mine and Van der Meer's."

"Will you go back for him?"

"Absolutely," he replied. "No other thought ever crossed my mind."

It was silent for a moment, as we each studied the stars.

"I suppose Lady Jane will go with you," I said.

He sat up, studying me in the moonlight. "Why do

you say that?"

"Because you're in love with her. And she's in love with you."

He sighed, and settled back down in the boat. "George, how can you be so perceptive and so blind at the same time?"

Thomas drifted off to sleep, and I returned to scanning the skyline.

Dawn arrived and sunlight filtered across the waves, revealing a distinct shadow in the distance. I studied the shape closely. After fifteen minutes had passed, it grew clearer and larger. I sat upright, peering intently into the distance.

"Thomas!"

He stirred but did not waken. I shook him, pointing to the north. He yawned, sat up, and rubbed his eyes.

"Look!" I yelled. "Land!"

"Row!" Thomas shouted. "Hurry! Before the tides take us past it."

I grabbed one pair of oars while he got the other. The mass appeared to be an island. As we came closer, trees that sprang from its hilly terrain waved to greet us.

"What's going on?" Sir Gregory asked sleepily.

I pointed at the atoll, my face flush with excitement.

He peered intently at the image, his eyes growing wide. "Jane!" he cried. "Land!"

She bolted upright. "Gregory, help them!"

He scrambled to my side. "Let me have the oars, George. I'll get us there."

He quickly proved his capabilities and steered us towards the atoll.

"We're saved!" I screamed.

"George," Thomas said sternly. "Look."

The sun had continued its climb, bathing the island in golden light. It was a small atoll, steep in elevation and dominated by a single hill that occupied most of the terrain. It rose steadily upward in all directions from the shore, reaching a height of several hundred feet at its center.

Perched on top of the hill was a Japanese flag.

CHAPTER 45

We stared at the flag, our elation rapidly replaced with despair. We had escaped death on the water only to meet the enemy on land. The southwest Pacific had become a giant chessboard, and the enemy had countered our every move.

"What should we do?" Lady Jane asked quietly.

Thomas studied the island and then shook his head. "We don't have any choice. We have to get to land."

"It seems fairly remote," I said. "It might just be a lookout post. Maybe there are only a few soldiers."

"Then let's hope they're still asleep," Thomas said. "If not, they'll be waiting for us when we get to shore."

We reached shallow water, and Thomas leaped from the boat and dragged it to shore. We climbed out and helped him, hiding the boat in the vegetation that met the water's edge and then covering it with branches from trees and shrubs.

Judging by the sun's position, we had arrived on the southern coast of the island, in a small cove shaped like a tear drop. We stood on an outcrop of land at the edge of the lagoon but couldn't determine if it was bridged to the island proper or a tiny islet separated from its larger sister. The vegetation was thick, with sporadic stretches of white sand and pools of turquoise water. Black rocks, probably born by volcanic activity, were scattered about the area ranging in size from pebble to boulder. We saw no sign of the enemy.

"We seem to be safe here," Thomas said as he peered through the shrubbery. "At least for now. We'll stay near the boat until we're ready to explore."

"Then we have to find the Japanese," Sir Gregory

added.

The enemy was everywhere. We should have been rejoicing, celebrating our survival. Instead, we were again planning to combat or elude them. Maybe it would have been easier to die at sea, drifting into a deep sleep, too weak to move as life slowly slipped away. But now we had to fight again, and somehow, we had to find the strength to do that.

Thomas had wandered inland a few feet, studying the terrain. "Look," he said. He pointed at trees sprouting large melons. "Let's eat."

We kept a wary eye on the approach to our hideaway. Thomas and Sir Gregory grabbed armfuls of melons, and we sat on the moss carpet and devoured them, overwhelmed with the succulent juice that spewed from the soft core. The sweet liquid bathed our parched lips and mouths and throats, sating our thirst and swelling our bellies.

"That was absolutely delightful," Lady Jane said, licking her lips.

"It was quite nice," Sir Gregory agreed.

"I suppose we need to find the lookouts," Thomas said. "We've lingered long enough."

"Should we all go?" Sir Gregory asked.

"I think it would be safer if you and Lady Jane stayed here," Thomas replied. "George and I will go and explore."

I was surprised he chose me to go with him. He knew I didn't have the strength or stamina that either he or Sir Gregory had. There must be some other quality I had that he sought; I just didn't know what it was.

"Agreed," Sir Gregory said. "While you're gone, I'll find a supply of food and water."

"Come on, George, let's get started," Thomas said.

We ventured from our landing spot and found that we were on a tiny sliver of land at the edge of the lagoon. A twenty foot wide span of water separated where we were from the main atoll. A few rocks and a palm tree lying on its side made it possible to cross the water without swimming through it.

Once we were on the main island, we walked around its circumference, hiding in the vegetation and carefully moving forward. The atoll was small, perhaps a mile around at most. We determined that we were on the southwestern tip, and we saw no sign of enemy activity until we reached the northern edge where we found a small harbor outfitted with a dock. Adjacent to the wooden wharf was an outbuilding, probably housing supplies. There were no Japanese.

"Maybe the island is deserted," I said.

"I don't think so," Thomas replied. "They wouldn't have built this wharf if they weren't going to use it. There has to be something here of value to them. It's either the geographical location, or what you can see from it. Or maybe its position lends well to radio transmittals. I suspect we'll find a Japanese contingent at the peak. Then our questions will be answered."

I pointed to the edge of the outbuilding. "There's a trail from the dock to a higher elevation. If we risk taking it, I'll bet we find the enemy where it ends."

I wasn't eager to face the potential dangers at the end of the trail, but it was the only way to locate the Japanese. If we didn't find them and avoid them, they would surely find us.

"All right," he said. "But let's be cautious."

We proceeded. The path had been hewn through

thick vegetation, and steps had been placed where the elevation was steeper. Considerable effort had been expended to construct it. We cautiously moved forward, climbing the mountain's face that formed the core of the island.

We were almost halfway up when we heard someone coming. They descended from the top, walking quickly, making no effort to conceal themselves. They brushed against tree limbs; their boots banged loudly on the wooden steps.

Thomas put a finger to his lips to signal silence, and then motioned to the shrubs adjacent to the path. We moved through them, carefully parting the branches and hiding ourselves a few feet away, ensuring we couldn't be seen from the path.

A few minutes later a Japanese soldier came bounding down the steps, walking quickly. He was shirtless, wore round black spectacles, and had a white scarf tied around his head. He didn't suspect our presence; the soldiers must not know we were on the island.

My breathing was rapid and shallow; my heart thumped against my chest. I could reach out and touch him, he passed so closely. I fingered the Derringer in my pocket and briefly considered killing him. But then I thought how senseless that would be. I didn't know how many more there were, and there seemed to be an unlimited supply anyway.

We waited until he disappeared from sight. Then we cautiously left our hiding place. Thomas paused on the walkway, searching for any other men. We listened for a moment, observing the landscape in all directions, and then continued.

"He's probably getting supplies at the dock,"

Thomas said. "This must be where they are stationed. I'm sure he'll be back."

"Do you think they saw us land?"

He shrugged and pointed upward. "We'll know when we get there."

We moved up the winding path, walking slowly and deliberately, always watchful of a place to hide if we encountered the enemy.

I was winded and weary, the climb had been physically challenging, the risk had taken its toll mentally. I didn't know how much longer I could continue. When we reached a clearing I looked towards the ocean and saw that we were quite high, several hundred feet, and I didn't think we had much farther to go to reach the summit.

A few minutes later the elevation leveled, and we reached the peak. Thomas motioned me forward, tiptoeing onto a small plain. He guided us behind some shrubs, and we moved around the edge of the clearing. After traveling about seventy feet, we found the camp.

There were four tents perched in the center of a clearing, a large tent flanked by three smaller ones. The sides of all were open to the environment, flaps secured along the sides. The center tent contained a table, upon which sat a series of short wave radios, all attached to a vertical pole beside the tent that acted as an antenna. Three chairs were scattered about the table, two adjacent to the radios and the third just behind them.

Two men sat beside the radios. We could hear them chatting between themselves; they smoked cigarettes. At the edge of the tent several rows of crates were stacked, probably filled with supplies. The smaller tents appeared to be sleeping quarters. I doubted if more than two men could fit comfortably, so I suspected that the camp contained three to six soldiers. Here were two, one was on the trail, so the question was were there more and, if so, where were they? At the perimeter of the encampment were two large telescopes, pointing to the northwest and the south.

We waited patiently, observing them. There was an occasional radio communication, short and limited, but little else occurred. After about fifteen minutes we heard someone approaching. We crouched down farther in our hiding place and saw the soldier we had passed on the trail returning. He carried a wooden crate on his shoulder. Once he reached the main tent, Thomas tapped me on the shoulder and pointed to the pathway.

We reversed our course, crawled to the trail, and started making our way down the hill. It was much easier than climbing up, and we slowed our pace, studying the path in detail and searching for signs of more Japanese, but we saw none. Eventually, some twenty minutes later, we again reached the wharf.

"Let's circle the remainder of the island," Thomas said. "Just to be sure. But I think their presence is limited to that lookout post."

"If they're searching the sea with telescopes and happen to scan the island, they may see us."

"We'll have to be careful," he said. "Do you know where we are?"

"Not exactly, but I think we're east of Sumba, which is a large island and certainly under Japanese control. But the telescopes confuse me. I understand why they are watching the south; an attack could come from Australia. But the telescope facing the northwest doesn't make sense. That area is firmly in Japanese hands, although it's open seas. And what about the east? It's being ignored. That makes me think Sumba is to the east."

"You would know if you could see through the telescope?"

"Oh, yes. I can identify everything. Or I'm sure they have maps. Once I see them, I'll know."

We continued our tour of the island, finding nothing but beautiful scenery: tropical lagoons with palm trees hanging gracefully over aqua water, volcanic rocks smoothly polished by nature, some as large as a small house, flowers with large buds of orange, yellow and lavender, trees sprouting succulent melons, birds and butterflies of every color of the rainbow, and white sandy beaches. There seemed to be few animals and no people, except for us and three of the enemy who inhabited the peak.

We cautiously made our way back, poking through shrubbery and vegetation, circumventing ponds and lagoons, Thomas steadfastly leading the way. I thought of Shanghai and wondered how Thomas had mentally survived such a horrible tragedy. It was difficult enough for me to cope with Maggie's loss. Thomas had lost his wife and children, all dying as he helplessly watched. My stomach churned at the images harbored in his mind, the nightmares they spawned, and the bouts of depression they created. I watched him now, relentlessly pursuing our survival, and I realized what a strong man he was, much stronger than me, and how much adversity he had overcome.

It took several hours to conduct our tour. It was early afternoon when we returned, stepping across the stones and crawling across the downed palm tree to reach our hideaway. When we returned to the rowboat, we found the area deserted. Lady Jane and Sir Gregory were gone.

CHAPTER 46

We cautiously approached the mossy area where we had eaten the melons, and found nothing but the rinds, half eaten by birds and riddled with insects. The rowboat was still beached and hidden as we had left it.

"Something happened to them," I said. "I hope it's not the enemy."

"I don't think it is," Thomas countered. "Our baggage is gone. The Japanese wouldn't have cared about that."

"Maybe they explored a bit of the island looking for fresh water. Or they could have gone to find more food."

I still had doubts about the Japanese force. We had identified three on the summit. Two manned the radios, a third supported them. But there were three tents large enough for two soldiers each. I wondered if three more wandered the island.

First we searched the islet where we had landed, and then we crossed the channel. We tried to stay sheltered, conscious of the telescopes we had seen on top of the hill. Although they seemed to be trained on the open seas, the enemy could easily adjust them to view the island if they had reason to.

"We came from the east after we explored the island and didn't see them," Thomas said. "Let's try moving towards the interior."

"I don't think they've gone far."

We proceeded through the underbrush, looking for signs that the vegetation may have been trampled by footsteps. While Thomas searched for broken branches, crushed grass, and footprints in the sand, I kept a wary eye out for the enemy.

We had moved about forty feet inland, past the undergrowth that hugged the shore to where the elevation started to rise, when we found a cave carved into the rock ten or fifteen feet above ground level. A winding trail led to it, formed by nature rather than man, and Thomas and I quickly made our way to it.

"They've been here," he said.

The cave was about twenty feet long and eight feet wide and offered generous views of the sea. Its southern face was open almost entirely to the ocean, making it more of a cleft in the mountain than a cave, but it would provide adequate shelter and a comfortable place to stay. We found our baggage along the back wall, as well as a stockpile of melons, coconuts, berries, bananas, and yams. Hunger would not be counted among our problems.

"Where could they have gone?" I asked.

"They have to be nearby," he replied. "They must be searching for fresh water."

"I hope they understand the danger."

We continued our search. Above the roof of the cave there was an indentation into the hillside that stretched to the west. We climbed upward and found a tiny plateau that rose slightly before stopping at the steep face of the hillside. The plants and trees sprouted abundant sources of food; they had supplied the stores in the cave.

"We know they were here," Thomas said. "Let's keep going. Be mindful of the telescopes."

We kept moving west, passing through the foliage. The area below was marshy, a swamp where salt water from the sea met fresh water from the island. A waterfall a few feet wide trickled down the hillside.

"Stay hidden," Thomas said. "We still don't know if there are more Japanese."

We stepped furtively through the jungle. After traveling sixty feet, we found another waterfall that originated near the summit, dribbling down the hill, providing unlimited fresh water that was easy to access. It fed a tiny pond, the overflow of which poured into a larger pool some ten feet below. The second pond's runoff had created the waterfall I had seen, spilling into the marsh. As we approached, we saw our canteens and water bottles lying by the upper pond.

We descended and saw Lady Jane and Sir Gregory bathing in the lower pool of water. They wore little clothing, Lady Jane dressed in her batrik and Sir Gregory was shirtless but wearing his trousers. The rest of their clothes were stacked near the water's edge. I felt a twinge of jealousy, watching them frolic in the water.

I sighed with relief. "All of this intrigue for a bath," I said. "Let's go and get them."

I started to exit the underbrush when Thomas held out his arm, stopping me. "Don't move," he whispered.

I looked at him curiously. "What's wrong?"

He pointed to the far edge of the pond to the shrubs that surrounded it. There, hidden in the brush, was the soldier we had seen at the dock. The sunlight reflected off his glasses; his rifle was at the ready.

I was startled. I had been so engrossed in finding Lady Jane and Sir Gregory that I'd forgotten the enemy might be looking for them also. I squinted in the sunlight, trying to see if the jungle hid more than one person.

"Is he alone?" I asked.

"I think so."

"What are we going to do?"

"You wait here. Watch the soldier. Shoot him if you have to."

Before I could protest, he was gone, waging his single-handed effort to defeat the Japanese army, determined to seek revenge for the atrocities of Shanghai, intent on killing every enemy soldier he could find. But I was sick of death. I had seen enough corpses in the last few weeks: vacant eyes, gasps and groans, vanishing souls. From the dead pilot in Singapore to the Japanese in Sumatra, the throats slit by Bennie to General Hakkan, his face turning blue as Thomas squeezed the breath from his despicable body, I had had enough. I couldn't take any more even though I knew it was necessary to survive.

I watched the soldier peering through the underbrush, waiting for the opportunity to capture his prey. I suspected he took a moment to admire Lady Jane, the batrik clinging tightly to her perfect body.

Sir Gregory and Lady Jane were oblivious to the attention, both from us and the soldier. They were enjoying the cool water, sunlight streaming through the trees, the absolute serenity that a tropical paradise offers. As I studied them closely, they seemed to be immersed in each other. Sir Gregory was smiling, touching her shoulders and running a hand over her wet hair. She was laughing, a flirtatious look in her eyes, coyly letting her hand brush against him. It was like the hands of the clock had spun backwards and they were in India again before their relationship had wilted and died. It now seemed very much alive. I didn't know when it had renewed, or to what degree it had recovered, but I didn't like it.

I returned my attention to the soldier. He still stared, watching the couple closely. I found it disturbing that he had no idea his life was about to end. He looked very young. He had joined the army, probably fought many battles, and he had survived. I'm sure he was ecstatic to be assigned to this remote lookout post, enjoying Utopia, free from battle, safe from the enemy. In the unlikeliest place in the entire Pacific Theater, he was about to lose his life, cruelly and coldly, paying for a crime committed by a Japanese general he had never met.

Thomas stealthily approached. The soldier was still unaware, focused on Sir Gregory and Lady Jane. Thomas crept closer. His knife was in his hand. I closed my eyes and prayed for the boy's soul. I had no desire to see another dead body, regardless of the consequences had he lived.

When I opened my eyes a moment later, the soldier was on the ground. Sir Gregory and Lady Jane stood and stared, wide-eyed and mouths agape.

CHAPTER 47

"We've got to capture the lookout post," Thomas said as we regrouped in the cave. "Then we can use the radio to contact Bennie. If he's in Timor he can be here in a day."

"What about the other two soldiers?" I asked.

Thomas patted the rifle he had taken from his latest victim. "We'll use this."

"We're still not sure how many there are," Sir Gregory said. "Should we scout the camp again?"

Thomas thought for a moment before replying. "No, we need to move now. Before the others find their companion."

"But we have less than an hour of daylight," Sir Gregory said.

"We have no choice," Thomas insisted.

We didn't want anyone left at the cave; it was too risky to separate. So we ventured towards the lookout post as darkness rapidly approached. Our progress was slow. We stayed hidden in the underbrush and advanced cautiously, not knowing if more soldiers were looking for us.

"The lookouts are probably studying the island with their telescopes right now," Thomas said. "We have to be careful."

It took much longer to move around the coast at night than it had during the day. We kept close to the beach, pushing through the fringe of vegetation that spread from the sand to the hillside. It took over an hour before we reached the sheltered cove where the wharf was. It was serene, the isolated wooden dock stepping into the harbor, the shack standing guard beside it. There were no lights and no people.

We cautiously traveled the path that Thomas and I had taken earlier in the day. Ever so slowly we advanced, carefully climbing, frightened by every shadow, startled by every noise. We peered into the darkness, trying to make sense of the eerie shapes and shadows the jungle produced, as we listened intently for footsteps, filtering the sounds of the owls and insects.

I knew this would be our most difficult endeavor, much harder than our rescue operations or many escapes from the enemy. Now we would attack, with one rifle, a knife, and a Derringer pistol. It didn't seem like the soundest plan, but it was what we had to do to survive.

When we reached the summit, it was lit with torches placed on poles and spaced evenly around the clearing. Thomas led us from the path into the underbrush where we crawled across the sandy soil, wary of the enemy.

As we entered the edge of the camp, there were three soldiers visible. Two were in the radio tent, studying maps and recording messages. The third was stationed at the telescope, but instead of scanning the sea, he held the lens at a steep angle. He was searching the island. He was looking for us.

"The soldier at the pond makes four," Thomas hissed. "Can two more be sleeping?"

"Probably," I said. "I'm sure they man the radios twenty-four hours a day."

"How can we ever defeat them?" Sir Gregory asked. "We can't shoot five at once."

"We can attack from two directions," I suggested.

"That's a good idea," Thomas said. "All of you circle around behind the tents. Like this." He drew a plan of attack in the sand with a twig. "But let me start the fight.

I'll take the soldier at the telescope. Then let the others focus on me. After the action starts, you attack from behind."

Sir Gregory, Lady Jane, and I moved stealthy through the underbrush, crawling closer towards the tents. I wanted to get near enough to get a good shot with the Derringer but not risk discovery. I only had five bullets. I wouldn't have time to reload; I had to make each one count. If I didn't, we were all dead.

As sick as I was of death, I knew the fight was necessary. There was no other way to survive. But we had to be clever, smarter than the enemy. We were outmanned and outgunned; we faced a superior force, five battle-hardened, intensely trained Japanese soldiers. We were four adventurers: two aristocrats, a journalist, and a spy. It didn't seem like a fair fight, but we did have the element of surprise in our favor.

Thomas waited for us to get in position. Then he vanished. We waited, crouched in the underbrush, searching for two more soldiers. We suspected they were in the tents, but we really didn't know. They could be anywhere — behind us, roaming the island. Or they might not exist at all.

I lightly touched Lady Jane's hand. She smiled nervously, and squeezed mine tightly. I wasn't sure what that meant, but I liked it.

The telescope on the southern perimeter was only fifty feet from where we had been. Thomas crept closer, inching through the vegetation, keeping a watchful eye on those in the tent. Minutes passed with agonizing slowness.

He finally emerged from the shadows and slipped behind the soldier. He covered the man's mouth, took the knife, and dispatched him with complete silence.

Thomas lay prone behind the fallen body, swung the rifle over his arm, and aimed it into the tent. He fired once, and missed. The second shot found the farthest radioman, hitting him as he stood to see what the ruckus was about. He fell backward, knocking over the table and crashing to the ground. Thomas fired again and missed. The second radioman grabbed a machete and ran after him.

Two more soldiers emerged from the smaller tents as we had suspected they would. The first soldier blinked with disbelief, surprised and shocked by the intrusion. The second carried a rifle. He aimed at Thomas.

"Come on, George!" Sir Gregory said. "Let's get them."

We left our hiding place and ran towards them. I held Lady Jane's pistol in my hand, squeezing it so hard my knuckles were white.

Thomas fired at the soldier with the rifle. The bullet hit him, and he doubled over, sinking to the ground before he could fire. The soldier with the machete then attacked, swinging the blade in a wide arc.

Thomas fell to the ground, dodging the machete, and rolled away. He fired the rifle, holding it freely with one hand as he avoided the menacing blade. The soldier kicked it aside just as he pulled the trigger, and the bullet went astray. The machete onslaught continued while the second soldier in the tent grabbed a rifle.

Even though the second soldier was closer, I fired at the man with the machete. I wanted to save Thomas. The bullet grazed his left arm, far from a mortal wound. The man turned to face me, his attack on Thomas delayed but not diverted.

Sir Gregory sprinted towards him, trying to grab the machete as he leaped upon him. They rolled on the ground, the soldier gaining the advantage. Too close to swing the blade, he started swinging his fist; the handle of the machete struck Sir Gregory's face.

I approached the soldier near the tent with Lady Jane behind me. I fired her pistol but missed. He fumbled with his rifle, his face an angry scowl.

Lady Jane started throwing stones at him. Her aim was remarkable. She hit him in the face, the shoulder, and the head. He couldn't focus or fire. I kept running towards him; I had three more shots before I had to reload.

I was six feet away when he raised his rifle. I pointed the pistol and fired, a split second faster than he was. The bullet caught his thigh, blood immediately oozing down his pant leg. He dropped to one knee, favoring the wounded leg, and tried to level his weapon. I fired again, hitting him in the throat. He fell, dead before he hit the ground.

I stopped and stared at him, then sank to my knees, struggling not to vomit. I coughed and gasped, turned my head away, and then ran towards Thomas.

Sir Gregory lay on the ground, unconscious. Thomas was on his back, wrestling with the bolt of his rifle. It was jammed. The Japanese soldier stood above him, the machete drawn over his head, prepared to swing the blade and sever Thomas's head from his body.

I quickly fired the last shot I had. The bullet hit the back of the soldier's head. He fell over dead.

I glanced at Sir Gregory, to check if he was all right, and saw Lady Jane helping him to his feet. With the battle over and victory assured, I dropped to my knees, fighting to overcome the nausea. The whole fight had lasted only two or three minutes. Five men were dead. I was again overwhelmed by how fragile life was, how only a few minutes can end it or alter it forever. I took a few seconds to ask God for forgiveness for the lives I had taken.

Thomas slowly got to his feet, breathless and pale. He came to my side, wrapping his arm around my shoulder.

"You saved my life," he said. "How can I ever repay you?"

I hugged him. "You already have."

CHAPTER 48

"Java Three, Java Three, come in."

Thomas repositioned the switch, and his request was met with static and garbled noises.

"Java Three, Java Three, come in."   Thomas continued working the dials.

Sir Gregory sat in a nearby chair. He had a large welt on the side of his head, bruised and purple. Lady Jane was beside him, dabbing a moist rag on the wound.

I sat next to Thomas, poring over maps. I ran to each telescope, observed our surroundings in all directions, struggling to see in the moonlight, and then returned to the charts.

"George, you have to figure out where we are," Thomas said. "And you can't be wrong. If you are, we'll wither away and die here. Or more Japanese will come."

I studied the maps. I had found land to our east with the telescope, larger than our present location but not a major island. A much bigger land mass spread beyond it to the east, extending northward. I looked at the sizes and shapes of the thousands of islands that comprised the Dutch East Indies and narrowed the search to where the ship had traveled. Then I focused on where we were cast adrift.

"Java Three, Java Three, come in."

Again the reply was met with static.

"George, this could be our only chance," Sir Gregory cautioned, repeating Thomas's warning.

"This is Java Three, come in."

We started cheering, and then Thomas hushed us quiet.

"Java Three, this is Java Two. In need of rescue. State location."

346

"Current location is Timor.   State location of rescue."

Thomas turned to me. "This is it, George. Can you do it?"

I nodded my head.

He put the microphone in front of me.

"Come on, George," Lady Jane said.   "We have faith in you."

I clicked on the microphone, studying the map before me.   "Java Three, current location of Java Two, is latitude ten degrees and twenty point one minutes south; longitude is one hundred and twenty degrees, six point eight minutes east. Java Three copy?"

"Java Three copy.   Latitude is ten degrees and twenty point one minutes south; longitude is one hundred and twenty degrees, six point eight minutes east. Java Two, describe?"

"What does he want?" I asked.

"He wants you to describe our location," Thomas said. "Just like you were giving directions."

I clicked on the microphone. Beads of sweat dotted my forehead.   "Java Three, location is a small atoll due west southwest of Salura Island, which is west of the southern tip of Sumba. Pick up location on north shore. Java Three copy?"

There was no reply.   We waited about thirty seconds.

"He must be figuring out where we are," Thomas said.

"Java Three, copy?" I asked again.

"Java Two, we copy. Location is island due west southwest of Salura Island, which is west of southern tip of Sumba. Pick up location on north shore. Java Three will arrive in twenty-four hours. Copy?"

"Java Three arrives in twenty-four hours."

"That's correct."

"Java Two signing off."

Thomas and Sir Gregory put the bodies of the dead soldiers off to the side of the compound, hiding them in a gully and covering them with branches and leaves. They placed rocks over top of them.

"I hope this radio station isn't too critical," Sir Gregory said. "If it is, the Japanese will send someone to investigate when they get no response."

"Hopefully, it'll take them a few days to figure it out," I added.

"It would probably be better if we stayed here for the night," Thomas said. "That way we can watch the ocean around the island. We can go get our baggage in the morning."

We went through the crates of supplies, finding hand grenades, bullets, cans of fish, crackers, rice, and tofu. We sat at the table, gorging on food, knowing in twenty-four hours we would be bound for Australia.

We slept restlessly, not in the tents that served the Japanese but sprawled on the moss on the mountain's peak. Thomas, Sir Gregory, and I took turns standing watch, gazing through the telescopes to ensure no one approached, and maintaining a constant vigil in case any enemy remained on the island.

As I stood guard, my thoughts drifted to the faces of the two men I had killed. I had taken their lives to save ours, so the cause was justified, but that didn't make it any easier. They had died in agony, twisted in pain, their bodies deformed and damaged. Maggie had died quietly in my arms, telling me she loved me.

We woke just past dawn and ate some fruit for breakfast. We then glanced through the telescopes again, and, when satisfied no danger existed, we started down the hillside, destined for the cave where we had left our belongings.

We moved quickly, perhaps a bit carelessly, but we were buoyed by our recent victory and looked forward to our rendezvous with Bennie. When we reached the wharf, we checked the crates contained in the hut. There were boxes of bullets and hand grenades, tins of fish and meat, bananas, and rice.

"When Bennie arrives, we should take these supplies," I said. "I'm sure we can use them."

"Let's take some bullets and grenades now," Thomas suggested. "Just in case we see more Japanese on our way to the cave."

We continued through the jungle, looking forward to the future while forgetting the past. I tried to erase the events of the prior evening, and the last few weeks for that matter, and enjoy the scenery. We truly were stranded in paradise.

"This island seems to be a natural habitat for swallow-tailed butterflies," I said as we wandered back to the cave. "They are also known as *papilio weiskel*, and they come in various colors: emerald green, sapphire blue, and golden yellow."

"Are the butterflies common?" Lady Jane asked.

"They are to this part of the world," I said. "And they are beautiful. But other species found here are very rare. Yesterday, I thought I saw a Queen Alexandra's bird-winged butterfly, supposedly native to New Guinea. It's the world's largest butterfly and has a ten-inch wing span. But I haven't seen it since."

"We'll keep looking," Thomas said. "It can offer you another story to write. This one can be about beauty and perfection. You can describe how fabulous these creatures are, how rare and exquisite. And you can let the people of the world know that somewhere in this living hell there's a symbol of what the future can be. I think they would like that."

We went back to the cave, feasted on fruit, berries, and a few tins of Japanese fish, and then spent some time at the pond, bathing and relaxing and enjoying our temporary paradise. For the first time since Singapore, there were no dangers lurking in the shadows, no darkness hiding the dawn, and no threats, fears, or anxieties. We knew Australia was a short trip, a day or day and a half, and once there we would be safe and secure. After I reached Australia, I needed to decide what path to follow: continued coverage of the war from the southwest Pacific or a return to London, hoping the memories of Maggie would no longer haunt me.

I thought about my parents, my sister Angie and her husband Tom, and my friends and coworkers. I wondered what had happened to them in the last five weeks. Had they continued the routine that life demands, muddling through each day with no time to enjoy it or savor its simple pleasures: flowers blooming, the smile of a child, a bird singing, a snowflake, the wrinkled wisdom of an octogenarian, or the purity of the color white? Probably, because that's what life was all about. It was a hectic race for survival - financial, emotional, spiritual, physical and mental. But it wouldn't be like that for me. I had seen death in so many faces, from Maggie's to General Hakkan's, that I vowed to celebrate and enjoy every single minute I was privileged enough to experience.

I looked at Thomas, floating on his back and staring at the clouds, and Lady Jane and Sir Gregory, whispering in a corner of the pond. It seemed as if she couldn't decide whether she loved Thomas or Sir Gregory or me. Balraj was a distant memory, barely mentioned since the day he'd walked out of her life. Was that my fate, an interesting diversion, pleasant but temporary? I suspected I would be forgotten as quickly as he'd been.

But I would never forget her.

Early that afternoon we collected our belongings along with some bananas and tins of fish and started our trek around the island destined for the dock on the north shore where our rendezvous with Bennie was scheduled.

"What do we do if George miscalculated our position?" Sir Gregory asked. "We'll miss Bennie and be stuck here forever."

"George did the best he could," Lady Jane said. "I'm sure he's right."

"And what would be so bad if he wasn't?" Thomas asked. "The whole world is at war. We have found a tropical paradise. There's plenty of food, perfect weather, beautiful scenery, the company of good friends. Who could ask for more?"

"There's also the Japanese," Sir Gregory reminded us. "We may have killed those here, but if the island was important enough to use as a base, I'm sure more will be sent."

I listened to the conversation but didn't comment. I may have made a mistake and chosen the wrong location. We might wait on the dock for days for a rescue that would never come. I could be off by hundreds of miles and never know by just how much. The only solace I had was knowing that I'd done my best.

We made our way through the vegetation, following the same path we had taken the day before in route to the wharf on the north shore of the island. We were not quite as cautious as we should have been, straying from the protective canopy of the foliage and talking louder than a whisper.

As we approached the northern side of the island, to where the wharf was located, Thomas suddenly stopped and held up his hand.

"Quiet!" he hissed.

"What's the matter?" I asked.

He pointed to the water. A Japanese patrol boat was docked at the wharf.

CHAPTER 49

The ship was some type of supply vessel outfitted with guns and manned by over a dozen men. It looked like they had just arrived; a line of sailors were strung across the deck, handing wooden crates to two more on the ground. An officer and another sailor stood near the path that led to the summit and stared skyward, shielding their eyes from the setting sun. I knew what they were thinking: why hadn't the soldiers come down to greet them?

We hid in the bushes, watching. They took about twenty minutes to unload, methodically stacking crates in the outbuilding and placing others at the foot of the path. When they'd finished, three sailors gathered around the officer while the rest lounged on the deck of the boat. They were engaged in a discussion, pointing up the hill.

"How many do you think there are?" Sir Gregory asked.

Thomas peeked from behind a shrub and studied the ship. "I don't know for sure. I count fifteen. But there may be more."

"Too many to attack," Sir Gregory said.

Lady Jane watched the enemy, her lips taut. "Maybe they'll drop off their supplies and leave."

"That's probably their normal routine," I said. "But they're wondering where the soldiers are. If they find the bodies they'll never leave."

As if he had heard me, the officer waved his hand forward and the three sailors started scampering up the hill, each carrying a crate. It would take ten or fifteen minutes to reach the top, some time to find the bodies, and then maybe ten minutes to return to the dock. We had little time to develop a plan.

"We have to think of something," Thomas said. "When they return from the summit, the others will search the island."

Sir Gregory eyed the enemy warily. "I have a half box of hand grenades. I could disable the ship."

"But we would still have fifteen Japanese to deal with." Thomas said. "We need a better plan. And we have to do it soon. Bennie will be here at dusk."

I thought for a moment, considering our options. It would be suicide to attack a force four times as large as ours, especially when they were better equipped. One shot from their canon would kill us all, and any attempt to attack the sailors would meet with disaster.

"We need a diversion," I said.

"What do you mean by that?" Sir Gregory asked.

"We need to make them leave, either because they think they are in danger or to launch an attack," I said. "And we have to get them to go long enough for Bennie to rescue us."

"Once they find the dead soldiers at the top of the hill, they'll radio for help," Thomas warned.

"I know," I said. "That's why the timing is so critical."

I realized that all eyes had suddenly turned to me. Somehow I had become the leader of this mismatched band of adventurers, although I'm not sure when or how. It was probably after I saved Thomas's life, or maybe it was my ability to use my mind to master muscle, and that's what I had to do; I didn't have the strength that others did. They now waited anxiously, wondering what plan I had created. They were ready to follow blindly, having developed a faith and trust in me that I couldn't explain, somehow knowing that any action I suggested would hold their safety paramount.

"Our best chance is to confuse them when they get to the top of the hill," I advised. "Then they won't think to look for their companions."

"I don't follow you," Sir Gregory said.

"We have to make them think that the soldiers left the summit," I explained. "And for a good reason."

"How do we do that?" Thomas asked.

My plan was formulating, I only had to refine it. "How many hand grenades do we have?"

Sir Gregory shrugged and grabbed the crate. "I don't know. Maybe twenty."

"Here's what I think we should do," I said.

Ten minutes later the first grenade exploded. It was followed by silence, and then two distinct rifle shots, spaced ten seconds apart. The sailors at the dock all turned, looking first at each other, and then towards the island's interior. They were confused and, even though they were probably well-trained and seasoned, some faces showed fright.

A sailor was dispatched up the path. He yelled for those on their way to the summit, trying to direct them back to the wharf. The officer then issued a command to the remaining men, and they boarded the boat, manning the two guns that sat on deck and standing by the railing with their rifles at the ready.

The second grenade exploded a few minutes later. It was followed by a third. The sailors responded to the apparent attack, prepared to retaliate. Some sought cover, crouching behind the gun deck and behind the bridge.

"Thomas and Sir Gregory are very convincing," I said. "They're certainly making it sound like there's a battle on the far side of the island."

Lady Jane pointed at a disappearing sun. "I just hope they make it back in the darkness. Do you think this will work?"

"First we have to get the sailors off the summit before they find the dead bodies. Hopefully, that was successful. Then they have to all get on the boat and go to the south side."

"What if the Japanese try to find them on foot?"

"I don't think they will," I said. "They've probably never explored the island before. They just deliver supplies. They don't know where to go. Especially in the dark. And they have their guns on the ship."

Five minutes passed before another grenade exploded. Then a series of staggered shots arrived, some in rapid succession. The sailors remained vigilant.

It took a while before the sailors came running down the hill. There were four, three that had gone up the path to investigate and the fourth that was sent to get them. If they had reached the summit, they were only there a matter of minutes, not enough time to find the dead soldiers.

The officer left the boat, a pistol in his hand, and waved the four sailors towards him. They huddled near the outbuilding, using it as shelter, and discussed the situation. The sailors were reporting their findings; the officer was revealing his strategy.

Another grenade exploded, followed by six rifle shots in a long string, indicating the escalation of the battle. The timing was perfect; the soldiers displayed a sense of urgency as the officer's conversation became more animated.

Two sailors and the officer returned to the boat. The other two sailors sat in the shadows of the shack armed with rifles. They guarded the supplies and the pathway to the summit where telescopes, valuable radios, and more supplies were housed. Along with five dead comrades.

The boat chugged from the dock setting course for the other side of the island, the sailors determined to combat an unknown enemy. Another grenade exploded as the vessel departed, legitimizing the threat.

"What are we going to do with the guards?" Lady Jane asked. "We weren't expecting them."

"I know," I said, fingering the two grenades that daggled from my belt. "I hadn't planned on that at all."

Twilight yielded to darkness, sounds of combat still evident on the distant shore. The Japanese boat had disappeared from sight, speeding towards battle. Lady Jane and I stayed hidden in the shrubs, watching the two sailors by the shack. Three torches lit the area, spaced around the dock and identifying the path to the summit.

"We need to do something with the guards," Lady Jane said. "Bennie will be here shortly."

They had to be killed. I would have to toss a grenade where they stood, letting the explosion eliminate the threat they posed. The faces of the men I had killed the day before, gruesome and grisly and disfigured and destroyed, had haunted me ever since. But if killing two more of the enemy got me back to London, if those deaths saved Lady Jane, then that's what I had to do. They wouldn't hesitate to kill me. Or her. And I had to protect her.

"Wait here," I whispered.

I moved through the brush, crawling when I had to, sliding on my stomach when the vegetation was scant, and slowly made my way towards the shack. In the distance, I could hear more rifle shots, but now the tone was different.

357

It was a Japanese machine gun firing into the island's vegetation. There were distant explosions, the grenades thrown by Sir Gregory and Thomas to mimic an attack, but they were dwarfed by a louder blast. The Japanese ship was firing on the shore, using the canons that sat on its deck.

Bennie's fishing trawler appeared at the edge of the harbor, still rolling on the waves but destined for the cove and guided by the lights that lit the wharf. I continued crawling towards the shack, warily watching the men I was about to kill.

The two sailors hid behind the building, watching the landscape, anticipating an attack. They weren't focused on the sea. They hadn't noticed the looming shadow approaching on the ocean.

I kept moving closer until I could see their faces. I saw fear, anxiety, courage, and conviction. They would fight to the death. There was no doubt, but that's what soldiers do.

I pulled the pin on the grenade. My heart was in my throat, thumping wildly. I said a prayer, asking for forgiveness. Then I lobbed the grenade towards the shack.

The explosion was much louder than the distant blasts from the south side of the island. It made my ears ring, and a gray smoke hid where it had landed. I crawled forward, moving closer, holding the second grenade in my hand, ready to pull the pin if needed.

When the smoke cleared, a corner of the shack was destroyed. The roof hung haphazardly where the support post had been. Splinters of timber were strewn about the edge of the dock, broken crates and metal containers of food lay scattered about. The two sailors lay prone.

I stood and walked towards them. A sailor was

groaning. I hung the grenade on my belt and took Lady Jane's pistol from my pocket. I disarmed the safety catch.

The sailor was moving, attempting to sit upright. I saw the barrel of his rifle, his finger poised around the trigger.

I dove for the ground as the shot fired. I could feel the breeze as the bullet whistled past me. I rolled away from the enemy and aimed the pistol. I waited, knowing the dying wish of the sailor was to take me with him.

As soon as I saw movement, I fired, one shot, clean and precise. I remained on my stomach, elbows balanced on the ground, both hands holding the pistol.

I didn't know if I'd hit him. I waited, patient and determined. I studied the shadows. There was no movement. Slowly, I rose.

I walked towards them, my pistol ready. Both sailors lay on their backs where the blast had thrown them. The one closest to the shack was dead. The second soldier lay beside him. There was a bullet hole in his forehead just above the right eye.

I sighed with relief and relaxed, letting my arms fall to my sides, easing my grip on the pistol. I turned away from the bodies. I didn't want to see any more.

As I walked towards our hideaway, Lady Jane rose to greet me.

"Nothing would have been worse than if something had happened to you," she said softly.

She hugged me tightly, willing away the fatigue and doubt, shame and shock. I wanted to stay in her arms forever.

She raised her head, her lips near mine, and kissed me. She buried her face in my shoulder. I kissed her neck and cheeks and eyelashes, and then her lips. My hands stroked her hair and then roamed over her shoulders down the length of her back.

"Jane," a voice called. "Jane, where are you?"

We separated abruptly, breathing heavily. She looked at me and smiled.

"I'm sorry," she whispered.

I pulled her towards me and kissed her again. She lingered a moment and then broke away.

"Gregory," she called. "We're here."

Sir Gregory and Thomas emerged from the vegetation. Their clothes were torn, their bodies smudged with dirt. They were tired and breathless but unhurt.

"Bennie's boat is coming now," I said as they approached.

"We have to hurry," Thomas said. "The patrol boat is returning. We raced through the jungle to get here before them."

We moved to the wharf, waving our arms, signaling to Bennie that he had the right location. The boat came closer, sliding up to the dock. Bennie threw a lanyard off the deck, and Thomas pulled it over a post, keeping the boat steady while we boarded.

"Are we happy to see you," Thomas called.

"I'm glad I could help," Bennie said. "Where are the Japanese? I saw the flag on top of the mountain."

"They're on their way," Sir Gregory said. "Hurry up, and get out of here."

CHAPTER 50

Bennie's fishing boat skimmed across the waves, the island shrinking in the distance. We sped due east, never encountered the Japanese patrol boat, and passed along the island of Salura before turning south, headed for Darwin, Australia. We sat in the kitchen and spent a few hours relating our adventures to Bennie.

"We have to go back and get Van der Meer," Bennie said.

"We will," Thomas assured him. "Let's get everyone to Australia first."

Bennie's tone and facial expression did not lend to compromise, and I expected him to turn the boat around and head for Java. There wouldn't be the slightest hesitation.

"He needs more time to recuperate," Thomas insisted. "We can go to Darwin. Then we'll go back and get him"

I lay on the deck that evening, awake long after the others had fallen asleep. I was haunted by images of the men I had killed, their faces cringing in pain, their bodies maimed and disfigured. Even though I proved myself worthy of the armed forces that had rejected me, that validation came with a tremendous emotional burden, and it taught me much about myself. I wasn't a killer; I'd never be a battle-hardened veteran, thirsty for the next victory. I took no pleasure in watching the life drain from someone's body, enemy or not. If I never did it again, I'd be a better person for it.

As the minutes passed, changing to hours, I realized God had forgiven me, but I had to forgive myself. I had killed to survive just as men had done throughout history. I had done what I'd had to do, and I had protected Lady Jane. I had to lock those memories, the haunting visions of death, in a separate mental compartment, like the tiny, little-used drawer in a roll top desk. I had to erase the sight of their faces, the thoughts of their families, the imagined promise of lives they would never live. I had to let it go.

I rolled over on my back, staring at the sky and listening to the water lapping at the boat. The ability to forgive isn't selective; it applies universally. If I forgave myself for killing Japanese soldiers, I must forgive myself for falling asleep on an English road in the wee hours of the morning and letting Maggie die. It was the only way I would ever heal.

I thought of all that had gone wrong that day. We had left London later than planned; I was delayed at the office due to a breaking story. We should have waited until morning. When I got tired I should have stopped, maybe walked for a bit to wake up or slept for a few hours, or awakened Maggie and let her drive.

We were almost there when the crash occurred, just a few miles from our destination, and I had relived that night in my mind every day since. There were a thousand things I could have done differently. But I hadn't. I'd kept going. And because I had, Maggie had died. Again, a few precious minutes defined life, when the rest ticked by unnoticed.

It's hard to make sense of tragedy. Why did she die when I was barely injured? I would never know. But somehow, I knew I had to forgive and forget, and live the rest of my life, not as a shadow, but as a man. If I didn't, my survival would be wasted.

Sometimes I thought Maggie died because she was better prepared. Her soul was pure, her laugh genuine, her heart large enough to hold the universe and all of those in it. Maggie was ready; she was deserving. I was not. As I finally drifted off to sleep, I realized that everything would be all right. God had just needed another angel, and Maggie was the perfect choice.

When we awoke the next morning, we were far from the islands of the Dutch East Indies, traveling in a southeasterly direction. We expected to reach Darwin in another day, and although we now faced the most daring part of the sea voyage, braving the ocean with no sight of land, it paled when compared to our adventures of the last few weeks.

"When we get to Darwin, I'll contact my friend in Perth," Sir Gregory said. "He'll help arrange our return to India. Your family will be thrilled to see you."

"I'm sure they will," Lady Jane said with a bit of annoyance. "But I think we've discussed this in detail the last few days. Remember our conversation on the ship? And at the pond?"

He ignored her like a parent tired of denying a child. I'm not sure why. I wondered if she really would return to India with him. It didn't seem likely. Somehow I couldn't imagine her stepping back in time, embracing the structured existence she had discarded. But maybe that's what she wanted. Maybe it was easier than an uncertain future.

Their interaction confused me. I had thought, given her recent behavior and our intimate moments, that we might share a future. But maybe we only shared a past.

It was near dusk with only twelve hours of our journey remaining when we heard the short wave radio. It was hidden alongside the engine, tucked in a compartment that appeared to be an auxiliary component. It was easy to miss. I had spent several days on board during the journey to Sumatra. I never knew it existed.

"Java Three, Java Three come in."

Bennie pulled a chair up to the radio and turned the dials.

"Java Three, Java Three come in."

"This is Java Three, come in," Bennie said.

"Java Three, this is Java One."

"It's Van der Meer!" Thomas hollered.

We all cheered, thrilled that he was all right. I marveled at the man's resilience. We had left him near dead only a few days ago. Now he called us on a radio.

"Java One, it's great to hear from you! I am with Java Two."

"Java Two, I was worried about you."

"Not nearly as worried as I was about you," Thomas said.

"State location," Van der Meer continued.

"Twelve hours from Darwin. Do you need pick-up?"

"Affirmative. Can be in Pamekasan in four days. Can you?"

Bennie looked at Thomas, who nodded.

"Affirmative. Pick up in four days in Pamekasan."

Affirmative. Over and out."

"How did he ever get to a radio in the countryside?" I asked.

Thomas shrugged. "I have no idea. And he'll probably never tell."

"He was so badly injured," Lady Jane said. "Can he get to Pamekasan in four days?

Bennie nodded. "If anyone can, it's Van der Meer."

At dawn the next morning, we saw the Australian

coast, fringes of green meeting white sandy beaches that stretched into the horizon. We watched as land approached and buildings, rooftops, church steeples, a water tower, and a railroad terminal became visible. Along the waterfront, ships of varying sizes sat at anchor: freighters, sailboats, ships from the Australian navy, tugboats, and a tanker. We watched with excitement, eagerly awaiting civilization unspoiled by the enemy.

Bennie guided the trawler into port, steering towards a deserted dock on the eastern edge of the city. The slender pier, which was adjacent to brick warehouses and a set of overhead cranes, stretched out to sea some two hundred feet.

The boat was secured to the dock. We gathered our belongings, just a ragged bag for each of us, and walked to the edge of the deck. Sir Gregory and I helped Lady Jane step onto the wharf. I piled our belongings on the walkway as Thomas handed them down from the vessel.

"This is where we part company, my friend," Thomas said. "Bennie and I are returning to Pamekasan to get Van der Meer."

"To start your spy ring again," Sir Gregory said.

"It's want we want to do," Thomas replied. "It's our contribution to the war effort." He looked at us sadly. "And it's revenge for Shanghai. It makes me feel like they didn't die in vain, that something that benefits the whole world will result from their deaths."

We were silent for a moment, out of respect.

"I think you're an amazing man," Lady Jane said softly. "And I can't think of a more prestigious profession than spying for your country. Or a more exciting occupation."

He would never forgive the Japanese, but he was

turning his loss into something positive. I should do the same, maybe something for Maggie's memory when I returned to London. It would help me move on.

"You're an unknown hero," I said. "And the world applauds you." I thought for a moment, asking the question I'd always wanted answered. "How do spies support such luxurious lifestyles? Isn't it volunteer work?"

"It is," he said. "But I used to be a banker. And I know a lot about banks." He grinned. "So now I rob them."

We were stunned, both from the sheer act and the ease with which he revealed it. There was a pause while everyone uncomfortably digested the information. We'd known there was something different about him. We just hadn't expected anything so astonishing.

"You rob banks?" Sir Gregory asked incredulously.

He nodded and shrugged. "Just when we need money. It's nothing personal."

"The banks that were robbed in Singapore and Batavia," I said. "That was you?"

"Yes, it was. Pamekasan also. That's why I left the cottage in the middle of the night."

At first his revelation sickened me. I would never have guessed he was a thief. But he had his reasons, and it wasn't my role to judge him.

Lady Jane wasn't surprised; it seemed she already knew his secret. It made me wonder what else she knew.

"That's certainly a unique talent," Sir Gregory said haltingly. "Not admirable but unique."

I knew Thomas was far from perfect, but I wondered what drove an international financier to rob banks. Why didn't he use his expertise to earn money instead? And how did that tie to revenge of his murdered family? It didn't. He probably subconsciously blamed the bank who'd sent him to Shanghai as well as the Japanese. I didn't know and didn't ask.

"We're ready, Thomas," Bennie called. "We've loaded petrol and supplies."

"Goodbye, my friend," Thomas said.

I noticed that, although he spoke to me, his eyes were directed at Lady Jane.

"Start the engines," Bennie said to the young lads.

Lady Jane looked at Thomas. "Wait!"

He held out his hand. She grasped it, and climbed on deck.

"I would love to be a spy," she said. "And I miss Van der Meer."

Sir Gregory gasped. "Jane, are you crazy? What are you doing?"

"I'm sorry, Gregory," she said.

"This is outrageous!" he exclaimed. "Jane, come to your senses! You just have an absurd infatuation."

"No, Gregory, I don't," she said. "It's about freedom, like a bird flying from its cage. I want to choose where I go and with whom. I don't want the decision made for me. We discussed this in Batavia. And then we discussed it on the ship. And we discussed it again on the island. We're much better off as friends. I'm not the little girl you fell in love with. I grew up. You fell in love with what you wanted me to be. Not with who I am."

He sighed, her explanation, which had apparently been provided several times, finally absorbed. "You won't consider coming back to India?" he asked, knowing the answer before he posed the question.

I watched their conversation, my heart heavy; a sick feeling welled in the pit of my stomach. So she had chosen

Thomas. I wondered when I had lost her. Was it in Singapore, in Sumatra during Sir Gregory's rescue, when she fell out of the train, in Pamekasan, or maybe on the rowboat? Was it before or after our kiss on the island? Maybe it was recent, on the voyage to Darwin. At what point had she decided that she loved Thomas? I would probably never know.

"Gregory, I can't do that," she said softly. "You're a wonderful person and a sweet man, attractive and strong. There are many women who would do anything to share your life."

He looked at her sadly and nodded. "And as you've already told me, you're not one of them."

"Not as a lover but as an eternal friend," she said. "You'll always have a piece of my heart, Gregory. And you know that."

"What do I tell your father?"

"Tell him I'll be home someday," she said. "But for now, I'll go where the wind takes me."

She leaned over and kissed him on the cheek. "Take care, Gregory. You're a good man."

He nodded his goodbyes, then turned and walked away, the heels of his shoes thumping loudly on the wooden dock. We watched as he slowly disappeared.

I felt sorry for him. He had spent his whole life loving her, but he had actually been losing her. Day by day, week by week, year by year she had drifted away, slipping farther from his grasp. Now she was gone.

Thomas turned to me. "Will you come with us?"

I flirted with the idea. But unlike Lady Jane, I hadn't inherited wealth, and unlike Thomas, I didn't steal it. I had to earn it. It would break my heart, anyway, watching her with Thomas, seeing her smile and live and love. It was already too painful.

"No, I can't," I replied. "I have my writing and..."

"To hell with your writing, George," Thomas said. "Come with us. I'll teach you how to be a spy."

I smiled. "And a smuggler and a bank robber."

"It's a lot of fun," he said. "Come on. We'll explore the Southern seas."

"Yes, George, please come with us," Lady Jane said.

Their offer was enticing. It would be interesting, traveling to parts unknown. But my own future was even more exciting. I had changed from the heartbroken, emotional wreck that tiptoed into Singapore, hiding from Maggie, having no idea what waited. I was stronger, more confident, and more mature. Conquering disasters make you grow as a person, and I had certainly endured my share. The world offered unlimited opportunities. I wanted to enjoy them. And I could. Maggie's shadow was still with me, but it no longer consumed me.

"As much as I'd like to, I must decline," I told him. "There are territories I want to explore, also. But they lie in a different direction. I want to go back to London."

I looked at them, standing side by side, studying me curiously. I owed them both. They had rescued me. They had picked up the pieces and made a man.

"Then good luck to you," Thomas said. He grasped my hand and shook it firmly.

"I'll never forget you," I said.

He smiled confidently. "We'll meet again. The world is smaller than it seems."

"Perhaps you're right," I admitted, even though I knew it was unlikely.

"Goodbye, George," Lady Jane said. She leaned over the side of the ship and kissed me on the lips.

"I'll miss you," I said, my heart broken.

"I know," she said softly.

I stared at her for a moment. I wanted to capture her image, the upturned nose and the smile that lit the globe, all framed by the golden mane blowing in the breeze.

"Take care of yourself," she added.

I loved her, and she knew it. But I couldn't hold on to something I'd never really had. I let her go.

And so I turned and walked down the weathered dock, tracing the empty, hollow footsteps of Sir Gregory Millburne. I knew just how he felt. But he had known there was little hope. I hadn't. The kiss and lingering embrace on the island had meant so much to me. It meant stepping from the past and into the future and tearing down the wall that Maggie had built. But it hadn't meant anything to Lady Jane.

I had walked about a hundred feet when I heard footsteps, someone running down the wharf. I turned to find Lady Jane standing behind me, out of breath. She was carrying her bag.

I stared at her, dumbfounded and confused.

"Will I ever get used to London after living in India?" she asked.

I couldn't believe what I was hearing. "What about Thomas?"

"Thomas? Oh, George, you are so silly. Thomas is my friend. And he always will be. It's nothing more than that."

"But I thought you wanted to be with him," I said. "And that he wanted to be with you."

She smiled, shaking her head. "George, all Thomas ever did was continuously tell me that you were the perfect man for me."

I was shocked. I thought he was my adversary, battling for her affection. But I couldn't have been more wrong. I looked to the end of the dock. The boat was starting to pull away. Thomas stood on the stern, watching. When he saw me looking, he waved.

I waved back, smiling. What if I never saw him again? There were so many things I had left unsaid, words he needed to hear. My eyes started to mist, but then I realized that I was easy to find. He could contact me at the *London Times,* and I was sure he would.

I watched as the boat sped away and he slowly vanished from sight. I knew I would never meet another man like him: spy, killer, smuggler, thief, and the best friend I could ever ask for. It was quite a combination.

I turned and started walking down the dock. Lady Jane put her arm through mine and snuggled up against me, kissing me lightly on the cheek. I looked at the dawn, the sun rising in the sky, splashing colors of the rainbow across the horizon, and for a brief instant I saw Maggie, shimmering in the clouds as her image washed across the heavens. She was waving goodbye.

The End